The Last Summer

Karen Swan is the *Sunday Times* top three bestselling author of twenty-two books and her novels sell all over the world. She writes two books each year – one for the summer period and one for the Christmas season. Previous summer titles include *The Spanish Promise*, *The Hidden Beach* and *The Secret Path* and, for winter, *The Christmas Secret*, *Together by Christmas* and *Midnight in the Snow*.

Previously a fashion editor, she lives in Sussex with her husband, three children and two dogs.

Follow Karen on Instagram @swannywrites,
on her author page on Facebook,
and on Twitter @KarenSwan1.

Also by Karen Swan

The Last Summer

Karen Swan

MACMILLAN

First published 2022 by Macmillan
an imprint of Pan Macmillan
The Smithson, 6 Briset Street, London EC1M 5NR
EU representative: Macmillan Publishers Ireland Ltd, 1st Floor,
The Liffey Trust Centre, 117–126 Sheriff Street Upper,
Dublin 1, D01 YC43
Associated companies throughout the world
www.panmacmillan.com

ISBN   978-1-5290-8437-5

1 3 5 7 9 8 6 4 2

A CIP catalogue record for this book is available from the British Library.

Map artwork by Hemesh Alles

Typeset in Palatino by Palimpsest Book Production Ltd, Falkirk, Stirlingshire
Printed and bound by CPI Group (UK) Ltd, Croydon, CR0 4YY

Visit **www.panmacmillan.com** to read more about all our books
and to buy them. You will also find features, author interviews and
news of any author events, and you can sign up for e-newsletters
so that you're always first to hear about our new releases.

For Laura Tinkl, who is part of our story now

Glossary

BOTHY: A basic shelter or dwelling, usually made of stone or wood

CATCH A SUPPER: To receive a scolding

CLEIT: A stone storage hut or bothy, only found on St Kilda

CRAGGING: Climbing a cliff or crag; a CRAGGER is a climber

DREICH: Dreary, bleak (to describe weather)

FANK: A walled enclosure for sheep, a sheepfold

GREET: To cry or weep

LAZYBEDS: Parallel banks of ridges with drainage ditches between them; a traditional, now mostly extinct method of arable cultivation

PEELY-WALLY: Looking pale or sickly

QUERN: A simple stone hand mill used for grinding grains

SOUTERRAIN: An underground chamber or dwelling

STAC: A sea stack – a column of rock standing in the sea – usually created as a leftover after cliff erosion

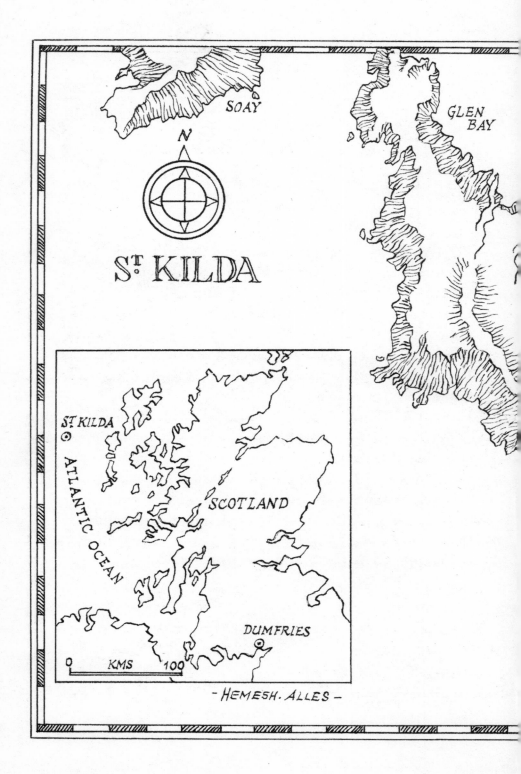

SOAY

GLEN
BAY

N

ST KILDA

ST KILDA
⊙

ATLANTIC OCEAN

SCOTLAND

DUMFRIES

0   KMS   100

— HEMESH. ALLES —

BORERAY

PUFFINS

AMAZON'S
HOUSE

CONNACHAIR

CLIMBING
EXHIBITION

BULL HOUSE

AN LAG

OISEVAL

EFFIE'S
HOUSE

FACTOR'S
HOUSE

AM
BLAID

STORM CLEIT

VILLAGE
BAY

RUIVAL

DUN

0   0·5   1
KILOMETRES

Prologue

21 June 1930

Glen Bay, St Kilda

The three young women sat cross-legged in the grass, their shadows long behind them as the sun softly dropped from its high arch. Sheep dozed on the slopes, tails flicking at the flies as they sought pale shelter against the stone dykes, waiting for the fluttering kiss of a breeze. It was summer's longest day and the sky was holding its breath, the dry heat suspended above their heads like a tethered veil. Their fingers worked in unison as they pulled feathers from the bird carcasses, plumes of white down speckling the meadow like daisies.

Flora pressed the back of her hand to her brow. 'I'll not miss this.'

'Of course you won't. You won't even remember it,' Effie said with a wry glance. 'You'll be a grand lady in your house with stairs and you'll have lipstick and a wireless and you simply won't believe that you ever had to pluck the fulmars.'

Flora preened, delighted by the image. 'You must come to visit. James says there'll be a bedroom for each of you and we'll get you a new dress every time you come to stay, and we'll go to shows and we'll dine in restaurants . . . '

Mhairi frowned. 'Real-life restaurants?'

Effie laughed. 'Yes! Actual places where they pluck and cook the birds for you.'

'Oh . . . That must be nice.'

'James says in Glasgow you could go out every night for a month and not eat in the same place twice.' Flora tossed her long dark hair back from her face.

'So long as m' belly's full, I'll not much care what's in it,' Effie shrugged.

Mhairi's hands had fallen still and the sudden absence of activity was jarring to the others. They looked up to find her biting her lip, trying to hold back tears.

'Hush now, Mhairi,' Flora said quickly. 'You'll be fine.'

'How can you say that? It's not the same for me as it is for you. When we cross over, you'll get everything you ever wanted. But I'm going to *lose* everything. And nothing can stop it.'

'A wave will rise on quiet water, Mhairi,' Flora said, smoothing back Mhairi's flame-coloured hair and reaching for her hand. 'You have to just trust your happiness lies in another place.'

Mhairi snatched her hand away. 'You keep saying that, but what's being asked of me . . . it's too much!' Her grey eyes burned. She was rarely given to anger. She had a gentle nature and an open heart, but neither had served her well in bringing her to this point.

'I know. And I'd be raging too. I'd be mad with grief if it was me who had to do it,' Flora agreed warmly. 'But you're a better person than me. You're good all the way through. I'm not even good skin deep.'

'You're not that bad,' Effie protested, rolling her eyes.

'Aren't I? I lose my temper if the wind messes my hair. I

curse if I bang my knee in kirk. If it wasn't for this . . . ' She framed her beautiful face with cupped hands. 'They'd have thrown me over the top years ago.'

There was a short silence. Slowly, Flora gave an impish smile.

Mhairi chuckled softly, in spite of herself. 'They would not,' she chided, fondly slapping Flora's knee. 'You have lots of good qualities.'

'I'm a beautiful monster,' Flora argued, looking not in the least concerned by it. 'And Effie's a tow-haired wildling . . .'

'Oi!' Effie protested, her long trousers covering the multitude of scabs on her knees and shins from scrambling over the rocks.

'You're the best of us, Mhairi. There's no way you're not going to get your reward. It is coming,' Flora said with her usual determination. 'Even if you can't see it yet. You have to believe it's coming.'

Mhairi shook her head sadly, but she gave no more reply. Flora's passion could normally convince them all that the sky was green and the sea was black, but Mhairi had no wish to imagine an unseeable future when all that she wanted, she already had. If they could only stay here . . . But their paths had been set and the outcome couldn't be altered now. Not for any of them.

'The same goes for you.'

Effie flinched, her breath catching high in her throat, as Flora's keen gaze fell upon her too. She closed her eyes, willing it to be true, but knowing that to get any sort of happy ending, she had to do more than step onto a boat. It wasn't a distant time or another place that blocked her future from view but the threat of something unspeakable. Unthinkable. It hung over her at all times, a swinging scythe above her head as she

KAREN SWAN

cut the peats or hoed the beds, a shadow that crept through her dreams.

'You'll be free there,' Flora said fervently.

Effie swallowed and nodded, wishing she could believe it. No one spoke for several moments. It still didn't seem possible that horror could touch them here on their secluded isle, but this summer everything had changed.

'There's only a few weeks to go now, but you must be ready just in case,' Flora said. 'You must dig your bait while the tide is out.'

'I know.' Effie had been slowly gathering what she needed, taking care to spread apart the petty thefts so that no one noticed the missing length of rope or the rusted knife that used to lie in the bottom of the skiff. There was one more thing she needed but she knew it couldn't be found anywhere on the isle. 'And I'm almost there, if Captain McGregor will help me.'

'When is he hauling anchor?' Mhairi asked anxiously.

Effie glanced towards the setting sun, gauging the time. It had dropped below the Mullach Bi cliffs; there was maybe another three hours of light. But with a two-hour walk back to the other side of the isle . . . 'Soon. I should be heading back.' She tucked her legs in to stand but Flora reached for her hand first.

'Before you go.'

They sat joined together in their small circle, the crash of the sea and the chatter of wrens a symphony around them.

'I know it's hard. Hardest of all on the two of you. In a couple of months, our lives are going to change forever. We'll leave here and everything we know will be different. Every single thing. Some will be better, some will be worse. But I also know a day will come when we'll look back on this

4

moment – on the three of us sitting on the grass, with feathers in our hair and dead birds by our feet – and there'll be something of it that still remains.'

'What?' Mhairi blinked.

'Us. *This*.' Flora squeezed their hands tighter. 'We'll always be Kilda girls, no matter where we end up. Ma's forever saying there's no secret if three know it, but she's wrong in our case. What we three do, only we three will ever know.' She pressed her finger to her lips. 'We're sisters. Yes?'

Mhairi nodded, Effie too; she felt an unfamiliar lump in her throat. She wasn't one for sentimentality but emotions were trying to press through her thick skin. She got up, her shoulders held high, her lithe body as brittle as a stick. 'I'll be back over when I can.'

She could feel their apprehension at her back as she turned away and began striding for the ridge. She wanted to stay with her friends. She wanted to pretend they were still just girls and life was, if not easy, then at least fair. But those days had sunk with other suns and she knew the moment was upon her to face her future. Flora was right; she was always right: the tide was out. It was time to dig the bait.

BEFORE

Chapter One

A month earlier – 13 May 1930

The dogs were barking on the beach. The old women came to stand at their doors, looking out with hard frowns across the curve of the bay. The tide was going out and there'd been a testy wind all day, whipping up the waves and making the birds wheel with delight.

Effie didn't move from her position on the milking stone. She had her cheek to Iona's belly and was filling the pail with relaxed indifference. She knew it could be another twenty minutes before a boat nosed around the headland, though it would probably be sooner today, given these winds. Her collie Poppit – brown-faced, with a white patch over one eye – sat beside her, ears up and looking out over the water, already awaiting the far-off sea intruders, though she wouldn't leave Effie's side.

She watched the movements of the villagers from her elevated perch. The milking enclosure was a good third of the way up the hill and she always enjoyed the view. It was a Tuesday, which meant washing day, and she could see the younger women standing in the burns, skirts tucked up and scrubbing the linens as they talked. They wouldn't like having their sheets flying in the wind if visitors were coming. None

9

of the tourist boats were scheduled to come this week, but if it was a trawler, it wouldn't be so bad; most of the captains were friends.

The indignity of airing their linens before strangers was taken seriously in a village where privacy was merely a concept. The layout alone meant anyone could see the comings and goings of the villagers from almost any point in the glen; it was shaped like a cone with smooth but steep slopes two-thirds of the way round, leading up to towering cliffs that dropped sharply and precipitously on the other sides to the crashing sea below. The cliffs only dipped, like a dairy bowl's lip, on the south-easterly corner, skimming down to a shingle beach. There was nowhere else to land on the isle but here. The seas were heavy and torrid all around but by a stroke of luck, the neighbouring isle, Dun – no more than a bony finger of rock – almost abutted the shores of Hirta, creating a natural breakwater and rendering Village Bay as a safe haven in the churning grey waters of the North Atlantic. During some storms they had as many as twenty ships taking refuge there.

Trawlermen, whalers, navy men, they all rhapsodized, as they took shelter, about the welcoming and cosy sight of the village tucked beneath the high-shouldered ellipse, chimneys puffing, oil lamps twinkling. The grey stone cottages – interspersed with the older traditional blackhouses, which had been steadily abandoned since the 1860s – sat shoulder to shoulder and fanned around the east side of the bay, bordered by a strong stone dyke. Looking down from the ridges on high, they were like teeth in a jaw. Giant's teeth, Effie's mother used to say.

The village's position afforded the best protection from winds that would funnel down the slopes at speeds that lifted rocks and tore the steel roofs from the stone walls (at least until the landlord, Sir John MacLeod of MacLeod, had had them strapped down with metal ties).

The Street – and there was only one – was a wide grassy path, set between the cottages and a thick low wall that topped the allotments. It was the beating heart of island life. Everyone congregated there, protected further from the wind by their own homes and able to bask in the sun on fine days. The old women sat knitting and spinning by their front doors; the children ran along the wall, cows occasionally nodding over it. Every morning, the men would meet outside number 5 and number 6 for their daily parliament to decide upon and allocate chores; and after tea, the villagers would amble down it to pick up from their neighbours 'the evening news'.

In front of each cottage, across the Street, was a long, narrow walled plot that ran down towards the beach. It was here that the villagers planted their potatoes in lazybeds, hung their washing and allowed their few cattle to overwinter. During the summer months, the cows were kept behind the head dyke, whilst the many sheep were grazed on the pastures of Glen Bay, on the other side of the island. Separated from Village Bay by a high ridge, Am Blaid, Glen Bay spiralled down to a sharply shelved cove. There was no beach to speak of over there, for the northerly waves were relentless and though the villagers kept a skiff there for emergencies, heading out and coming ashore were only possible on the rare occasions when the prevailing wind switched and the sea lay fully at rest.

Iona stopped munching and moved with a twitch of irritation. Unperturbed, Effie reached down for the pile of dock leaves she had picked on her way up and wordlessly passed her another few. The cow gave a sigh of contentment and

Effie resumed milking. This was their usual morning routine and both were accustomed to its gentle rhythms.

A few minutes later, the pail was almost full and Effie sat up, patting Iona on the flank. 'Good girl,' she murmured, standing up off the milking stone and looking down the slope. As predicted, the prow of a sloop was just nosing round the headland of Dun.

She watched keenly as the ship slipped silently into the embrace of the bay and threw out an anchor, sails drawing down. Not a trawler, then. The women would be displeased. This vessel with its slim-fingered triple masts and low curved hull was a finessed creature, more likely found in the azure waters off France than the outermost Hebrides.

'Friend or foe?!'

The question echoed around the caldera.

The crew were just black dots from here but she could see the locals already readying the dinghy; the men would need to row powerfully against waves that were pounding the shore. The passengers aboard the sloop had chosen a bad day to sail. The open water would have tossed them like a cork and although Dun's presence granted mercy, it was no free pass; a south-easterly made the bay's usually sheltered water froth and roil like a witch's cauldron and there was no guarantee they would be able to disembark.

Only one thing was certain: if the men were able to land them, no one would be coming back dry, and the villagers knew it. Already faint twists of grey smoke were beginning to twirl from the chimneys, people rushing in and out of the arc of low cottages that smiled around the bay and taking in their washing, sweeping floors, putting on shoes, moving the spinning wheels to their prominent positions so that their visitors might watch.

They all knew the drill. Catering to the tourists had become a quietly profitable sideline. It couldn't help feed them – with not a single shop on the isle, they had little use for money on Hirta itself – but it was useful for asking the more familiar captains to bring back treats when they were next passing, or to give as extra credit to the factor when he came wanting the rents. Or in Flora's case, to purchase a brightly coloured lipstick she'd once seen on one of the well-heeled lady visitors – even though it would be wasted on the three hundred sheep she was currently herding in Glen Bay for the summer.

None of the villagers understood quite why the world at large took an interest in them, but the postmaster, Mhairi's father, Ian McKinnon, had been told by colleagues on the mainland that a St Kilda-stamped postcard was now considered desirable, if not valuable. Their way of life, they were told, was being rapidly left behind by the rest of the world. Industrialization meant society was changing at a more rapid pace than any other time in centuries and they were becoming living relics, curiosities from a bygone age. Some people pitied them, perhaps, but the St Kildans cared naught for sympathy. They had learnt to play the game to their advantage – Effie chief among them.

She lifted the pail and began to walk down the slope, her eyes never fixing off the black dots as they transferred from one heaving vessel to the other. Once they'd dried off and recovered from the swell, she knew they were going to want a show. And she was going to give it to them.

'Where'll they do it?' her father asked gruffly as she finished with churning the butter. He was standing by the window, looking out, his pipe dangling from his bottom lip.

'Sgeir nan Sgarbh, I should say,' she replied, closing the lid

13

of the churn and going to stand beside him. 'It'll be more protected from the wind round there.'

'Over the top, aye, but will they get the dinghies round on the water?'

'Archie MacQueen's got the arms on him,' she murmured.

'Just not the legs.'

'No, not the legs.' She watched a trio of men walking down the Street. One she recognized by his distinctive gait – Frank Mathieson, the factor, their landlord's representative and the islanders' de facto ruler – but the other men were strangers. They were wearing well-cut dark brown suits and wool hats, but from beneath one of them she caught the gleam of golden blonde hair and a tanned neck. She willed him to turn around, wanting just to glimpse the face that went with that hair and elegant physique; but the path curved, taking them out of sight.

The group that had come ashore had been disappointingly small – a private contingent, Ian McKinnon had said with his usual authority. It meant the tips would be meagre. If the women were to take their sheets in, there had to be good reason for it and two men alone could hardly reward everyone. The captain had been put up in her Uncle Hamish's cottage and the other two men would stay at the factor's house, for it was the largest on the isle. She didn't envy them having to endure Mathieson's hospitality.

'I'm just going to put this in the cool,' she said, lifting the churn onto her shoulder and walking out, Poppit trotting at her heels. She could see the visitors further down placing pennies into the palm of Mad Annie as she sat carding the wool and telling stories about broomstick marriages and snaring puffins. Unlike most of the village elders her English was good, but that didn't mean the others couldn't communicate, and Effie gave a small grin as she saw Ma Peg make a play of bustling and hiding from their camera, even though those days of shock at the new technologies were long past. More coins crossed palms.

She went round the back of the cottage and a short way up the slope that led to the plateau of An Lag, where they herded the sheep into stone fanks in bad weather. Beyond it, Connachair – the island's tallest mountain – rose majestically like a stepping stone to heaven. For some it was. Many had met their fate over the precipice, tricked into distraction by the summit's rounded hummock on the village side and caught unaware by the sheer cliffs – 1,400 feet high – that dropped suddenly and vertically to the sea, as if cleaved.

The lush grass was speckled with buttercups and thrift and felt springy underfoot as she moved past the countless identical stone cleits to the one where she and her father stored their butter and cream. She ducked down as she stepped inside and set down the churn. It was the very store her family had been using for this purpose for over three hundred years. There may have been over 1,400 of the hump-topped, stacked-stone huts on the island, but she could identify every single one that belonged to her family – this one below An Lag for the dairy; that one on Ruival for the bird feathers; that on Oiseval for the fulmar oil; that on Connachair for the salted carcasses, that for the peats . . . There were plenty that lay empty, too, but they also had their uses as emergency larders, rain and wind shelters, hiding places for courting lovers . . .

She came back down the slope again, jumping nimbly over the rocks nestled in the grass and seeing over the rooftops that everyone was beginning to gather on the beach, preparing for the visitors' exhibition.

'Are you joining them, Effie?' a voice called.

She looked over to find Lorna MacDonald coming out of the postmaster's hut, fixing her auburn hair. She worked there sometimes with the postmaster.

Effie skipped over, Poppit beating her by two lengths. 'Aye,' she grinned. 'You never know, there might be some pennies in it for me.'

'And more besides,' Lorna said with a wink.

'What do you mean?'

'He's a fine-looking fellow, the young one. A smile from him would be payment in itself,' Lorna laughed, her brown eyes twinkling with merriment.

Effie gave a bemused shrug. 'I only caught the back of him.'

'That's pretty enough too, I should guess.'

Effie chuckled. It was a wonder to her that Lorna was their resident old maid – all of thirty-three years old and still unmarried – for she was a terrible flirt. Alas, the visiting men never stayed for long and the St Kildan bachelor nearest in age to her was Donnie Ferguson, who had no interest in a wife seven years older than him, cleverer than him and almost through her child-bearing years.

'Who are they, anyway?'

'Rich,' Lorna shrugged. 'If that ship's anything to go by.'

Lorna knew about such things. She wasn't a St Kildan by birth but a registered nurse from Stornoway who had chosen to make her life here; she had seen another world to this one and what money bought.

'Good,' Effie sighed, catching sight of the men beginning to head up the hill with their ropes, the dogs running ahead in a pack. 'Well, then I'll still aim for some pennies from them and you can have the young gentleman's smile. What do you say?'

'Deal,' Lorna winked as Effie took off again and darted back into the cottage to grab their rope. It was thickly plaited from horsehair, supple and rough in her hand. Her father was sitting in his chair by the hearth now – he could never stand for long – tamping his black twist tobacco.

'Well, I'll be off then.'

He looked back at her. His eyes had a rheumy look, the whites yellowing with age, but they still revealed a strong man within an infirm body. He gave a nod. He wasn't one for sentimental farewells. 'Hold fast, lass.'

'Aye.' She nodded back, knowing those had been his last words to her brother too.

For a moment she thought he might say something else; the way he held himself, it was as if an energy for more words lay coiled within him. But the moment passed and she left again with just a nod.

Some of the men were already walking the slopes, ropes slung over their shoulders too. As she'd predicted, they were heading for the easterly cliffs. A small rock stack just out in the water provided enough of a break from the broadside waves for the dinghy to rope up in relative comfort whilst the show was put on.

She ran and caught them up, listening in as they chatted about the visitors and the news from 'abroad', meaning Skye.

'. . . friends of the landlord,' David MacQueen, Flora's eldest brother, was saying. 'So we're to make it good.'

'Shame the wind's up or we could have gone further round,' her cousin Euan said.

'There'll be no tips if they're sick as dogs,' Ian McKinnon replied.

'But the cliffs are lower here.'

'This will do them fine. It will all be high to the likes of them.'

She fell into step with Mhairi's older brothers, Angus and Finlay.

'What are *you* doing here?' Angus asked with his usual sneer.

'Same as you,' she shrugged, slightly breathless as their longer legs covered more ground than hers.

'We're not fowling. This is just for display.'

'Aye, so there'll be tips.'

'Then knit them some socks!'

'You know I'd get a fraction of what I can get up here and the agreement is whenever you're all on the rocks, I'm allowed to be too.'

'You're a pain in my side, Effie Gillies,' Finlay groaned.

'And you're a pain in mine,' she shot back.

They rolled their eyes but she didn't care. Her brother's friends, her friend's brothers, they had been teasing her all her life and she knew to give as good as she got. They had all grown up playing hide and seek in the cleits as children, learnt to read together in the schoolroom beside the kirk, and kicked each other during the minister's sermons.

But she couldn't ignore that things were changing. Or had already changed. A tension existed now, a low-level hum, that hadn't been there before. Her brother's death had profoundly affected them all and she was no longer John's little sister to them – or anyone but herself; sometimes she caught them looking at her in a new way that made her nervous. Finlay's eyes seemed to follow her wherever she went and Angus had tried to kiss her as she cut the peats one evening; he hadn't yet forgiven her for laughing.

For visitors wanting to take in the view – and they always did – this would be a forty-minute to hour-long walk, but she and the men did it in under thirty and were already spread across the top and looping out the coils of rope by the time the dinghy appeared around the cliffs. Birds whirled and

18

screeched around them, feathers lilting on the updrafts. From this height, the boat looked no bigger than a bird either. Effie glanced down a few times, scanning the rock face for the line she wanted to take, then casting about for a rock with which to drive in her peg.

Looping the rope around the peg, she leant back, checking its firmness and tension. It vibrated with pleasing freshness and she wrapped it around her waist in the St Kildan style.

She looked down the drop once more. Cousin Euan had been right; it really wasn't so high here. Seven hundred feet? Half the height of Connachair. A single drop of the ropes would take them maybe a third of the way down. Still, they were merely going to be playing up here today. No bird hunting, no egg collecting, no saving stranded sheep. Just playing.

'You're looking peely-wally there, Eff,' Angus drawled. 'Sure you're up to it?'

She looked back at him with scorn. Angus prided himself on being the fastest climber on the island. He had won last year's Old Trial, a climbing race among the young men to prove they were worthy of providing for their families – and future wives. If he had wanted to prove anything to her, the point had been well and truly lost. Effie was certain she could have beaten him (and the rest) had she only been allowed to enter too. But as a girl . . . 'Actually, I was just wondering how quickly I could get down there.'

A smirk grew. 'You think you can do it *fast*?'

'Faster than you.' She pulled her fair hair back, tying it away from her face in a balled knot. The last thing she needed was a gust of wind blowing it about and blinding her on the route.

'Ha! You're all talk and no trousers, Effie Gillies.'

It was her turn to smirk. 'Well, yes, even I won't deny

19

there's not much in *my* trews.' Angus McKinnon might be the fastest man on the isle, but he wasn't the brightest. As if to make the point, she hitched up her breeches at the waist; they had been John's and were the only suitable attire for climbing, but she didn't wear them purely for reasons of practicality.

Finlay blushed furiously. 'Ignore her,' he said. 'You know she's only trying to rile you. Everyone knows you're the fastest, brother. Just give the rich people a show. This is an exhibition, not a race.'

Effie shrugged as if she couldn't care less either way, but they all knew the gauntlet had been thrown down. She – a girl! – was challenging Angus for his crown; the competition could happen here between the two of them. Why not? It was as good a chance as any. She watched him looking down the cliff as the islanders did final checks on their ropes and took their positions on the cliff edge.

Effie kept her eyes ahead, her hands already around the rope. Waiting. Hoping—

'H'away then!' Archie MacQueen cried. Flora's father, he had been an experienced cragger himself, but he left these shows to the younger ones these days; already lame in one leg, his grip wasn't what it used to be either. Besides, someone had to stay up top in case anyone needed hauling up.

It was the cue to go, to perform, to show off their derring-do and the skills that made the St Kildans famous around the world as they all but skipped and danced over the cliffs. Without hesitation, Effie leant back and stepped over. She felt the swoop of her stomach as her body angled into open space and the rope tightened. She pushed off, allowing the rope to swing on a pendulum, her bare feet already braced for contact with the rock face, ready to caper across it in a bold defiance of gravity. A visitor had once told them it was like watching spiders drop from the top of a wall. She herself loved the sound of the ropes under tension – a *huzzahing* – as she and the men scampered and sprang from side to side.

'First to the boat then?'

She looked across to find Angus on his rope, staring straight at her. She smiled at his tactic – finishing the race at the boat, not the bottom, when neither one of them could swim . . . 'Aye. But I'll wait for you, don't worry.'

Angus's eyes narrowed at her insult, but she was already off. Abandoning the acrobatics, her foot found a toehold and she brought her weight to bear on it as the other foot searched. The St Kildans never climbed in boots, always bare feet. The cliffs were too unyielding to give any more than a half inch to grab and there was nothing that compared to skin on rock. Shoes and boots – the hallmarks of civilization – had no place on a granite cliff.

She left the older men to the games, their powerful arms and legs flexed as they made a point of playing on the rock faces, bouncing off with their feet, reaching up for a fingerhold and pulling themselves up like lizards, before repeating again. Others scrambled sideways, scuttling like crabs over the rocks.

Effie just focused on going down. She could see the boat between her legs, far below her, as she descended on the rope, her arms braced as she lowered herself, hand over hand. She didn't have biceps the size of boulders to help her, but as she always said to her father, she didn't need them. She was wiry and light, skinny even, but that didn't mean she was weak. The less there was of her, the less she had to support. She wouldn't tire so quickly. She was more nimble, more flexible . . .

From her peripheral vision, she sensed she was already ahead of Angus, but only just. He had power, height and gravity on his side.

Soon enough she was out of rope. Balancing on a narrow ledge, she unwound the rope's end from her torso.

'What are you doing?' Ian McKinnon called sharply down to her as she began to free climb.

'Winning! Don't worry. It was Angus's idea.'

It always felt different scaling without the rope and she knew it was reckless, but there was something about the intensity it brought – her brain and eyes seemed to tune into hyper-focus, the adrenaline refreshed her muscles – that meant she could remember her mother's eyes and smile, hear again her brother's ready laugh. Somehow, by thinning the skein of life, it seemed she could almost reach the dead.

Down she went, agile and sharp until the horizon drew level, then hovered above her, and the crash of the waves began to intrude on her concentration. White splashes of cold sea were beginning to reach towards her, spraying her bare brown calves, but she didn't care about getting wet or cold. She just had to win. She had to know – and crucially, Angus had to know – that she was the fastest and the best.

She saw the dark sea, ominously close. She was less than thirty feet above the waves now, but the cliffs just sliced into the ocean depths, and as she scaled ever downwards, she realized that the only place where she could stand and pivot was a narrow ledge perhaps six feet above the surface, no wider than her hand's span.

For a moment, she felt a visceral spasm of fear. This was madness! If her father was to hear of the carelessness with which she was treating her life . . . Or maybe that was the point of it. Maybe she wanted him to hear of it. His heart had been broken by death too many times, and she was the only one left. He couldn't – or wouldn't – love her in case he lost her too. Was that it? If she was to slip, to go straight down, under the waves . . . would he weep? Would she be mourned like the others? On the other hand, if she won, would he be proud? Would he see that she could be enough?

There was no time to think. Everything was instinct. Her feet touched down and her arms splayed wide as she hugged the wall, gripping its surface with her fingertips, her cheek pressed to the cold, wet granite. Breath coming fast, she gave her muscles a moment to rest. They were burning, but she knew she wasn't there yet.

She glanced up. Angus was only a few feet above her. What he lacked in nimbleness, he made up for in power. In a few more seconds . . . She looked carefully back over her shoulder and saw the dinghy tied to a rock just a short distance away. Her Uncle Hamish, skippering, was frowning and watching her intently, the way Poppit had watched for the boat earlier. He saw her movement and seemed to understand she wanted in; that she was going to launch herself towards it, one way or another. If he was alarmed, he didn't hesitate nonetheless. Not in front of the guests. Quickly he pulled in on the rope, hauling the small dinghy as close as he dared to the cliff wall, knowing that if he went too far, the swell risked tossing them against the rocks.

A nervous flinch inside the boat betrayed someone's nerves as her intentions became commonly understood. Effie knew she would have to time the next wave and then leap. She hugged the wall as she watched and braced for the next break – just as Angus landed beside her.

A blast of white water broke upon them both, making them gasp with the shocking cold as they were soaked. She didn't care. As she felt the draft pull back, she twisted and leapt blind. Death or glory then!

For one stunning, protracted moment, she felt almost as if she could fly, like the very birds that soared and wheeled and sliced around her in this island sky. Then gravity took hold, and she landed – half in the dinghy, half in the water. She took a hard knock to her chest but her arms gripped the prow as the boat rocked wildly, water slopping over the sides. But it was flat-bottomed and made for heavy weather; it righted itself almost immediately, and she laughed victoriously as her uncle Hamish hastily got a hand to her waistband and dragged her aboard in one swift movement like a landed salmon.

'I didna' know you had decided to make it a race to the bottom,' Uncle Hamish said to her with a stern, disapproving look. It was the most he would reveal in front of the tourists, but she already knew he'd be telling her father about this. There would be trouble to come, most likely a hiding; but it was worth it. Effie's eyes were bright. She'd beaten Angus McKinnon! The fastest cragger on the isle. Not just that – he could make no further claims now of providing for her when she herself had beaten him.

'It was Angus's idea,' she panted, scrambling to her knees and looking back to find him still clinging to the ledge. With her leap to victory, he now stood frozen in place and was becoming more soaked with every breaking wave. He either had to jump too or climb back up, but he couldn't stay there.

With an angry sigh, he jerked his thumb upwards, indicating the latter. He had lost. What good was there in riding back with them now? She would only crow her victory at him.

Uncle Hamish nodded, understanding perfectly what had just happened between them. It was a man's look, the kind that cut her out, but what did she care? With a satisfied smile, Effie sat on the bench, pulling out her hair tie and wringing her long hair. Seawater puddled in the dinghy floor.

'Heavens above!' a voice said. 'It's a *girl*?'

She twisted back to face the visitors properly at last. In all her ambition to beat Angus, she'd forgotten who they were trying to impress in the first place. The three men seated towards the back were staring at her in wide-eyed amazement: Frank Mathieson, the factor, and the two men she'd glimpsed from behind earlier.

'Well, I can't climb in a skirt, sir,' she grinned, wringing out her tweed breeches as best she could.

'It wasn't just your clothes that fooled me. The speed! I've never seen a spectacle like it. You scaled that cliff like a squirrel down a tree!' It was the older man speaking. He was portly, with a dark moustache, lightly salted. Spectacles made it difficult to see his eyes past the reflection, but he appeared friendly as well as impressed. 'Do you mean to say females climb here, too?' he asked their skipper.

'Only this one,' Uncle Hamish said with a resigned tone, untying the rope from the mooring rock and beginning to row. 'This is my niece, Euphemia Gillies.'

'Effie is Robert Gillies's daughter. They live at number nine,' the factor added, as if that information was somehow enlightening. 'How are you, Effie?'

'Aye, well, sir, thank you for asking.'

'Becoming bolder, I see.'

'If by bolder you mean faster.'

He laughed. 'Allow me to present the Earl of Dumfries and his son, Lord Sholto,' he said. 'I'm sure you will be aware that they are great friends of Lord MacLeod.'

'Ah,' she said blandly, although she was aware of nothing of the sort. Who their landlord kept as friends was no business of hers, though it confirmed Lorna's observation that the visitors were rich.

'They were visiting his lordship at Dunvegan when they heard I was planning on making the voyage here—'

'It's been something of an ambition of mine to get over here,' the earl said brightly, interrupting. 'I'm a keen birder, you see, and Sir John very kindly agreed to my proposal that we might sail Mr Mathieson here ourselves. Two birds, one stone and all that.'

'Aye.' She could feel the younger man watching her keenly as she talked, but for as long as the others spoke, she had no such opportunity to cast her gaze openly over him. 'So will you be staying for long, then?'

The factor inhaled. 'Well, a lot will depend upon the wea—'

'Certainly a week,' Lord Sholto said suddenly, allowing a dazzling smile to enliven his features as she finally met his eyes.

'A week?' Effie smiled back at the blue-eyed, golden-haired man. Finally she could see his face at last. And she liked it.

'Miss Gillies.'

She turned to find the factor hurrying up the beach after her. Uncle Hamish was tying up the boat, the distinguished guests having been appropriated by the minister again the moment they'd set foot on shore.

'Mr Mathieson.' She tried not to show her impatience, but her tweed breeches were soaked from her half-swim and she wanted to get back and change. Their progress round the headland had been slow as they'd met the headwinds and she was shivering now.

He stopped in front of her, slightly downhill from where

she stood, so that she was aware of standing taller than him. He wasn't a tall man, stocky but not conspicuously short either, and the consequence of not standing out in any way seemed to work to his advantage; many times an islander had been caught saying things they shouldn't, not realizing he was within earshot. His relationship with the St Kildans was highly taut, for as the bringer of supplies every spring, and the collector of rents every autumn, he was both carrot and stick to the island community. He could smile and be charming when it suited him, but no one could ever quite forget that the power he wielded over them was almost absolute, and few – apart from Mad Annie – would clash with him. He wore finer suits than the village men and affected the manners of his employer, but reddened, pitted cheeks and the forearms of a wrestler betrayed him as a fighter first.

'Well, that was quite a display,' he said.

Effie wasn't sure this was intended as a compliment. 'That's the idea,' she replied vaguely. 'They always like it.' A sudden gust blew her long, wet hair forward and she had to use both hands to pin it back. The sky was growing ominously dark.

'Indeed.' He gave what she had come to learn over the years was his customary pause. It preceded a direct contradiction of what came after it. 'Although I'm not sure such daredevil antics require the added *novelty* factor.'

It took a moment to understand his meaning. 'Of a girl climbing, you mean?'

He shrugged. 'I understand your obligations to your father impel you to undertake men's work in a regular capacity, but when it comes to making a good impression on visitors . . . '

'But they seemed to like it.'

'Well, they're polite, of course, but things are quite different in the wider world. I know it's not your fault that you don't know any differently – why should you? – but decorum and good taste are held in high regard. Women scrambling over cliffs like monkeys . . . ' He pulled a face. 'No. It's important to think about the impression you make on these visitors and how you and your neighbours will be conveyed in their onward conversations. I'm sure you wouldn't want to embarrass Sir John, would you?'

She had never met Sir John. '. . . Of course not.'

'Very well, then. So we're agreed there'll be no more fits of vanity on the ropes. We must strive to make sure the guests are not made to feel uncomfortable by what they witness here. Best foot forward, yes?'

She stared back at him, shivering with cold and anger. '. . . Aye, sir.'

He looked over her shoulder, along the Street. 'How is your father, anyway? Still lame?'

Her eyes narrowed. 'And always will be.'

'Which only makes him all the luckier to have you,' he nodded, oblivious to her terse tone. 'But please tell him I shall need to find him later and discuss the rent arrears.'

'Arrears?' Alarm shot through the word.

'As I recall, you were short thirteen Scotch ells of tweed last year. Your uncle picked up some of the slack, but you were also down nine gallons of oil and seven sacks of black feathers.'

'It'll be fine this year,' she said quickly. 'We were only short because I twisted my ankle and couldn't walk for ten days. It was just bad luck that it happened when we were fowling.'

The factor looked unconvinced. 'I'll need to reappraise the quota with him. You will remember I extended a great kindness in not reducing the oatmeal bolls after your brother's accident and as a result you have enjoyed more than your share for nigh-on four years now—'

Effie looked at him with wild panic. What he said was true, but it still wasn't enough. The past few winters had been hard ones and their harvests had all but failed, save for a half-dozen potatoes and those oats that were only half blackened by frost.

'—I have been both generous and patient, but it's not fair to expect others to compensate for your shortfalls. Accidents will always happen, Miss Gillies. You cannot expect to be fit and well every day of the year.'

'But I do. And I will,' she said urgently. The factor didn't know it yet, but she and her father had lost four of their sheep over the top this year already, so they were already down on their wool yield. Her father had bartered 100 extra fulmars instead with Donald McKinnon and it had been a rare endorsement of Effie's climbing skills that both men believed she was capable of bagging the extra haul, on top of the usual harvest.

'Miss Gillies, you don't need me to remind you that you are a girl doing a man's job. The odds are already grossly stacked against you.'

'But I'm eighteen now, and I've grown this last year. I can do anything they can and I'll prove it to you. I'll show you, sir.'

The factor looked at her keenly. 'You receive more than you are due and you deliver less than you owe. You see my predicament? I must be fair, Miss Gillies. Why should I make – and keep making – exceptions for you? If the others were to know—'

'But they won't. I'll make sure we're square and level come this September.'

'So you're saying you want me to keep this a secret?'

'Secret . . . ?' Behind him, the reverend and the two gentlemen guests walked past on the path back to the village, the minister holding forth on the repairs made to the manse. Lord Sholto glanced across at them talking as he passed by and she found herself smiling back at him, as though he'd pulled it from her on a string.

'From your neighbours? And your father too?'

She looked back at the factor in confusion. He was watching her intently. '. . . No, please don't tell him. I don't want him to worry. I can make the quota this year, I know I can.'

He tutted. 'I don't know why I allow you to manipulate me, Miss Gillies—'

She frowned. *Did* she manipulate him?

'A "thank you" doesn't pay the fiddler, now, does it?' he sighed. 'Still, I have sympathy for your predicament and although I have a job to do, I believe in being a friend in the hour of need.'

Effie bit her lip – she had to – to keep from laughing out loud. What? There wasn't a person on the isle who would have considered the factor a friend. He bought their feathers at five shillings a stone and sold them at fifteen, and the supplies he brought over – oatmeal, flour, sugar, tea and tobacco – cost them three times what he paid. Was it any wonder the villagers tried to bypass him with money they earnt from the tourists and could spend directly themselves?

'Talking of which, I have brought you something, again.'

'For our studies?' She had finished her schooling four years ago, but he never seemed to remember this.

'I've left it in the usual spot. Just . . . be discreet, please. I can't oblige these sorts of favours for everyone.'

Favours? Secrets? 'But—'

'Good day, Miss Gillies,' he said briskly, assuming his usual manner as he noticed the three men now ahead of him on the path. 'I must get on. Our visitors will be requiring some refreshments after the afternoon's . . . excitement. Just remember what we discussed. We shall have to hope first impressions don't stick.'

Chapter Two

The next day dawned clear and bright, brown puddles winking in the sunlight. It had rained in the night, the day's excitable winds steadily agitating throughout the evening and tossing storm clouds into their path. When the rain had come – as she climbed from her bath – it fell like silver knives, confining the villagers to their cottages and the visitors with the minister and factor. As expected, Effie caught a supper from her father for 'showing off'; Uncle Hamish had been quicker than usual to come round and enlighten him of the afternoon's events. It seemed to be Angus McKinnon's humiliation, and not her mortal danger, that was the principal issue.

Now, though, everything felt washed clean and fresh again. It was a new day and Effie had slept well; her exertions always meant she fell into oblivion as soon as she lay down but she had woken to an effervescent feeling in her stomach that she couldn't quite explain. Her body felt as if it had tuned to a higher frequency.

She went about the morning duties with her usual rigour – collecting a slab of peat from the cleit for the fire, fetching water from the burn, cooking oats for their breakfast and milking the cow – but with one eye out, as if casting around for something. She was both distracted and highly focused.

Her gaze came back time and again to the magnificent yacht now sitting serenely on the glassy sea.

Would its owners really stay a week? Most visitors only managed three days at the very most; they struggled to adapt to the simple ways over here, no matter how pretty or charming they first thought it on arrival. It was unfortunate it was such a busy time for the village, too. As it was the second Wednesday of May, they were leading into the fulmar harvest. The towering cliffs, and the rock stacks that rose like needles from the sea, were bleached white with the legions of seabirds come to nest and brood, and any day now – today even – the men (and Effie) would catch and kill thousands of fulmars that the women would then pluck, and the feathers would be stored. Finally the carcasses would be salted to preserve through the coming winter and transferred to the cleits. The days would be long and hard; there'd not be much time for play.

The men were already gathered on the Street for the daily parliament by the time Effie wandered up, Poppit by her side. From a distance, they all looked the same, wearing brown woollen trousers and waistcoats, their shirt sleeves rolled up and cloth caps on their heads, no shoes. She, wearing the same, minus the cap, loitered on the periphery near to Mad Annie, who was sitting at her spinning wheel by the front door of her cottage. The men were debating between digging in the potato crop, starting the fulmar harvest or planning a trip over to neighbouring Boreray to pluck the sheep. Effie looked out to sea. The water was mirror-calm through the four-mile stretch.

'We should take the window while we've got it,' Norman Ferguson said decisively. 'You saw the winds yesterday, there'll be a few days o' doldrums now before the next spring storm. If we leave it till after then, the sheep'll go into moult and—'

'Aye, but with the winter we've just had,' Donald McKinnon argued. 'I say we should get the crops in now while the ground's warm. It'll buy us some time to lift early if need be—'

'What about the birds? Stac Lee's thick w' them,' Angus said, wanting to get out on the ropes.

'We've a few more days on that. They were a week late in comin' this year,' Norman said dismissively. 'But if we get over to Boreray and pluck now, the factor can take the wool back and we free up some space in the feather store. It's always fit to bursting on his return.'

Her father gave a derisive laugh. 'Get the wool now, aye, but if ye think he'll credit ye that come September, think again. Half o' it will be conveniently lost or forgotten.'

A silence greeted his bold words. It was one thing to cheek the factor in his absence, quite another to risk it while he was in residence. Heads turned to check they'd not been overheard, the factor a silent shadow at their backs.

'Then he can write it down and we can show proof he took it,' Norman said in a quieter voice.

'Because we read and write so well?'

Norman's cheeks coloured. 'Lorna MacDonald can do it then.'

Uncle Hamish cleared his throat. As one of the older men but still active in the island duties, he often moved as an unelected leader. 'We'll have a show of hands. Those for the tatties.'

Two hands went up – Donald McKinnon and old Finlay Ferguson. Old Fin was in his eighties, but digging lazybeds was one of the few chores he could still partake in.

'Sheep plucking.'

Twelve hands went up, including Effie's.

'Boreray it is then.' Uncle Hamish looked across at her. 'Effie, you know full well you'll not be coming.'

'But—'

'No buts.'

'But the water's like glass!' she said hotly anyway. 'You could run over there!'

'Ah, good morning!'

They all turned at the hearty greeting. The minister was walking towards them, his guests and the factor a step behind. Had they all breakfasted together? Effie felt her stomach pitch and roll as she caught sight of the young lord again. If it hadn't been raining so hard last night, he might have taken an evening walk down the Street; they might have talked. One whole precious evening had been lost already.

'I trust we're not too late for this morning's parliament?' the minister asked with rare brightness. Reverend John Lyon was a young preacher who had bitterly resented his posting to this remote outpost. He had been ordained only three months when the news came he was to sail to the ends of the earth and for the first year he had struggled with everything – the constant winds, the relentless sun, the roar of the crashing sea, the screams of the birds, the paltry diet. The islanders would sit in the kirk every evening and watch with scorn, pity and bemusement as he mumbled through his sermons, white with exhaustion, malnourishment and despair.

Gradually, though, in the manner of adapt or die, he had acquired a taste (of sorts) for roasted puffin and had come to realize that in a community of only thirty-six people, all of whom depended upon him alone for spiritual guidance, he could wield a certain power. His religious fervour began to rise, and his warnings of damnation and the eternal fight against sin saw the villagers sent back out into the nights with increasingly furrowed brows. They greeted him in the Street with raised caps and when important visitors came to the isle, it was with him that they were obliged to socialize. The minister was never happier than when mainlanders came over, bringing supplies and news of the wider world, and it was a new source of amusement for the villagers to watch him become more Kildan than the natives.

'I'm afraid you are, Reverend,' Uncle Hamish said. 'We've decided to take advantage of the flat sea and make the expedition to Boreray.'

'Boreray? Now that's the large island over there?' the earl asked, stepping into the meeting too and pointing an arm out to his right.

'Aye, sir,' Uncle Hamish nodded. 'It's where we keep our sheep. They need plucking before they moult.'

'Your sheep *moult*?'

'They do. A very ancient breed, sir. We pluck them, bring back the wool, then card and spin and weave it into tweed as rent for his lordship.'

'Truly a cottage industry! Well, may we join you? My son and I are keen to experience your Hebridean ways.'

Effie saw looks skate from one man to the next.

'You would be welcome, sir, but you should know there's always a strong risk of the weather changing and us getting caught over there. If that happens we could easily be there for a week, ten days, and I'm afraid there's none of the creature comforts there as here.'

Both visitors laughed – until they realized the man was completely serious; that supposedly there were creature comforts *here*. The earl cleared his throat. 'Quite. Yes, I see. How long are you planning to be there for?'

Lord Sholto caught Effie's eyes; she could see the laughter in his look, though he stood perfectly composed. He was wearing a light brown suit and, unlike his father, no tie.

'Three or four days, most likely. It's not comfortable when we have to fit in the Stalker's House. All thirteen of us.'

'Fourteen!' Effie piped up.

'. . . Fourteen, aye,' Uncle Hamish confirmed, but with another of his stern looks.

She didn't care. She'd caught him on the hop and secured her place. She beamed, feeling satisfied.

'It sounds rather . . . crowded.'

'It's very rustic, Your Lordship,' the factor replied, po-faced. 'It's an ancient souterrain. An underground dwelling. No more than a ditch walled with stone slabs, really.'

If he had been trying to put him off . . .

'Good gracious. What a shame we can't join you, I should have loved to see it!' the earl exclaimed.

'You still can, sir. We have a couple here on Hirta. The Fairy House is not far away. I'm sure we could find someone to show you.' Uncle Hamish looked straight at her. 'Effie, you could make yourself useful and take their lordships to Tigh Na Banaghaisgich.'

She looked back at him with pink-cheeked indignation. 'But I'm going to Boreray!'

'I just told you you're not.'

'No. You just said it – fourteen of us going over.'

'Aye, the factor will want to come. That makes fourteen.'

The factor looked as surprised by his automatic admission to their party as she was to be excluded from it.

'I trust you will want to make an inventory of the sheep numbers and check their condition for the laird?' Uncle Hamish asked him.

There was a pause. 'Indeed.'

'But you all agreed it's my right to do our share,' Effie said, pushing her way forward and refusing to be ignored.

'Effie,' Finlay McKinnon said warningly, trying to pull her back as he always did, as if she was heading towards some danger only he could see.

'On Hirta only. You know this.' Uncle Hamish looked away, pointedly ending the discussion. 'It's agreed, then. Tell the women to pack the supplies. We'll set off in the hour.'

The band of men turned to disperse.

'I wonder . . .' The earl let the words hang in the air. His rank meant the men could not turn away when he spoke; sure enough, they all turned back. 'Will there be anyone left on the island who can act as our guide?'

'I'm afraid the men will all be gone a few days now, sir,' Archie MacQueen said, touching his cap apologetically.

'Ah, that is a pity,' the earl nodded. 'To have come such a long way to see your famous birdlife. Sir John said it was worth making the trip especially.'

There was a silence. Everyone knew from the casual mention of 'Sir John' that this was an elegant warning: it would not be in their best interests to disappoint their landlord, or his close friends.

'If it's birds y'like, there's no one knows more about the birds here than Effie. She saw the fork-tailed petrels up by Mullach Sgar just the other week, did ye no', lass?' Mad Annie piped up from her position at the spinning wheel. 'And she's a good climber too, equal to many of the men.'

Angus McKinnon immediately bristled. As did Effie. Hadn't she, only last night, proved she was *better*?

'Well, we certainly saw a display of her speed and courage last night,' the young lord said, one hand pushed casually into his trouser pocket as he leant against the wall. 'I wouldn't hesitate to place my trust in Miss Gillies. Would you, Father?'

The earl considered for a moment, watching Effie from behind his spectacles. For the first time, she wondered what he saw, how she appeared to outsiders – a girl dressed as a boy, showing off on a rope, arguing with the men . . .

'After what we saw yesterday, no. What do you say, young lady? Will you be our guide for the next few days? We'd pay, of course – say, two shillings for your time?'

'Two . . . ?' Effie looked at her father with disbelief. She only earnt a pound for looking after the bull for a whole year! It would mean abandoning any hope of getting over to Boreray, but . . .

She nodded back to the gentlemen. 'For two shillings, I'd be happy to guide you, sir.'

'That's agreed, then,' Uncle Hamish said, effectively dismissing the meeting again with his pronouncement. The men quickly disbanded, but Effie stayed where she was as the earl and his son walked over. Poppit pressed herself against her legs as she petted her head.

'Well, we are now in your hands, young lady,' the earl said. 'Can you lead us to the fork-tailed petrels?'

'Aye, sir. Or to the Fairy House. Whenever you're ready.'

'I'm not sure this is entirely regular, Your Lordship,' the factor said, stepping in.

'Why not?' the earl asked briskly. 'She's proved she's equal to the men in her abilities. And she has personally sighted one of the very birds I've come here to spot.'

'But, as a young woman alone, guiding . . .' The factor let his words fade, allowing an insinuation to speak for him instead.

'Yes . . . ?'

There was an awkward silence as the factor looked between her and their esteemed guests, his employer's personal friends.

'It's nothing, sir, you're quite right. I'm glad an arrangement could be found.' Frank Mathieson went to withdraw, looking like a kicked dog.

'Mr Mathieson, before we leave,' said Ian McKinnon, the postmaster, stepping towards him. 'I'd like to talk with you about the matter we raised on your last visit in September . . . ?' He tailed off into a diplomatic silence, not wanting to go into details in front of their guests.

The factor's mouth settled into a flat line. He often seemed displeased by the realities of his work. As the laird's man on the ground, he had to not only bring over supplies but listen to and address their problems, illnesses, needs and wants: the roofs weren't secure, it rained inside the houses as well as out, the harvest had failed . . . On his second trip of the season, at the end of August, he would collect the goods they bartered for rent and would again leave any necessary supplies to see them through the long, hard winter, when the isle was cut off from the mainland by the heavy seas.

'Can it not wait till we return, Mr McKinnon?' he snapped. 'I've just endured one hellish crossing only to find I must immediately take another.'

The postmaster looked clearly affronted. 'Well, I dare say it can, aye, sir.'

'Good,' the factor muttered with a look of scorn as he turned on his heel. 'Now, if you'll excuse me. I've to prepare for counting *sheep*.'

The decision to see to the sheep put the village into a spin. Chores were abandoned as the women put together food supplies and blankets were sought, old sacks retrieved from cleits and folded down for the plucked wool that would be coming back with the men. The dogs ran along the shore, barking excitedly and sending the birds scattering skywards as the boat was pulled towards the water.

But within the hour they were ready, and the women and children waved with handkerchiefs in their hands till the village's boat rowed around the headland of Oiseval and out of sight.

'Shall we get such a fond farewell when it is our turn to leave, Miss Gillies?' Lord Sholto asked, amusement dancing through his eyes. He had emerged from the factor's house as he heard the commotion and had come to stand on the beach with the rest. Now, somehow, they were standing together.

'I'm sure we shall be quite sorry to see you go, sir,' she said, keeping her eyes dead ahead. She could see the factor looking back to shore from the boat and knew he still wasn't happy that she would be guiding their most esteemed visitors, no matter what he'd said to the contrary. In the six years that he had occupied the role as MacLeod's factor, there hadn't been a single visit when he hadn't called her 'a wild thing', as though she was an animal and not a girl. 'We always take care to say proper goodbyes, for there are never any guarantees we'll be reunited.'

She turned to walk back up the beach, but he moved too and walked with her. He had changed from his suit into climbing tweeds.

'But they are not going far. The isle is just over the way, is it not?'

'Aye but you don't need to go far for danger. We had three men drowned right here in the bay and we couldna' save them.'

A deep frown puckered his smooth brow. 'That's terrible, I'm sorry. Was it recent?'

'No. Fourteen years past now, but to their families it is like yesterday.'

'Was there a storm?'

'Not a bad one, but there was swell. They went out to catch some birds off the stack over there. Stac Levenish. The men were tied to one another, ready to climb. One fell in . . .' She shrugged.

'And the others went down with him,' he murmured. 'Could they not swim?'

'None of us can.'

'None—?' He looked shocked.

'We've no need to go in the water. The waters are too heavy to fish in any numbers. We can fish a little off the rocks but it's why we mainly hunt the birds instead.'

'But yesterday, coming down the cliff . . . You leapt into the boat.'

'Aye.' She looked back at him blankly.

'If you had missed . . .'

'But I didn't.'

'You barely made it, though.'

'Barely was still enough,' she shrugged. 'But perhaps if I had really needed it, you might have thought to save me, sir.'

He laughed at her wry tone. 'I hope you know I wouldn't have hesitated.'

She shrugged.

'And are you going to tell me you risked your life just to beat that fellow who was racing you?'

'It was important that I won.'

'But worth dying for?'

'Well, I would always prefer not to, naturally.'

He laughed again.

The earl, who had been watching the departure from the

window of the factor's house, stepped out, and she headed for him. 'Are you ready, sir?' she asked.

'Indeed. Though I should warn you – my son may be up to keeping up with you on the ropes and slopes, but I'm afraid those days are very much behind me.'

Effie gave a guarded smile. Manners barred her from exclaiming that his son wouldn't have a chance of keeping up with her on a rope. 'We'll mainly just be walking today, sir. I last saw the Leaches circling near Na h-Eagan, on the far side of Ruival there.' She pointed to the mountain to their left, on the opposite side of the glen.

'You call them Leaches too?' The earl seemed impressed. 'So then you know something of the birds, other than by sight?'

'Aye, sir.' She jutted her chin defiantly. Poor didn't mean ignorant. Like all the younger generation on the island, she could read and write and spell in both English and Gaelic. 'I read a lot.'

'Quite so. And your dog . . .' He glanced at Poppit, standing close by her legs, her head positioned as ever beneath Effie's palm. 'She won't disturb the birds?'

'On the contrary, she's my secret weapon. She can smell them.'

'What's her name?'

'Poppit.'

'That's an unusual name.'

'It's on account of a meadow pipit she befriended as a pup.'

The earl laughed. 'I see.'

'I trained her myself. Her mother rejected the litter so I hand-reared her.'

'Yes, I can see the bond from here. She doesn't take her eyes off you.'

43

'She's a loyal lass.' Effie couldn't keep the warmth from her voice as she stroked the dog's head. She looked back up to find both men watching her with curious looks. Didn't they talk to their animals too? '. . . Shall we, then?'

They walked through the Street, Effie nodding and sharing a smile with Jayne Ferguson and a crafty wink with Lorna MacDonald as she passed by with the distinguished guests. Effie knew the gossip that would spill out now the women had charge of the village and she felt their sharp-eyed gazes at the men's backs as they walked along. Even Mary McKinnon, who was rarely out of her bed these days – she was with child but carrying poorly – looked up from her knitting as they strode past her door.

They walked three abreast, the earl centrally placed as they began the climb up Mullach Geal. It was too steep to talk much, although Effie pointed out as many birds as she could – snipe and meadow pipits, wheatears and the native wrens particularly who hopped on the walls and cleits, singing loudly as they fought to be heard above the sea, wind and shrieking seabirds.

At the top of the Am Blaid ridge, an hour or so later and twice the time it would usually take her, they stopped.

'Miss Gillies, a brief rest, if you will,' the earl panted, leaning on his walking stick. 'At my age, the spirit may well be willing but the flesh is sadly weak.' Gingerly, he sat himself on the ground.

Effie flopped down where she was standing, his son too, all of them leaning their elbows on their knees as they took in the view over the glen and out to sea.

'You're lucky to call this home, Miss Gillies,' the earl said once he'd got his breath back, a sense of wonder in his voice.

'Aye, I am,' she sighed, looking down upon the smoking settlement, her kingdom, with pride.

'Have you ever left here?'

'Why would I do that, sir? I have all that I need here.'

'Quite so.' He smiled, seeming bemused by her reply. 'Still, for all its wild majesty, it's not an easy way to live. Sir John often shares the problems you face living somewhere so remote – the failed crops, the sickness and lack of medical care.'

'There is that. But the beauty outweighs the problems.'

'So you've never thought of moving elsewhere?'

'Only during the particularly bad storms.'

'I imagine they can be quite wild. The rain last night was ferocious.'

'It's the winds that are really fierce. We've had roofs ripped off, the boat flipped over . . . It's not much fun if you get caught away from home, I can tell you.'

'Do you take shelter in the cleits?'

'Aye. If the sheep don't beat us to it.'

Lord Sholto gave a low laugh. He seemed entertained by her conversation.

'But you're still not tempted by an easier life?'

She sighed. 'Oh, sometimes we get visitors over who tell us stories about your side of the water and I get to wondering what it must be like not to . . . struggle. But this is what I know. It's what I am.' She stared down at her home, her eyes tracing the long wall of the head dyke behind the cottages, the symmetrical roundness of the burial ground's high wall, these dots and dashes the small impressions made by her ancestors into this landscape. Nature had carved, whittled and whipped this rock in the sea into a home. And that home had shaped her, its wild forces honing her like a parent.

'Besides, my father would never leave here and I would never leave him, so . . .' She gave a shrug.

'Then he's a lucky man to have such a loving daughter.'

'He'd prefer a living son.' The comment was out before she could stop it. She gave a tight smile, seeing the visitors' surprised looks. '. . . Sorry, sir, I shouldn't have said that. I forget, sometimes, not to say every thought that comes into m' head.'

'Please, my dear, speak freely,' the earl said. 'If we cannot be free here in the middle of nowhere, then where?'

'This isn't the middle of nowhere,' she protested with hurt pride.

'No?'

'It's the middle of everywhere – for me anyway.'

'Of course. My apologies. My remark was tactless.'

Lord Sholto was regarding her with interest. 'Are you an only child too, Miss Gillies?'

She swallowed. 'I am now. My big brother John died four years back . . . He went over the top.'

He frowned. 'You mean he . . . ?'

'Fell, aye. The rope snapped.'

There was an appalled silence. The visitors had seen the height of the sea cliffs for themselves yesterday. 'Is that sort of accident common?' the earl asked.

'No, but it happens every few years or so. My father hasn't recovered.'

'And your mother . . . ?'

Effie inhaled sharply. 'Knew nothing of it, thankfully. She died when I was ten. TB.'

'My dear girl, I'm so sorry,' the earl said softly. 'So it's just the two of you then?'

Effie nodded. 'My father was married before. His first wife died delivering a baby. They had five wee 'uns and none lived past seven, for various reasons – lockjaw, the boat cough.'

'That is a heavy burden for any man to bear.'

'Aye.'

The earl was watching her. 'And for you too.'

She was surprised by the observation. No one had ever commented on *her* loss before. 'It's fine. I get on with it.'

There was a small pause, the men digesting her revelation with pitying eyes, but tragedy was a part of life here, like the wind.

'So is that why you stood with the men at their meeting this morning? You've taken on your brother's duties?' Lord Sholto asked.

She nodded. 'We need craggers to catch the birds and their eggs we eat for food, but out of the thirty-six of us, there's too many as are too old or too young to go over the top. My father's too old for the ropes and his bones are bad anyway, so I go.'

'But wouldn't your neighbours help you?' the earl asked.

'Aye, they would, as they do for the widows and Old Fin. But why should we rely on charity when I am young and strong and able-bodied? Should we put out our begging bowls just because I am a girl and not a boy?'

They saw the defiance in her eyes. '. . . That's a very modern view, especially in a community such as this. Has it been well-received among the men?' the earl asked.

'Not really. The old ways run deep, but it's tolerated because they've no other choice. Whatever their prejudice against a girl doing men's work, there's just not enough of them to do it without me. I've proved to them I can do it and they need my help, even if they don't want it.'

The son was smiling at her again as she spoke. 'And what exactly do you do, that girls shouldn't?' he asked.

'Cragging. Fowling for fulmars, kittiwakes and guillemots. Snaring puffins, working the dogs.'

47

'So why weren't you allowed to the other island?'

'That's just their way of stopping me. The sheep wool isn't food, clearly, just rent, so they can get by without me. They need me for the bird quotas here and they know they can't prevent me from climbing the cliffs anyway, but they can stop me from getting into a boat with them.'

'Their justification being?'

'I can't swim.'

Lord Sholto frowned. 'But they can't either. You said to me on the beach that—'

'I know. It's just the excuse they give.'

He didn't reply, but his eyes flashed with something that looked like anger.

'Can I be honest with you, Miss Gillies?' the earl asked after a short pause.

'I hope you will, sir.'

'Before we left, Sir John mentioned to me in confidence that he had received a letter from the islanders. He said you've petitioned the government, asking for evacuation to the mainland.'

Effie looked at him, then away again. She clenched her jaw. 'Aye.'

'Did you sign it?'

'I had to. We either all go or all stay, that was the arrangement.'

'Even if it's not what you want? You just said you never want to leave.'

'That's just how it is here. The voice of one is the voice of all. We can scarce support ourselves with the numbers we've got, it's true, and if any more young men were to leave . . . I try to show them every day that we could manage it if the women could be allowed to do the men's jobs too but . . .'

'They're not as brave as you?'

'They just don't want it. Every month, we have more tourist boats, people coming over and telling us about life on the Other Side: Luxury. Comfort. Heating. Shops. Cars. Indoor bathrooms. Talking pictures . . .' She sighed, shrugging her shoulders in a hopeless gesture. 'Their heads have been turned. They're tired of island life.'

'But you're not?'

'I don't want easy. This is all I know. Besides, there's nothing for me over there. I'd have nothing to go to.'

'So if the government grants your request—?'

'But they won't. They never do, that's why I agreed to sign. For years we've been asking for a radio tower, a regular mail boat, a bigger boat instead of the skiffs, even just herring nets! Nothing. Why should this be any different? No one cares about us.'

Her voice faded out as it occurred to her she had said too much, revealed the dissatisfaction and unhappiness of the villagers to people who were friends of their landlord, a man about to lose the considerable income they generated for him. Why should she think they would understand, much less side with her? If the factor was to hear about what she'd just said . . . Wasn't she behaving in exactly the way he'd feared? She forced a smile and an end to the conversation.

'Well, if you're ready, sir?' she asked, gathering in her feet.

He nodded, seeming to read her sudden apprehension, and they all rose, setting off again. They bore south-westwards, walking with more ease now along the high plateau. Effie loved it up here. The ocean puddled around them in every direction, the horizon forming an unbroken line for 360 degrees, no land in sight. On really clear days, the distant peaks of North Uist and Harris could just be glimpsed as faint shadows, but not today. A slight haze kept them locked in their own universe, quite alone.

They walked another hour, the men forming a line behind her as the path narrowed to single file. They skirted the cliffs, the land drawing sharply inwards in parts, the sky becoming sketchy with white and grey arrows, birds swooping as they circled their perches on the vertiginous cliffs. The earl was an experienced birder. Even at height he could identify the shag from the cormorant, the fulmar from the lesser black-backed gull, the flight pattern of the gannet and the kittiwake. Effie walked with focus, her gaze catching on one bird, then another, following, assessing, searching . . .

'There,' she said suddenly, pointing ahead of her as she stopped walking. The men flanked her on either side, following the direction of her finger. She motioned for them to get low, her eyes scanning the long tufty grass. They all lay on their stomachs.

'What do you see?' the earl whispered.

'A Leach nest, straight ahead.'

'Here? Not on the cliffs?' the earl asked.

She shook her head. 'The fulmar petrel nests on ledges, but the fork-tail burrows.'

'I can't see it,' Lord Sholto said.

'It's right there, look.' She pointed to the remains of an ancient cleit. Only a few rocks remained, the remnants now barely even a wall, but tucked between several stacked boulders could be seen some wildly placed stalks of grass and displaced patches of lichen. It was almost impossible to discern in the sprawling wildness, only the tiniest vagaries of mismatched placement drawing the eye.

'How on earth did you spot that?' the earl asked. 'I can scarcely make it out even now you've shown it to me.'

'Come left a little.' They all shuffled leftwards a few feet and the new angle better revealed a small bird the size of a swift, roosting upon the scant nest, sitting tight between the stones. Its feathers were bluish-grey with white upper tail-coverts and a small dusky black bill.

The bird ruffled its wings, twitching as if sensing their scrutiny.

The earl inhaled sharply. They had all seen, in the movement, the bright ovoid perfection of its egg. 'Tell me what you know of them,' he whispered.

Effie considered for a moment. She knew a lot. Her books were the only distraction to be had on long winter nights, and if it was a choice between that and the Bible . . . 'They're pelagic, spending up to eight months at sea. Their forked tails make them good divers. They're slightly larger than the Stormies, with an erratic, hesitant flight pattern. They often appear to walk on the water . . . What else?' She thought harder. 'Oh. Yes. They don't recognize their own chicks and will switch mates if a hatching fails. They usually only lay one egg. It's rough-textured, chalky white with a few small red dots at the larger end and they're highly prized.'

'I'll say,' Sholto murmured, glancing at her. 'Papa's been after one for six years. And you've just walked him straight up to one!'

'I'm afraid I really must have it,' the earl murmured, as if he was breaking bad news to her. But he wasn't the first rich man to have arrived here on an egg hunt and he wouldn't be the last. 'Sholto, seeing as you're nearer . . .'

His son nodded.

'Wait,' Effie said as he moved to go forward. 'If you invade the nest, they'll spit oil on you.'

'That's nothing to what Papa will do if I don't get it for him.' Lord Sholto gave a bemused smile.

It was the sort of smile that probably meant he always got what he wanted but she held firm. 'Just wait. She'll move.'

'Today?' But it was a gentle joke, and he moved back into position again.

'During incubation, both parents frequently abandon the egg for days at a time. Their eggs incubate at much lower temperatures than other birds. Look, see how she's twitching again. I think she's getting ready to fly . . .'

'How do you know all this?' Lord Sholto asked.

She felt offended he expected so little from her. Did he assume her to be primitive just because she was an islander? 'I watch and I learn, sir.'

As if to make the point, she pulled a small notebook from her climbing bag and – watching intently – began making notes of the bird's behaviour, sketching its bill, the crown of its head . . . They lay in the grass for a while, all watching the bird as she fussed, moving on the egg and off again as much as she could in the confines of the nook. She pulled at a stalk of grass that wasn't laid to her liking. Her feathers ruffled again, stretching out her wings.

'That's it . . .' Effie murmured, eyes narrowing in concentration. 'Go on . . .'

A few moments later, the bird took off, skimming and half-circling over the cliffs and out above open water.

'Hurrah!' the earl exclaimed as the egg was exposed in its brilliant perfection.

'And now you may take it without having your clothes ruined.'

'Well worth the wait – and I can get it myself now.' He struggled back up to standing.

'My mother's always telling me patience is a virtue. She

says the best things are always worth waiting for,' Lord Sholto said.

'Then your mother and I are in agreement,' she said evenly, resisting the light in his eyes as he lay on his stomach watching her. For all his easy laughs and gentlemanly charm, she sensed there was something in them that could lift her up and carry her away. She broke cover, sitting up into a cross-legged pose now that the petrel had flown. For something to look at, other than him, she watched the birds pitching above them, her pencil still poised in her hand.

Lord Sholto rolled onto his side and rested his head in his hand, watching her as she sketched. The earl had gone over to the nest and was crouching, cradling the egg tenderly. 'It's wonderful,' he called over. 'Quite a rough texture, as you said.'

'You shall need to blow it properly, sir, if you want to preserve it.'

He glanced over at her. 'I suppose you have expert tips for that too?'

'I'm no expert, I can only tell you how we do it here, sir.' Blown bird eggs were one of the main things tourists liked to buy from the islanders, along with their soft tweed and home knits.

'Au contraire, Miss Gillies,' the earl said, baffling her completely. 'I can see that when it comes to your sea birds, you are indeed the expert and we your humble students. Tell me again, who was the lady who recommended you to us? We must thank her.'

'Mad Annie?'

Lord Sholto laughed. 'Heavens. *Is* she mad?'

'No,' Effie grinned. 'But she smokes the pipe and curses and doesn't go to kirk. The minister despairs of her.'

'Why doesn't she go to church?'

'She hasn't since the day her husband died. He was one of them that drowned. She said God had abandoned her so she would abandon him.'

'She sounds a strong character.'

'We've a few of those,' she agreed. 'Ma Peg's not to be messed with either and Old Fin can still spit in your eye from ten paces.'

Both men looked shocked by the comment and Effie had a sense again that she'd been . . . embarrassing. But they laughed again in the next moment.

Effie watched as the earl pulled a small box from his knap-sack; he knelt down and pulled at some moss and grass, padding the box with it before setting the egg in the middle. She watched on, discomfited. It wasn't a hobby she understood. She could see the beauty of it, but for her – for all St Kildans – eggs were food, not pretty objects to collect. She was no hypocrite; she knew she had and would continue to take thousands more eggs from their nests than either of these men ever would, but that was a matter of her survival; it struck her as somehow against the natural order to take an egg from the nest, the only egg the bird would lay this breeding season, just for the sake of display. It felt very close to avarice.

She watched Lord Sholto pluck a stalk of rye grass and begin to chew on it, his eyes flitting to her again and settling there as he found her gaze already upon him. She felt, again, that sense of being lifted, of the ground dropping away beneath her, and it made her stomach swoop. She didn't understand the feeling. She was a St Kildan, an intrepid climber who swung from the ropes without a care; but for the first time in her life, she understood what others felt when they watched her as a spider on the wall: the fear of falling.

Chapter Three

They returned to a village very much at rest. With the menfolk away, the women were moving about with a rare leisured air as the sun sank softly behind Mullach Bi. The children were playing hide and seek behind the dyke, their shouts echoing around the glen, water pails ready filled for the morning, their chores done.

Effie could see the smoke puffing from their chimney on the approach, her father sweeping the threshold, his body stooped. Along with Archie MacQueen, who had rowed back from dropping the men, he and Old Fin were the only village men left on the island – Old Fin on account of his age, her father on account of his bones. Mad Annie was sitting on the low wall, knitting as she talked to him. Several dogs were strewn about her dangling feet. Effie could see her father's white shirts, including his Sunday best, were still pegged to the line. She would need to take them in, the dew would be coming soon.

'So did you enjoy today, sir?' she said to the earl as they stepped into the Street. She was determined to earn and keep her two shillings.

'My dear, it's been a revelation,' the earl replied, his bag jostling with eggs from razorbills, turnstone and guillemots, as well as the fork-tailed petrels. She had been on the rope for most of the afternoon, stealing eggs to order for him.

'In more ways than one,' his son added.

'Never in my life have I seen such a proliferation of birdlife,' the earl continued.

'Well, if there's one thing we have here, it's birds.'

'And the noise they make is quite extraordinary.'

'We're used to it, I suppose. That and the wind. There's ne'er a break in either,' she said, glancing in the windows as they walked past Mary McKinnon's house. The door was closed but Effie glimpsed shadows moving at the back of the room. At least she was up. There was another four months before the baby was due and she couldn't spend all of it off her feet. Her husband Donald worked every hour he could.

Ma Peg was walking slowly ahead of them on the path, leaning on her stick as she carried a cut of peat. She was wide-hipped, with swollen ankles and legs like salted hams. Her long white hair was piled atop her head in the same loose bun she had worn for seventy-five years, the red plaid head-scarf all the married women wore wound around her head to keep it neat in the breeze.

'Let me take that for you,' Effie said, lapsing into the usual Gaelic as they advanced upon her quickly, taking the slab of turf from her hand. The old lady did not resist, but to Effie's astonishment, Lord Sholto reached across and took the cutting from *her* hand. He said not a word but simply smiled as she looked over at him.

'Tell me, lass,' the old woman said as they walked side by side. She hadn't lifted her head as she trod carefully, but she didn't need to see Effie to recognize her voice – and skinny shadow. 'How was it up top?'

'Fine today. Quite the view, though we couldn't see the isles.'

'Naught worth seeing there anyway,' the old woman tutted.

In all her years, she had never once left the archipelago. 'Were you there to hunt?'

'No, we were collecting today. All the prettiest eggs. Ma Peg, have you met their lordships? The Earl of Dumfries and his son Lord Sholto. They brought over the factor.' She looked at the men, switching back to English. 'This is Mrs MacDonald.'

'Earl?' The old woman stopped shuffling in order to be able to turn and look at the men. Her lookover was thorough, an inquisitive look up and down. 'No crowns?' she asked, resuming walking again. 'How disappointing.'

The earl, not speaking the native tongue, looked at Effie for help.

'She's very pleased to meet you,' Effie said.

Ma Peg said something else about the tyranny of aristocracy. Effie translated to a more polite remark. 'And she hopes you are enjoying our beautiful home.'

'Ah, yes!' He nodded exaggeratedly. 'Among the most beautiful I've seen, Mrs MacDonald. We consider ourselves fortunate to be here.'

They had reached her cottage and waited for a moment as the old woman pushed on the open door.

'Allow me to bring this in for you, Mrs MacDonald,' Lord Sholto said, enunciating as though she was deaf and stepping forward into the gloomy interior. 'By the fire?'

The old woman watched with a twinkle in her eye as he set it down by the hearth. She nodded her thanks with a toothless smile and looked back at Effie, dismissing her with a conspiratorial wink.

The trio walked the short way further down the Street to Effie's own cottage. The factor's house was at the far end, nearest the quay and the beach.

'Well, I'll leave you here,' she said as they drew close. 'This is me.'

Poppit had trotted ahead to greet the other dogs after her day's absence. Her father had disappeared into the house with the broom, leaving Mad Annie sitting on the wall. Her hands were still moving as she watched their group approach with open curiosity, the needles clacking away incessantly.

Effie quickly made the introductions. Mad Annie was ten years younger than Ma Peg and had the spirit and nervous energy to prove it, looking back at the men through dark inquisitive eyes, her steel-grey hair caught in a tight bun.

'Ah, you're back,' her father said, reappearing at the sound of their voices.

'Mr Gillies, may I commend you on instilling in your daughter an impressive education,' the earl said. 'She's a credit to you.'

'I'm afraid he has no English, sir. Just a moment . . .' Effie quickly translated, but not *his* words. 'He says they've had a good day and are pleased to give us the two shillings,' she said instead, not mentioning anything about her education. Her father knew nothing of the books hidden beneath her mattress. She had never known how to explain that the factor brought them over for her. It had started as a kindness after John's death, a diversion now there was no brother to talk to, but several years on, she didn't merit this special attention and she knew it. But she loved her books . . .

She heard a momentary pause in the clacking of Mad Annie's knitting needles before they started up again. She had forgotten that Mad Annie, sitting there, spoke English as well.

Effie's cheeks flamed at having been caught out in the fib.

'Will you be all right getting back to the factor's house? You know the way to go?' she asked the two men.

Even out of the corner of her eye, she could see Lord Sholto's grin. The short journey back was but a straight line after all.

'I think we'll manage. Thank you, Miss Gillies, for an illuminating day.' For all their directness and bright-eyed smiles yesterday, she had found it increasingly hard to hold the younger man's gaze. Something she couldn't quite grasp, an undercurrent, seemed to pass between them and as the day had progressed, she had fallen into a pattern of directing her comments, conversation and looks almost entirely towards his father.

Her own father said something to her. She looked back at the guests.

'Oh. My father says the minister came round earlier, asking if you were back. With Mr Mathieson gone on the expedition, he has invited you to dine with him tonight.'

There was only the barest of hesitations. 'How kind,' the earl murmured.

'Very,' Lord Sholto added.

There was a pause.

'And what shall we be doing tomorrow, Miss Gillies?' the earl asked.

'Well, I thought I might show you how to snare the puffins, if you're willing,' she said.

'Indeed we are.'

'And perhaps you might be interested in teaching me some of your roping skills too, Miss Gillies,' Lord Sholto said.

'Have you climbed before, sir?'

'I've done some mountaineering in the French Alps,' he replied. 'But from what I saw today, I think you can probably still teach me a thing or two.'

'If you like, then, I'll pack both ropes. And you, sir?'

The earl shook his head with a surprised laugh. 'I rather think not. I'm here for the birds, not the thrills.'

'Very well. I've chores to get on with, but I'll be ready whenever you are in the morning. Just come here, I'll not be far.'

'Very well. Good day, Miss Gillies. Mr Gillies,' the earl nodded. Lord Sholto simply smiled.

Father and daughter watched the father and son walk away, both tall and imposing, both with a similar erect gait. Even from behind, they looked like lords, elevated to all the rest. Their suits were well cut, the cloth fine, their manners impeccable. They smiled and spoke easily to the villagers, to her, but she sensed there was an invisible shield around them, their own sense of remove.

'Are you running hot, missy?' Mad Annie asked, needles still clacking.

Effie pressed a hand to her forehead. 'No. I don't think so,' she said warily. 'Why?'

The old woman shrugged. 'Your eyes are bright. You look feverish.'

Effie turned back into the cottage. Now that she mentioned it, she did feel out of sorts, somehow both agitated and worn out. She felt . . . edgy. But why? She had done her job well today. She hadn't liked the taking of the bird eggs for mere possession, it was true; but they had had plenty of ornithologists come to the isle before and do just the same. And she had never earnt so much money so easily. Uncle Hamish was always saying that the more they – the villagers – could earn on their own through the tourists, the less they would have to rely upon the factor to trade for them. That had to be a good thing.

A pan was on the stove, a broth bubbling away and filling

the room with a damp steam. She peered in at the bones, her tummy rumbling. She'd not eaten a meal since her oats this morning, although the earl had produced some apples from his bag and given her one. The sweetness had made her mouth water and the two men had been openly surprised that she had never eaten one before. They seemed to forget that to have an apple, one must first have an apple tree and there wasn't a single tree – apple or otherwise – to be found in the whole archipelago.

She walked into the closet that sat between the kitchen and main bedroom. Her room. It was tiny and had no windows, with just enough room for a narrow bed and a chair. It had been John's when he was alive – she'd always slept in the byre next door with Poppit and their cow – but after he'd died, it had been a comfort to smell his hair on the pillow. (She could still remember the stabbing guilt the day she'd pulled on his clothes and realized they no longer smelt of him but of her, as though she had overwritten him. Perhaps she had. She wore his clothes, slept in his bed, did his chores. But she was still never enough.) The cupboard room always had an immediate calming effect upon her, like putting a bag over the bull's head, and she lay down on the bed – but a minute later she was up again, wringing her hands.

'Where are you going?' Mad Annie asked as she strode back out into the sunshine.

'To take in the laundry,' she said over her shoulder, jumping onto and over the wall and walking down the plot to the washing line. Poppit was by her side again, tail up and bounding over the grass.

'Definitely a fever,' she heard Mad Annie say to her father as she began unpegging the shirts.

'Miss Gillies!'

She looked up to find the earl's son walking back along the Street towards her. They had been separated all of a few minutes but she felt a rushing of her blood to see him again. His father was no longer with him and he had taken off his jacket, now slung over one shoulder as he walked. The formality of only a few minutes earlier seemed to have gone as quickly as a sea mist.

She waited, the shirts clutched to her body, as he hopped athletically over the wall and came towards her. 'Hello again.' His smile was like a dawn, a promise of something bright and new.

'Hello, sir.'

'Oh . . . please . . . don't bother with all that. At least, not when it's . . . just us.'

Just us.

'What should I call you then?'

'Just Sholto,' he shrugged.

'Just Sholto. That's a funny name, Just Sholto,' she deadpanned, revelling in how he laughed at the joke.

'And may I call you Effie?'

'Aye. Everyone does.'

'Short for Euphemia, I think your uncle said?'

'Aye. My mother's name.'

'It's beautiful. I imagine she was too.'

'Why should you imagine that?'

'Like mother, like daughter, isn't that what they say?'

She was bemused. 'Not here.'

'Well, then they should.'

He was charming her, she could see, plying her with his gentlemanly manners. She turned back to the washing line and continued unpegging the shirts, but with no real desire to complete the task – they provided a useful barricade between the two of them and her father and Mad Annie on the Street, both watching.

'Are you not staying in to rest, then?' she asked him.

'No. My father is still tired from the crossing but I'm feeling . . . restless. It seems wasteful to have spent so long getting here, only to spend it in recuperation. I wondered if we might have another adventure?'

'You and I?'

'Yes. If you've time.'

'. . . Adventure? Like what?'

'You tell me. What do you do for fun here? Apart from swinging from ropes.'

'We read the Bible.'

His expression changed. 'Oh.'

Effie wasn't able to contain herself, a giggle escaping her. 'Not really. The minister wishes we did, but I'm a terrible disappointment to him.'

'Only to him, I'm sure.'

She finished unpegging the shirts.

'Actually, I do have an idea myself,' he said, shoving his hands in his trouser pockets as he watched her. 'But I'm not sure you'll be game.'

She bristled, turning to him. '. . . Try me.'

The water was at its coldest, when the days were warming up but the sea still held winter rivers in its belly. She was used to wading up to her knees but she'd never in her life gone any deeper than that. Lord Sholto – or Just Sholto – though, wasn't taking no for an answer.

'Ready?' he asked, holding his hand out for hers. They were standing on the shore together. Apparently this was the only way in – at pace.

Reluctantly she put her hand in his, feeling his fingers close around her, skin on skin. There was an awful lot of skin on display. He had changed into bathing shorts, the likes of which had never been seen on the isle and had almost caused Old Fin to swallow his false teeth as he'd emerged, changed, from the factor's house. She was wearing a winter chemise of her mother's – boiled wool the colour of porridge that hung away from her body with angles she didn't possess. She was painfully aware, too, of the tan line on her legs, which stopped quite abruptly at her knees, but her new swimming tutor seemed not to have noticed. 'Three, two, one – go!'

Without hesitation, he led the barefoot charge over the stony shore, tugging her along into the icy water. She gasped, she shrieked, but – propelled by him – her legs kept moving, and as the depth increased quickly, the water tangled around her knees, bringing her down. She landed with an almighty splash, surfacing moments later with wide eyes and a lungful of air. 'Oh! Oh!' she gasped, laughing, feeling borderline hysterical from the shock. 'That is *so* cold!'

'I know,' he gasped back. 'It's horrific. Which is why you have to keep moving. Quick now. Come here.'

She shook her head. 'I don't want to go deep.'

'We won't. You'll be able to stand at all times, I promise.'

She waded over to him, her elbows held high. Already she was shivering, her skin covered with goosebumps. 'Now lie back. I'm going to hold your shoulders so you don't sink. You must trust me. I won't let go at any point. I just want you to feel the sensation of lying in the water, of floating.'

She shook her head. 'No. That doesn't sound good. I don't like the sound of that.'

He pulled back. 'Oh, I'm sorry, you must be the wrong

Effie Gillies. How terribly embarrassing – I meant to teach the other one, the fearless one who can beat the boys at their own game.'

Her eyes narrowed at his tease. In the next instant, she lay back, her toes sticking out of the water and feeling his hands upon her shoulders, buoying her up.

'There? It's not so bad, is it?' he asked, looking down at her as he began to walk backwards slowly, pulling her along. 'Keep your mouth closed, your eyes too if you like. Just get used to the feeling of floating in the water.'

She did as he instructed but she was too aware of his eyes upon her and she opened them again. She could feel her feet beginning to drop below the water.

She felt a hand on the small of her back. 'Try this. Take a deep breath and hold it for a moment. See how your body lifts and rises in the water? Now when you exhale, blow out slowly. You should feel yourself sink.'

'But—'

'Trust me. I won't let you go.'

She closed her eyes again and inhaled. Just as he'd said, she felt her body rise from the water for a few seconds, before gently falling back into its embrace.

'See that? You can control your buoyancy with your breath. It's an important thing to know if you're in a sticky spot.'

'A sticky spot? You mean – potentially drowning?'

'Indeed.'

They looked at one another – both upside down to the other; he could see the amusement in her eyes. 'No, don't laugh, you'll sink,' he chuckled.

But it was too late and as her body folded, Sholto had to hoist her up under the arms to keep her from going under the water. She shrieked. For a moment he held her aloft, half in and half-out of the water, and she could see he was about to throw her. She gasped in fright.

'Tempting,' he grinned, placing her back down gently. 'But not yet.'

'Not ever!'

'Well, we'll have to see about that. I make no promises.' He flicked the surface of the water with his index finger and thumb so that a small spray hit her full in the face.

Effie gasped in astonishment, before returning with her own double-handed version. It was his turn to be surprised. For a moment they fell still, eyes locked, time holding its breath as the brittle walls of formality – respectability, the factor would have said – began to crack. Within seconds, they were engaged in a full-blown water fight, slapping the sea with their palms and shoving great swathes of it into waves upon each other, the sound of their games ricocheting around the glen like an eagle's cry.

Chapter Four

The moon was just a few days off being full. It slipped silently over the glassy sea, throwing down a silvered glow as the water kissed the shore with a gentle hush. Effie closed the door behind her and tiptoed down the lane. There were no pools of light puddling on the path from the cottage windows, the villagers now asleep in their beds, the animals nodding in the byres. The encircling mountains formed a dark, protective embrace around the village and even the ever-calling birds were at rest.

Effie moved with practised flight, nimble on her feet. The key felt heavy in her palm as she crept past the unlocked cottages of her neighbours. She could hear Old Fin's snores as she passed by his window. The tiger-striped cat lay curled up on the sill in Mary and Donald McKinnon's. A rack of fulmar eggs sat on Jayne and Norman Ferguson's. At the factor's house – the grandest on the island, being white rendered – nothing stirred at all. She had never been inside, but she wondered now which room the visitors were staying in.

Once past the white house, there were only cleits between her and the featherstore and she relaxed a little more, walking more easily, pressing the key tightly into her palm so that she could feel its teeth against her skin. The storehouse was located at the very end of the Street, right upon the beach near to the jetty, and she looked about her as she slid the key into the lock. Only two people had a key. Officially. The factor and the postmaster. Hers was kept hidden with the books under her bed. There would be no way of explaining that, either.

The door opened with a creak and she stepped inside. The space was warm and stuffy, with little ventilation. The familiar waxy smell impressed itself as she closed it behind her. It was half full already with the products that would be due in September when the factor made his return trip for the landlord's rents: bolts of tweed in light blue, light grey and brown were piled high against one wall, sacks of feathers against another, some drums of fulmar oil.

Effie moved immediately towards the feather sacks. Their contents supplied the upholstery trade on the mainland and she knew the grey fulmar feathers fetched five shillings a stone but that the finer black ones from the puffins fetched six. She'd never slept on a feathered mattress but she didn't much care to; she'd slept well enough these past eighteen years on her horsehair mattress and it did her fine. The feathers had only one value for her . . .

She pulled one of the frontmost sacks away and set it to the side, working her way back through the stacks, her eyes down until eventually she saw something – a single sharp-edged corner peeking out from a sack of black feathers.

She hesitated, feeling herself teeter on the edge of temptation. She had been determined to leave it this time; after the factor's cruel words on the jetty yesterday she had wanted to reject his kindness, push back in the only way she could – but curiosity got the better of her, as it always did. The novelty of anything that came from the mainland was hard to resist. But it wasn't only that. If she was honest, the earl's compliments had swelled her head; she liked that she knew more than him. What if there was something more to learn? Another fact with which to impress him – and his son?

She reached for it, pulling out a large heavy book and feeling her heart quicken as the page ends glinted gold. The book was huge, the length of her arm from her elbow to her fingertips and weighing the same as a new-born lamb. For a few moments, she couldn't move, crouched on her haunches, as she stared down at the tome, her palm sweeping over it as if in communion. Never had she seen the like. It was clearly very old and felt as important and rare as the Bible the minister clutched to his bosom during his passionate sermons.

Effie took it over to the single small window, to see better by the moonlight. THE SONGBIRDS OF SCOTLAND was inscribed in handsome gold-stamped lettering, the spine stiff and pristine, as if it had never been opened. Her finger ran along the edges of the gilded pages. Could a book be too precious to read?

She opened it as if she was peering into a jewellery box. On the inner page was a circular motif of a bull's head, crossed flags either side of it. She flicked past the title and contents pages, her eyes wide at watercolour illustrations which were separately glued to the sheets, like paintings within a book. The colours were gentle yet precise, capturing not just the birds' likenesses but their personalities too. Every page of vellum was bordered with a hand-drawn green ink line with scrolls in the corners, decorative whimsy.

She'd never seen anything so beautiful. All the other books had been factual and informative, with sketchy line drawings scattered through, studies of heads, bills or claws, wing and tail patterns. Some had broken into colour drawings or had leather covers, but this was an entirely different beast.

She closed it gently, tenderly, as though closing a door on

a wondrous sight. Hugging it to her, she leant back against the wall and stared out through the window. She had never owned anything so precious before and she felt . . . unworthy of it. A book like this had no place here, literally – not even a shelf to sit on. If she was to keep it, it would have to be hidden under her mattress along with all the others, keeping its beauty and workmanship hidden, and that felt . . . wrong. This book belonged to a better life than hers.

She stared out sightlessly, trying to imagine who she needed to be to warrant it. A girl with silk dresses and a house full of literature? Of art? Music drifting from windows and song-birds singing in trees . . . ? Not the girl dressed in boy's tweeds. Not the girl for whom birds were not just beauty, but food. Who slipped snares round their necks as they sat in their burrows. Who swung from ropes with one hand and wrung their necks with the other. This book belonged to a life she would never know. One that couldn't be lived here, on a rock in the ocean. For the first time in her life, she felt a flicker of resentment towards her home.

The sea was slumbering, occasional sighs rising and falling, and she watched a seal swimming near the shore, its dark head rising and dipping below the surface.

She watched it disappear below the waves, then rise again in a rhythm.

Wait . . .

It was no seal. An arm, two arms, emerged, cutting through the water like blades. A man was out there and he was swim-ming the width of the bay. She sat straighter. A midnight swimmer on an island of landlubbers? There was only one person it could be, of course. No one here could navigate water like that.

She watched, transfixed. She had never seen someone swim

70

before. Some of the men, when they'd toppled off the boat, acquired a strange frantic paddling motion, much like the dogs', which was passable till they could grab on again. But this was nothing like that. His body was synchronized and streamlined. He moved like silk.

Her own swimming lesson – after the brief attempt at floating, and the water fight – had ended with a sprint back to the beach (which she won) to warm up again. They hadn't come close to anything like this.

She watched as he ploughed back towards the mid-point of the bay and stood. He tipped his head back, wetting his hair again before shaking it out and combing it back with his fingers. His body was an inky silhouette but its line she already knew well. She had traced it from his very first hours here.

He began wading in, heading towards the beach.

She was unaware her breath had caught high up in her chest, closing her throat, all reflexes on hold. Had he already been in the water as she had walked down? Had he seen her enter *here*? Or had he slipped from his bed as she unearthed her new treasure? Either way, they must have missed each other by mere moments, surely? She felt that tension again, the ratchet tightening deep inside her, at the thought of having met him in the moonlight. Was it fate that they were both out of their beds in the dead of night? Or was it fate keeping them apart? Her in here and him out there?

She watched as he walked from the sea, back onto the grainy beach where his towel lay. He twisted it into a thick rope and vigorously rubbed himself dry, his gaze towards the village as he dried his back, pulling the towel diagonally between his shoulder blades. Then he stepped into his trousers and walked up the beach onto the grass, out of sight from the window at which she sat.

She felt a surge of panic, a need to keep him in her sights until the moment the factor's door closed behind again. In haste, she ran outside, clutching the book close to her chest, and went to stand behind the corner of the featherstore; but to her surprise, he hadn't borne right and headed for the factor's house. He had gone straight ahead and walked almost all the way up Old Fin's plot at number 8. It was right next to theirs, where her father's shirts had flapped in the wind this afternoon, where he had jumped the wall and sauntered over to her. Effie watched as he stared at the cottage. Her cottage.

He had the towel draped in a twisted loop behind his neck, a hand at each end, elbows down. What . . . what was he doing? What was he thinking? If her father was to stir and get up, if anyone was to see him, the young lord, standing staring at their cottage in the moonlight . . . She didn't stir. What would happen if he was to discover her watching him, watching her? What would he do? And what would she?

Eventually he turned, walking briskly back through the Street, past all the cottages without even turning his head, lost in thought. She watched until he slipped back into his home here and the factor's door closed behind him.

She fell back against the wall, biting her lip as she tried to understand what she had just seen, and his secret sojourn. Mindlessly, she clutched the book tighter to her chest, already forgotten. It was no longer the most precious thing she had been given.

Chapter Five

'Any word from the men?' Effie asked, staring down from the steep grassy bank at Lorna MacDonald, who was standing in the burn, skirts tucked up around her thighs as she filled her pails. Effie clambered down to join her, sitting on a rock on the bank and grateful for the cool rushing water around her legs too. Poppit lay down and watched, head between her paws. The sky was already a burning blue with not a breath of wind, the birds orbiting listlessly. The sloop sat in the bay as still as if packed in ice, its tall, elegant lines mirrored perfectly in the dead calm water, projecting an upside-down world.

Effie half wondered if she had stepped into that world instead, for she felt strangely untethered from her own. After a night in which she'd tossed fitfully, she was moving around and completing her chores the same as she ever did, the familiar landscape immutable around her – and yet something had changed. There had been a shift, even if it was just in her perception.

'Aye. All's going well over there,' Lorna MacDonald said, filling a bucket and passing it to her. 'Wee Fin and Donnie Gillies ran up top this morning to make the check. The men were right to head out when they did. It's rare so calm as this.' She gave Effie a wink. 'Lucky for us they timed it to take the factor with them too.'

Effie gave a roll of her eyes. 'Aye. I've already caught a supper from him.'

'Already? Strong work, lass. What did you do?'

'Showed off on the ropes in front of the guests.'

'Ah. Stole his thunder, did you?'

'Apparently, I'm an embarrassment and a disgrace.'

'As far as he's concerned, we all are,' Lorna chuckled as she passed up another of the pails. Effie carried it up the bank for her. She often tried to help her, even though Lorna never asked for it. She lived alone, so the burden of chores fell solely upon her shoulders, but she never complained. She was young enough to take care of herself very well – she could rake, hoe and plant her own crops, milk her own cow and churn her own butter. She washed her linens, spun her yarn and dyed her wool. She was quick on her feet for catching the sheep and quiet on them for snaring puffins. The only thing she couldn't do was work on the ropes. She had moved over from the mainland too late to overcome the natural fear that came with scaling those cliffs; the ease had to be instilled from childhood or it would never come at all.

'Well, lucky for you, they left behind his guests,' Lorna said, now rinsing out a pan.

Effie felt a jolt at the words. Was Lorna jealous that Effie had bagged a smile as well as a tip from the handsome visitor? Or was it worse than that – had Lorna seen the young lord standing outside her cottage last night?

'Two shillings, I heard.'

'Oh. Aye.' Effie kept her gaze down as she scrambled back down the slope. 'Father wants to buy another cow.'

'It'll cost more than two shillings to get a cow.'

'Not if we buy it ourselves.'

Lorna glanced up from scrubbing. 'You mean, cut out the factor?'

'Why not? We're not obliged to spend every farthing we make through him.'

'That's true enough. But still, he wouldn't be pleased.'

Effie shrugged. 'Father says we should sail to Harris and buy the cow ourselves.'

'I daresay you could. But that'd be a rough crossing in the skiff, even on a day like this,' Lorna warned. 'The damp would be no good for his bones.'

Effie knew she was right. The villagers' boat wasn't intended for open water crossings. 'We could travel back with a trawler, like Mary did.'

'Mary?' Lorna frowned.

'When she was sick and had to go to the mainland. Captain McGregor took her on his way past.'

Lorna frowned. 'I don't remember that.' As a qualified nurse, she had immediately assumed a role as the island's medic when she arrived; she knew every villager's medical history and complaint.

'It must have been before your time,' Effie shrugged.

They had finished filling the pails now. They scrambled back up the steep grassy banks of the stream, Lorna untucking her skirt and straightening herself, before walking together down the slope.

'Of course, it might not be necessary to buy another cow,' Lorna said meaningfully.

Effie gave her a pained look. She knew the nurse was referring to the petition. Since signing their names a few weeks earlier, the islanders had lived in a suspended state – the request to evacuate had been formally delivered and the ball set rolling, but the endless debates and arguments preceding it through the harsh winter and dreich spring had now fallen quiet. No one had mentioned the evacuation since the letter had been taken to the Other Side with the trawler-men; it was as if they were scared that to mention it at all would somehow determine the outcome. The will to leave was not unanimous by any means – the elders wanted to stay and so did some of the younger ones, like Effie and Mhairi. In Mhairi's case, she had too much to lose by leaving; in Effie's, simply nothing to gain. Most of the time Effie consoled herself that it would never happen. They had been denied everything before; why should they be heard now? But occasionally doubt crept into her mind and she felt a cold clutch around her heart at the prospect of leaving. It was too much to consider and the islanders had collectively resigned themselves to waiting, silently, patiently, for the judgement that would declare their fates.

'. . . Have you heard back, then?' She swallowed, feeling a rush of dread.

Lorna had been the architect behind the petition. She had taken it badly when poor Molly Ferguson had died this past winter from an illness that would have been treatable on the mainland. Lorna had declared enough was enough and raised the idea of evacuation. The harvest had failed for another year, they were all exhausted, too few doing the work of too many. She had led the village discussions on the matter, then when the vote was in, written the letter. She had decided on a new life with the same determination and vigour that she'd once applied to this one and it seemed only natural that she would be the one to deliver the verdict.

'No, not yet.'

Both women were silent as they walked, their bare feet treading over ancient sunken rocks, moving past the beehive stone structures that had first been built by men thousands of years before. Effie couldn't imagine a life beyond here, she simply couldn't see what it might like look like – the lie of the land, the houses, all those crowds of people? They moved into single file, walking down the narrow path between her cottage and Old Fin's. Lorna lived in number 16, at the furthest western end of the Street. It had been one of a few cottages available after Dougie MacDonald's family of thirteen had emigrated to Australia a few years earlier. Logic might have dictated – Effie's father always muttered – that as the village's nurse she should be more centrally located, but the privacy seemed to suit her and the abandoned neighbouring black-house, which predated her 1870s cottage, was in good enough condition to serve as a clinic.

They turned onto the Street, to find the visitors being entertained by Effie's aunt Mary Gillies, several cottages down at number 10. She was sitting in her chair by her front door, spinning the yarn as she spoke, seemingly oblivious to the fact that they spoke no Gaelic and she no English. Effie could see she was giving a demonstration, hoping to earn a coin.

Effie and Lorna swapped bemused looks as Effie handed her back the other pail.

'Good morning, gentlemen,' Lorna said brightly on her way past, looking demure in her skirt that only moments before had been tucked into her undergarments.

'Good morning,' the earl said brightly, doffing his hat. His son did the same, but his gaze was already casting around. It stopped as he found Effie, standing by the narrow alley.

'Miss Gillies,' he said, coming straight over to her. His skin had tanned a little already after yesterday's exposure on the slopes and it had the effect of brightening his teeth and eyes further. 'We were looking for you.'

If she hadn't seen him standing outside her cottage in the moonlight, she would never have known it from his casual demeanour here now, which picked up from their adventure together yesterday afternoon. But she did know, and she couldn't forget it. She felt as wooden as he was languid. 'My apologies if I kept you waiting. I'm just back from feeding the bull.'

'You were feeding the . . . ?'

She saw how the corners of his mouth twitched, wanting to turn into a smile. She supposed it might make for an odd image – a scrawny thing like her, tending the bull – she'd never stopped to consider it before. But only his eyes gave away something of his contained laughter. 'Does the bull have a name?'

'Aye. Tiny.'

'Tiny.' The corners of his mouth twitched further. 'Splendid. Well chosen, I'm sure.'

The earl ambled over, also sporting a burst of ruddy colour in his cheeks. In Effie's opinion, they both looked the better for it. 'Miss Gillies, another brilliant day dawns,' he said heartily. 'Are you ready to show two hopeless birders how to snaffle some puffins?'

'Aye, sir. I'll get the snares and we can away.'

'We brought more apples,' Sholto said, as they followed her back to her cottage. He stood by the threshold, discreetly looking around as she reached for the long-handled snares that were suspended from nails on the first rafter. The ropes were coiled on the floor and she glanced inside the large climbing bag that hung from a hook by the door, checking for pegs, her notebook and pencil. 'Seeing as you liked them so much yesterday,' he said quickly, as she turned back to him.

'Thank you,' she nodded, handing him a snare as she passed, their eyes grazing over one another like fingers in sand.

'Do you paint as well as draw, Miss Gillies?' he asked, seeing a pot with several brushes peeking from the top on the windowsill.

'I try.'

His fingers brushed absently over the tips. '. . . Are those *sable*?' he asked in surprise, looking back at her.

She wasn't sure what sable was – they were supplies from the factor – but she felt discomfited by his evident shock. She shrugged. 'A brush is a brush to me,' she said, moving past him into the Street.

Effie had already determined they would only need to go to the Gap, the dip between the summits of Connachair and Oiseval on the east side of the isle, behind the cottages. The land was fairly gently sloped on the bay side and she knew exactly where the puffins liked to burrow there. The three of them walked together past the cleits, through the narrow gap in the head dyke and up to the plateau of An Lag. Jayne Ferguson was hoeing her lazybed, so lost in thought she didn't hear them approach until they were almost passing her.

'Hallo Jayne,' Effie waved, the snares in her hand and the ropes looped over her shoulder, looking much the same as she usually did but for the esteemed company beside her.

Jayne waved back at the unlikely trio, watching as they began the steeper ascent, Poppit running ahead of them and circling back in continuous loops, never stopping, never tiring. Effie didn't stop either till they reached the top.

'What a view!' the earl exclaimed, much as he had the day before, and she knew this was his cue to take a rest. She let the bag drop from her shoulder and sank to the grass, knees up, but Sholto remained standing with his hands planted on his hips, looking out over her domain. His eyes were slitted against the bright light, enjoying the wisps of warm breeze over his skin. She remembered again the sight of him cutting through the water in the moonlight. Was he a master of every element he ventured into?

'I hadn't expected the weather to feel so clement,' the earl remarked, getting his breath back.

'It's often good here in May, sir,' she said. 'May and June are the best months.'

'Not July or August?'

'Not so much. It always blows a gale in July and August is usually wet, which brings out the midges.'

'Blasted things,' the earl tutted. 'They always go for me, I'm afraid. I look like a pin cushion by the time they've finished feasting on me.'

'How about December, what's it like here then?' Lord Sholto asked.

'December is often calm, often mild. Sometimes it feels like a sort of spring.'

'How odd. In Ayrshire you could swear the house will get blown down.'

'Ah, that's January for us. Roaring gales that *do* bring the houses down. This year there was a storm with winds so fierce, we were all deaf for a week afterwards.'

'Deaf?'

'Yes, the wind batters you here. It doesn't just howl, it screams. There's no escaping it and I suppose the shape of the glen helps it echo. It's usually a north-easterly wind then and it's bitter.' She shrugged. 'Then it snows in February. Drifts so deep – forty feet sometimes – we have to rescue the sheep; it piles up by the fank walls and they'd suffocate to death if we left them.' She laughed softly. 'Although Father always says the sheep are so stupid, they'd die twice if they could.'

Both men laughed and they resumed the hike.

They skirted the side of the island in full sun, the density of birds increasing as they drew closer to the edge. To their right, the land fell away sharply, down sea cliffs that were the highest in the British Isles. Many times a misstep had been fatal.

'It looks like someone's just had a pillow fight,' Sholto remarked, smiling up at the sight. 'Don't you think? White feathers everywhere.'

They walked along the path that led to Aird Uachdarachd, the small peninsula that jutted out below and behind Connachair mountain. It was the easternmost point on the island and the ground was a series of layered grassy ledges that the puffins loved. Effie stopped at a particular point she had been looking for and walked carefully to the edge. She looked down, scanning the landscape below. She nodded to herself, then took the rope off her shoulder and dropped to her knees. Opening the bag, she selected a wooden peg, chose a nearby rock and began to drive it into the ground.

The men went and looked over the drop. She saw the earl's visible relief as he saw a grassy ledge a mere fifteen feet below where they stood, slightly too far to jump but nothing like the precipitous cliffs they had passed on the way up here.

'One of you will have to stay up as a counterbalance to the other's weight,' she said, still knocking in the peg.

'But what about you?' the earl asked.

'The advantage of being a skinny girl,' she smiled. 'The peg does me fine.'

She stood there with the rope, waiting for them to choose which one would go first.

The earl's cheeks were deeply flushed from their exertions. 'You go, my boy. I need to get my strength back from that walk. It's exhausting just getting anywhere on this island!'

'Very well then.' Sholto held his arms out wide as Effie wrapped the rope diagonally over one shoulder and around his waist, knotting it in the St Kildan style. She did the same to herself, looping the other end of her rope to the driven peg.

'Sir, if you wrap the rope around your middle and sit yourself down here, that'll give enough support. If there's any strain or pull, dig your heels in and lean back. Don't try to stand. We'll let you know when we're down with two sharp tugs, and you can rest.'

'Very well.' The earl sat down as instructed as Effie and Sholto walked over to the edge.

She peered over the ledge again. 'The birds are just over there, can you see?'

Sholto frowned as he peered at the rock face she was pointing out. 'No . . .'

'Just there. Not in the rocks, the grass.' She stood closer so that he could follow the line of her finger.

'Oh.' His voice was almost in her ear. She could smell his soap. 'How the devil did you see them? They're almost completely camouflaged.'

'It's just a matter of knowing where they like to roost. For puffins, it's ground burrows ideally but also clefts in the rock. They're also smaller than most people think.' She turned back to face him. 'We'll need to be quiet or they'll fly off. Just follow me and do as I do. Lean back and trust in your anchor.' She smiled over at the earl, who was already sitting with his feet flexed, heels dug down. 'Ready, sir?'

'Ready when you are, Miss Gillies,' he called back.

Effie pushed the snares down the length of her spine, held

in place by the rope twisted around her waist, and positioned herself at the cliff edge. Poppit knew to lie down and wait. She tugged on her rope once, twice, then leant back. She stepped over the edge and looked across at him. 'Legs straight, trust your anchor, hand over hand. Make sure the fists touch, keep the movements small,' she murmured, lowering herself easily. She didn't even need to look. They could fall from here and have a soft landing, so long as they didn't roll.

He climbed down with apparent ease, giving two sharp tugs of the rope, as promised, to let his father know he was on the ledge. They could hear the puffins clearly now, over the screech of the skuas and guillemots. The sound was distinctive, like the lowing of a cow, followed by a clacking sound.

'Keep the rope tied about you,' she whispered, crouching down and reaching for the snares positioned along her spine. She pulled them out and handed him one.

'What are they made from?' he asked, inspecting his more closely.

'The wing bones of gannets.'

He smiled. 'Ingenious.'

She looked over at the bird. 'Now, no rushing movements. The snare tightens like this.' She showed him how pulling on the twine closed down the loop. Sholto nodded, watching her every move closely. They were sitting close, their bodies almost touching on the ledge. 'I'll get the first. You have to bring the snare in slowly, above the bird as it's roosting. Then over the head and close the loop.'

'Will that kill it?'

'No, it'll just trap it. You'll have to wring its neck.'

'I see.' They both watched as a couple of puffins flew in,

landing a short way down from where they were crouched, their distinctive brightly coloured bills filled with several limp mackerel held sideways.

Effie tiptoed into position by the edge of the ledge and waited, the snare held in one hand as she watched the puffins roosting, choosing the best bird to take. One came out of its nest, waddling on a rocky ledge, holding a short stick in its beak. Silently, fluidly, Effie moved closer, extending the snare out and down towards where it stood. She spent a few moments positioning the loop in the air above its head, then prepared to lower—

She stalled.

She watched as the puffin – the stick in its bill – turned its head and began to scratch its own back. Effie couldn't believe what she was seeing. She looked back at Sholto but he seemed more surprised by *her* surprise.

'What?' he mouthed.

She crept back to him. 'Did you see that?' she whispered excitedly. 'Just then – when it scratched its own back?'

'. . . Yes,' he said slowly, still looking baffled.

'Do you know what that means?' She stared at him with bright eyes. 'It used the stick as a *tool*. Less than one per cent of animal species are able to use objects as tools!' She racked her brain, trying to think of precisely which animals. '. . . Chimpanzees . . . otters . . . but it's never been recorded in sea birds, as far as I'm aware.'

He was staring at her. 'How on earth do you know these things?'

'I told you, I read. Do you think I must be ignorant or stupid, just because I'm a poor islander?'

'Of course not. I simply meant that you know so much. More than most professors seemingly.'

84

But she wasn't listening. She was looking back at the puffin. 'Och, why didn't I bring down my notebook?' She bit her thumbnail as she watched it, trying to commit to memory what she saw: it was still holding the stick in its bill, scratching between its wing feathers. 'Is it just scratching an itch,' she wondered aloud. 'Or is it cleaning itself? Parasites can cause them a lot of bother . . . What do you think?'

She looked back, to find him already watching her. His eyes were even bluer up close, with a startling purity of colour. 'I'll think whatever you think. You're the expert.'

She couldn't respond immediately. All of a sudden, her thoughts and words seemed to have vanished.

She looked away again and felt them return. '. . . I can't kill it now,' she said quietly. 'Not now I've seen that. I know it's silly. I've killed thousands but . . . I'm sorry.'

'Don't be.'

'Really?' She met his gaze once more.

'If we kill it we'll have to eat it, won't we?' His eyebrow twitched ever so slightly, a pervasive humour bubbling beneath his polished manners.

'Ha! Roasted puffin is as good as it gets here. You'd be *lucky* to get it. We wait all year for the puffins to come back.' She paused. 'What did the minister serve you last night?'

'Boiled fulmar and most of the Book of Job.'

Effie laughed out loud, startling the birds, and they began clacking, alarmed now by the open presence of intruders. 'Well, what did you come up here for, then, if not to catch your dinner?' she chuckled.

'Oh, to . . . admire the view,' he replied, but something in the way he glanced at her suggested he didn't mean the commanding panorama over their shoulders. Quite suddenly, she felt their close proximity, their aloneness, birds flapping around them in a whirling white confetti. On this ledge, they were hidden from the entire island. 'Although, I can't tell if you feel the same. About the view.'

She didn't respond immediately. She sensed he was playing word games – saying one thing, meaning another. 'The view is . . . beautiful.'

'I think so. It's taken my breath away. I never imagined it could be so lovely.'

Was he saying what she thought he was? No one had ever flirted with her before. Could he hear her heart pounding?

'I saw you last night!' The words burst from her before she could stop them.

He paused. 'Last night?'

'You were swimming.'

'. . . Yes. I couldn't sleep and the water looked so inviting.' He glanced down. 'I hope I didn't disturb you. If I had known there was any chance of meeting anyone, much less you . . .' A small flicker of memory passed through his eyes and she knew what he was thinking. Had she seen him get out? He had been swimming nude after all.

Her cheeks burned at the memory. 'And after?' She couldn't stop herself from asking. She had to know. What did it mean?

'After?'

'When you stood outside, staring at my house?'

His eyebrow twitched the way she was learning it always did when he was concealing his impulses behind manners. 'Your house? Was it?'

'You know it was.'

He didn't respond immediately. 'What makes you think I was staring at your house – and not past it, up to the mountains?' he asked nonchalantly. 'It was almost a full moon last night. The moon glow was quite wonderful.'

She stared back at him, her heart beating dully. Had she been wrong, then?

'Although—'

Although?

'—there'd be nothing wrong with a fellow admiring the home of a girl who intrigues him, would there?'

A sound of disbelief escaped her. 'I don't *intrigue* you.'

'Au contraire: your climbing skills and bravery, your prodigious knowledge of the natural world, your forthright spirit, the way you meet me as an equal, your utter lack of awareness of your beauty . . . I'd say there's an awful lot about you that intrigues me, Miss Gillies. I've never met anyone quite like you.'

Their gazes locked again and she had it again – that sensation of falling, far scarier than anything she'd ever known on a rope; a tension seemed to exist between them that paid no heed to barriers the factor had warned must keep them apart. She couldn't seem to ignore it. Avoiding his eye didn't work, and the way he was looking at her now, it felt so private. Was he going to kiss her? Gravity seemed to be pushing them towards one another. Or was it fate? Or just the wind?

. . . I shall need to find him later and discuss the rent arrears . . . The factor's words echoed through her mind, pressing for her attention. *You wouldn't want to embarrass Sir John, would you?* She couldn't risk angering him further than she already had.

'We should go,' she said briskly, pulling back and putting a distance between them.

'Effie—'

'Will your father want an egg?'

It was an abrupt switch back to the mundane, the territory they must publicly occupy. It wasn't even a question she wanted to ask; like the fork-tailed petrels, a mating pair of puffins only laid one egg per season. But she felt an obligation to provide some sort of trophy for the experience, if she was to earn her two shillings.

But Sholto shook his head, seeing how she withdrew. 'He has some already. It's the snaring he's interested in today.'

'Ah. Well, then, we'll climb back up and explain to him what we saw.' And before he could stop her, she scrambled back up at a dizzying speed, leaving him watching after her.

To be fair, he was a fine climber himself. He was tall and strong, with an instinct for the right handholds in the rocks as he pulled himself up. She had moved quickly, even by her standards, but Sholto climbed over the ledge less than twenty seconds after her.

'What happened? Weren't there any?' the earl asked them with evident disappointment, seeing them return empty-handed. Poppit ran around her legs excitedly, pleased to have her mistress back.

'It wasn't that, sir,' Effie faltered as she watched Sholto untie the rope around his torso; his gaze was fixed determinedly downwards. She looked back at his father. 'It was just that I . . . observed a behaviour which I don't think has been recorded before – at least, not as far as I'm aware.'

'What sort of behaviour?'

'The puffin used a stick to scratch its own back. It used the stick as a tool.'

The earl looked gratifyingly surprised. 'A tool?'

'Aye, sir. It's not a behaviour associated with sea birds.'

'Indeed.'

'I hope you understand it didn't feel right in this instance to kill the bird, just for the sake of a demonstration as to how to kill the bird.'

'I do. Miss Gillies, you have the astute instincts of a scholar.'

'Of a what?'

He laughed, as though she'd told a joke.

Effie glanced at his son but Sholto, having untied himself, had turned away and was staring out to sea. He had his hands jammed in his pockets, his jaw jutting forward slightly. Had she offended him with her abruptness? Had she been rude when she'd been trying to stay 'polite'?

'Seeing as we're up here, I can take you to see something special if you're interested – a sooty tern?' she offered. 'I only saw it a few days past. It's not nesting here. It's resting on migration, so it might have left already, but I could show you where I saw it, in case. As I understand, the sooty tern's only been recorded in the British Isles three times.'

Sholto turned suddenly on his heel, cutting into the conversation. 'Is that Boreray over there?' His voice was unusually sharp as he looked at her and she knew she had insulted him.

'Aye. It's where the men have gone to pluck the sheep.'

He frowned as he looked back at the small isle. 'So then what's that?'

'What's wha—?' But as she said it, she saw it and she knew. She knew immediately.

Two huge slabs of turf – each the length of three men – had been carved from the grass and turned over. From this distance, four miles across the water, they appeared like dark cuts, a wound in the land. 'No,' she whispered, growing pale at the sight.

'Miss Gillies?' the earl asked with concern. 'What does it mean?'

It was a moment before she could reply. Only once in her lifetime had the semaphore been used for this.

'It's for sending the boat. One cut means they're ready to come back. Two means there's been an accident or someone's sick. Three means there's been a death.' She looked back at them, already beginning to tread backward, preparing to run. 'I can't stay, I'm sorry. I've got to get back and tell the others. Are you able to get yourself down? Just follow the path.'

'Of course. Go! Go!' the earl urged.

'I'll come with you,' Sholto said.

'No, stay with your father,' she said, turning back. 'You shouldn't separate. Stay together.'

'But I can help row. Only one man came back, didn't he? With two rowing over there, we can make better time.'

It was a good point. And they knew that Effie, for all her determination to stand toe to toe with the males, couldn't match a man's strength on the oars.

'My son's right,' the earl said. 'You need manpower and he rowed for Oxford. Take him. I'll be fine. Both of you make haste. I'll make my way down in my own time.'

With only a nod, Effie turned on her heel and began to run along the faint track of worn grass. She had the snares in one hand, the rope and her bag slung over the opposite shoulder. She was grateful they got to run downhill and not up; no emergency could help a man climb these slopes any quicker than the islanders already did.

She was aware of Sholto running behind her, panting hard, trying to grip in his leather boots, but they didn't speak. A man was injured or sick, possibly dying, and every second counted. They rounded the neck of Connachair and ran the ridge back to the Gap, then down the grassy straights back to the An Lag plateau. Jayne Ferguson was still at the lazybeds, working some manure over them, and she looked up in surprise as they sprinted past. 'Two cuts,' was all Effie could manage to say. It was all she needed to. Jayne dropped her rake and began running behind them too.

They ran through the gap in the dyke, past the cleits, down to the back of the crescent of cottages. Effie darted down the nearest alley and swung left, heading for Archie MacQueen's house. He'd skippered back after dropping the men the other day. He had strong arms, but an accident years back had left him lame in one leg and not much help for running after sheep.

'Archie!' she yelled. 'Two cuts! Two cuts!'

At her cry, heads emerged from cottage doors, above the Street wall, around spinning wheels and washing lines. Archie, who was repairing a section of wall for Ma Peg, looked up as the words carried and the villagers were rustled into the same frenzied panic as the puffins on the ledge. He saw Effie running towards him, her arms like pistons and the whites of her eyes on show, and he knew the words had come from her. He dropped the rock he was lifting and began running with his distinctive limp, down the plot towards the beach. There was no point in asking 'What?' or 'Who?'. None yet knew.

The boat had been pulled just past the high tide line. In the winter it had to be weighted down with stones and sod to stop the winds from lifting it or the storm surges from grabbing it, but now it sat ready for a return trip they were still a day or two due from making.

Together with the women who got there first – Rachel McKinnon, Mhairi's mother and Effie's own Aunt Mary – they began to push the boat down the beach. Effie, Sholto and Jayne arrived moments later, all of them putting their weight behind the effort.

'Where's Lorna?' Effie asked, looking about for the nurse.

The women looked at one another. Everyone in earshot had heard the shouts, they'd all been brought forth by the commotion.

'I've not seen her in hours,' Aunt Mary said. 'Did she go fishing? She mentioned she might.'

Rachel McKinnon shrugged. 'Or is she with Mary? She said she had to check on her.'

'Shall I look?' Effie asked, poised to sprint again.

'No, there's no time,' Archie replied grimly. 'She could be anywhere and we can't afford to wait.'

The boat was nosing the waterline now.

'I'll help you,' Sholto said, wading into the sea with Archie and jumping into the boat as it began to float.

Archie McKinnon simply nodded, his face grim set; there was every chance it was one of his own sons they were saving. The two men grabbed the oars and began to pull, their bodies dipping back and forth in unison as they coaxed the boat into cutting a line through the water.

Along with the other women, Effie stood up to her knees in the water, watching them go. Their hands were pressed to their mouths, tears gathering in their throats, but there was no use in crying. Not yet. Though they were racked with alarm, it would be several hours before the men got back here and they knew who to worry for. All they could do now was watch and wait.

It was the children's idea to run tags from Rubha Cholla, the point where the boat would round the headland at Oiseval and slip back into the embrace of Village Bay. The older ones formed a broken line along the track, Neil MacQueen, Flora's younger fourteen-year-old brother, taking up position as the sentry. 'He's got wheels,' their father always said of him, and sure enough the boy sprinted like Hermes himself once the boat came closer.

The name had been passed four along before they could hear it on the beach. 'Donald McKinnon! Head wound!'

Lorna gave a sombre nod in reply and turned to her medical bag. Effie knew she had been hoping for a broken arm to set, something mechanical. Heads were never simple. They kept injuries as hidden as thoughts and lies, promises and secrets.

'Should I tell Mary?' Effie asked her. It had turned out Lorna had been tending to the expectant mother after all; she had been a few hundred yards away from the drama on the beach, their shouts drowned out by a pan on a rolling boil. More vital time had been lost.

The nurse considered for a moment. 'Yes. You had better. She'll need time to get down. We'll not know how grave it is till they beach but she should be here, in case.'

Effie ran up onto the grass, sprinting through the Mac-Queens' plot, accidentally planting a bare foot in the freshly manured lazybed as she went.

'Mary,' she called. 'Are you there?'

Effie peered her head in to the cottage. Mary McKinnon was standing in the bedroom. She had her back turned and was holding onto the wall. 'Mary,' she gasped, running forward. 'Are you—?'

'Get back!' Mary cried, alarm in her voice.

Effie stopped dead in her tracks.

'Please . . . don't touch me.' The woman was holding herself awkwardly, pressing her hands to the walls as though holding them up. Effie could see from the rumpled bed that she'd just been lying in it.

'Are you in pain?' Effie whispered. 'Shall I get Lorna back?' But of course, the nurse was already on the beach, awaiting Mary's injured husband . . .

Mary shook her head, letting it hang down as she took several slow, laboured breaths. The baby wasn't due for several more months, Effie knew that much. 'I'll be fine. I just need

93

a minute . . . I heard a commotion.' She turned her head slightly, in question.

'Oh. Aye.' Effie felt troubled to be bringing bad news when the poor woman was already suffering. '. . . I'm afraid it's Donald, he's been injured. Head wound.'

She saw Mary's fingertips press into the walls, blanching the skin. It didn't need to be said how hard life would be for the woman if her husband died or was even incapacitated and she was left with a new baby. The neighbours would rally, they always did, but . . .

'Lorna thinks you should come to the beach. In case . . .' She didn't spell it out. She didn't need to.

Mary simply nodded. 'You go. I'll be right down.'

'Do you want me to help you walk?' Effie offered.

'No. I'll be fine. It was just the sudden movement that got me . . . Go.'

Effie waited another moment more, still not sure she should leave her, but Mary was a firm character. They'd all heard her husband catching a supper off her on many nights over the years. If she said no, no was what she meant.

'Just call if you need me, then,' Effie said quietly, retreating from the room.

She walked back out into the Street. The rowing boat was almost at the shore now and all the women were gathered, ready to nurse, feed, wail, greet. The minister was pacing along the water's edge, the Bible in his hand. Effie's gaze fell again to the magnificent yacht that had started to become a familiar part of the landscape over the past few days, the emblem of an alien world beginning to settle into theirs. She had been staring at it the whole time she and the women had been waiting for the dinghy to return. If Donald's injury was bad enough that he needed a hospital doctor, it would be the yacht that would get him there . . . In a matter of minutes after their return, Sholto and his father might be gone from here and she knew they wouldn't be coming back.

A cry of voices startled her from her thoughts and she saw the women wading out to the boat. She had to get back down there. She ran again, in perpetual motion it seemed, back to the beach. Her Uncle Hamish and oldest cousin Euan, who was her age, had jumped out and were helping the women haul the boat onto the shore. It stopped with a jolt as the prow met the shingly sand and the men that had come back – only half of those who had gone out – leapt into the water. Donald's limp body was carried between them, an ungainly method as each arm and leg was held, his head hanging back, his skin cloud white.

Some of the women gave a cry, the smallest children clutching their mothers' legs. Effie looked back for sight of Mary. She was coming down the grass, moving well given the distress she'd been in minutes earlier.

They carried him up the beach and set him down on the grass edge. Lorna immediately laid a blanket over him and crouched over, peeling back the shirt sleeve that had been torn off and used as a bandage. Blood had seeped through, drying dark and clotted in his hair. The minister stood beside them, offering up a prayer as the nurse worked.

Effie felt a stab of guilt. Why hadn't she looked over at the island as she'd roped up? She'd have seen the semaphore immediately. Vital minutes might have been saved. Instead, she'd been too busy trying to avoid a young lord's bright eyes to even notice the SOS across the water.

'What happened to him?' Lorna asked, examining the wound more closely. It was a deep, nasty gash to the back upper corner of his skull.

'He fell against a rock,' the factor said, back again.

'You saw it happen?' Lorna asked.

'Aye. We were covering Sunadal together. He was lunging for a sheep, caught it but it wriggled free and in the struggle, he lost his balance and fell.'

Lorna frowned, looking back at the cut. 'It's deep,' she murmured. 'He must have fallen heavily.'

'He did, aye. Went down like a stone.'

'When did it happen?' She was peering at his pupils now.

'Six, seven hours ago? The sun was still low.'

'Seven hours?' There was rebuke in Lorna's voice.

'It took me an hour alone just to get enough folk to help carry him down to the disembarking point! Then we had to wait for you to see.'

Effie felt his words like a punch to the stomach. She felt like she'd been the reason there was a delay.

'It was fine on the morning check,' Jayne Ferguson said defensively. 'The boys went up to check as usual.'

'Bad luck for us then that he fell that bit too late for the breakfast lookout,' the factor snapped.

'Donald?' It was Mary, her voice breathless as she made her way over the uneven ground. 'Oh Donald!' Her hands flew to her mouth.

'It's all right, Mary,' Lorna said quickly as his wife sank down beside her, beside him. 'He's got a nasty cut to his head. It's deep but it's not bleeding out. He's going to be a wee bit doollally a few days but as long as we can keep it clean, and he rests, he should be well.'

'You promise?' Mary looked at her urgently, her hands on her swollen belly.

Lorna swallowed. 'As much as I can. I'll take good care of him . . . I'll stay with you for the next few nights, it's the most critical time.'

Mary looked comforted by the thought. She was hardly nimble on her feet. How could she nurse him?

Lorna looked up at the men. 'We need to get him into the house and onto the table so I can clean him up. Infection will be the biggest risk now.'

The men moved as one, lifting the injured man as the women ran ahead, gathering their skirts and fussing. Only one man stayed back.

Sholto reached for his jacket in the boat. There was a rip in his shirt by the shoulder and as he turned she saw great smears of blood across the front of it. His face was flushed and he looked utterly spent. She supposed he had never had to row an eight-mile medical emergency before.

'Thank you,' she said quietly as he trudged up the beach to where she stood.

'Why are you thanking me?'

'For helping Donald and Uncle Hamish.'

He frowned. 'What kind of a man would I be if I hadn't?'

She could feel that the offence caused by their earlier 'moment' on the ledge, the one that she had rebuffed, still sat between them. Their careless ease together and childlike spontaneity had gone.

'. . . You look tired.'

He gave a small smile. He had just run down a mountain and rowed to Boreray and back. 'Yes.' He wouldn't be restless today. No midnight swim tonight.

'You should rest. Have something to eat.' She remembered their earlier joke. Boiled fulmar was no reward. 'You said you had some apples?' she asked, willing the edginess between them to ease. 'You can have those.'

'True. I can have those.' He blinked back at her. 'At the very least I need to change my clothes.'

They walked together up the path. Neither one of them spoke but the silence between them seemed swollen with unsaid words, and as they reached the factor's front door he turned to face her. 'Well, it is a relief to hear that Mr McKinnon will likely recover,' he said, falling back into his usual mannered mode.

'Aye,' she agreed. 'Mary was awful worried.'

'Of course.' He cleared his throat. 'And also it means we shall not have to leave in a rush.'

Her mouth parted as their eyes locked once more. So he had thought it too? All the while he'd been gone, her mind had tried to run through the inevitable sequence of events that was coming, be it sooner or later: her on the shore, watching the anchor lift, the sails bowing out and having him glide away from her. It had left her dismayed, but more than that – shocked by the extent of her dismay. He had been here not two full days and she knew they were already in the shadow of the moment when he would leave again, that it couldn't be stopped. But . . . not yet. She wanted more. She didn't know what exactly, but she knew she needed more than just this.

And her wish had been granted! They had a stay of execution and he was still here now. For today. Tonight. The question was – what were they going to do with the time left?

She saw the hope dial up in his eyes as he saw his turmoil reflected in hers, a smile beginning to flicker on his lips—

The front door opened suddenly and the factor went to step out, looking startled to find the pair of them on his threshold, standing together in silence. Sholto immediately stepped back. Effie too, creating a space wide enough for the man to pass. But he did not. 'Lord Sholto,' he said, pointedly turning his back on her. 'I was just coming to find you! You must be hungry after your exertions. I've prepared a meal for you.'

'That's very kind,' Sholto said after a pause.

Effie looked down, feeling reality bite again. For a moment there, she had allowed herself to believe he was within her reach. Had he noticed the factor's snub to her? Would he understand it was the reason why she had to step back – not just earlier, and right now, but every time? Would he see that what *she* wanted didn't come into it?

'Was there anything else, Miss Gillies?' the factor asked, turning slightly as she stood frozen on the spot.

'. . . No.' Her voice was flat as she stared back at Sholto.

'Perhaps Miss Gillies would care to join us?' Sholto asked quickly.

A flush of high colour swept through the factor's cheeks, his nostrils flaring with anger at the suggestion.

'Thank you, but I should go,' she said stiffly. 'The bull needs fresh hay.'

There was no light in Sholto's eyes this time at the mention of the bull but she saw the factor's approving nod at last and she left without another word, doing what had to be done.

Chapter Six

Effie walked around the bull house, raking the manure into a pile. She had let Tiny into the enclosure and he was grazing, the sun bouncing off his back and making his hide gleam. Below her in the glen she could see the women fussing with meals now some of the men were back, children being dispatched to others' cottages on errands. They had safely carried Donald McKinnon to his own tabletop and rested him upon it – Lorna was still there with him, cleaning the wound – before the men went back to the boat and unloaded the bags of wool.

Effie shovelled the manure into the pails by the back wall, but as she glanced out, she caught sight of someone flying down the hill from Mullach Mor, dark skirt billowing, a red scarf tied around her waist. Effie frowned. There was only one person who would wear a headscarf like that . . .

'Flora?' Effie called, setting the fork against the wall and waving wildly. She'd not seen her friend in over two weeks, since she and Mhairi had taken the livestock over to the summer pastures in Glen Bay. To walk there and back again was almost four hours and she'd not enough hours in the day as it was. The best she could hope for was a chance visit such as this – no doubt the girls needed more food. 'Flora!'

The girl's head turned at the shout and she swerved in the direction of the bull house as she saw Effie climbing onto the wall and waving her arms above her head.

'Where's the fire?' Effie smiled, hugging her excitedly a few minutes later.

'Uff,' Flora panted, leaning her arms and head on the wall and trying to get her breath back. She turned her head to smile up at Effie, her face flushed appealingly. It was commonly acknowledged that she was the most beautiful girl on the isle, with long raven-black hair that gleamed like oil, hazel-green eyes and a rosebud mouth. Her big brothers, David and Donald, called her 'the Kelpie'; it wasn't intended as a compliment, but Flora still knew the power she wielded. 'I'm dead. She made me run the whole way here.'

'Mhairi did?'

'Aye.'

'Why couldn't she run? Is she hurt?'

Flora put up a hand to stem Effie's fast-rising concern. 'She's fine. But we were over on Cambir when we saw the cuts on Boreray . . .' She gave another sigh, unable to catch her breath. 'Who is it?'

'It's Donald McKinnon—'

'What?' Flora snapped up to standing again.

'He's got a head injury.'

'Is he going to recover?'

'Aye. He fell catching a sheep and cut his head, but Lorna thinks he'll be fine with some rest. She's going to stay with them for the next few nights too.'

'She is?'

'Aye. Poor Mary's not up to much.'

'No,' Flora said quietly, looking pensive. 'But he's definitely going to be all right?'

Effie couldn't help but feel bemused by her friend's excessive concern. Although they shared the same surname, Donald McKinnon wasn't a relative of Mhairi's. 'Is absence making the heart grow fonder?' Effie teased. 'Are you missing us all over there while you idle the summer away?'

'Idle?!' Flora huffed, grabbing a stalk of grass from the wall and threading it through her fingers. 'We've three hundred sheep over there.'

'Aye, grazing and giving you no bother, from the look of things.'

'What does that mean?'

'Just that you look bonny as ever. I thought it was hunger that had driven you back, but evidently not.' Flora's hair had an especially glossy shine to it and her skin a dewy plumpness. 'The look of love.' Flora always preened as the others complimented her.

Effie wasn't sure she herself looked like that – she felt she must look more haunted than contented – and besides, she wasn't even sure if this *was* love. She didn't know what this feeling was.

'There's nothing bonny about spending a fortnight alone with Mhairi, let me tell you. She's grown up with her brothers telling her tales about the McKinnon curse and dash if she doesn't believe it! She's frightened everything's going to kill her or hers.' Flora rolled her eyes. They both knew their sensitive, gentle friend suffered more than them in this wild life.

'Well, you can tell her it's all fine. No relatives harmed.'

'But Donald's not out of the woods yet?'

'No, but if Lorna thought it really bad, she'd have sent him to the mainland.'

'How?' But as she asked the question, Flora lifted her gaze, fixing upon the yacht anchored in the bay. She gave a gasp. Effie was more surprised that she hadn't seen it as she tore down the hill, but supposed it spoke to the level of her concern as she had run. 'Whose is *that*?'

Effie sighed, staring at it too. It was an emblem of the distance between her and Sholto, a motif of their very different worlds. When she was with him, she could believe he was just a man with bright eyes and a ready laugh, who swam naked in the moonlight and flirted with her on mountain ledges, but the yacht was a constant reminder he wasn't 'just' anything. 'They're friends of MacLeod. The Earl of Dumfries and his son. They brought the factor over.'

Flora gave a groan. 'Eeesht.'

'I know. We thought we got lucky that the men decided to make the trip to Boreray on account of the weather and they took Mathieson with them, giving us some peace. Only . . . two days later and they're back again.'

'Bad luck.'

'Worse for Donald,' Effie shrugged.

They watched as Tiny walked back up the enclosure, tossing his head and snorting happily.

'He looks pleased with himself,' Flora murmured.

'He should be. He's had a long mating season,' she quipped.

'Men! Man or beast, they're all the same,' Flora said in that knowing way of hers that seemed to belong to women of great beauty. She gave a garrulous laugh, pressing her head to Effie's like they had always done as girls; but Flora had long outgrown her childish ways. She was engaged to be married to James Callaghan, a rich textile merchant from Glasgow. He had come over the previous spring to try and strike a deal with the villagers to buy their tweed direct, but the quantities he wanted were too great for the St Kildans to

103

meet. They had to fulfil their quota obligations for their rent first. But he'd not come away empty-handed. One glance at Flora and he had sailed over as many times as the seas would allow that summer. He was building a grand home in Blythswood Square and he promised her that as soon as it was completed, they would be married and live there.

In many ways, Flora had already left. She had always been a restless spirit, this rock in the ocean too small to contain her passionate life force, and Effie had grown up somehow knowing that her best friend was destined for a bigger stage. Ironically, it was her engagement and the confirmation of a future on the mainland that meant she now embraced life on their wild isle with an unnerving grace and good humour that had been lacking before. She constantly sang and did her chores with a smile, and when it was asked who would spend a summer in isolation with the grazing animals in Glen Bay, she had willingly agreed to join Mhairi McKinnon there. Effie simply couldn't imagine this place without her.

'Will you stay for dinner?' Effie asked her. 'They'll be pleased to see you. Your pa had to skipper the boat back to Boreray so he's worn out. David and Donnie are still over there and your ma's upset by the fall.'

'If they see me, they'll make me stay,' Flora said. 'But Mhairi's got the jitters. She made me promise to come straight back.'

Effie scowled impatiently. 'I don't understand why if Mhairi's got the jitters, she didn't come over here herself instead of sending you?'

But Flora didn't hear. She was staring down at the village. Specifically, at Lorna standing talking to Mary round the back of her cottage. The nurse was holding her hand consolingly as she spoke. Was it bad news she was giving? Was that why they'd come round the back, so Donald couldn't hear?

Both women frowned. 'That doesn't look promising,' Flora murmured.

'No,' Effie agreed.

'Perhaps I should stay a wee while after all then. See if the situation changes.' She looked back at Effie. 'Have I missed much?'

Effie's mouth parted. Where did she begin? How did she begin to explain the predicament in which she found herself, drawn to a man she had no business calling a friend, much less anything more. But with no mother to advise her, no sisters . . . Her life had been lived on a male plane, especially since her brother's death. How was she supposed to know what to feel, do, *be*?

'There's been some excitement, aye,' Effie murmured non-committally. She felt vulnerable even broaching it. The girls had teased her for the way she'd ruthlessly chopped their elder brothers at the knees when they'd started to look at her through a new gaze but now she was the one with a fresh perspective. Why had no one ever told her it felt like *this*?

Flora's eyes brightened as she saw her friend's uncharacteristic hesitancy. 'Speak to me. Tell me.'

'I've been guiding the visitors while the men were gone.'

'Aye.'

'I'm being paid two shillings for my trouble,' she hedged.

'*Two*?'

She felt so nervous. 'And we've become friends.'

Flora frowned. 'I thought you said they were lords.'

'Well, yes, but . . . you wouldn't know it. Not really. There's no airs and graces when we're all out walking together.'

Flora's eyes narrowed. 'And . . . ?' she prompted. She had always had an instinct for secrets. The minister's wife had torn her hair out trying to teach Flora to read, but even as a young girl, she'd had an innate ability to read people. 'What else is there?'

'Miss Gillies! I've been searching for you.'

The voice was sharp through the air and they looked up to find the factor striding towards them.

'Eeesht,' Flora said under her breath. 'If it's not the devil himself. I'll catch you later.'

'Flora, wait—' But her friend was already in motion, sauntering off and deliberately swinging her hips as she passed by. The factor was one of the few men seemingly unmoved by Flora's powers – she used to joke he could only be aroused by a profit margin – but she flaunted them in his presence anyway, if only to provoke his opprobrium. Flora wasn't one to be ignored and she well knew that her womanly wiles, and how she used them, did not fall under his jurisdiction.

'Mr Mathieson,' she said breezily as she passed him, her nose in the air.

The factor gave a terse nod, coming to a stop beside Effie. 'Where the stream is shallowest, it's noisiest,' he muttered, watching Flora go with a frown. He waited until she had passed through the dyke and was almost upon the cottages before turning back to Effie.

He gave a short smile, but there was something unnatural in his manner. Was he here about the arrears again? Had he heard about those four sheep they'd lost? Or had she done something else wrong? 'Miss Gillies, I'm aware we haven't really had any time yet to speak.'

'Really, sir? I thought we spoke well enough the other day.'

She stared back at him with her usual impassive look, but she hadn't forgotten the way he'd castigated her by the jetty after the climbing display, as Sholto and his father had gone past. 'Besides, I thought you were dining with your guests.'

'Yes, well, Lord Sholto was weary from the day's exercise, so he has decided to take his meal in his room.'

'Oh.' Effie couldn't help feeling pleased to hear it; she knew how much it mattered to the factor to chalk up these social encounters with dignitaries and improve his familiarity with them. Sholto's elusiveness would be a victory of sorts against this man's snobbery, even if he didn't know it.

There was a moment's pause as the factor took in her reserved demeanour. Did he even remember his cutting words on the quayside? Or the snub on his own doorstep just an hour ago? Probably not, she knew. Tiny was lighter-footed than this man.

'. . . Are you well?'

She was surprised by the enquiry. It wasn't his usual form of conversation. 'Yes, sir,' she replied suspiciously.

'You look . . . very well. I hope it hasn't been too taxing for you, having to entertain his lordship's friends the past few days?'

Her eyes had narrowed to slits as she talked. 'Not at all. They have been kind to me and I've endeavoured to do my best for them and show them the birds they wish to see.'

'Indeed, indeed.' He was staring at her with a scrutinizing gaze, as though trying to read behind her eyes. Had Sholto betrayed something of their . . . it couldn't be said to be intimacy, but familiarity, certainly? 'His lordship has conveyed how pleased they've been with your efforts and wanted me to thank you for them.'

Effie felt herself grow cold, her heart giving a flutter of

panic. 'You make it sound like they don't need me to help them anymore.'

'Yes, that's right.'

So that was why he was here. 'But I was to guide them for as long as they're still here . . .' She was aware her voice had risen fractionally.

'No. You were to guide them for as long as they're still here and while *we* were away. But we're back now, so I'll pick it up for the rest of their stay.'

That strange, awkward smile sat upon his face again. 'Miss Gillies, there's no need to look so aghast. You're quite busy enough with looking after your father, without having to add to your duties.'

'But I didn't mind, sir.'

He nodded. 'Because you're a generous person, Miss Gillies. And I commend you for it. But as I said, you were only ever commissioned during our absence, and it wouldn't be appropriate for you to continue now the circumstances have changed.'

Appropriate. There it was, that word again.

Effie desperately tried to think of a way to talk him round. If she lost her opportunity to guide the visitors, the only times she would see them – him – would be down here in the village, with the eyes of every islander upon them. She longed suddenly for the privacy of the ledge again, where they had stood suspended between will and action, as the puffins lowed at their feet. 'But what about my money?' she blurted. 'I was promised two shillings and I've not earnt it yet.'

Mr Mathieson hesitated, then reached into his pocket and fished out two coins for her. 'You're quite right. You deserve to be rewarded for all you've done. I'll make sure his lordship knows upon my return.'

He stepped forward and tipped them into her palm. The coins were warm and she had to resist the urge to tip them out, to step back. There was something repellent about the way he was so obsequious around the visitors and so hectoring and bullying to the rest of them.

'While we're here . . .' He turned back to her, lowering his voice in spite of their evident isolation. 'I see you found it?'

Effie swallowed as she remembered the book. In all truth, she'd completely forgotten about it, her mind elsewhere during her waking hours. 'Aye, sir. I did.' She saw the expectation in his eyes, the need to have his generosity acknowledged. '. . . It's beautiful,' she added. 'I've never seen anything so lovely.'

'No, I thought probably not,' he sighed. 'Still, just because you come from nothing, it does not mean you should die with nothing. The world is changing fast and we can all improve our stations in this life. You may be coarse and rash, but you're no fool, Miss Gillies. There's still hope for you to better yourself and make your father truly proud.'

A small silence opened up and it felt like a tear in the very fabric of the universe. She felt hot tears sting her eyes; the clear intimation was that he wasn't proud *yet*.

'Actually, I was going to talk to you about it. I love the book, but I can't accept it, sir,' she said with quiet determination, seeing his shock. She realized it pleased her to be able to push back for once.

'What?'

'Yes. It's too fine. It doesn't belong here, with someone like me.'

'Nonsense. Haven't you been listening to a word I've said? Besides, who else has a finer mind for these things than you? You have schooled yourself into an expert on these birds.

When I saw it, I knew you had to have it. That book was written for you.' She could feel the weight of his stare upon her. 'You may be poor, but—'

'But I'm *not* poor, sir,' she replied with sudden defiance. 'That's just it. I have everything I need here. A poor man needs what he does not have, but I want nothing more.'

'Miss Gillies.' A small smile curved his mouth. 'How many times must it be said? You are not a *man* – and wearing your brother's clothes and doing his chores will never make you so. That is evident to us all, and yet not to you? You seem unaware that you have bloomed into quite a beauty.'

She swallowed, perturbed by the change of direction in the conversation. 'I am not concerned with how I look, sir, only with what I can do.'

'You may be unconcerned, but I assure you others are impacted by it. And a woman should take care with where she places her attentions.' There was a rumble of threat in his words.

'I don't understand,' Effie faltered.

'Don't you?' He let the scepticism chime through his words like a bell.

She stiffened. What did he know? Had Sholto said something? Had he betrayed her because of her boldness, because she had turned away from his flirtation, left him on the doorstep . . . ?

The factor stepped closer to her, a five-foot-ten pillar of might and musk. 'A word of advice. The power you wield is only an illusion. Do not toy with a man's affections, Miss Gillies. Go carefully with a full cup.'

So Sholto *had* said something. He was still angry about what he saw as her rejection. It went against the natural order of things – her, refusing a man like him!

The factor stepped back and inhaled sharply as he looked around at the village again. He gave a nod, surveying it as though it were his own. He turned back to her, a new look upon his face. 'Well, I am pleased you like the book. I shall aim for something equally special on my return trip.'

'Please, it's not necessary—'

He gave a stern look that stopped her words in their tracks. 'Miss Gillies, it is merely a book. Hardly a gift of any merit or substance. There is no cause for such fuss.'

'. . . Sir.'

'Good day, Miss Gillies.'

She watched him walk away down the slope, her heart clattering in her chest as he became smaller and smaller, before walking past the McKinnons' cottage and turning out of sight.

Tiny had grazed his way up the enclosure and snorted heavily over the wall, making her jump – but it wasn't the bull she was frightened of.

Chapter Seven

'Eff, have you seen Jayne?'

Effie looked up from the quern; she was sitting on the three-legged stool in the plot, grinding down the oats and feeling grateful for the physical exertion. She needed to vent. Flora was leaning on the other side of the wall, her shirt sleeves rolled up and her hair twisted in a messy topknot. Even hot, she looked beautiful, though she did look bothered. 'You're still here? I thought you'd gone back.'

'I'm heading back shortly but I need to talk to Jayne before I go and she's not home.'

Effie had to think for a moment. She had passed Jayne on the Street earlier and the woman had been heading towards the jetty. 'Did you try the fishing rocks, past the featherstore? She often likes to sit there at this time.'

Flora arched an eyebrow. They both knew Jayne avoided being at home with her husband as much as she could. Norman Ferguson was handsome and dynamic but he had an ugly temper and ready fists, and many was the time the neighbours had had to run in to save Jayne when voices became raised. The irony was, she had the gentlest nature. Effie thought it was his wife's meek goodness, contrasting his own black soul, that drove Norman to such rage.

'Ah,' Flora nodded. 'Want to come with me?'

Effie looked back up at the cottage. Her father, like their neighbours, was inside in the shade, weaving at the loom. The morning's sharp sun had grown steadily more sultry through the afternoon, the air growing so still and heavy the birds almost dropped. At this time of day, the front of the cottages were exposed to the full blast of the afternoon sun and the shadow from the wall stopped a full foot short of where she sat, providing no relief at all. Effie realized she was sweating, her cheeks red, her long fair hair worn in loose plaits that aired her neck. After coming back from cleaning out the bull's pen, she had taken off her tweeds and pulled on the light blouse and navy wool skirt that was the summer uniform of the St Kildan women. She tried never to wear it except for Sunday best, when the minister had made it clear she would not be accepted into the house of God in men's clothing, but in this heat, even she couldn't deny the merits of anything that permitted bare legs.

'Aye, c'mon then,' Effie said, getting up and letting her skirt fall back down her thighs; she knew this would be their last chance to talk before Flora went back over the ridge. She jumped over the wall, expecting they would walk down the Street, but Flora turned instead up the alley between theirs and Old Fin's, and round to the back. Effie felt a reflex of both disappointment and relief that it meant they wouldn't pass the factor's front door.

'Why do you need to see Jayne?' Effie asked as they immediately linked arms while they stepped past the cleits and over the sunken stones in the long grass. They had walked together like this since they were children. There was only eight months between them and Effie often felt they were more like sisters than friends.

'It's Mhairi and all her talk of curses. It's got me spooked.'

'You?' Effie laughed. 'But you don't believe in such things!'

'I didn't used to,' Flora sighed. 'But I don't know, when someone keeps telling you over and over that something bad's coming . . .'

Effie was surprised by her friend's newfound superstition. 'You don't really think that, do you?'

'I didn't till something bad did happen,' Flora shrugged. 'I'm just hoping this is it. Donald's had a knock, but he'll be fine, and the danger's all passed.'

'Flora, it was just an accident. There was nothing more to it than that.'

'Wasn't there? He is a McKinnon.'

Effie laughed. 'Oh, Flora! The McKinnons' curse isn't real!'

'Just like Jayne's visions aren't real?' Flora asked back.

Effie didn't reply. She might not understand it – no one did – but the islanders knew that when Jayne had a certain type of dream or waking vision about someone, within a few days, they would be dead. Second sight was no new phenomenon – Ma Peg's own mother had been in possession of the same power, she had always said – but it made the islanders edgy nonetheless. Jayne had only had five such visions in Effie's lifetime and she never spoke of them in advance; only if the deceased's loved ones came to her afterwards would she confirm what she had seen. She had told Effie's own father – after her brother John's death – that often it was difficult for her to understand what she was seeing; the visions were always different in form and not always clear, and she certainly never knew when or how death would come. The rest of the villagers – excepting her own husband – treated Jayne with a wary respect, but Effie couldn't imagine how terrible it must be for the poor woman to be possessed of such a burden, for it was no gift. How must she feel during the days after a dream, just waiting, knowing what was to come . . . ? Little wonder she kept herself to herself.

'Honestly, I don't know what I think anymore, but when I came over here, I had no idea who it was that was injured. How can I go back and tell Mhairi it's a McKinnon?'

'But he's not her family.'

'But he's got her name. And if I can tell her I've spoken to Jayne and she's reassured me it's not the curse . . .'

'Then you'll have a quieter life.'

'Precisely.' Flora glanced at her. 'I want to know nothing will go wrong, at least till I can get through this summer and off the isle, back to James.'

Effie had to laugh at her friend's reversion to her old self-ishness. 'Ah – but all's well if something goes wrong *after* you leave?'

Flora laughed too, unashamed and not denying it. 'I've missed you.' She squeezed Effie's arm to her waist; something rough pricked her skin.

'Ouch, what's that?' Effie pulled her arm back just in time to see a thistle-shaped brooch pinning the scarf around Flora's waist. '. . . Who gave you that?'

But Flora didn't even need to answer. Who else but James?

'Did you not tell him it was inappropriate, giving you gifts like that before you're married?' Brooches were the only jewel-lery worn on the isle and were reserved for the married women alone. Flora's premature gift defied the usual modesty of waiting till marriage – and was suggestive of other things not being held back till marriage, too.

Flora's cheeks flushed a deep pink. 'Sssh. You didn't see that,' she said quickly, rearranging the shawl so that the brooch was hidden in the folds.

'Of course I didn't,' Effie murmured, watching her friend

with a mix of jealousy, intrigue and concern. 'I've missed you too. I don't know why you had to volunteer to spend the summer over the other side – especially when you know you're leaving.'

'Mhairi needs me.'

'*I* need you! Mhairi's got sisters who could have gone with her.'

'But they're too wee. You could have come too, you know,' Flora suggested.

'You know I've got Da and the bull to look after.'

Flora shrugged. She was used to being fought over. 'What did Mathieson want, anyway?'

'Oh.' Her shoulders slumped. 'He came to tell me I'm no longer needed as a guide for the visitors now the men are back. *He's* going to do it now.'

'Of course he is. He's such a hideous snob,' Flora muttered, her eyes narrowed upon the haze beginning to blur the horizon. 'There's another storm coming.'

But Effie didn't hear; she was distracted. They were walking by the back of the factor's house now. The dyke curved in at this far end of the village, herding them closer to its curtilage, and Effie glanced at the back bedroom windows as they passed but they stared back like dark eyes, revealing nothing. Flora looked back at her, catching Effie's inquisitive stare at the impassive building. '. . . It'll mean the visitors will have to haul anchor if they want to get ahead of it.'

This time the words registered and Effie stiffened before she could stop herself. Flora must have felt it; their arms were looped together tightly. 'Why didn't you mention the young visitor's fine-looking?' Flora winked, squeezing her arm tighter and giving her a crafty grin.

'Who told you that?'

'Lorna.'

Effie rolled her eyes. Who else?

'Well? *Is* he fine-looking?'

'He's fine enough,' she said lightly, but she couldn't keep the light shining from her eyes. Flora gave a squeal of delight.

'Have you taken a fancy to him?' she gasped.

'Flora, he's a laird!'

'A lass can look, can't she?' Flora laughed. 'Ooh, I never thought I'd see the like! Finally the seal around Effie Gillies's heart is broken! Wait till my brothers hear!'

'They'll hear nothing of the sort,' Effie said quickly. 'Don't start putting talk about. You know what Father's like.'

'I don't know what you're so worried about. A girl's perfectly safe flirting with a man she knows can never marry her, especially the son of an earl. It's the men who *can* marry you that you should be wary of.'

'You, maybe. They're hardly lining up for me.'

Flora tossed her head back and laughed. She flirted with the flowers, the clouds, the minister, everything and everyone. 'Well, it all sounds a lot more fun than listening to Mhairi greet about the McKinnons' curse!'

Jayne was sitting on the rocks just ahead, knitting away. She cut a solitary figure, the sea glinting behind her as the headland peeled back towards Boreray.

'Jayne!' Flora called as they approached. 'I've been looking for you all over.'

The brown-haired woman looked up. Her face was plain and lined for one so young, but she had a ready smile, despite her many burdens.

'Flora, you're back,' she said warmly as the girls veered from the grass, their tanned legs flashing as they gathered their skirts to see better while they climbed barefoot over the rocks. They settled themselves on some boulders either side of her, looking out to sea towards the Great Beyond. Effie often thought that living here, they were like the sailors with Christopher Columbus – believing there was something over the horizon, though they could not see it.

'Aye. Mhairi saw the cuts and had me tear back here. She was worried about the McKinnon curse.'

Jayne gave a low chuckle. 'She's a vivid imagination, that one.'

'Like you?' Flora asked meaningfully.

'It's not imagination that I've got,' Jayne murmured, immediately getting the gist of the visit. Flora was many things, but subtle wasn't one of them. 'What is it you want?'

Effie felt uncomfortable and looked away. Jayne wasn't a clairvoyant; the visions couldn't be summoned at will. What could this achieve?

'I'm sorry, I know we shouldn't ask,' she said, asking anyway, 'but I just need to know before I go back – is it done now?'

Jayne frowned, her gaze meeting Flora's briefly. 'Is what done?'

Effie watched, almost hypnotized, as Jayne's needles flicked up and down as she talked; she never needed to watch the stitches as she went.

'The bad spirit that led to Donald McKinnon's accident today.'

A gleam of amusement came into Jayne's eyes. 'Who said bad spirits were at play? As I understand, he fell trying to catch a sheep.'

'So you didn't have any of your dreams about him?'

'About Donald?' Jayne smiled outright now. 'No. There's been no dreams about Donald.'

'And no visions about him either?' Flora clarified, determined not to be caught out on a technicality.

'No visions either.'

Flora gave a loud sigh. 'So then I can go back with good news and she'll give me some peace.'

'If it's the McKinnon curse she's so worried about, surely she should be more concerned about the McKinnons in her own family?' Jayne enquired with her usual good sense.

'Aye, of course,' Flora said quickly. '. . . You've not had any dreams about them either, have you?'

Jayne seemed to grow calmer in the face of Flora's panic. 'Flora, you can tell her I've not had any dreams – or visions – about any of the McKinnons, family or no.'

'Then that should guarantee I'll have a good night's sleep tonight. Thank you.' Flora sighed again with more relief, but her eyes seemed to catch on something over Effie's shoulder. She sat straighter. 'Who . . . ?'

Effie twisted to look. For a few moments she could see nothing beyond a dark silhouette winked out by a harsh gleaming sunlight that bloomed around it with every step. And yet she would know that physique anywhere, in the light, in the dark. It was like feeling a heat moving towards her.

Sholto walked closer and she automatically rose to greet him. He was carrying a fishing rod over his shoulder, two silver fish dangling behind on a hook. 'Miss Gillies. What a surprise to see you here.' He seemed pleased, but she heard the reserve in his voice too.

'Have you taken to catching your own dinner then, sir?' It had become their private joke, but neither of them was much in the mood for laughing.

'Guilty as charged, I'm afraid,' he said, coming to a stop just a few feet away and looking back at her. There were questions in his eyes, as there were in hers. That sense of easy connection that had sparked between them at their first meeting had, over the ensuing hours and days, become steadily more complicated: looks had weight; words had hidden meanings. But what could come of it? Something primitive in her recognized something primitive in him, but if it drew them to one another, equally powerful class boundaries were pulling them apart.

She jolted. '. . . Forgive me – these are my friends. This is Mrs Ferguson. And Miss Flora MacQueen. This is Lord Sholto . . .' She realized she didn't know his surname.

'Crichton-Stuart,' he said quickly. 'But please let's not concern ourselves with formalities.'

All the same, the two women rose, nodding their heads respectfully, demurely.

'A pleasure to meet you, sir,' Jayne said, as the elder and therefore more senior woman.

Effie felt a sudden jab of alarm at how Sholto would react upon seeing her beautiful friend. Would he fall in love on the spot, like every other man?

'Mrs Ferguson, Miss MacQueen, the pleasure is mine,' Sholto said, his gaze lingering slightly upon Flora. He frowned. 'Miss MacQueen, I have not yet seen you in the village, I don't think?'

Effie's heart fell to the floor. And so it began . . .

'No, sir. I'm summering with Mhairi McKinnon with the livestock over in Glen Bay.'

'Glen Bay,' Sholto echoed. 'Now that is up Mullach Mor and over the other side of the ridge?'

It was a moment before Effie realized he had directed the question back to her, and not Flora. 'Oh . . . aye . . . it's the northern bay, not far from where we saw the petrels yesterday.'

'We have not explored there yet. Perhaps that can be tomorrow's excursion?'

Effie stared at him. He wanted to go to the bay, to see Flora? Her heart felt shrivelled to a nut. 'I'm afraid I cannot, sir.'

'Why not?' he frowned.

For a moment the words wouldn't come as she saw the confusion on his face. But she saw the factor's face too, his hard eyes and hard words throwing shame upon her. 'Now the men are back, the factor will continue guiding you—' She looked away.

'Mathieson?' He sounded appalled. 'Whilst I'm sure . . . I'm sure Mathieson would do a splendid job of guiding us . . . your rope skills . . . and the birds . . .' His voice faltered as he tried to catch her eye.

'The factor is proficient too. Or perhaps one of the other men could take you,' she said, speaking to the ground. 'Angus McKinnon's a good climber. He's Mhairi's elder brother.'

She could feel him still staring at her, the silence becoming heavy, but she would not meet his gaze.

Sholto gave a small, embarrassed laugh. 'Well, I see you cannot be persuaded, Miss Gillies. It is our loss indeed. I know my father will be terribly disappointed.'

'I'm sorry, sir,' she said awkwardly, but made no move to offer anything more.

There was another pause.

'Well,' he said finally, bringing his attention back to the others. 'I really ought to get these back, before they start to turn. It's been a pleasure meeting you ladies.'

'Good evening, sir,' Jayne nodded. Flora too.

'Mrs Ferguson. Miss MacQueen.' He looked back at Effie. '. . . Miss Gillies.'

She didn't look up again till she saw his feet moving off.

The others didn't move at all. Only when he was back on the path and passing the manse did they stir.

'We'll be off too,' Flora said firmly. 'I've to get back to the other side or Mhairi'll die of fright. At least I can tell her the McKinnons are safe, thank you, Jayne.'

'See you anon, Jayne,' Effie muttered as Flora marched off in a sudden rush towards the grass. She clambered over the rocks back to the narrow path and together they walked in silence for several moments. 'Well, that's good news about—'

But the words were torn from her.

'What's going on?' Flora demanded, whirling on her heel as soon as they were out of earshot. 'Tell me everything that's happened with him.'

'Nothing's—'

'Don't lie to me, Eff! I know what I just saw. Has he kissed you?'

'Of course not!'

'Made any declarations?'

Effie shook her head. 'N—'

'But he's going to.'

Effie shook her head again, but this time Flora stopped her with a nod. 'It wasn't a question. He's going to and you have to be ready for it. You can't allow it, Eff.'

It felt like an age before Effie could get the words to her throat. '. . . Why can't I?'

'You know why. Nothing can come of it.'

Effie stared at her, feeling rage at her friend's words and the finality in them. She had longed for the moment to confide her feelings, her confusion, in her worldly friend, but without even getting the chance, this thing that hadn't yet taken a breath was being condemned. 'But it has with you and James! He's rich! He's from another world!'

'Aye. But he's self-made. It's different. He can choose his path. That man . . .' Flora jerked her thumb over her shoulder in the direction of the village. 'He may as well be the king.'

'But you just said I was allowed to flirt with the son of an earl!'

'That was before I saw you together. That was no game. It can't happen.'

Effie felt devastated by the wholesale dismissal of her dreams. 'I never said it would.'

'You didn't need to! It's plain as day what's going on between you and where it's heading.' Flora looked back at her fiercely. 'Why did you not say anything to me? You could have come over the ridge! You could have told me at the bull's house! On the way here!'

'I was going to. I tried to earlier at the bull house.' The factor had interrupted them. 'Nothing's happened,' she repeated, her voice shaky. 'He hasn't said a word to me that's been . . . inappropriate. Or intimate.'

'Because he's a gentleman. But he's no actor, I'll tell you that.'

Effie looked away. 'You're worrying about nothing. Even if it was as you say, I'm not to go near him. The factor says I'll embarrass him in front of the laird's friends. I'm to stay away.'

Flora stared at her. 'So that's why you stood there just now and broke his heart? Because the factor said?'

Effie shrugged. 'He keeps talking about our rent arrears. I can't risk angering him.'

'Eff, you know I'd never willingly agree with that bloody man,' Flora sighed. 'But in this instance he's right – *not* because you're an embarrassment, but because this can only have one ending, and I don't want to see you get hurt. The stakes for

123

him are different to you.' She gazed at Effie with soft eyes. 'This rarely ends well for girls like us.'

Effie didn't need her to spell it out. Everyone knew the story of poor Kitty McQueen, Flora's cousin, a fallen girl ruined by a love affair with a naval officer stationed during the war. When the fighting ended, he had left for home and she had thrown herself from the rocks, her belly already swelling.

She felt desolation sweep over her. 'Then what do I do?'

'Nothing. Let Mathieson do the guiding till the storm hastens them off. All you have to do is just stay out of sight and keep away from him till then. Can you do that, Eff?'

Effie blinked back at her oldest friend. Could she?

Chapter Eight

The glen was still in shadow when she crept from the house. Her father had been snoring in his bed as she had tiptoed past, Poppit lifting her head from the old blanket that served as her bed and trotting out with her, no hesitation. The yacht bobbed silently in the bay but the water had lost its glassy tension, small waves rippling the moon's reflections out of shape and landing with a sigh upon the shore.

Behind tattered night clouds, the sky was a magnificent red, like a fire beneath ashes, just waiting to burn through. Shepherd's warning. The sun was only just beginning its climb, like her, but the temperatures had scarce dropped through the night and she had been sticky and restless beneath her sheet, sleep a mere kiss that fluttered upon her sporadically.

Girl and dog moved swiftly past the cleits and through the gap in the head dyke, heading straight for the steep slope of Mullach Mor. She swung her arms, the climbing bag with peg and her ropes over one shoulder. She would eat on the other side with the girls and stay there till the ship slipped from the bay, till it was safe again to come home. She had brought a salted fulmar carcass in from the cleit for her father and left it in a pan of water, along with a note explaining she was helping with the summer herd for a day or two. He'd not starve.

Her breath came hard as her legs strode, her gaze downwards as she concentrated on the next step, each one taking her away from a man she scarcely knew, who came from a place she had never known, but who had managed in a few short days to shift her world – and this tiny rocky isle – off its axis. Flora's words the evening before had left her shaken but she trusted her friend. Flora couldn't wring a fulmar's neck or tie a stopper knot but she knew men and how they were with women – what they would do for beauty, for love, for fun. Effie wasn't to see Lord Sholto Crichton-Stuart again.

She stopped marching only when she got to Am Blaid, the cradle of the isle and the plateau from where she could look out over all points: north, south, east and west – but it was only the village to where her gaze fell, the solid, rooted grey stone cottages that lay low to the ground, spread in a fan.

It had been her plan to walk straight to the Amazon's House, the souterrain where the girls were staying, but she had marched at a clip that was speedy even for her and she could feel her heart clattering like a stone in a box. She sank to the ground, her knees up and elbows resting, not yet wanting to commit to the steps that would take her down into the back glen and out of sight of the village. At least from this distance she might watch the islanders – and their guests – unobserved, for a while. No matter they would be indistinguishable from here, where the yacht was an inky shadow, the factor's house just a bright dot; it was just something to know he was still down there for now.

Her heart squeezed like a fist in her chest every time she thought about his departure. It was imminent, she knew that. Yesterday's grace had succumbed to today's weather. Pressure building, clouds climbing . . . The skipper would be reading the skies and listening to his host – her Uncle Hamish – making ready to leave.

Colour was beginning to leach into the day, the sky growing brighter with every passing minute, a bleed of green spreading upon the westerly slopes and a single golden sunspot glowing upon the tip of the yacht's masts. All around her, the ancient cleits sat silent like old friends, her hidey-holes of childhood. How many times had she crept into them as a little girl, playing hide and seek with Mhairi and Flora and their many brothers? Why couldn't one of those boys have grown into a man who made the very edges of her world flutter and fray? Why had God sent a man she could never have, to own her heart?

It was utterly silent up here. The world slept at her feet, even the symphonic St Kilda wren quiet for once.

Only . . . she wasn't fully alone. There was a pulse through the ground. A vibration of something travelling. Beside her, Poppit's head lifted from between her paws, her ears up as she looked down the slope. They were perched on a blind summit, the land dropping away so sharply that she couldn't see the hundred yards that fed to her feet – but she could hear something breathing. It was heavy and rapid and drawing closer quickly. Effie felt a rush of alarm, her palms pressed to the ground, ready to push up and run as Poppit gave a low growl that reverberated through her belly. 'Who's there?' she asked fiercely.

'Friend! Not foe!' a male voice called up, mere feet away now and a moment later, a golden-haired head appeared above the ridge like a second sun.

'Miss Gillies, you are a very fast walker,' Sholto panted, placing his hands on his thighs as he tried to get his breath back.

She stared at him, aghast. 'What are you *doing* here?'

He sighed and smiled in the same motion, his head tipping to the side. 'I was swimming in the bay when I saw you creep out from your house.'

She stared at him in disbelief. It wasn't even dawn! Did he never sleep?

'. . . I wasn't creeping,' she said defensively, seeing that his hair was wet and his clothes dishevelled, the buttons on his shirt mismatched so that the tails sat at different lengths. He had dressed in haste and it had the effect of making him look boyish. Less lordly.

'Well, I assumed you were trying not to disturb your father,' he shrugged. 'But as you wish.' He stared down at her. The look on his face to have found her suggested he had absolutely no idea he was the one she was trying to escape.

'. . . Why would you be swimming at such a time?' She hadn't seen him as she'd looked over from the Street, but then she hadn't been looking either. Her only focus had been on leaving.

He missed a beat, his smile faltering a little. 'Trouble sleeping.'

Oh.

He sank onto the ground beside her. '. . . You? Should you be alone out here, in the half-light?'

'There's no danger here.'

'No? You looked like a wild rabbit just now.' His eyes burned into her. 'Why are you out walking at this time?'

It was her turn to miss a beat. 'I'm going over to Glen Bay.'

A flicker of a frown crossed his face. 'To be with your friend?'

She nodded. 'She needs help . . . with the sheep.'

He looked like he didn't believe her. 'It's an early start.' Scepticism rang through his words. 'Lucky I was swimming then or I might not have seen you.'

'Aye, sir.'

He winced. 'Please . . . none of the "sir" nonsense.'

She looked away. There was little point in arguing about it now.

There was a short silence.

'Our captain says we must leave on the tide tonight.' He ran a hand through his damp hair. 'Apparently a storm is coming.'

She pulled at a tuft of grass. It gave her something to do, somewhere to look. 'Aye, I know.'

'You know?' His eyes narrowed, the intimation clear. 'And yet still you went? Without a goodbye?'

'I didn't think you would worry one way or another about my goodbyes, sir.'

A small laugh of disbelief escaped him, followed by a studying pause. '. . . But we are friends, are we not?'

'. . . If you say so, sir.' There was a tremor in her voice.

He looked pained now. 'Effie, don't call me that.'

'Why not? It's what you are.' She felt the anger begin to overflow, finding leaks in her seams. She was eighteen years old but she felt ragged and worn. 'You're a lord and I'm just a wild thing. A wild rabbit.'

'No—'

'It's what you just said.'

'I know what I said,' he cried, losing the composure that had marked his every movement, his every word since he'd set foot on this island. 'But you must know there's a difference between what I say and what I mean? That there are things I cannot say even though I . . . I would like to?' He moved towards her but Poppit gave a low growl. He stopped and looked at the dog. Looked back at her. 'But if . . .'

'But if what?' She stared back at him defiantly. She wanted him to say it, to make the words real and give shape to the void that existed between them. A chasm they could never cross. It had to be said and acknowledged. He had to go. He knew far better than she there was more that divided than united them. He came from a bigger world than hers.

'But if I am to leave here tonight, then perhaps they should be said,' he replied, watching her head snap up.

Effie felt her heart begin to pound, as though she was still striding the slope. Poppit growled and Sholto looked at her again warily – but the dog wasn't looking at him.

'Friend! Not foe!' a voice called from below, making them both startle.

Sholto jumped to his feet. 'What?' he murmured incredulously as the sound of footsteps became distinct, laboured breathing marking a new arrival. Effie scrambled to her feet, trying to see further, better, sooner.

'Who is it?' she asked him.

'Friend not foe,' the voice said again, closer now, with a weary sigh; Sholto and Effie watched in silence as their unwelcome intruder finally crested the blind summit with a smile. 'Well . . . Good morning!'

Chapter Nine

For several moments, no one spoke. They just watched the factor pant and sigh, his head bowed, hands on his thighs as he got his breath back. Effie wanted to cry. What . . . ? What was he doing here?

'I thought it was you, but I couldn't be sure,' the factor said, straightening up finally and directing his sole attention, as ever, to the guest. He frowned to see his dishevelled state – wet hair, a wrongly buttoned shirt. 'Are you quite well, sir? It's early for a walk.'

Sholto looked as baffled as she felt to find the factor standing there with them, in the half-light. '. . . I had gone for a swim when I saw Miss Gillies coming up here,' he replied stiffly.

'Early for a swim too, sir,' the factor simply replied.

'I've not been sleeping well.'

'Oh, I'm sorry to hear that.' As his host on the isle, the factor took personal responsibility for the comfort of his guests. Effie watched with a barely disguised sneer as he bowed and scraped. 'Is the bed lumpy? Or perhaps the room is too warm?'

'No, no. It's just . . . me.' Sholto stared back at the factor, his mouth set in a flat line. He looked imprisoned by his own manners. Effie knew he didn't want the factor here any more than she did but there was no reason either one of them could give to be alone. 'And you, Mathieson?'

'Why am I here?' The factor shrugged easily. 'I heard the door close behind you; at least I think it was that. I got up to check, and once I was up, I was awake.' He talked casually, conversationally. 'No matter. There's much to be done before our departure this evening anyway.'

'Indeed. Well, I'm sorry if I disturbed you. Please don't let us stop you from getting on.'

It was a weak shot.

'Not at all, not at all. Under the circumstances it's all worked out for the best. I was able to check the featherstore and run an inventory while you swam.'

'While I . . . ? I hope you're not *spying* on me, Mathieson?'

'And why should I do that, sir?' the factor asked with a hearty laugh. 'No, your comfort is my only concern. Sir John specifically asked that I keep a close eye on your wants and needs. It is beautiful here but wild too – bitter, savage, merciless . . . I mean the place, not the people.' It was a joke but only he laughed.

Sholto looked straight across at Effie, their eyes meeting in silent despair.

The factor looked at Effie too, with a cold expression that belied the lightness of his words. 'And Miss Gillies, you're not usually up at this hour?'

'I'm going to help Flora and Mhairi with the sheep for a day or two. Mhairi's not been feeling so well.'

His eyes narrowed. 'Does she need medical attention?' he frowned. 'If Nurse MacDonald is . . .'

'It's not so bad as that. Just a few days' rest, is what Flora said.'

'I see,' he said slowly. Effie swallowed, feeling her nerves pitch. If the factor believed she had arranged this dawn meeting with the earl's son, if he believed she had gone behind his back after everything he'd said, the consequences would come straight back on her father. 'So then we each have our reasons for being here for the sunrise.' The factor's words rang with a sardonic glint. '. . . It is bewitching, is it not?'

They all looked at the fast-rising sun, the red skies reaching overhead as the world trickled back into colour. Birds were beginning to speckle the air and throw phrases of morning melodies into the silence, but Effie couldn't sink into the beauty of a new day. Sholto was as brittle as a stick, the factor too friendly by far – and she was caught between the two of them.

'How was your father when you left him, sir?' the factor asked, bringing the attention back to Sholto again.

'Still sleeping,' Sholto muttered.

'Sleeping? Well, that is a positive at least. Let us hope his ankle will have started to mend well through the night. Getting onto the boat will be tricky with an injury.'

'Injury?' Effie looked at Sholto questioningly.

'It's nothing to be concerned with,' he said. 'Father twisted his ankle on the way down yesterday, that is all.'

Effie was mortified. The earl had been in her care and she had just run off, left him.

'It was the right thing to do, Miss Gillies,' he said hastily, reading her thoughts. 'Mr McKinnon's needs were urgent. He might have been far more gravely injured. Father will be fine. It simply took him rather a long time to descend, that was all. He shall rest up today and it will be fine in no time.'

Sholto stood impassively, his manners correct, but as his words settled she heard what else they contained: he had been free today. They would have been alone – the very thing she had tried to escape and the only thing she wanted . . .

Their eyes met again and she saw the urgency in his. The clock was ticking. This time tomorrow he would be gone.

'So what made you follow Miss Gillies up here, sir?' the factor asked him with fresh curiosity. 'If you had only come out for a swim?'

There was a pause.

'Well, given that this is my last day on the isle, I was hoping I might persuade Miss Gillies to impart some of her roping skills before I leave.'

As ever, the factor was quick to block. 'Sadly, as Miss Gillies has explained, she is needed on the other side—'

'No, it's fine, Mr Mathieson,' Effie said quickly. 'I'm not expected for a while yet. I had left much earlier than I needed to.'

'Had you trouble sleeping too, then, Miss Gillies?' Sholto asked. They were veiled words, she knew. He was asking her something more than it seemed.

'. . . Yes.'

'Yes, *sir*,' the factor snapped. 'Nonetheless, I can assist you with the roping, sir . . .'

'Good! I hoped you would, Mathieson,' Sholto said with a sudden, dazzling smile.

Effie frowned, looking at him in confusion. Surely . . . ?

'. . . If you would be so kind as to serve as my anchor, then Miss Gillies and I may descend together and she can instruct me better.'

The suggestion left the factor momentarily speechless. For once, he had been boxed in.

'Is that acceptable to you, Miss Gillies, sharing an hour or two of your time and expertise before you leave?' Sholto asked her.

She tried to stop her eyes from shining too brightly. She

134

would take whatever she could get. Flora could hardly be cross with her if they had the factor as a chaperone! 'Aye, sir. It's the least I can do. I feel I've not earnt my two shillings . . .'

Sholto's face changed as he remembered the matter of her payment. 'My word, I'd quite forgotten. Here—' and he reached into his pocket.

'Oh – no sir, it's already taken care of,' she said quickly. She didn't care for the money. She had only meant to corroborate his story to the factor.

He looked up. 'Father's paid you?'

'Not the earl, sir. Mr Mathieson.'

Sholto looked back at the factor, whose face had flushed a deep red. '*You* paid Miss Gillies, Mathieson? When? . . . And *why*? It was not your responsibility. This was a private arrangement between us and Miss Gillies.'

There was a pause. How could the factor explain his generosity without conveying his desperation to corral the guests for himself? 'It was after the excitement with Donald yesterday. I didn't want you to be troubled after your exertions. Miss Gillies was asking after it . . .'

Effie startled at how he twisted the truth – he made it sound as though she had been chasing the money when in truth she had only wanted an excuse to remain in Sholto's company – but she knew she couldn't publicly defend herself. Sholto's eyes flittered upon her momentarily, registering her silent protest.

'. . . So it seemed best to settle up the arrangement myself, especially as she was due to be heading over here today and we would be leaving tonight.'

'But did you know Miss Gillies would be coming over here today? She's only just told you her plans this minute.'

'Well, I'd heard the McKinnon girl was sick. It seemed likely help would be needed for a day or two.'

Effie stared at him, amazed he could tell such bold, outright lies and call himself a Christian.

Sholto simply smiled, his manner placid. 'I see. Well, that was very good of you, Mathieson. I'll be sure Sir John hears of it.'

The factor's expression changed. It was clear he had been expecting to be reimbursed, that his token of largesse and professional efficiency would be settled up later between gentlemen.

Effie had to suppress a smirk as Sholto appeared to take his explanations at face value. His obsequiousness had cost him this time.

'So, Miss Gillies, where shall we climb?' Sholto asked, fixing her with a triumphant look.

She thought for a moment.

'Well, there's a good bluff just by the narrow inlet over there,' she said, turning and pointing to a spot over to her right. 'Seeing as we're up here now anyway. The ground drops a little on the approach, so the cliffs aren't quite as high, and the fall line is off vertical. It's not Connachair, in other words. You'd be quite safe.'

But he didn't look concerned by safety. In fact, she felt sure danger was what he sought. He had pinned her with his eyes again, holding her up, the factor locked out once more. '. . . Shall we, then?'

They walked as a unit over the plateau, in the direction of the place where they had collected the fork-tailed petrel's egg the first day, coming quickly to the inlet which burrowed back into the land like a cleft.

'Why is that cleit so much larger than the others?' Sholto asked as she spooled out the ropes into coils on the ground, checking them over in silent concentration.

She glanced up. 'Oh, it's a storm cleit – for if you get caught up here when the weather turns and there's no time to get back to the village. We keep it clear especially.'

'Ah, yes, you mentioned – when you have to race the sheep.'

She smiled, dividing the ropes into two sets of two and laying them flat on the ground. Retrieving her thick, trusty peg and finding a suitable rock, she began looking for the best place to anchor.

'May I?' Sholto asked, offering to do it for her.

She shook her head. 'We each take responsibility for our own anchors, sir. That way, if the worst happens . . .'

'Oh I see, no blame. Very wise.' He watched as she drove the post into the ground with the rock and began securing the rope.

'And what type of knot are you using to secure yourself to the post there, Miss Gillies?' he asked, coming over and crouching beside her so close that their thighs touched.

She took a small breath at the daring closeness. 'It's a bowline knot, sir.' She sensed he already knew this. She knew he had rock-climbed in France and she had seen the way he'd climbed after her the day before. He was already a proficient climber, in no particular need of her tuition. This was a ruse.

'Might it not slip?'

'I'll back it up with a stopper knot.'

'Ah.' He watched her dexterous manoeuvrings with intense focus, the factor standing by like a shadow.

Eventually, satisfied with her fixings, she rose to standing. Sholto followed.

'Mr Mathieson,' Effie said, handing him one of the ropes. 'I know you know how to fasten yourself.'

The factor looped the working end of the rope around him with an unhappy look.

'Sir, if I can just rope you up.' Sholto held his arms out wide as she carefully wound the rope diagonally over his shoulder and around his torso, watching her all the while. She knew they were both aware of how her body lightly grazed his as she reached over and around him. Her eyes fell to his incorrectly buttoned shirt and it was all she could do to resist the urge to redo it for him, even though she liked it. It felt like this new sense of 'undoneness' brought him more within her orbit, as though the isle was rewilding him. 'There. Now you've your harnesses, we'll join the ropes so you are connected one to the other.'

All eyes were upon her as she expertly knotted the ropes together. 'And what do you call that join, Miss Gillies?' he asked, standing close again.

Effie felt her heart skip several beats at his audacity. There was something flagrant in his manner. The factor was right there! But it wasn't *she* who was standing by him; she was simply doing what Lord Sholto had asked. The factor could make no complaints.

'A bend, sir.'

'Ah . . . In France, I think they called it a figure eight follow-through.'

'A figure eight follow-through,' she echoed, trying out his words like they were clothes to fit.

Satisfied with their ropes, she tied her own harness and tested the fixings several times. 'Ready then, sir?'

Sholto nodded, coming to stand by her.

'A little space between you is better, sir,' the factor said. 'In case of swinging.'

'Swinging. Right.' Sholto took a single step to the side.

Effie studied the descent. It was an eight-hundred-foot drop to the water below; the first hundred feet or so being mainly large grassy areas which lay like blankets between rocky outcrops – still too vertiginous to walk down without being roped – before the turf gradually gave way to sharply tilted scree, and then a sheer face of granite.

'We'll go together on my word, then,' she said, looking up at him and trying to sound like a guide in front of the factor. 'Remember, as yesterday – lean back on straight legs, tilt your body in, small movements. Trust your anchor.'

He looked back, bemused, at the man sitting on the grass, the rope looped around his waist, his legs bent before him, heels dug in. 'Do you hear that, Mr Mathieson? I must place all my trust in you. Don't drop me, will you? I'll be depending on your strength and stability. This is a true compliment of your abilities.'

'Very kind of you, sir,' the factor nodded, but he didn't preen at the flattery as usual, doubtless aware of the risk that if Sholto fell, he might well be pulled after him.

Sholto and Effie locked gazes again, then on her command, they stepped over, walking backwards down a slope even the sheep struggled with. Effie saw the factor brace as he took the other man's weight, his jaw clenched and knuckles blanched as he slowly spooled out the rope.

They rappelled side by side for the first bit, past grass-roosting puffins and petrels, smiling as the birds screeched their protests, wings flapping and bills wide as they protected their eggs. If the factor had been able to sit nearer to the edge, he would have been able to see them as they scaled backwards, but he was now out of sight, blind of their position and actions. Effie had to smile. Sholto could not have immobilized the man more if he'd broken his legs.

He followed her lead with surprising concentration. He didn't talk as they belayed down to the change point, where the grass became bare rock and vertical; but as they moved into the technical part of the climb, he didn't pause either, stepping straight down and off the incline so that he dangled in space. Only now would the factor be taking his whole weight, rooted to his spot and braced at a steep reverse incline to counterbalance him. Effie watched from a few feet above as he steadied himself on the rope and was able to find a footing on the rocks, creating a bit of a slack for the factor again. Then she hopped next to him with a smile. They had entered a new topography here with the ground-nesting birds swapped for the shearwater and auk breeds – guillemots and fulmars taking to the air in an indignant flurry. They all cried and screeched in agitation as the two humans moved slowly past the shallow crevices and ledges where they had lain their large, perfectly white eggs; it always amazed Effie how only the shallowest of rock lips and rills stopped them from rolling or being blown off the precipices.

For several minutes they didn't speak, each engrossed in the thrill of scaling the wall, their bodies reaching, stretching, flexing as they found ledges to grab, moving ever downwards towards the roar of the waves. Occasionally, though, he would glance across at her and they would smile, sharing the moment.

'Effie, have you eaten this morning?' Sholto suddenly asked her as they climbed down towards a shallow, protruding ledge.

Effie. It was the signal they were alone again. Just the two of them, no one else. No 'Sir' or 'Miss'. No factor.

'No. Why?'

'We could have eggs for breakfast?' he smiled. To his far side, she could see an egg, just about within touching distance, his arm already outstretched, a fulmar standing on the crevice watching him defensively.

'Oh—' she began as he reached a hand towards it. 'Sholto, no!'

She was too late. The bird leant towards him, opening its bill aggressively and spewing, in fast succession, several emissions of a foul-smelling oil. Sholto gave a loud yell as he was caught in the face and neck, his hands coming away from the rock as he instinctively recoiled. The rope snapped taut as he spun, his hands smearing the oil that had momentarily blinded him.

Without thinking, Effie gave a small sideways jump and reached over, grabbing the rope to stop him from colliding with the jagged cliff, but she misjudged his weight and was pulled off the cliffs too, spinning and becoming the buffer herself. She gasped as the rough rocks scraped her back. She could feel the rope humming with tension but her foot managed to find a crevice upon which to place her weight, steadying her and taking some of the force.

'Effie!' Sholto shouted, reaching out and managing to grab onto a jutting rock with one hand, holding the rope with the other, but he was unable to see as the oil ran into his eyes. 'Are you all right?'

'I'm fine. Don't worry about me. Everything's fine,' she called back, managing to balance on both feet now. 'Just try to get yourself on the rock.'

Blind, his feet reached for the cliff wall. She scaled down a few feet, grabbing one of his legs and helping guide his foot to a small crevice. His other foot found purchase too and she climbed back up to him again as she saw the rope slacken as he bore his own weight.

'You hold on there. I'll try to get the oil away from your eyes,' she said, straining to reach him. She wiped the palms of her hand over his face but there was so much of it and nothing with which to blot her hands – no grass, no leaves, only her own clothes. 'It's not toxic, just . . . oily,' she said, standing on the ledge and balancing with just one hand on the rocks, a sudden strong gust of wind blowing her hair into her face and momentarily blinding her too.

'It appears attack really is the best form of defence,' he said, standing patiently as she ran her free hand time and again over his face, the contours quickly becoming familiar.

'Aye. Although they're not actually trying to blind you. The point of the oil is to coat the feathers of the bigger seabirds that are their predators. It makes their feathers lose their waterproofing and then the birds, needing to rest at sea, eventually drown.'

'My God, what a strategy,' he murmured as her hand repeatedly swept over his face, fingers following the lines of his brow and cheekbone. '. . . Merciless, too. It's a long slow death . . . for a predator just . . . wanting his lunch.' His speech had slowed.

'Well, that's how it is on St Kilda. Kill or be killed,' she smiled, becoming distracted as she noticed the length of his eyelashes. He leaned in slightly to the curve of her hand. '. . . How's that?'

She watched his eyelids flicker as he tested out his vision, saw his pupils constrict and then dilate as he focused upon her.

'Beautiful.'

They stood suspended on the cliff face, a moment of whistling silence whirling around them as even the birds were tuned out. Nothing else existed. Only the two of them.

She knew he was going to kiss her even before she saw the muscles in his forearm flex and he drew himself towards her. She closed her eyes as his lips met hers and the harsh, jagged landscape to which they clung became soft and diffuse, gravity ceasing to have any meaning. She couldn't have said whether she was flying or falling.

When he finally pulled away, his eyes were aflame. 'All this, to get you alone.' He gave a low chuckle at their extreme situation. 'Although it seems fitting that I should kiss you in the setting where I fell for you.'

He had fallen for her? She felt her heart punching against her ribcage. 'It's fitting that in this setting you should talk of falling,' she said, a wry smile on her lips.

He laughed and she could feel the vibrations through his body onto hers. He kissed her again. 'I could do this all day,' he murmured when they finally broke apart, both of them breathless, wanting more.

'Mathieson can't. He's going to be holding on awful hard up there,' she said.

'Good.' His eyes glittered. 'That man's been a thorn in my side from the moment I set eyes on you. I could swear he's been trying to get between us.'

'Well, he has,' she said, almost surprised that he hadn't seen it.

'Really?'

'He thinks I'm not good enough to look after the likes of you.'

'What?'

'He thinks he's the only one fit to talk to the laird and his friends.'

Sholto stroked her cheek. 'Little does he know you're better than all of us put together.'

It was a lie, but a charming one.

'I wish we could stay right here,' he said. 'Just you and me. It's all I've wanted from the moment you jumped into the boat. I've racked my brain trying to find ways to be alone with you. But last night, by the rocks, when you were so determined not to be with me today—'

'It wasn't what I wanted. But the factor's been so angry with me for embarrassing him with you. I was scared he'd put up our rents.'

'He's a bully.' He kissed her again but it was so hard to balance; and holding a static pose became more taxing with every passing minute. He swapped the hands he was holding on by, shaking out the muscles in the arm. They were tiring. Accidents happened when people grew tired.

'We should probably start heading up,' she said reluctantly.

'No. Let's stay here.'

She laughed softly at his desperation. 'We've put a lot of strain on the ropes.' They had been rubbing against the jagged rocks all the while.

'Wait!' He put his hand on hers. '. . . Stay with me today,' he said fiercely. 'Don't go over to the other side. Give me every second that is left to us.'

She swallowed. 'But how? The factor won't allow it.'

He thought hard for a moment. 'Leave him to me. He's not the first sycophant I've dealt with and he won't be the last.' He raised a hand to trace her cheek again, looking at her like she was something beautiful and rare. 'How could I ever have known that I would come here and find someone like you?'

Effie wondered where she would have had to go to find him. What was the world like, where he hailed from?

'Just go along with whatever I say. I'll get rid of him, I promise.'

They began to climb. She insisted he went first so she could advise on his route if it was needed, but his alpine experience showed in the decisions he made for where to reach, when to lunge. She went to catch him up, but as she drew nearer . . . she felt him pull away. Accelerating. She looked over to find him grinning.

'Oh I see! You want a race?' she laughed, knowing she could easily switch up a gear. And she did.

'No!' he cried as he quickly fell behind her. Although he was taller and stronger, he couldn't compete with her sure-footedness; she was barefoot and able to get a toehold in the smallest cracks; he, in his boots, could not.

She didn't go so far ahead as to leave him in the dust but once they were over the ledge and off the scree, back onto the grass slopes where they could use their legs to run as they pulled up, he narrowed the gap.

'Hurry up!' she teased, scrambling over the jutting, craggy rocks. 'Why are you so slow?'

She was only just ahead – the mercy she had shown on the technical climb now compromised on the grassy patches – and she gave small screams as he repeatedly lunged for her, his arm outstretched, nearly, so nearly catching her. She leapt onto the flat just in time, laughing breathlessly, her eyes as bright as a child's and forgetting – momentarily – all about the person waiting for them. Sholto arrived a moment later, rolling onto the grass in a breathless heap, his arms and legs sprawled.

The factor was looking at them like he couldn't believe what he was seeing. 'What . . . ?' he almost whispered, seeing their playful game. 'What happened? I thought the rope was going to snap.' His gaze fell to Effie's clothes, now stained with great oily streaks.

'Sholto was attacked by a fulmar,' she panted, seeing how the rope on her torso had twisted and untucked her shirt so that her midriff was exposed. She began untying the rope as quickly as she could, knowing it would only confirm the factor's low opinion of her wildness.

There was a pause as he watched on. '*Lord* Sholto,' he

corrected her sternly as she failed to recognize her error. Her appalling familiarity.

'Lor—' she automatically began to repeat, but the man in question interrupted.

'Actually, I asked Miss Gillies – Effie, if you will – to drop the formality. It seemed rather silly when one's dangling off a rope, being attacked by a seabird.' His eyes were dancing with amusement.

Effie stared at him, having to resist the urge to break into laughter herself, to throw her arms around his neck. She felt giddy with happiness, her lips still tingling from his kisses.

'I see,' the factor said, after a long pause. He looked furious that she had – against all his wishes, warnings and threats – garnered for herself the friendship he had wanted. 'I trust you are recovered now though, sir?'

'Absolutely. Although . . .' He sat up and sniffed at his shirt, pulling at the fabric. 'I'm afraid I smell rather high.' He wrinkled his nose as Effie couldn't help but laugh. She knew she must too; her clothes were smeared with the oil.

'It's nasty stuff, that oil,' the factor said. 'Gets into the hair. You'd be best dipping in the sea.'

'That's just what Effie said!' Sholto exclaimed.

Effie looked at him in surprise. Had she just said that?

'I do hope it wasn't too dull for you, being stuck up here while all the action was going on down there,' Sholto said, untying his rope from the harness. 'Although it was probably a mercy that you were saved it! We had a few dramatic moments down there, didn't we, Effie?'

'Very dramatic,' she grinned.

Mathieson looked flabbergasted by Sholto's repeated use of her given name, this flagrant evidence of friendship.

'I appreciate your anchoring, though, Mathieson. You were

steadfast throughout, even when I was blind and spinning like a top.'

'I did wonder what was happening down there,' the factor muttered.

Sholto gave a carefree laugh. 'It was wild. Absolutely wild. I've never been in such a predicament before! Wait till my father hears.'

The factor was standing as erectly as if he'd got a poker down his back. Effie had released her harness and quickly rearranged her shirt, coiling the rope into spools that would fit back into the bag and over her shoulders.

'I shall have to clean up in the sea,' Sholto said, inspecting his shirt for oil stains and running his hands through his hair, his fingers coming back sticky.

'Or we'll arrange for your clothes to be washed, sir. I'm sure Miss Gillies won't mind, seeing as she'll be cleaning her own too,' Mr Mathieson said.

Sholto gave almost a howl of disbelief. 'Mathieson, we're *your* guests, aren't we?'

The factor gawped.

'Heavens, man, I wouldn't dream of asking a friend to do my laundry.'

Mathieson didn't reply, but his colour was high with swallowed fury. Every punch was thrown with a velvet glove.

Packed up again, they began to walk back towards the ridge where they had all met only an hour or so before. The day had fully dawned now and they could see the villagers up and about along the Street, in the plots and by the burns, smoke puffing from chimneys. The night clouds had slunk away but a thick haze lent a heaviness to the sky. The storm was building, slowly but surely, promising to take Sholto from her.

'We shall leave you here, then, Miss Gillies, and bid you well,' the factor said as they reached the part of the plateau where the path divided, reaching on one side to Village Bay and on the other to Glen Bay.

'Oh, no, Miss Gillies is coming with us,' Sholto said lightly, not missing a step.

'But the sheep . . .' the factor spluttered, hastening after him.

'The sheep? What do they matter? She can't possibly go over in this state. Look at her – she's covered in the oil, just like me! Her clothes are ruined! She'll need to dip in the sea just to get it out of her hair.'

'Is it in her hair?'

'Oh yes,' Sholto said firmly. 'Unless of course you can use the beach in Glen Bay?' he asked her directly.

'There isn't a beach that side,' she said. 'Boats can land in some conditions but it's generally too difficult.'

'Far too dangerous for a non-swimmer, then. No, I'm afraid you'll have to come back with us and get sorted before you can do anything else. It wouldn't be proper to let you go off in that state.'

The factor and Effie walked behind him in silence. Effie saw the spring in Sholto's step as he walked. He was a man on top of the world.

'Tell you what, I could give you another swimming lesson if you'd like,' he said jovially, turning around.

'Oh, that's not necessary,' she replied quickly.

'Nonsense. One good turn deserves another. You did, after all, just save my life.'

Effie bit her lip, wanting to laugh at his games. She'd done nothing of the sort and the factor would know it, too – but he couldn't contradict his superior.

'I'm beholden and fully intend to make it up to you. I can't leave here in good conscience knowing you can't swim. If anything should happen, I'd never forgive myself. Besides, we'll be going in the sea to clean up anyway. We can kill two birds with one stone.' He gave her a glittering look. 'Although knowing you as I now do, you can probably kill ten birds with one stone.'

Effie couldn't keep from smiling back.

The gaiety that had characterized their first moments together had returned and they were both giddy with joy. 'How about you, Mr Mathieson – can you swim?'

'Well—'

'Come, I can teach you too,' Sholto said with exuberance.

'I can swim well enough already, sir.'

'You don't want to learn a new stroke, perhaps? I'm a strong swimmer myself. I'd be happy to teach you what I know. In fact, I'd consider it a public service, something *you* could then pass on to the islanders too. It would be a way for me to give back after their hospitality.'

'You're very generous, sir,' the factor muttered. 'But with this being our last day, I shall need to tie up my loose ends with the men before I return at the summer's end. There have been a lot of distractions on this trip, what with doing the sheep and then Donald McKinnon's injury.'

'Ah, of course, yes, I'd not considered that. Well, that's a pity,' Sholto said, without any hint of regret. 'It shall just have to be you and me then, Effie. I hope you don't mind?'

'Not at all, sir—'

'Sholto,' he guided, before she could slip back into old habits.

'. . . Sholto,' she echoed.

Chapter Ten

'People are watching.' She could see faces at the window of the featherstore and the manse, by the postmaster's hut, in the Street.

'Let them. We're not doing anything wrong.' His hands were around her waist, holding her up in the freezing cold water. 'We've offered for them to join us. I'm happy to teach any one of them.'

'But you know they won't accept.'

He shrugged.

Neither one of them wanted to get out, in spite of the breathtaking temperature; but they both knew it was like being on the ropes – sooner or later they'd be forced back to the wider world. They couldn't exist indefinitely in these hidden margins, concealed from prying eyes off the edge of a cliff, or underwater.

'Now kick again, let's at least give them a show.'

She moved her arms in the way he'd shown her, her chin up, but she had none of his elegance in the water, her body more like a bladder than a blade. His hands lifted off her waist but he stayed by her side as she inched forward in jerky movements, caught somewhere between panic and delight. 'That's it, that's it!'

'Am I doing it?' she gasped. 'Are you holding me?'

'I'm right here, you're doing fantastically well. Don't stop, keep going.'

One of the dogs had come down to the beach and was barking beside Poppit, who was sitting silently on the sand, her ears up and watching them with a hint of anxiety.

A small wave lifted Effie up; she could feel its muted power as it swept under her body, but it did her no harm and she gave a laugh of delight – only for the next wave to come at her unawares so that she caught a mouthful of sea water. In an instant she was coughing and spluttering, her confidence gone. Instinctively she straightened up and began to sink, but Sholto's hands were back on her immediately, holding her up as she struggled to catch a clean breath.

She could feel the salt in her throat, her body wanting to gag. 'Are you all right?' he asked, rubbing her back as she continued coughing. 'Do you want to go in?'

She shook her head. She wanted to stay here, half hidden in the water, no matter what, because when they came out . . . what could their excuse be to be together then? She could feel his fingertips digging into her waist, knowing exactly what she wasn't saying, wanting more than this too. 'I know,' he whispered, dropping the public act.

But she couldn't stop coughing, she had swallowed too much water, and this time he lifted her without asking, carrying her into the shallows where she could stand with her hands on her knees and catch a breath.

'Ugh,' she groaned when eventually the coughing had stopped, her head hanging. 'That was *awful*.'

'It is, yes. But you won't do it again, I can assure you.'

She looked up at him. They were all but out of the water now and the shock of air on her sea-soaked skin sowed a field of goosepimples over her body. The wind was coming in more strongly, in ever more frequent gusts.

'Your lips are going blue,' he said, looking like he wanted to kiss them pink again. 'We need to get you warm and dry.'

'No, I'm fine. I don't want to stop yet. I want to keep going. Let's try again. I'll keep my mouth closed this time,' she said desperately, even though the fun had gone now. Earlier she had screamed and laughed as he had splashed her when she hadn't wanted to get wet, she had helped scrub his hair with her fingertips to remove the oil. Everything had felt alive, like a new beginning – when really it was only the beginning of their ending.

He shook his head. 'We can't. Your temperature's dropped. You'll get sick.'

'But . . .'

His eyes met hers. 'Another time.'

It was like when they were on the ropes, when he had wanted to stay longer . . . only they both knew there wouldn't be another time. Their elation of earlier – that surprise meeting in the dark, the capitulation to their first kiss, recognition that they both felt the same – was giving way to a more melancholic desperation. Time was slipping by, fast running out and this was all they had, and would ever have: hidden touch, furtive glances, private jokes, a few stolen kisses . . .

They stared at one another longingly but her teeth began to chatter uncontrollably, proving him right. It was adrenaline that had kept her in the water for so long, anything to have another few moments . . .

'Come on. In.'

'I'm fine.'

'Now,' he said firmly, taking her by the arm and towing her out of the waves.

She staggered out of the water, surprised by how weak she felt. The dogs were lined up on the shore, barking as they waded through the shallows. She hadn't really noticed them before now.

'Why are they barking at us?' Sholto asked as they walked past them, to where they'd left the towels.

'It's not us they're barking at. There's a boat coming,' she said as he pulled a towel tightly around her.

Sholto looked back but there was only his yacht to see. He frowned as he pulled a towel around himself, seeing how she huddled under hers, shivering. They stood there together for a few moments, heads bent, bodies stiff.

'. . . I don't know how I can do it, Effie,' he said in a low voice. She looked up to find him staring at her sorrowfully. 'I don't know how I can get on that boat tonight and leave you.'

'So then don't,' she said urgently. 'Stay. Be here with me.'

Despair flooded his eyes. '. . . I can't.' His body seemed to wilt with the word. 'I have . . . responsibilities back home. Ties. It's not as easy as just . . . doing what *I* want.'

'Why isn't it?' Pain flecked her voice.

A sigh carried his. 'You don't understand.'

No, she didn't. Surely if she meant anything to him . . . He was the one who had come to *her* home, stepped into *her* life . . . Only four days earlier she had been oblivious of what love was, but now she knew it in its full spectrum. It was dizzying and electric, painful and agitating, it made her whole and hollowed her out in the same breath. She'd never been so happy, nor so wretched. None of it was fair. If it had been one of the village lads, everyone would be celebrating that – finally! – Effie Gillies's wild heart had been captured; but lords didn't count as suitors here. It would be a scandal.

He stepped closer, still huddled in his towel.

'Effie, if it was down to me I'd have made you mine the moment we got off that dinghy on the first day. I never imagined this could happen, but . . . I can't make things be different to what they are,' he said desperately, willing her to understand. She could only look at him blankly. She had no context beyond this isle, this life, and he looked away, frustrated and angry.

He gave a groan. '. . . And now someone's coming.'

She twisted back to see Lorna striding down the path. Her heart sank too.

'Lorna, I learnt to swim!' Effie said as brightly as she could, blue-lipped and huddling under the blanket.

'Was that what it was?' Lorna asked. 'It looked like you swallowed the sea from where I was standing.' There was a shortness to her words, a warning in her eyes, and Effie instantly understood how their 'swimming lesson' had been perceived by her neighbours. It wasn't just the factor who'd be furious.

'Aye. That too.'

'Well you'd best get warm – and you too, sir. You both look perished with the cold.' Lorna spoke firmly and with the authority of the resident nurse.

The dogs went into a higher state of frenzy just as the boat Effie had predicted was coming nosed round the headland. It was *Vaila*, a trawler well known to the villagers. Callum McGregor was the skipper; he lived at Applecross in Skye and had become a friend to them all when a fierce storm several years back had stranded him with them for a whole week. He had earnt his keep by entertaining them with stories of life on the mainland that sounded like they belonged to another time and not just another place. His visits were always welcome. He fished for cod and ling in the deeper waters and always stopped by Village Bay, their archipelago being the only land between here and the Faroe Islands.

'How's Donald?' Effie asked, stalling for time, even though she couldn't stop her teeth from chattering.

'He had a fitful night but he's growing more lucid and resting well now.'

'Good. I must look in and send my best wishes to Mary.'

'No need, I'll pass them on for you. I'll be going back there shortly once I've dealt with this.' She was looking at McGregor's boat and Effie realized Lorna's reason for being here was not to drive them back in – she was waiting for the mail sack. Ian McKinnon, the postmaster, was still on Boreray. McGregor often brought their post over with him and he'd take their letters back on his return leg too.

Effie's heart sank as she realized the older woman would continue to stand there for as long as it took for the trawlermen to unload and disembark. Her time alone with Sholto was already at an end.

'Hurry along now, Effie. Your father's heated the water for a bath for you,' Lorna said, still looking dead ahead.

Effie looked back at Sholto, feeling desperate. '. . . Well . . . thank you, sir,' she said, lapsing into their public personas again; they felt like pantomime roles now. 'You have taught me to swim at last and for that I'm very grateful.'

'Not at all,' he said stiffly, looking pained as he too realized the clock had run out. Uncle Hamish and Archie MacQueen were making their way down to the dinghy, to row out. 'You . . . uh, must practise, though.' He glanced at Lorna. She was standing beside them watching the boats, but still clearly listening in. '. . . And then if you become strong enough yourself, you might teach your neighbours, too.' His voice was flat, the words just a cover to stretch out their last remaining moments together.

'. . . I'll do my best, sir.'

'Good . . . Good.'

They were all out of public niceties.

'Well, g'bye then, sir,' she said, beginning to walk up the beach towards the long grassy plot that led to her front door.

'Goodbye, Miss Gillies,' he said, the words falling behind her like paper aeroplanes, nosediving to the ground.

The tin tub had been placed in front of the fire in the main bedroom, her father sitting at the loom in the kitchen by the window. He couldn't see down to the water from where he sat, but she knew just from the way he glanced at her that he'd already heard. A secret couldn't be kept in this place.

'I'm back, Father,' she said quietly, standing shivering in the doorway with the towel clutched at her neck, the bag and ropes held in her free hand. The air in the cottage felt stuffy and stale, thicker than outside, as though she had to swallow it down; the pan of broiled fulmar was simmering gently on the stove.

'You look like a skinned cat,' he said after a moment's pause, his arms and legs never stopping their work at the machine. 'You'd best get in the tub before you rattle your bones apart.'

She shut the front door behind her, dropping the bag and ropes. She walked through the bedroom into her closet room, struggling to pull off her wet clothes, but they clung to her like the kelp that wrapped itself around her legs whenever the tide came in after a storm. She let them fall to the floor in a sodden heap. There was no point in drying them by the fire just now; the oil marks would need scrubbing in the burn first.

She slipped into the water. It felt almost scaldingly hot to her body numb with cold. She sat with her knees hugged to her chest, her teeth chattering as she closed her eyes and tried to think of something, anything, that would make this feeling go away. Her heart was racing, her mind overwhelmed with panic. Right now, he was still here. Right now he was down the street, but by the time she went to bed tonight, he would be on a yacht home, sailing on a high tide to outpace a storm. She'd never see him again. He'd be lost to her.

'So they didna' need you over the other side after all then,' her father said from the other room.

She mashed her lips together, hating the charade. 'No, the plan changed. I'll go over tomorrow instead.'

'And why did it change?' His voice was hard and she knew he knew she was lying.

'Because I ran into Lord Sholto and the factor at Am Blaid. His lordship asked me to teach him some roping skills before he leaves tonight,' she muttered, keeping as close to the truth as she could. 'I couldn't say no. He and his father have paid me two shillings to guide them. I felt obliged to honour my duty to them first. The girls will understand.'

'You can still go over this afternoon. It's light enough.'

Effie felt her heart pound. He was calling her bluff, tying her up with her own lies. 'I'm too chilled to sleep out. The cold went to my bones. I'll stay warm tonight and go at first light.'

There was a pause, just long enough that she thought he might have decided to let it pass. 'And how did you end up from teaching his lordship to climb, to that display in the water just now?'

'Display?'

'Aye,' he said firmly.

'He was teaching me to swim. I can teach the kiddies now. It's safer if they know. We should all kn—'

'Enough!' he snapped suddenly. 'I wasn'a born yesterday, girl. You think I don't know why you been like a cat on a hot tin roof these past few days? You're sweet on the man!'

'No, I'm not!'

'Don't lie t' me! The whole isle's just watched you auditioning t' be a lady!' His tone was mocking.

'I wasn't!' she said hotly. 'I don't want to be a lady. I canna think of anything worse.'

'And *he* canna consider anything else! It's his lot.'

She pressed her face into her knees, trying not to cry. Did he think she didn't know that? She wet her face with the hot water, still shivering.

'It's as well that storm is coming,' her father muttered from the other room, the shuttle constantly moving side to side with a rhythmic clack. 'It's time they went now, before things get ugly. There's those that aren't pleased by you carrying on.'

'It's none of the factor's business!' she cried, losing her temper.

'I was talking about the minister!' he shouted back. 'He cares about the protection of your soul and not just your reputation!'

'But I've done nothing wrong!'

'The whole village saw you – cavorting on the beach, laughing and playing like you were bairns.'

'And why shouldn't we? I've just spent the last three days with him and his father. We've talked all the while. We're friends.' She could feel her voice becoming strained, the tears pressing, her emotion too high to keep pushed down.

'*We* do not become friends with the likes of *them*. You mistook manners for something else and you've humiliated yourself and me. Not to mention Mathieson is livid, aye – you've dragged his name through the mud too.'

'Why is it anything to do with him?'

'He's the laird's man! He'll report back on you getting high and mighty, being too familiar with the laird's friends. You need to accept the natural order of things and understand where you belong. He's not one of our kind and you're not his, no matter how much you may like the look of one another. You can make eyes and play games but that's not the foundation for a real life.'

'No!' A sob escaped her. 'Supposedly *I've* to choose between Fin or Angus McKinnon or Donald or David MacQueen – but they're all lumps! Angus is mean; Fin is timid; Donald is stupid and David's clumsy. I'd have to spend my life either taking care of them or hiding from their fists.'

'Nonsense! They have their faults but they're good men who'd any o' them make a fine husband. What makes you think you're any better than the other lasses?' he growled.

'I don't!'

'No? Then why do you always have to have different rules applied to you?'

Tears were streaming down her face now. 'I just want to be free to live my life, instead of having labels put on me! I can't crag because I'm a girl? I can't love him because I'm poor?'

'That's not love!' her father shouted, his own voice becoming ragged with the strain. 'It's an infatuation, nothing more! And now you've brought shame upon me. You're a disgrace to our family. What would your mother think if she was to have seen this? She'd be ashamed of you!'

Effie hid her face. Any mention of her mother felt like a slap.

'You'll no leave here now for the day. Stay where I can see you till that ship leaves and he's on it. You hear me?'

She pressed her face into her knees, crying silently and still shivering, the chill settling in her bones.

'You hear?' he repeated, demanding an answer.

'. . . Yes, Father.'

Chapter Eleven

The afternoon dragged wretchedly. Effie went limply about her chores. With her cheek pressed to Iona's belly, she watched mauve clouds thicken as she milked. She saw the sudden, erratic gusts flatten the grass and make the women's skirts billow as she tilled. But she didn't see him. The door to the factor's house didn't open, though she kept it in her sights all the while.

Poppit lay on the grass beside her as she worked, smiling and panting hard as she tried to cool off in the muggy heat, occasionally taking herself off to the burn to drink. The horizon had blurred from sight, the sun just a bright smudge behind the haze. Everything felt heavy, gravity redoubling on itself, as the villagers moved slowly, sullen in the heat.

A sudden shout carried down the Street, puncturing the malaise.

It was Rachel McKinnon, Mhairi's mother. 'They're back!' she cried, fast walking down the Street, arms aloft, and leaving her knitting behind her on the stool.

Effie looked down to the beach to see the small rowing boat enter the mouth of the bay. The *Vaila* trawler was now anchored there, along with the earl's yacht, but the dinghy that had brought in McGregor and his crew had gone straight out again as her Uncle Hamish and Archie MacQueen had rowed to Boreray to bring back the remaining men. It had become a race against time, for the storm was blowing in faster than expected and the ripples that had lapped the beach this morning now broke with a rushing, hissing foam; further out in the open sea, past Dun, white horses galloped. The sky was full of whirling, chattering birds dancing on the thermals like it was a London ballroom and conditions were fast becoming too wild for a rowing boat. It was a relief to all to see the small craft bob and stagger through the choppy water, filled with hulking silhouettes of sunburnt husbands, brothers and sons – the men she had grown up with. Some were cousins, or uncles; others were simply the brothers of her friends or the friends of her late brother. She knew their characters and stories and routines with a mundane intimacy, but while they had spent three days chasing sheep and plucking them of their winter coats, she . . . she had been fundamentally altered, as if rebuilt in a new shape. Would they see it, this change in her? Would they see she wasn't the girl she'd been when they left?

Further down the Street, she could see Lorna standing by the door at Donald and Mary McKinnon's house; she had taken the post sack back with her to work there. It would be a relief for her to see that Ian was now back and could resume his postmaster duties; she was needed full-time on her nursing post at the moment.

Effie turned back to find her father standing by the door, roused by the fuss. 'Will I go down to help, Father?' she asked him.

He couldn't very well say no, they both knew – once the men were all back on land, they would need to unload, check and stow the cargo. They would then feast; stews had been bubbling on stoves all day to feed them on their return.

Her father nodded.

Effie put down the hoe and walked slowly down the plot towards the shore. All the other women were holding their skirts and running barefoot over the grass, but she had no need to rush – there was no one on board for her. All the immediate family she had was already on dry land, and his eyes were on her back.

The dogs were barking with their usual agitation, even Poppit mustering some energy as she was caught up in the excitement. Effie didn't dare to sneak even a single glance across to the factor's house as she waited on the beach with the women, but it made her heart pound to think that perhaps he could now see her.

The boat was drawing closer now and the women waded out as far as their hitched skirts would allow. Effie kept well back, not wanting another touch from the sea today; the shivers still tremored in her bones. The women formed a line and one by one the sacks of sheep wool were passed back to her, on the shore. She stacked them in neat piles, noticing as the factor's door opened at last and the owner came striding out. He was always remarkably visible when money or power was around.

Effie kept her head down as he approached, pretending to count the sacks even though she had already counted them in, all fifty-three of them.

'You're still with us, Miss Gillies,' he muttered, reaching a hand into the nearest bag and inspecting the quality of the dark wool.

'Yes. I'm going to go over tomorrow now. It was a bit late by the time I—'

He looked up at her, one eyebrow arched, waiting for her own description of the events in the water earlier.

'Finished swimming,' she murmured.

'So you learnt then,' he said after a pause.

'Aye, sir, and now I'm going to teach the kiddies next. It's a matter of safety.'

'Safety? Indeed,' he said, pulling apart some of the fleece between his fingers, feeling the density of the yarn. ''Tis a wonder you've all survived on the isle this long.'

His sarcasm stung her but she gave no reply. Over his shoulder, she could see that his guests had come to stand in the doorway and watch the islanders' return. The earl was leaning on a set of crutches, his ankle and foot heavily bandaged; Lorna's work again. Sholto stared openly at her from the threshold. Had the two men been forced to endure the factor's hospitality all afternoon? Certainly the earl couldn't possibly get away.

Mathieson was now stuffing the wool back into the sacks and lifting them to gauge their weight and likely yield. He had a way of moving that implied discontent with what he found, as though he suspected the islanders were swindling or defrauding him. Effie shifted her weight uncomfortably, wishing someone else would stand by them too, but behind her the men were disembarking. She could hear the sound of their feet splashing through the water as everyone heaved the boat up and onto the beach.

'How is he?' Flora's brother David called up as he wound the mooring rope once around the boulder. Effie turned to see who he was talking to – Lorna was coming down the Street to join the welcoming party now, her arms swinging in her usual manner; she always moved with great purpose.

'Recovering. Still in bed,' Lorna replied, stopping short somewhat of the beach and remaining on the grass. 'I've moved in to keep a closer eye for the next few days. Poor Mary's in a state, she can scarce move herself.'

'I've said it before but I'll say it again – we're lucky to have you, Lorna MacDonald. We've been saying our prayers over there, not knowing if he was hovering at death's door.'

'I'm confident he's through the worst,' she said briskly. 'But if you're all here now, come up to the meeting place. I've something to tell you.' And with that she turned on her heel and moved back up the grass again.

Effie looked past her towards the Street. She could see her father, Mad Annie, Ma Peg and Old Fin already gathered and seated on the wall. There was a murmur of perturbation, everyone looking to their neighbour for an answer, and finding none.

The villagers moved en masse from the beach to the Street, the men more heavily bearded and a little leaner than when they'd left, wives fussing as they picked grass and wool from their husbands' shirts. They had grass stains on their trousers, some blood too from Donald's accident, and they smelt high from no bathing or changing of their clothes all week.

The children, all thirteen of them, skirted the group with idle curiosity, sensing that something important was happening with the grown-ups. Effie kept her head down as she walked with them all, but she knew Sholto was watching her from the door. He had changed too, their oil-streaked, sea-soaked morning washed away, leaving only scorched memories. He murmured something to his father and the earl nodded as Sholto followed behind the pack, keeping his distance but clearly intending to hear.

They all stopped at the parliament's usual meeting place outside Mad Annie's, a nervous silence falling over them. It was unusual for a woman to address them, but Lorna was a nurse and that carried a unique authority.

'My friends and neighbours, you'll be aware of the decision we came to a few weeks back and the letter we sent requesting assistance with an evacuation to the mainland—'

A sound of alarm jostled the group, making them stir as though they'd been shoved.

'Well, today we've received our reply.' She held up a folded letter.

Effie caught Ian McKinnon's scowl. As the resident postmaster he felt it was his job to impart news from the mainland to the islanders.

'So soon?' Uncle Hamish asked, sounding shocked – he wasn't a man easily surprised. 'But the letter's barely left us!'

'It appears things have moved quickly. It's been debated in parliament and our plight discussed—'

No one spoke, the air becoming as frigid as ice as they awaited her next words.

'. . . And they've agreed to our request! We're to be evacuated to the mainland!'

A shocked cry rang out, the women gasping, their hands rushing to their mouths. They looked to their husbands, their children, their brothers and sisters, their neighbours as the enormity of the news settled – after over two thousand years of continuous human settlement, their days on the wild isle were now numbered. Several of the men stared at the ground, Effie's father included. Mad Annie and Ma Peg reached for each other's hands in rare silence. Some of the children had gone back to their games of cartwheels and playing leapfrog, already bored.

'When?' someone asked breathlessly.

'Where will we go?' asked another.

'Are they keeping us together?'

'What about jobs?'

'Everyone, please,' the minister said, raising his voice above the rabble. 'Let Miss MacDonald continue speaking. We have many questions but she will have only some of the answers at this stage.'

Lorna nodded her thanks to him. 'It says only that we will be evacuated by the end of the summer, just as soon as new homes and jobs have been found. Every effort will be made to keep us together but no guarantees can be given. Further details will follow in due course but we are to start making our preparations now for a wholesale removal at the end of August, before the weather turns.'

Effie's heart was pounding in her chest. Could this really be true? They were leaving here?

She looked around to find Sholto staring at her. She was leaving here.

She was coming to live on the mainland, on his side of the water. The island life she knew here – cragging, fowling, knitting and spinning – was going to be left behind. She would live in a different house in a different place and have a job. She blinked back at him, the two of them locked in a private world . . . If she lived differently, in a different place, would she be different too? Different enough to be good enough? For him?

The villagers were beginning to disperse already. People needed to absorb the news. They needed to go away and think upon the consequences of being granted what they had asked for. The old way was already dying. Rachel McKinnon and Effie's aunt, Mary Gillies, were crying into their handkerchiefs, the men walking with deeply etched frowns back to the beach to fetch the sacks of wool to take to the feather-store. The group on the Street became smaller, contracting into a tighter unit, Sholto edging slowly ever closer to her.

'Does Mary know?' Archie MacQueen asked.

'I've told her, aye,' Lorna said.

'I'm not leaving my spinning wheel,' Mad Annie was saying firmly, her dark eyes bright with apprehension. 'It was my ma's.'

'You won't need to,' Lorna said to her. 'We may all take all our belongings. Nothing can or should be left.'

'This is momentous news, Miss Gillies.' Effie turned to see Sholto standing beside her finally. '. . . How do you feel?' He was addressing her as if for an audience.

She glanced around to see who was nearby but everyone was talking intently with their neighbour; her father and Old Fin were walking slowly up the Street, her father having momentarily forgotten about the family shame. Jayne and Norman Ferguson were sitting apart on the wall, both lost in thought.

She looked back at him. '. . . I never thought it would happen. I don't know what to think. I can't believe . . .' Her eyes wandered over the bay, grazing over the nobbled spine of Dun, the sweeping slopes of Ruival, the soaring majesty of Mullach Mor and Connachair – an old-as-time backdrop that sat behind every memory of her life. To leave it behind . . .

Tears gathered in her eyes, the reality of it hitting her. She couldn't leave here! It was absurd. Unthinkable.

'Effie, I know it must be a shock. I know this is all you've ever known . . .' He cleared his throat, returning with a whisper. 'But could it not also be—?'

'Miss Gillies, we can rely upon you, no doubt, to inform Mhairi and Flora of the news when you see them tomorrow?' The factor stepped forward, making his presence known. How long had he been standing there?

'Mr Mathieson,' she said wearily. '. . . Yes, of course I shall.'

She was eager not to provoke him this afternoon. He was already known for being bloody-minded, hectoring and ruthless but he had been in a particularly foul mood all day – no doubt on account of the early start. From inside the cottage, she had heard him quarrelling with almost everyone he met – her Aunt Mary had gone off in tears after he criticized the heel turns on her knitted socks, she'd heard him arguing with Lorna over their need for more medical supplies, and he'd even butted heads with Mad Annie as she requested another two sheep. Effie didn't want to catch a supper from him again. Not right now.

But if she had thought her swift accommodation would appease his black mood, she was sorely mistaken. He seemed almost to twitch with anger, the emotion rising from him like a humming swarm of flies.

'Well, this is all . . . a great surprise, Mr Mathieson, is it not?' Sholto asked, falling back on a lifetime of manners as he saw how the official made no move to sidle off.

'Oh, it certainly is to me, sir, yes.' The factor nodded with barely concealed rage. 'I knew nothing of it. Nothing at all.'

Effie frowned. That wasn't true. Ian McKinnon had tried to raise it with him the very morning he had arrived, straight after the parliament, and he'd been sent away with a flea in his ear.

He glowered at Effie again. 'Please tell me you people had the decency to let his lordship know before you petitioned the British government?'

You people? Effie realized suddenly the reason behind his palpable anger – he was going to be out of a job. No islanders meant no tenants and no rent to collect. No factor.

No factor?

She straightened herself up. She no longer had to cower to

this man. It was like having a boulder lifted off her chest. 'I wasn't involved in the formalities, sir. I simply signed where I was told to sign.'

He looked at her incredulously. 'And would you jump from a cliff too, if asked to do that?'

'If you asked it? Absolutely not, Mr Mathieson.'

His eyes narrowed as he absorbed the new tone in her voice, saw the contempt in her eyes.

'Have you forgotten yourself, Miss Gillies?' he snapped.

'Mathieson, there's no need for that tone. I understand feelings are running high. Everyone is rightly shocked but Miss Gillies is not responsible for this process, nor its un-intended consequences,' Sholto said sharply. 'It appears that Miss MacDonald is governing the events. You may wish to cover the bureaucracy of it with her.'

It was a dismissal, they all knew.

The factor glowered like a hot coal for several moments and Effie wondered whether the temper that had soured so many of her neighbours' days today would overrun him again now. But he regained just enough self-control to walk off without another word, his manners fast beginning to dis-appear along with his career prospects.

'Odious man,' Sholto said under his breath. 'Sir John can't stand him either.'

'Why does he keep him on, then?'

'He's good at his job,' Sholto shrugged. 'But let's not waste time talking about him.' Almost everyone had left now. They would have to disperse in the next few moments too or be conspicuous by their lingering presence, and she couldn't afford the attention after this morning; her father was as angry as she'd ever known.

'I have to go.'

'What? No. Stay. Just a few more minutes.'

'I can't.'

'But we have to talk. We can talk, can't we?'

She shook her head. 'My father's furious with me. I caught a supper off him when I got back and he's kept me in his sights all afternoon. He's said I'm not to go near you. He'll realize any minute I'm not with him and he'll come looking . . . I have to go.'

'But that's not fair. There are things we have to say. Everything's different now.' Her right hand was resting on the wall and she felt his fingertips inch onto hers, covering them by the tiniest of margins. He glanced up, his gaze catching on something briefly, before he leant into her. 'Effie, you said to me when we met that you would never leave here because you'd never leave your father. But now he is leaving.'

'Aye, I know—'

'And you said you had nothing to leave for anyway, nothing to go *to* . . . But that's changed now, hasn't it? . . . Hasn't it?'

She looked away. How could she possibly answer that? 'I don't know.'

She saw him look over her shoulder, watching someone. 'I know you're blind-sided by this. You can't imagine what the future looks like now. And I know it's still months before you leave here, but if we could talk . . . I don't know, make a plan?'

She blinked. 'A plan?'

But he kept looking over her shoulder distractedly. He looked concerned. 'Can you get away? Meet me somewhere before we go,' he whispered urgently. 'We have to talk. I'll get a message to you . . . at the bull's house.' His eyes rested upon something that made him straighten up sharply.

The factor *again*?

'Mr Gillies,' Sholto said loudly, managing a smile. 'What news!'

Effie turned on her heel just in time to see her father nod in reply. It wasn't deferential, but neither was it an outright slight. Like the factor, he sat right on the boundary of politeness. The balance of things had changed. It no longer mattered that the Earl of Dumfries and his son were close friends of their laird, when Sir John MacLeod was now soon to be their *former* laird.

'Home,' her father said gruffly, taking her by the elbow. 'There's things to discuss.'

'But—'

'No buts.' He pulled her away before another word could be said.

Chapter Twelve

The winds had arrived, hot, torrid squalls catching and smashing the waves upon the shore before barrelling up the slopes. Effie's hair flapped wildly in front of her like a bird's wings, catching her in the eyes several times and making them water, but she couldn't pull it back. Her hands were full, carrying a fresh bundle of hay and a bucket of soaked oats as she made the walk from her cottage to the bull's house.

She walked alongside the burn, past the mossy-topped cleits where they stored the peats and sidling sideways through the gap in the head dyke. The dusk sky looked bruised by the turbulence in its atmosphere, purple clouds hanging low and setting off one of her father's headaches.

In the bay, lights were already shining from the yacht, the skipper making final preparations to leave with the tide. They would be gone within the hour. She could see dark figures moving up and down the Street to the quay, carrying bags and some bundles of tweed that the earl had ordered. Was Sholto one of them?

In spite of his pleas earlier, she hadn't been able to leave the house before now. Her father, far from picking up their earlier argument and scolding and railing at her, had come home – and wept. The shock had almost floored her. The only other time she had ever seen him shed tears had been when

John had died and he, her father, had been left on the clifftop holding half a rope. This was almost as bad and it had knocked her own confusions out of her mind as she sat with him, trying to find comfort in the news – but his two wives were buried here, six of his children lay in the ground. How could he leave them behind?

Like her, like others, she suspected, he hadn't believed the petition would be granted. Everything else was always refused – a telegraph tower, a dedicated mail boat . . . Why would the politicos in London grant this? He had signed his name only because he had felt obligated to move with the pack. His arthritis meant he couldn't crag like the other men, he couldn't provide for the widows or her, his own only remaining child. *She* supported *him*. She worked like a man and took the risks they took because he could not. Who was he to say they all must stay, when he could not do anything to contribute to the islanders' survival effort? In a village of thirty-six people, they had only twenty-three adults – thirteen men and ten women – and once he, Old Fin, Ma Peg and Mad Annie were discounted, that number of able-bodied providers dropped to a critical level. He could not stand in the way of easier, better lives for those he burdened with supporting his own.

And she could not leave him. Not right now, not ever. Though he resented her for not being John, he was her father and he needed her. Her spirit twisted inside her body, agitating her to go outside and meet Sholto, but she had instead sat with him as he wept, then cooked for him as he sat in the chair staring into an unlit fire. They had eaten together quietly, not saying much. And when she'd left him just now, saying she would feed the bull and come straight back, he was puffing on his pipe, looking older than he had yesterday.

She walked quickly around the sheep fanks by the head

dyke and up towards the bull's house. There was no sign of Sholto that she could discern from here, but she could see Tiny running up and down his enclosure, snorting heavily as the wind buffeted his back. Storms always unsettled him and she would need to shut him in the pen tonight once she'd changed the hay.

'Hey big lad,' she called over as she drew closer. She always talked to him; he seemed to listen, if not understand. She reached over the wall and pulled the gate across, dividing the spaces and allowing her safely into the house while he prowled outside. 'Did you hear the news? There's been some big excitement today.' She poured the soaked oats into his feeding trough. 'We're leaving here. All o' us . . . It's big news . . . Some are happy 'bout it. Others not so much. Father's sad.' She looked around as she talked and worked, remembering how she'd felt as Sholto's fingertips had touched hers, as he'd asked to make a plan . . . But where was he now?

'Of course, it's going to mean changes for you too. You can't stay here on your own,' she said, grabbing the pitchfork from its hook on the wall and beginning to toss out the dirty hay. She was faced towards the back of the building but she could sense Tiny behind her. She wasn't watching him, but she could feel his presence at her back, the sound of breathing.

The sound of breathing . . . Sholto?

She whirled around, her heart beating wildly.

Tiny blinked back at her, his head over the gate, trying and failing to reach the feeding trough.

She gave a relieved laugh as he snorted and moved off again. 'Look at me, so jumpy,' she said out loud. 'I guess I'm a bag of nerves too.'

She shook her head and finished changing over the hay, replacing the pitchfork on its hook. She could only stay for a few more minutes. She had to get back; she couldn't put her father through any more worry. But where was Sholto? Had he been and gone? Had he waited for her here and thought she wasn't coming? Two hours had passed since Lorna had broken the news. Perhaps he'd had to get back to dine with the minister before he left? Or to pack?

She looked out. Tiny was at the bottom of the enclosure again and she quickly slid the gate back and climbed onto the wall. At the sound, he turned and charged back up the field, knowing he could get to his dinner at last. Effie waited for him to trot into the house before sliding the gate back, safely penning him in for the night.

She crossed her arms across her body, fingers drumming on her skin as she walked around the back of the bull's house. Would Sholto have seen her walking up here from the factor's house? Perhaps he was keeping watch from somewhere hidden? But she'd been working in the pen for fifteen minutes now, doing everything slowly, buying time . . .

She turned on her heel and began walking back around the cleit, when she noticed something small and white peeking out of the stone wall. She rushed over and pulled out a pinched sheet of paper: *Meet me at the storm cleit from this morning. I'll be waiting for you.*

She gave a cry. The storm cleit was up near Am Blaid, easily a twenty-five minute run away from here – but all steeply uphill! Why there? Why couldn't he have waited for her here? But she knew that was the only private place *he* knew of, somewhere precise he could stipulate. The tide was turning in forty-five minutes. She'd barely get there before he'd have to leave again. Or he might already have left! He might have thought she wasn't coming. Could she intercept him?

There was no time to hesitate. She ran. She ran past the

cleits across Lag Aitimir and leapt across the burn. She passed on the upper side of the of the quarry and quickly scaled the crags of Creagan Breac. She covered the land as expertly and innately as a mountain goat because she was a part of this landscape and it was a part of her. The pitch was steep but it was grassy here in the back of the bowl and her bare feet were silent across the earth, her body fast growing tired from the extreme exertion. She pushed herself onwards anyway. They would have only minutes. Ten, perhaps fifteen at most?

She could see the ridge now, the plateau smoothing away behind it. He was up there. She prayed he was still up there, waiting for her. She was almost running with her hands to the ground as she got to the flat, staggering forward towards the storm cleit. There were fourteen hundred cleits but precious few were empty of bird carcasses or feathers or milk churns or peat turfs.

'Sholto!' she called out, hoping her voice could get to him before her legs. Hoping he could meet her halfway from here now, up high, in the fading light . . . They could meet, be together, no one would see or hear anything now. 'Sholto!'

The wind taunted her, throwing her own voice back upon her, returning only with a whistling silence. Was she too late? Had all this been in vain? Had he gone already?

She approached the storm cleit, staggering on the spot for sight of him, her hair flying like streamers. Lights were glowing from the cottages down below, those on the yacht masts dipping forward and back as the sea rocked the boat with simmering menace.

'Sholto!' She ran to the cleit, ducking slightly to look in, just as he was walking out.

Effie felt her heart miss several beats. She felt her blood pressure dramatically fall as she staggered backwards.

What . . . ?

'His lordship's not here,' Mathieson said, stepping out into the evening too.

'I . . .' she whispered, her voice fled. She couldn't get her breath back, couldn't control her heartrate. Her body was in a high state of exhaustion and alarm. Where was Sholto?

She looked around again, bewildered by what was happening. The note . . . the bull's house . . .

'I'm sorry, sir. I—' she panted, turning back and trying to gather her wits.

'Ah. We're back to "sir" again now, are we? Now that you no longer have the protection of a powerful man by your side?'

What? She felt her bewilderment begin to shift, become something else. '. . . What is it you want?'

He didn't reply immediately. He was watching her through dark, narrowed eyes, reading the changes in her like they were coloured lights, seeing her dawning fear. '. . . I want what I've always wanted, Miss Gillies. What I've been waiting for, most patiently, these past six years.'

Six years? The timing didn't have any immediate significance for her, other than that was when he'd become MacLeod's factor, when he'd first come over here.

'I don't understand. What have you wanted for six years?'

He gave an abrupt laugh, but the sound was ugly. Joyless. '. . . You, Miss Gillies! I want you!'

She looked at him with slow-dawning horror. The gifts, nothing to do with education and socialist aspirations at all? His agitation any time she was near Sholto – not to do with sucking up to the laird or furthering his career, but blocking them because he wanted her for *himself*?

He read her understanding and grabbed her arm suddenly, holding her in place.

'He who would enjoy the fruit must not spoil the blossoms. I've been patient long enough. You didn't think I was just going to let him swoop in and take what was mine, did you?' he hissed, his mouth pulled back in a grotesque sneer.

Her head was shaking from side to side in disbelief. This couldn't be happening. He couldn't mean these things. 'But . . . I'm wicked. I'm wild, you always say. You hate me,' she whispered.

'Love. Hate. It's a fine line. But you've spirit, Effie Gillies, and I like that. I can use that.'

She felt sick. She was trembling. His eyes looked black with madness, crazed with alcohol, for she could smell the whisky on his breath. How long had he been drinking for? Since the news about the evacuation, when he'd learnt he was out of a job? When he'd realized his control and power over her was about to end? He was a man who had lost everything in one afternoon. A man with nothing left to lose.

'Please. Just let me go,' she whimpered. 'I'm not good enough for you. You deserve someone better.'

'I know,' he agreed, almost calm. 'But for reasons my better self doesn't understand, the heart and body wants you. Only you.' The twisted smile came back. 'When I lie with other women, it's always you I imagine beneath me—'

A scream, a cry of horror, escaped her then. She tried to rip her arm free, terror and disgust shooting through her, but he only held her tighter. Tears were streaming silently down her cheeks and she hadn't even realized.

'Please, just let me go. Sholto's coming. He'll be here any minute.'

The sneer grew wide. 'No, he's not. No one's coming. But thank you for confirming my worst suspicions. At least I know now that I'm *not* going mad.'

Going mad? He was mad already! He twisted the skin of her arm so that it burned, felt like it would split. She gasped but he didn't stop. 'Did you know, I wait all winter for the snow and the rain and the winds to pass, for the spring tide to bring me back here again; and during those long months of waiting, I think of what might make you happy. The things I might bring to you that will make you smile. But you never do smile. You look at me with that look of yours – like you're better than me, like I disgust you.' A sound, almost of anguish, escaped him. 'Why do you do that?'

'I . . . I—'

'I told myself it was because you were green. You didn't know how to love a man yet. You scarce know yourself as a woman. You don't dress like one, behave like one. It's like you want to deny what you are.'

'I just try to support my father,' she whispered desperately.

'Why? He's ashamed of the way you go about,' he scoffed. 'Can't you see that? He just wants a son like Archie MacQueen, like Ian McKinnon.'

'That's not true.'

'Oh, but it is. I see it on his face when you're standing there in your dead brother's clothes . . .' She crumpled at the mention of John; she knew it was true. 'Which was why I knew that when I came out this time and asked him for your hand—'

Her eyes widened in horror.

'That he would say yes. Because I was determined to do it right, I knew he'd be proud at last, that you'd made a good match. Better than he ever could have hoped for you.'

'No—'

His lips pulled back. 'But then . . . you started up with *him*. Right in front of me, like you were trying to taunt me.'

'No, I wasn't, I swear—'

180

'And I saw then that you *did* know how to love a man. That you did know yourself as a woman. I saw you throwing yourself at him, behaving like a whore in front of me, and your father and the whole village.'

'No—'

He slapped her then, so hard that she would have fallen over had he not been holding her up.

'Yes. You're a whore, Effie Gillies, and now everyone knows it. You've brought shame on your father. On your family name.' He gave another joyless laugh. 'And yet, still I'm prepared to forgive you. To give you a chance of respectability, of a good life. Am I a madman? Am I?'

He appeared to genuinely be asking her. He looked crazed; the whites of his eyes were threaded with red veins.

'Please—'

'Why could you never look at me like that? Just once? Why did you always act like there was a bad smell around me, even after all the things I gave you. Gifts. Tokens of love . . . And you accepted them.'

'I didn't know—'

'But you did. You did, Effie. You knew no one else got special favours . . . The hand that gives is the hand that gets. Did you really think there would be no payment in kind?'

He looked deep into her eyes but she couldn't answer. Her brain had frozen.

'No, perhaps you didn't. You're a simple girl. An idiot, really. Perhaps you thought there'd be a happy ending with *him* . . .' He laughed, laughed long. 'As if it could ever happen. You have no idea of the society he belongs to, his place in the world . . . I pity you, Effie. He's been playing with you . . . and you don't even realize it.'

'It's not true,' she sobbed.

'Aye, it is. Every word . . . It's just lucky for you I'm a man of honour.'

Honour? The word promised a glimmer of hope.

'What . . .' she hiccupped. 'What are you going to do?'

The smile came back, slow and menacing, as he pointed to something lying on the ground by their feet, the broomstick just a dark shape she hadn't noticed before now. She looked back at him as she realized his plan.

'No!' she cried. 'No! No!' She wrestled furiously, fighting him now. 'You can't make me!' She began to scream but he slapped her again, twice, so hard it made her head ring, dazzling her. His grip tightened around her arm so that his fingertips touched.

She stared back at him, dazed, still shaking her head desperately but already she could feel the momentum building as he pulled her forward. Onward. 'No!' She sank back, trying to keep her weight down, to root herself into the very earth – but nothing grew in this soil. Not strongly.

'Yes! Now, Effie – jump!'

Her feet left the ground and she felt herself fly – for a moment. They landed again not a second later but in that wink of time, her entire life had changed. She was no longer Effie Gillies. A silence pulsed between them but it contained all the horror, all the fear she now felt as Mathieson grinned back at her in the darkness. 'You're mine now.'

She shook her head as the wind howled, making her hair fly and flap like angry birds. 'No.' Her voice was just a whisper, unconvincing even to herself, and she felt his hand grip harder on her arm as he took a step closer, holding her in place, his mouth suddenly upon hers in a clash of teeth. She tried to push him away but he was twice her size and pressing her into him with his other hand, as though mashing their bodies together.

She felt his spittle on her lips, his breath in her mouth as he pressed against her harder, pushing her backwards so that her knees began to bend. Desperately she tried to wriggle, to wrench herself free, but it was impossible. She could feel the ground almost rising up to meet her . . .

She was down and another scream tore through the sky – but it was several moments before she realized it hadn't come from her. Effie looked up from where she lay sprawled in the grass to find Poppit attached to the factor's calf. Her teeth were sunk deep into his flesh and he howled in agony as she brought him down.

'Poppit!' Effie cried, scrambling back, away, trying to stand again on shaking legs. 'Poppit!'

'Hai!' someone called out, panting. 'What's going on up there?'

Effie wheeled around to see Mhairi coming around the cleit, her wild flaming hair like a burning halo around her head. If Effie was stunned to find her dear, gentle friend – absent for the past few weeks – suddenly there, it was nothing to Mhairi's shock.

'What . . . ?' Mhairi took in Effie's pale, stunned face, the factor on the ground and clutching his leg, Poppit's aggressive stance over him, growling with bloodied jowls and her hackles up. Mhairi looked back at the factor again as though she understood it in a glance.

'What has he done?' she cried, running towards Effie and holding her, scanning her for injuries or a hurt she could not see.

'I'm all right, I'm not hurt,' Effie said shakily. Things were bad – but that didn't mean they couldn't still get worse. 'Really.'

Mhairi looked frantically between them, clearly not believing a word of it. 'Effie? What's going on?'

183

Effie's mouth opened but no words came, for over Mhairi's shoulder, she saw the factor glowering at her, threat still in his eyes. For as long as she and her father were in debt to him, he still had power over them. She understood nothing had been stopped here, only stalled, and she had to find a way back; she needed to calm him and not enrage him further. If this had all happened because he believed Sholto was 'stealing' her from him, then she had to make him believe otherwise. She had to convince him he was mistaken. '. . . There was a misunderstanding, that's all. I was just about to head back.' Her voice was quiet but firm; she kept her gaze steady.

Mhairi looked at her through narrowed eyes, seeing how she shook. 'But why are you all the way up here?'

'Why are you? I thought you were over the other side?' Effie heard the question burst from her as though this was any normal conversation between two old friends. But her voice shook and her body trembled.

Mhairi tipped her head to the side, trying to understand what she had stumbled upon and why Poppit had attacked the factor. 'Aye, I was,' she said warily. 'But David MacQueen came over to tell us the big news and I thought I should check how Ma and Da were taking it. Then Poppit tore past me at Am Blaid and shot up here like a rocket. It got me worried. She never leaves your side, but she looked like she was just going to race off the cliffs.'

Effie dropped her gaze, despairing at the sheer bad luck of it all. If Poppit had only come a minute earlier – thirty seconds! – she would still be free. Still Effie Gillies. She dropped her head in her hands, trembling violently and feeling the tears come. It was too much—

'Effie, just tell me what's happened.' Mhairi placed her hands upon her shoulders. 'Let me help.'

Effie looked up but there wasn't time to scream. Everything happened at once. The factor, in those brief few moments of distraction, had managed to stand and – his face contorted with pain and rage – he lunged forward, catching Mhairi by her hair. He yanked her head backward, throwing her to the ground like she was a dirty sheet.

'No!' Effie cried, too late, as Poppit, her lips drawn back menacingly in readiness for round two, leapt at him.

The world stopped spinning then. Time became elastic. Effie could see her pet, her beloved dog, almost hang in the air, her silky coat ruffled by the winds, lips pulled back to reveal glistening white teeth. The factor's leg – the bloodied one – lifted and wheeled around in an arc, connecting with utmost precision his boot to her body. Poppit folded and changed trajectory, travelling not forward now, but sideways, into the rocks that had once formed a cleit. Her body slammed against a boulder with shattering force, falling to the earth and lying limp, where seconds before it had rippled with dazzling, intense life.

'*Poppit!*'

Effie's scream alone almost tore her in half but the factor was upon her in the very next instant. His hands pinioned her arms as he shook her violently. He could kill her, she didn't doubt it. 'One word about any of this and I'll see to it that your father doesn't see the sun rise. Do you understand me?' he hissed.

She nodded desperately, tears streaming down her cheeks. She felt delirious with terror.

He sneered, looking at with her contempt. 'You should be thanking me. I've thrown you a lifeline. You'll never survive the mainland. You're already saddled with debt and you've no skills of use over there. If you want a future for him, you'll accept the way things are and not try to fight me, do you hear?'

She nodded frantically again. Anything to appease him.

'I'll be back soon enough. Now I have an evacuation to organize, I'll need to come back here multiple times this summer.' His sneer grew. 'You'd better be ready for me. We've jumped the broom and that makes you my wife now—'

She kept nodding, her heart threatening to leap from her chest.

'—I'll be back for what is mine! Lawfully *mine*, do you hear?' he spat, his face pressed against hers so that even their lashes touched. 'I will take what is owed to me – if it's the last thing I do!'

His breath made her want to retch but she was saved by him slapping her hard and throwing her to the ground, sending her rolling over the grass. For several moments she lay stunned, her hair streaming over her face so that she could only see him hobble away through narrow blonde slices.

With effort, she lifted her head. Mhairi, groaning, was curled up on the ground, a hand to the back of her head as she blinked, groggily. She had no idea what had just happened to her. With her back turned, she hadn't seen the factor coming. One moment she'd been up, the next down.

'Eff . . . ?' she groaned.

'It's fine. I'm here. He's gone,' she whispered, looking over towards the inert dog. She stretched an arm to her warm body, fingers moving hopefully through her silken pelt. 'Poppit?' she whispered.

Nothing.

'Pops?' She felt the tears stopper her throat.

The hazelnut coat didn't stir – but for a minute twitch of an eyelid. A low whimper brought a sob from her. 'Oh, thank

God!' Effie crawled on her hands and knees to where her pet lay, dropping her face into Poppit's coat and weeping pitifully. She was alive! They both were . . . But what sort of life was this, now she had lost her freedom and her name? How could she smile or rest or know a moment's peace, knowing that he was coming back for her? This wasn't over. Far from it. The worst was yet to come.

AFTER

Chapter Thirteen

Three months later – 29 August 1930

They were drowning the dogs.

As the boat bobbed and the villagers streamed down to the jetty, the hounds that had herded their sheep, rustled puffins into their snares and sat by their chairs every evening were having their heads held under a calm sea, bubbles escaping in silent protest.

The process was viciously, mercifully quick, but it was no comfort to Effie. She'd watched in horror as the men dragged the dogs by their scruffs to the water's edge and she'd turned instead for the hills, Poppit limping beside her. She sat now, shaking and unable to move, against a black cliff as the rising sun bloomed like a white rose upon it.

This was goodbye? Death and violence under a blue sky? She knew her neighbours had all been hardened by the realities of living on this rock in the Atlantic, that they were simply doing what had to be done. This was economic reality. Life on the mainland came at a cost and dog licences were a burden the villagers couldn't afford. Money might never have meant much on an island where they ate what they caught and reaped what they sowed, but their new lives would depend upon what they could earn, not catch; it would be every man for himself. But to have not even left St Kilda, and need money . . . For these to be the last memories of her home . . .

Every few minutes, her name carried intermittently on the wind, wheeling around her head like the pretty kittiwakes.

'Effie Gillies!' Her father's voice rebounded around the caldera. His legs might no longer have much strength, but there was no doubting the power still in his lungs; she had grown up to the sound of his instructions bellowing around the hills, competing with the winds and the birds to be heard. He hadn't seen her halfway up Ruival, one arm around Poppit and a rope around them both. The granite bluff on which she sat gave onto precipitous scree. A fall from here wouldn't kill them but they wouldn't walk away from it either. (Not that Poppit walked from much these days; her leg had set badly from the break and she didn't now stray far from the cottage.)

Still Effie didn't stir.

The collie leant into her, warm and trembling, as though she understood the mortal threat, and Effie's arm tightened around her as they watched the happenings in the bay. These were the death throes of their lives here.

The evacuation had been going on for days. Ever since the *Dunara Castle* steamship had rounded the headland the villagers had been packing up, frenzied by the prospect of departure. She had watched her neighbours carrying tables, chairs, beds and spinning wheels on their backs, seen the potatoes dug up several weeks too early (still better to have than to leave). She had even laughed as the cows were towed through the water behind the dinghies, ropes around their horns, protesting loudly as they were dragged to the ship.

The three hundred sheep had been brought over last from Glen Bay. Mhairi and Flora had gradually herded them from their scattered perches into the enclosures on the far side and

Effie, along with Lorna, had brought them over the ridge a herd at a time to the fanks at An Lag. The holdings there were large and not far from the jetty where they could be transferred in batches to the dinghy and rowed to the ship. But even that painstaking method hadn't been foolproof, the dinghy almost capsizing a few times as the sheep jostled in panic on the water, and Uncle Hamish now sported a black eye from where he'd been headbutted numerous times by the simple creatures. The activity had been incessant all week and when the villagers weren't packing, they had been in the kirk, the minister leading prayers asking for the protection of their souls as though they were heading for the Seven Circles of Hell and not the Scottish mainland. Sleep this past week had been as fleeting as rainbows, until now there was nothing left to be done but . . . go.

The *Dunara Castle* had finally left yesterday evening and gone ahead with all the livestock and their worldly possessions. Now the elders were standing in the wall-encircled graveyard, saying goodbye for the last time to their own blood – withered grandparents who'd never seen land beyond this isle, eight-day-old babies that had never seen beyond their mother's breast. Flora's eldest brother David was throwing a bucket of dirty water into the run-off as he cleaned a floor that would no longer be walked upon. Ian McKinnon was bent double, fastening the last of the letter sacks; the St Kildan postmark had become so highly collectable in these final weeks, he had been up most of the night, stamping over eight hundred postcards. Mhairi was haltingly leading her weeping mother and six younger siblings like a flame-haired pied piper along the Street for the final time. Her hands kept reaching for the walls, palms pressing against them, her face downturned.

Jayne Ferguson was standing alone on the jetty and staring

intently back at Mullach Mor, at the village where the cottages already lay empty. She was oblivious to the navy men in their white ducks waiting to help her into the rowing boat and take her out to the SS *Harebell*, the ship sent to them by the British government. After years of neglect, with no MP to represent them, no way to vote, no postal service, now they were being given the gold standard, with three braided officers on board to welcome them on the first step to their new lives. Effie's wide eyes skimmed over the parting scenes, coming to rest again upon the men standing in the shallows and now tying rocks around the dead dogs' necks to sink the bodies.

'Effie Gillies!' Her father's voice boomed again. She could see him standing on the Street. His body was bent as if worn down and reshaped by generations of howling winds but it was the arthritis in his bones that had the greatest power in pulling him earthwards. She watched him look up to the hills – Connachair; Mullach Mor; Ruival . . .

He found her at last. A bright speck against the dark rock, his eyes as keen as the eagle's. 'Get yourself down here!'

'No!' The wind, carrying his words, threw her own behind her, but he knew from the very set of her shoulders what she'd said. She wore her defiance the way Flora wore her scarlet shawl.

He shuffled forward a few paces in warning, his weight heavy upon the stick, but he had no influence here. She had been up close and personal with real threat; she knew the metallic tang of it, the way it hung in the air, silent and fetid.

Effie looked back at the beach. The drownings done, the men were wading back to shore, leaving the shadowy shapes in the water behind them like a kelp forest.

'Damn you, girl! This is no time for your devilment! Get down!'

Time was speeding up, it seemed. Behind him, the cemetery had emptied of life. Mad Annie, Old Fin and Ma Peg were shuffling down to the jetty with bowed heads; Mhairi was on the rowing boat now with her mother and young siblings, and Jayne. The three youngest MacQueen children and Effie's own cousins were already clustered around the *Harebell*'s bow-rails with her Aunt Mary, who was calling out with mournful laments. Within the next few minutes the last men would expect to row out with them to the ship and St Kilda, after two thousand years of human settlement, would finally fall into silence.

Only, people were beginning to notice the ruckus on shore. The smart navy men were staring from the jetty at the sight of her father waving his stick. Figures on the boat – red hair, black hair – and faces on the beach were turning, searching, finding her bright, spry form on the rocks, the brown dog in her arms. Her name carried like the birds' cries, layered and criss-crossing one another. She heard the exasperation that always covered it like a coat.

'Effie!'

She looked down. Lorna was running towards her over the grass, her dark skirt like a sail. She was a few hundred feet below the ledge where Effie was perched, but the wind carried her voice like it was a petal to be caught.

'What are you doing?' Lorna called up, panting.

'I'm not going!'

Lorna looked at her with astonishment. There had been an excitement earlier when Mr Bonner, the reporter from *The Times* newspaper in London, had been found hiding in one of the cleits. He had had an idea to stay behind after the evacuation; no one could understand why. It had been one thing to winkle out his foolish notions. But hers? After the night they had all lived through?

'You know it's impossible. We must depart.' Lorna's tone was kind but firm and Effie knew what she really meant: she might not want to leave, but she certainly couldn't stay.

The woman who had travelled to live here, who had embraced island life with a vigour even the natives didn't possess, was now urging her to quit and leave without looking back. And Effie would have. After a fretful, heart-quaking night, she'd have been first on the boat and away from here if she could have. But the drownings had sent her running instead, the instinct to protect stronger even than self-preservation.

'I won't let them kill Poppit!' She looked across and saw the white-uniformed navy men were standing now beside her father, listening as he waved his stick angrily in her direction.

A couple of the men – Uncle Hamish and Angus McKinnon – were crossing the field from the beach. Coming for her. They walked with long, loping strides, their bare feet inured to the uneven ground and countless sharp, frost-shattered rocks that dotted the grass. She knew this bluff would be nothing for them. Expert cragsmen, they could get to her without ropes, no bother.

Effie pulled her legs in and got to her feet, the dog wriggling in her rope harness as she became suspended again. She shifted the dog onto her back and Poppit began pawing at the air, as if offended by the indignity of being carried like a sheep. But they had to move. The men were almost at Lorna's shoulder, already scanning the cliff for the fastest route up. Effie hugged the rough, cold granite, her cheek pressed to it as she waited for the dog to settle.

'Effie!' Lorna cried.

'No!' Effie yelled back, looking for handholds and beginning to reach.

'I won't let them harm her!'

But Effie knew Lorna – for all her education and mainland skills – had no more power than she did in this. The only thing that could save her dog was money. Anything that cost the villagers was a liability to be cast off, and there would be no value given to a lame dog.

She began to climb, her knees pointing outwards so that she could keep her body flat to the rocks and counterbalance the extra weight on her back. She moved confidently, her hands and bare feet grabbing small, sharp, jutting rocks, her fingertips finding narrow crevices. She was strong but light and moved up the bluff quickly, even though the dog's weight was added to her own.

'Effie, where are you going? You know there's nowhere to go!' Lorna called up, her voice ever more distant.

Effie glanced down. The men were on the rocks now and narrowing the gap as they advanced without the encumbrance of a dog.

She heaved and pulled herself up with a power she'd never known she had. If she had wanted to beat Angus McKinnon in the past, it had never mattered more than today. Panting hard, she scaled the bluffs, one hand, one leg at a time.

They were gaining on her but when she looked up, she saw the clifftop was only fifty feet above her. She might not outclimb the men today, but she could outrun them. If she could get to the top with enough of a lead, she could force them into an agreement. They wouldn't listen to sentiment or vain promises, but there was one thing she could leverage.

With a burst of power, she scaled the last stretch, heaving

herself onto the grassy slopes of Ruival with a cry of effort. Poppit squealed and wriggled as Effie rolled onto her side, rejoicing as the strain and weight was immediately relinquished. Poppit squirmed, frantic to be released, her muzzle hitting the back of Effie's head as her hands struggled to loosen the rope around them both. Her ribs felt bruised, her arms depleted from the strain. The collie broke free in the next instant, breaking into an excited, ungainly run as Effie shrugged off the makeshift harness.

On her hands and knees, she scuttled back and looked over the cliff. The men were fifty feet below and advancing quickly.

'Stop there! I'll make a deal with you!'

Both men stopped from sheer surprise rather than obedience, their sunburnt faces turning up to her.

'If you let me bring Poppit, then whatever we get for the cow at auction – once we've bought the licence – we'll give you both the rest to share.'

'No, lass!' her Uncle Hamish shouted back. 'I'll no' allow that. Your father would never agree to it. You'll need all the pennies you can get on th' other side. I'll not let you and your father starve on account of a dog.'

'Then you'll have to sail without us! By the time you get up here, I'll have run and hidden somewhere you'll not be able to find us.'

'There's nowhere to hide on this isle. We know all the spots,' Angus said with his usual bombast.

'Aye, but will you find us in time? Or will you have to go without us? The tide won't wait. The skipper's pacing the deck already. I can see him!' The factor had drilled into them all week that there was a strict timetable for the crossing.

Both men's eyes narrowed as they realized her plan.

'Why, you devious . . .' Angus began.

'No,' Uncle Hamish said, cutting him off. '. . . She's right. We'll no' find her in time if she hides now – and it's not worth delaying the departure on account of one cur.'

'Then we'll leave her here, just as she wishes!' Angus snapped. 'Give her what she wants.'

'That's not an option and you know it.' Uncle Hamish looked up at her again, his black eye shining; he was angry at her game but he was also a rational man. Slowly he nodded. 'Come on now, lass. We'll do it. Bring the dog and we'll find an arrangement for its licence till you can pay.'

'You have to give me your word,' she said fiercely, her hair hanging and framing her face as she looked down at them. A St Kildan's word was equal to his handshake – much store was put by it.

'Aye, you have our word. Get down now. Enough of this nonsense and heap no more shame upon your father.'

Effie's eyes flashed but she had her agreement; her uncle might be brusque but he had honour; everyone knew his word was his bond. She scrambled to her feet. 'Come on then, girl,' she said, looking back.

Looking around.

'Poppit?'

She turned on the spot, seeing grass and sea and sky on all sides. But no dog.

'Poppit?' Her voice inflected strangely, eyes focusing to pinpoints, like they did when she was out searching for birds.

A short bark, whickering into a squeal, made her head whip round.

'Poppit?'

A silence came back at her as she stared into the distance from where the sound had come. There was a shallow dip over there, near the storm cleit. Beyond it lay the narrow inlet where the land tore apart into a vertiginous crevasse.

With a gasp of horror, she began to sprint, her feet flying across the hard ground, her arms like pistons – but limbs were no good. The drumbeat of her feet seemed to make no difference; she might as well have been dancing. She needed osprey wings that would make her soar and not stumble; she needed to cover ground. She needed—

A dark head appeared. Broad forehead and heavy brows above hard eyes and a thick beard.

'Where's my dog? Where's my dog?' she screamed as Norman Ferguson, Jayne's husband, strode towards her. 'Hamish has agreed! She's to come with us! It's agreed! Where is she?'

The wind carried her voice like feathers in the moult, scattering them through the sky. She saw his face – impassive, unmoved – and knew it was already done. Her spirit cleaved, a confetti of pain and panic that made her legs buckle, bringing the ground up to her. No! She could still feel the weight of her pet on her back, still smell her coat on her hands. Shock and disbelief racked her. How long had she been turned away from Poppit? One minute? Two?

She screamed. Everything, all her efforts, had come undone in those few mere moments and she was alone now. Utterly alone. She couldn't move. She wouldn't. She lay on the hard-packed ground and sobbed, her fists clutching mindlessly at the grass and heather.

Norman's bare feet stopped in front of her, inches from her face. She stared blindly at the dirt ingrained beneath the nails, the muddied skin that had been stained since his early baby steps. She felt his hand close around her bicep, fingers digging uncomfortably in her armpit as she was hauled to her feet, onto legs that wouldn't lock. He held her askance until he felt her feet take the weight.

'How could you be so cruel?' she cried, her voice tearing in half as the grief overtook her again. Where was his compassion? His heart?

'There's no money for her,' he said simply. Not a bad man. Just not a sentimental one.

Chapter Fourteen

'Effie.'

Flora held out her arms as Effie climbed aboard, flanked by Norman Ferguson, Uncle Hamish and Angus McKinnon, the villagers watching on in silence. If they pitied her, their expressions also told her it had been inevitable. Hard choices were made on a daily basis. Her fight, her last stand, had been a futile one.

'Effie, I'm so sorry,' Jayne said quickly, reaching an arm out to her in consolation as she passed. Effie stared at her. She could see the sorrow in her eyes, but was she sorry because she had foreseen this horror? Or was she apologizing for her brutish husband?

Ma Peg was sitting on a bench, singing an old lament and rocking herself slightly, Mad Annie sitting beside her in turgid silence for once, patting her hand. Old Fin was sitting next to her father, who had been boarded by the white-suited navymen as Norman Ferguson was escorting her down Ruival; her father gave a single tut as she passed, perfectly conveying all his disappointment and shame in that solitary gesture for the fuss and slight delay she had caused. And for what? A dog that had been killed anyway.

Her boots in one hand, Effie staggered over to her friend, weak with despair. She sank down to where Flora was sitting and dropped her head on her friend's shoulder, hiding her face away.

'I'm sorry,' Flora whispered as she wept. 'I know how you loved her.'

'She didn't need to die,' Effie hiccupped wretchedly. 'We had made a deal. I'd saved her.'

'I'm sorry.' Flora's fingers gripped her shoulder more tightly as she cried harder, the tears sliding fast and plentifully. Her dismantling was complete. She had nothing left to lose: John's accident, Poppit's killing, Sholto's departure and the factor's return . . . they had each and all stripped her of any joy or hope. She felt hollowed by grief.

Flora had been sitting alone on a bulkhead by one of the lifeboats, her knees drawn up, and gradually Effie became aware that she too was trembling. She lifted her head to see Flora staring back to the village. Her cheeks – usually so rosy – were pinched white. 'Are *you* well?'

Flora nodded, swallowing hard. '. . . I just can't quite believe it's actually happening. We're really doing this.'

'Aye, I know.' Effie, sniffing, looked back to land too. Neither of them had really seen their home from this vantage before; the women and children were very rarely allowed in the boats and never this far out in the bay. She could see now what the fishermen meant about Village Bay being a glad sight. The stone cottages curved with the land, bedded into the jaw of rock, withstanding the worst of the elements, stubby protectors in a wild place. Could they really be abandoning them? Would no more children play on the grass, no more fires puff up the chimneys? Was this to be left to the birds and the landlord's own remaining sheep?

'Where's Mhairi?' Effie asked, realizing that their friend

was missing. She had seen her last in the dinghy with her family, looking stricken.

'Below deck. She's not up to it.'

Effie felt her tears catch in her throat. 'No.' Losing Poppit was a devastating blow. Mhairi, though, faced far worse. The day she had dreaded was finally here.

Effie looked at her beautiful friend. Only Flora was to get a happy ending, a bright new beginning, but she didn't look overjoyed. She looked stony and rigid, holding back emotions she didn't want to show. She had always boasted she would leave at the first opportunity and find a bigger life than this, a grander one, but now that she was getting what she had wished for . . .

The captain blew the horn three times and the chain of the anchor rattled as it was winched in. Flora's hand gripped her tighter as they began to untether themselves from this place. Their home.

Slowly the boat began to swing round, engines beginning to roar and thrusters grinding the water. Effie felt her emotions surge to a peak, tears brimming her eyes again and her throat stoppered shut as she looked back to land – taking in for the last time the sweeping but infertile slopes that had tried their best to support them, the ancient majesty of Connachair and Mullach Mor on whose cliff-faces she had played with cocky delight. Her eyes followed the line of the dyke that had been their sole distinction between civilization and wildness; she took in the empty fanks and the abandoned bull house; the whistling loneliness of the burial ground where her mother and her brother lay; the babbling burns still rushing regardless of whether anyone stood in them; the featherstore, the bright white factor's house . . .

She stared at the stony beach as they began to pull away.

She saw *him* – golden-haired and smiling, splashing in the shallows, his laughter rebounding through the glen and settling in her bones. He wasn't from here, or of it, but he had become a part of her and she couldn't see it now and not see him.

Tears streamed her cheeks in silence, down Flora's too. Both were trembling as they gripped hands. Ma Peg's lament grew louder as she sang as one voice for the villagers, the ship steadily pulling out of Village Bay, away from the protective embrace of Dun, until they lost sight of the stoic settlement.

Immediately the sea began to heave and breathe more deeply as their horizon expanded to give them last views of Boreray too, where Donald McKinnon had almost died this spring; of the towering, ancient stacks – Stac Lee and Stac an Armin – feathered white with birds, where the men would hunt for gannets. She could just see the iron peg at the base of Stac Lee where they would throw the rope to disembark; one of many everyday feats of bravery and skill, the simple acts of heroism required to feed their families.

The ship began to pitch and roll, though they were sailing beneath a flawless blue sky. It was barely past eight in the morning and they had ten hours ahead of them. Effie watched the birds whirl in the sky, a dancing confetti lifted on thermals. She took in, for the last time, the avian kingdom on the cliffs of which, she realized, she had been a part: the gannets roosting on the highest perches and the fulmars below them; guillemots and razorbills on the ledges below and the kitti-wakes darting in and out of the caves . . .

Gradually, as the boat steamed away, the isles changed colour, fading from green to grey; details became lost so that only shapes remained. The women were waving their hand-kerchiefs at it, as if the rocky archipelago was watching their retreat, scornful and imperious as they abandoned her. She grew smaller and smaller, and it looked to Effie like the mountain itself was slowly sinking back into the sea.

She felt an intense yearning to place her feet on the jagged rocks one last time; she wished she had taken a moment to grab the rope and swing over the top for one final thrilling play – but it had been a risk she couldn't take. This entire last week, she had made sure there wasn't a moment she could be caught off guard, by shadowing her friends and neighbours' actions closely: she fetched water with Jayne, carried the furniture with Fin McKinnon, brought over the sheep with Lorna. She had waited in terror all week for the factor to set foot in the cottage and tell her father what they had done, but it hadn't happened. Poppit had been her protector, baring her teeth and growling, her hackles up, any time she saw him, near or far. He had regarded her distance with suppressed rage, giving only bewildered shrugs as the villagers questioned what he had done to trigger the gentle dog's ire . . . Her dog had kept her safe.

Until last night, when he had caught up with her outside the kirk. The dogs were in the byres and she was momentarily alone as Jayne spoke to the minister. He had got a hand to her arm and hissed in her ear, in a single instant bringing back all the horrors of that stormy May night. But she had been prepared this time. She had dug her bait and her plan had worked. It had actually worked.

She stared back at the wild isle as it disappeared from sight, her heart still beating like a frightened bird. But the nightingale was no longer caged.

She was free.

Hands tilting through the afternoon sky. That's what Effie noticed first as the ship's progress slowed to a stately glide through the silky sheltered waters. The captain gave a valedictory toot of the horn as they approached the harbour and it sent the crowd waving harder.

The crossing had been long and arduous – ten hours to here – with a heavy Atlantic swell that even the admiralty sloop couldn't iron flat beneath her broad beam. Some of the islanders had been ill from the heave-ho. A few of the men had chatted with the sailors, but most had lapsed into increasingly pensive silence. Occasionally the cries of a day-old baby escaped from below deck: Mary McKinnon had her child in her arms at last, born last night, a St Kildan for one day.

Now, though, the silence grew trepidatious as the navy men threw thick ropes to the harbourmaster, the St Kildans standing watchful along the decks. For once, the women's hands, always knitting, were still; the men, always toiling, stood idle; the children, always running, clutched their mothers' skirts. Palpable disbelief sat upon their faces, not just that they had dared to leave, but also that they had now arrived.

Already, the ease of their new lives announced itself. In Village Bay, disembarking was a treacherous job in all but the calmest conditions, but here, the sloop docked with almost careless nonchalance. From stepping off a boat to eating a meal, their survival would no longer be dictated by the season or the weather but by personal will. It was an extraordinary concept.

Effie's puffy-eyed gaze moved dully over the gathered, waving mass, seeing how the mainlanders scanned them with rapacious interest, assessing their weather-beaten faces and clothes. The older women here appeared not to wear the red headscarves that were customary back home and she had a feeling of one tribe meeting another. Ma Peg and Mad Annie, who were standing at the prow of the ship, reached down and threw the feather broom tied to a ladder – made by one of the men – into the water. The good-luck tradition seemed to cause a stir among the local crowd and several bright flashes exploded in quick succession.

'It's just the cameras from the press men,' one of the sailors explained as the St Kildans stepped back, startled. 'There's a lot of interest in your move over the water. They've been reporting it as far away as Australia and America and Canada.'

Effie frowned, unable to understand why. They had all grown used to the small cameras wielded by the tourists who came over on the steamships and paid them a few farthings to stand still, so that they might somehow freeze their images and show them to people at home; but these big, bright dishes were altogether larger and more violent, and she scowled at the trilby-hatted men standing behind them, their own faces obscured.

The gangway was thrown down with a clatter and the captain came to stand at the top, ready to shake the hands of the families that were alighting. Of the thirty-six islanders, all but nine were stopping here in Lochaline. The others – her Uncle Hamish and family, and Mary and Donald McKinnon with their new baby – would go on to Oban further down the coast, arriving tomorrow morning. It hadn't been possible to keep their tight-knit community tightly knitted after all. There weren't enough houses, or jobs, in just one place.

On paper, it hadn't sounded too bad. She wouldn't especially miss her uncle's strict, self-imposed authority over them and although Donald was kind, Mary had always been a prickly and sour woman.

But as the moment came for the villagers to leave behind their old neighbours, an outpouring of sorrow escaped them. Was it the people or the place they would miss? Effie watched numbly as arguments, feuds and old debts were forgotten, as her cheeks were kissed and the men shook hands with characteristic solemnity; they put much store by a man's grip – for an island nation of craggers, a solid grasp was as good a test of character as any. They would meet again, they assured. Letters would be written. Promises were made.

And then that was . . . it. The true moment of leaving their old lives was happening not as they had stepped off Hirta, but now, here, as they prepared to step ashore at Lochaline. For as long as they remained on the ship they were still as one, but the deep and profound entanglement of their island community was finally unbound and they would scatter now like dandelion seeds on the wind.

Who would take the first step? Everyone had gathered in their family groups. Flora had clutched her hard one last time, her body rigid, before going to stand by her parents.

A new silence fell, weighted with expectation. The islanders, aware of their audience, became inhibited again. The sailors – their duties completed – were standing to attention beside the captain; the crowd on dry land didn't stir, their waving hands fallen still now too. Effie could see a line of officials waiting for them on the pier. They were distinguished from the local men's tweed and cloth caps by their uniform of dark suits and bowler hats.

Lorna took the lead, offering a steady arm to Ma Peg and helping her down the gangway, a blizzard of camera flashes accompanying their every step, the spell broken as they stepped onto the level. Mad Annie and Old Fin followed after, arms linked and talking closely to one another all the while; it wasn't clear which of them was supporting the other as they descended into the mass of strangers.

Beside her, Effie's father's body shook as he leant on his

stick and prepared to go next. She went to give him her arm but he was still angry at her and he gave a pointed look to the navy men in their white ducks, one of whom stepped in and escorted him with rigid ceremony instead. Effie followed three steps behind, thinking her father looked like a prisoner, which was ironic for someone walking to an easier freedom.

'Name, please?' one of the hatted men asked, moving forward as the crowd shifted closer too.

'My father speaks no Engl—'

'Robert Gillies. Euphemia Gillies,' her father said proudly, guessing what information was required. His head was tipped back as he strove for dignity amid the strangeness of the unknown.

'Welcome to Scotland, Mr Gillies, Miss Gillies,' the man said with a brief smile.

Effie didn't smile back. Part of her wanted to point out that they had always been in Scotland, that they were every bit as Scottish as he.

'My name's Mr Croucher. I'll be escorting you to your new home today.'

But Effie wasn't listening. Her attention was diverted by the proximity of the onlookers, all so close now and staring at her with open interest. She was tall, taller than most of the women, but only half their width. She could almost feel their temptation to reach out and brush a hand against her salty skin, her rough skirt, her wind-tangled hair. But her own curiosity was pricked too as she stared back – what was that powder on their faces? How did their hair settle into smooth, regular waves like that? Why were their ankles wrinkled? Were they in Sunday best too, or did they always wear shoes—

'No!'

A loud wail from the deck made everyone startle and look back. Mhairi had collapsed to the ground, sobbing pitifully. She was clutching a bow rail and tossing her beautiful red mane like it was a dancing flame. 'I canna, I canna!' she cried frantically, looking up at her neighbours, her hand reaching blindly towards them for help. 'Don't make me! Please don't make me—'

Effie frowned as a murmur rippled through the titillated crowd. Was hysteria what they had come for, then? Hoped for? She could feel the weight of their scrutiny, had a sense of awaiting judgement from the welcoming party.

Mhairi's mother, with six other children to herd including an eighteen-month-old toddler, shot a single look to her husband.

'Father! Leave me be!' Mhairi cried as, without a word, Ian McKinnon hoisted her to her feet again and escorted her, weeping, off the ship in a thin-lipped display of dignity. Effie could see the whiteness of his fingertips against Mhairi's arm, the only visible sign of his anger as his daughter's legs kept buckling, her head hanging down heavily as she staggered, sobbing pitifully.

'No! No! No!' she wept.

For one fleeting moment, the crying girl glanced up, as if noticing for the first time the many faces of strangers turned towards her, as if she alone on the boat hadn't been looking to shore. Her reddened eyes had a bleak look that bordered on utter capitulation.

Effie wanted to run to her friend – Mhairi had never been strong-willed, like her and Flora – but the family was corralled by another of the government officials stepping forward and thoughtfully herding them away from the spectators and press men, who seemed more excited than ever. Mhairi's little brothers, oblivious to their sister's distress, gave whoops of delight as they slipped their hands from their mother's and bolted towards the shiny black cars parked in a row alongside the pier. They had all heard of cars, of course, but to finally see one . . .

'Alasdair! Murran!' Effie heard their mother yell as she ducked after them. The crowd seemed pleased by the commotion, moving as one to watch the action, so that within moments Effie had lost sight of the family. Her friends. Her neighbours. Just like that they were gone.

A frisson of fear juddered through her own heart, the way it did when she missed a toehold on the sea cliffs or was startled by a ground-nesting bird. She knew the McKinnons were being housed near to her and her father, that they would remain neighbours – but what did 'near' mean over here? Were they two cottages apart, or two miles?

She looked back at the ship and met Flora's gaze. A look of concern passed between them, but the camera dishes began popping again as the press men caught sight of her too. Her parents were coming down the ramp now, Flora bringing up the rear and holding the hands of her own little siblings. Immediately, Mhairi was forgotten, her dramatic anguish overshadowed by Flora's riveting beauty. Her long black hair streamed in the wind like a witch's skirt, her waist cinched by the red scarf in her signature act of defiance. But if she looked beautiful, for once she didn't know it. Her lips were pursed together to keep from weeping and her pallor was wan, even on such a bright day as this.

'Effie, come,' her father said, half-turning towards her. 'We're away.'

Effie looked back to the ship in a panic, still not ready to step away from the only people she had ever known. Norman and Jayne Ferguson were disembarking now. She sneered to see Norman walk with the buoyant stride of a pilgrim arriving in the Promised Land at last. There was blood on his hands but, broad-shouldered and long-legged, his eyes were bright as he addressed the official assigned to them; like Flora, he had been waiting to step into this life for a long time. He had been one of Lorna's main advocates of the idea to petition the government for evacuation, arguing alongside her that they wouldn't survive another winter.

'Effie!' her father barked.

'. . . Coming, Father.' She faltered in his stooped wake as they both followed the bowler-hatted gentleman to one of the glossy cars across the way. It seemed strange that her father should be so sure-footed in this new place, as she – young and strong – stumbled behind, unable to tear her gaze from the passengers remaining on board. She might never see them again – Uncle Hamish and Aunt Mary, her cousins, Mary and Donald McKinnon . . .

'Your carriage, Mr Gillies, Miss Gillies.'

Effie and her father stared at the vehicle. It was bigger than she had expected, and shinier too, the low sun bouncing off it. What she liked most was that the wheels were so perfectly round. The only round things on Hirta had been the stone querns used for grinding the barley and by comparison, they could only be described as round*ish*.

A door was opened at the back of the vehicle and for a moment, Effie and her father stared in. The bench where they were to sit was not wooden, as she had supposed, but covered in smooth leather the colour of plums. It had a rich smell she had never encountered before.

'Ahoy!'

The shout made them both stop and turn. Her Uncle

Hamish was waving down from the deck, as much the leader of their ship as he had been back home.

'Where's Mathieson?' he called down to someone on the pier, one of the men in cloth caps sorting the cargo now that all the Lochaline passengers had disembarked. 'MacLeod's factor?'

'Not here,' was the reply.

Hamish cast an enquiring glance to the other men working alongside him, but they muttered back the same. 'Not here.'

'He's got my money!'

'Not here.'

'The smack left after the *Dunara Castle* yesterday!' Flora called up to him.

Yesterday? Hamish scowled, his quizzical look carrying over the crowd and finding her father, who merely shrugged.

'Oban, then!' someone shouted.

'Aye.' Hamish gave a reluctant nod, pulling back from his position over the rails, but his scowl made plain he was displeased.

'What was he doing entrusting money to that man anyway?' her father muttered, shuffling into the car.

Effie sat beside him without comment, her hands flat on the smooth seats that were the colour of plums, her heart beating fast.

Chapter Fifteen

The journey was mercifully short. Just the sound of the car starting up had almost done for her father's heart, and neither one of them enjoyed the rolling sensation along the bumpy roads. For two people who had never moved off their feet in their lives – with not even a horse on the island – it was an altogether disconcerting experience. On all but Sundays, they walked the earth barefoot, connected to the land in a way that already felt alien here.

Effie restlessly wiggled her toes in her boots again, forced into them by Lorna, who had gone around the deck and done a 'check' as the mainland drew into sight. It only added to her feelings of restriction and unease here now. It was difficult enough to change lives, much less in heavy shoes. Then again, her entire body felt like it belonged to someone else. Her hands – now idle and cold – were used to the familiar comfort of Poppit's fur coat, threading silky ears through her fingers, tapping out a single pat on her thigh that brought her companion straight to her side. Her ears were used to straining to distinguish the thick lattice of bird cries that always criss-crossed the sky in a shrieking cacophony around them; but here, only singular notes rose into the dusk, solitary songbirds twittering out of sight, hidden in that feature most curious to St Kildans – the trees.

Mr Croucher stopped outside a low stone wall and cut the engine. 'Home sweet home,' he said, seemingly without irony.

Both Effie and her father peered past the glass windows at a low cottage. But for the fact that it was white and the roof wasn't tethered down with iron straps, it wasn't so very different from their old home: a single-storey building, with a window either side of a centrally placed door.

Effie climbed out of the car and went round to pull her father out too; the seats were dashed low to get out from and they had to link arms to get him up. He steadied himself on his stick as Effie turned slowly on the spot, trying to orientate herself. The road had swept back from the pier and then looped round to the left. They had come over a low hill and now faced towards distant purple hills. From the brackish wind that blew her hair forward, she sensed the sea was behind them. The land was rolling and gentle, thickly heathered moors butting up to the cottage's stone walls with a stand of trees just beyond a small rocky outcrop. It occurred to her that there was nothing to climb – no mountains, no crags, not even any boulders – and she felt the yawn in her body again, the urge to stretch and reach.

In all, she estimated they had probably travelled the length of Hirta. It had taken minutes in the car, but by foot – unless there was another route – it was likely a mere half-hour walk back to the village, for there were no mountains to climb. It would be nothing for her, but for a lame man with a stick . . .

Her eyes narrowed as she looked further down the lane. She could see another white cottage, a hundred yards along; and another a hundred yards past that. Perhaps this was considered close by the mainlanders, but coming from a village where the entire street had been a hundred yards long, the cottages standing shoulder to shoulder like weather-beaten sentries, people dipping in and out of each other's houses just like the gannets diving for fish . . . Their village was really just a ribbon of different rooms. But here there was space and gaps and roads and trees.

The glistening hulk of another of the black cars sat outside the nearest cottage and she wondered who had been placed there. She hoped it was the McKinnons and the MacQueens, though they were both large families and these cottages – from the outside, at least – looked small.

'So you are in number three,' Mr Croucher said, opening the gate for them and leading them down the short path. 'Your belongings were unloaded from the *Dunara Castle* last night. Everything should be there, but if there's any problems, speak to Mr McDougall down at the harbour.'

'Did they bring my stool? I need it for my leg,' her father said.

The man looked back at him blankly and Effie quickly translated, for he appeared to have no Gaelic.

'They'll have brought everything of yours there was to bring, Mr Gillies,' Mr Croucher said, sliding a key into the lock and turning it as Effie relayed his reply. He stepped back to allow them to pass.

Effie was itching to charge in and see for herself, finally, what all the fuss was about for mainland life, but her father already had a hand to the doorframe as he shuffled over the threshold and she was forced to wait her turn. Her fingers flexed with frustration.

'Be careful as you go,' Mr Croucher warned. 'The light's fading fast now and I'm afraid there's no electricity here as yet.'

They wouldn't miss what they'd never had, Effie supposed.

A tiny, arms-width lobby opened to rooms on each side

and they instinctively moved into the right-hand room in silence. It was suffused with gloom and musty with damp. Even on such a beautiful summer's evening, it felt chilly inside. Shadows pressed forward from the lumpen walls, and the small window was so ineffectual at letting in any light that Effie expected it threw a dark shadow on the ground outside instead.

She shivered, her heart plunging to her unwelcome boots, and she realized by her sharp disappointment that in spite of her resistance to leaving the isle, a part of her had been hoping to be seduced here after all.

Mr Croucher lit a candle-holder set on the deep windowsill and an aurora of pale amber light lit up the front half of the room. The spiny fingers of her grandmother's old spinning wheel spread and reached towards her, and she could see her father's wooden chair balanced upside down by the corner wall.

Mr Croucher walked towards the small chimney breast on the left wall and lit another candle. The room revealed itself fully – but needn't have bothered. Their scant possessions were as meagre in this house as they had been on the isle.

'A cord of wood has been prepared and left for you at the back,' Mr Croucher said. 'For lighting the stove.'

Effie translated for her father as he stared at the cast-iron stove. It was much the same as the one they had had back home. 'What's wrong with peat?' her father scowled to her.

Effie relayed to Mr Croucher again.

'Nothing at all, Mr Gillies. It's just that we use wood here. You saw the trees on the drive over, I take it? Plenty of them here.' Mr Croucher walked towards the door in the back wall. 'There's a stream out the back for water and away to the side is the outdoor toilet—'

Effie wandered through to the room on the other side of the cottage. It was identical in layout and size to the kitchen but for a pale blue sheet hanging across the centre. She peered past it to find her parents' narrow wooden bed roughly pushed against the far wall. On this side of the hanging was the single bed her brother had slept in all his life. It had a star notched in the headboard, the bed left askew in the middle of the space, as if tossed there.

She looked about her. The fireplace sat to her right-hand side but the hanging sheet meant her father, to the left of it, wouldn't get any benefit from the fire when it got colder. She gave a tentative tug of the sheet; it would have come to down. It would be a sore loss of privacy for them both but there was nothing to be done. On Hirta, before John's accident, she'd shared the byre in the original neighbouring blackhouse with their cow and Poppit and it had suited her fine, but there was no such luxury here.

Mr Croucher and her father followed her into the room as she went to pull down the sheet.

'Leave it,' her father commanded.

'But Father, you'll get cold.'

'It'll do fine,' he said. Effie could see he was leaning heavily on his stick, his joints bad today.

Mr Croucher went straight to the window and lit the taper there, before repeating the same at the fireplace. Weak light sputtered then flared, casting shadows about the stone room. The flagged floor looked cool and reassuringly ancient and a yearning to press her bare soles to the stone rushed through Effie's body; she'd been suppressing her physical instincts all day and she didn't think she could stand it any longer. She stared at Mr Croucher in anguish, willing him to leave.

Mr Croucher smiled, as if believing her to be happy about

their new circumstances. 'A rudimentary map has been drawn for you of the area,' he said, speaking over his shoulder as he disappeared into the kitchen, before reappearing a moment later with a sheet of paper. 'But you'll work it out for yourselves soon enough, I should imagine.' He held the map towards the light. 'You are here,' he said, pointing to a small black X in an otherwise unmarked part of the sheet. Blue waves, seemingly drawn by a child's hand, lapped due west. 'The Forestry Commission is here; this is where the men will report for work on the morrow.' His finger stabbed upon an area due east, demarcated with looping green squiggles. 'The village is a mile and a half thence. As well as the harbour and fish market, there's an inn, a general store and post office,' he said, tapping due south. 'There's a bus to the Corran ferry and over to Fort William twice a week. Mondays and Thursdays, I believe, but Mrs Lamont in the store is the person to keep you straight. Not much happens round here without her eyes and ears on it, so I'm given to understand.'

He looked back at the young woman and her crooked father staring at him with stern expressions. 'Well, you must be weary. If you're settled in, it only behoves me to equip you with the keys to your new home and to take my leave. I've a journey back to Glasgow before the night train to London.'

Effie arched an eyebrow. Officials from London. Braided sailors. Press men. A waving, staring public. All to ship thirty-six islanders sixty miles off a speck of rock in the Atlantic. Why was there such a fuss?

He wasn't at the car before Effie had her boots unlaced and her bare feet were pressing to the stone floor. Immediately she felt her pulse settle, her blood cool. 'I thought he'd never leave,' she said to her father's back as he shuffled to the kitchen again.

'Aye,' he said flatly.

She looked up. With that one word, she knew his feelings about the place too. This move had been a mistake.

Her heart beat a little faster and she followed after him, quickly turning his chair the right way up and setting it down at the far side of the stove. His low, three-legged stool she set as he liked it, in front, just to the left. Her father sank down with not a sound but the small wince that accompanied the release of his standing bones told her he'd been suffering. He reached into his jacket pocket and pulled out his black twist tobacco and clay pipe.

Effie carried on righting the few pieces of furniture they owned as she listened to the distinctive tap-tapping of him tamping the tobacco. She brought over the candle so that he could bring the flame to the bowl and he took three sucky sips.

He exhaled slowly and the smell of St Kilda was suddenly around them. She closed her eyes, transported: she could hear the birds again, see the bay in all its moods, feel the grass beneath her feet, overhear the chatter of the 'evening news' on the Street as everyone walked after dinner. She could feel, still, the embrace of her neighbours living together in that small glen, the joy of childhood games and the kiss of a bright-eyed man as she had clung to a rope. But there was heartbreak too – a collie airborne over a cliff, a storm shelter that had been anything but a refuge, half a rope swinging from a cliff . . . All the memories were marbled into a swirl inside her and she could no sooner remember one than conjure the others too. They all lived on in her still, the moments gone now, but not forgotten.

She opened her eyes again and looked around at the gloomy place. Perhaps it was to her advantage the damp was so bad, the light so poor. They couldn't settle here and now her father would see it too.

The sooner they left, the better.

The heather moor was in shade but a blade of pink light still glanced off the treetops as she flung back the garden gate and began walking, arms swinging, up the road to their neighbours at number 4, an hour later. She had unpacked the trunks of their linens, made up the beds and aired their clothes from the salty sea crossing; the pots and pans now hung from hooks inside the walls of the chimney. The furniture was all set on its right sides and with a clear path so that her father wouldn't trip. The sheet still hung halfway between their beds.

Her eyes darted like dragonflies as she strode out, trying to get the measure of her new landscape. Incredibly, it was more barren in many ways than the place she had left – fewer seabirds, no cliffs – but she couldn't deny the trees were a marvel, their canopies like many-fingered hands from a land of green giants, hiding and housing whole other kingdoms; creatures she had only seen in books – red squirrels, pine martens – leapt and scampered through the woody branches, disappearing into secretive homes before she could approach. Hirta held no such mysteries; she was what she appeared – a land of granite rock and ancient immovability. She could weather, withstand, endure; she would not falter but neither would she protect. It had been for the villagers to find their own shade behind painstakingly stacked rock walls, to learn to climb the vertiginous cliffs where their sustenance awaited if only they were brave enough to dare.

The car had long since left the verge in front of number 4 and Effie was both happy and dismayed to see the graceful figure of Jayne Ferguson sitting on a stool outside the front door, knitting a sock, as if she'd always sat there. For where Jayne was to be found, Norman was too and Effie didn't want to see him, not ever again. She wouldn't forgive him for what he'd done.

'It is you,' Jayne smiled, as Effie approached. 'I'm glad.'

'Are you?'

'Of course. I'll sleep better knowing we've got you to protect us, you know, in case the headless piper comes.' Her feet too were bare in the grass, her boots neatly placed by the front door.

'Don't tell Mhairi that.' Effie rolled her pale eyes. 'Besides, you've got Norman.'

'Aye, but there's none so fierce as you, Effie Gillies, everyone knows that.'

Effie stood at the gate. 'Is he here?'

Jayne heard the contempt in her words and knew exactly Effie's feelings about her husband. 'No, he's walked back to town to get a measure of the distances. He has an early start in the morning and he wants to make a good impression.'

At that, Effie let the gate spring back behind her as she walked up the path. 'Can I?' she asked, thumbing towards the front door.

'Of course,' Jayne smiled, her hands never pausing from their work. Click-clack, click-clack. It was as much the sound of her home as her father's pipe was the smell of it.

Effie walked through the cottage quickly, lest Norman should unexpectedly return. The layout was identical but there was no need of a dividing sheet in the bedroom, a jug of heather already sat prettily on the kitchen table and Jayne had hung curtains at the windows, bringing a shock of colour and sense of homely cheer. The small distinctions between their two homes seemed more significant, amplified even, than if they'd been back on the isle and Effie felt a sense of failure that she couldn't – or hadn't – done more to bring a feminine touch to their own home. Would that kind of thing matter here? She had never thought her duties as a good daughter needed to extend to fripperies before; what little pride her father had in her stemmed from her ability to climb a rope faster than any other on the isle. But she already sensed there would need to be new ways of pleasing him here. She resolved to pick some heather on her way back down the road again. It could sit in the milk pail till they got their cow back.

She wandered back into the gloaming and sank cross-legged onto the grass beside Jayne. She picked a blade of grass and threaded it between her fingers as she looked around. The pink light had slipped off the treetops now and the shy crescent moon, delicate as a fingernail, was beginning to peep in the sky.

'So, we've actually done it . . .' Jayne sighed, her hands still busy with industry even though she no longer needed to knit for rent. The habit was as much a comfort as a trade. 'How are you feeling?'

Effie hesitated, countless words rushing into her mind, wanting to be heard like impatient children. But none of them could be said. '. . . Furious,' she said finally, choosing the least of them.

'Furious?'

'Of course. Aren't you?' But it was a pointless question. Effie didn't think Jayne had ever felt fury in her life. 'Is this *it*? Is this what we left our homes for?'

'What's wrong with it?'

'There's nothing right with it, that's what's wrong! It's all so . . . gentle.'

'No near-death experiences just to get dinner, is that what you mean?' Jayne smiled, looking at her sidelong.

'At least on Hirta we knew we were alive,' Effie huffed, knowing she was being gently mocked.

'That's true enough. We did.'

Effie picked a buttercup and looked up at her. 'How about you? Are you pleased we came?'

This time, it was Jayne's turn to hesitate. 'I believe I will be. In time.' She gave one of her enigmatic smiles.

'And Norman? Is he pleased?' She couldn't keep the bitterness from her voice.

'As a wee boy,' Jayne smiled again. 'He's like Columbus reaching America. As far as he's concerned, this is the brave new world we're in now.'

'Going to make his fortune, is he?'

'Aye, whatever that means.' Jayne gave a shrug. 'How's your da?'

'Quiet.'

'It's to be expected. It's harder on the older ones.'

'Aye, maybe,' Effie murmured, plucking at the grass, although that would be no comfort to Mhairi; she'd taken it harder than anyone. 'I'm just glad I thought to make some extra oatcakes before we left. It's saved us the bother of trying to get sorted with the stove tonight.'

'I wish I'd have done the same. You know how Norman gets in a temper with an empty stomach.'

The entire village knew. 'So have you eaten?'

'No. Norman had to get to the village anyway, like I said, so he's going to eat at the inn and make himself known to the locals.'

Effie frowned. 'But what about you?'

'Oh, I'm fine. I've no appetite tonight.'

There was a silence; for all her outspokenness, Effie knew when to remain quiet. As her mother had always said, what happens in a marriage is private.

'So who's our other neighbour?' she asked, jerking her chin in the direction of the last white cottage within sight.

'Old Fin.'

Effie was shocked. '. . . On his own?'

'Aye.'

She felt a rush of blood to the head, a familiar feeling as indignation flooded her bones. 'But what are they thinking, putting an old man on his own in a house all the way up the road there?' Her voice was pinked with feeling.

'Don't worry. I've been to check on him just now and he seems right enough,' Jayne said, seeing her high colour. 'He's worn out from the journey so he's in bed already. I'll look in on him in the morning too.'

'But it may not be tonight or tomorrow that he needs you, Jayne. Once the novelty wears off—'

'I'll check in on him every day.'

'But checking in isn't enough! What if he was to fall? He's isolated up there. Who is there for him to talk to? What can he watch? Back home, he sat on the Street from sun-up to sundown. No one could pass by without him and Mad Annie and Ma Peg passing comment on the size of the lambs or the burn on our faces or the holes in our shirts. How's he going to get food? And don't tell me there's the shop. He's as unable to get it from there as shin down the ropes for a bird.'

'You're right, of course. They should have thought it through better.' Jayne mollified her with a smile. 'But he's got us. We'll not abandon him.'

Effie checked her temper, the guilt that she *would* be

abandoning him – all of them – an effective silencer. She stared at her hands, wishing she could say something of what she had gone through; wishing she could at least explain. 'And the others? Where are they all?'

'We'll know more when Norman gets back. I'm hoping they've kept Ma Peg and Mad Annie together.'

'I doubt it, if they've put Old Fin out on a limb. They're of the view that we're lucky to be given any homes at all.'

'Well, I'd prefer to think that when they were looking on the maps and allocating homes, they believed they were placing your father and Old Fin as close neighbours, with us in the middle as . . . helpers. Though I agree the distances are more than we're used to.'

To take her father from Old Fin . . . Another flutter of guilt tremored through her heart. How could she separate them? Neither one of them spoke English. Their companionship was vital for both. But last night had proven they unequivocally could not stay. This wasn't a choice. It was survival, and whether he would believe it or not, this was the only true way she could protect her father.

A small bird landed on the far garden wall and hopped on the stones. It was exquisitely pretty, though understated, with brownish-green plumage streaked with yellow, a creamy belly and an eyebrow stripe. Effie squinted closely, her upset momentarily forgotten as it sang a few notes of a tune before flitting off again in the next instant. Had its legs been dark grey, she'd have assumed it a chiff-chaff, but the pale legs confirmed it for her as *phylloscopus trochilus*. A willow warbler.

She leant back on her sit bones with a rapt expression. She had never seen one in real life before, but she had read all about it, of course. She knew it was highly migratory and would soon be on the wing to southern Africa. She knew it liked to feast on insects but would eat berries and fruit too. If she remembered correctly, it also moulted twice a year, a highly unusual habit for a bird—

'Perhaps it's not *all* so bad?' She glanced over to find Jayne smiling at her, her body entirely motionless though her hands were still moving rapidly. Click-clack went the needles, their bone heads dipping and bobbing. Effie could guess that all the women from the island – from Mad Annie to Ma Peg to Mary McKinnon still on the boat and heading for Oban – were this very moment engaged in identical labours. Old habits would die hard. 'Let's give this side a chance before we condemn it to eternal damnation. They may not have cliffs and seabirds here, but there's a different beauty in trees and songbirds.'

'Maybe . . .' Effie said non-committally. It wasn't beauty she needed here but prospects. Refuge. Somewhere safe to go next. She and her father had to leave here and disappear sooner, not later. Once the factor was found . . . 'I should be getting back,' she said, getting to her feet and dusting the shredded grass blades off her lap. It would be dark soon, and she didn't yet know the lie of the land well enough for bare-foot walks. 'I've an early start tomorrow.'

'At the factory? Aye, I'll see you there.'

'No, Jayne, the forestry,' Effie admonished her. 'You've got a man to feed you but in our house, *I'm* the man and I need a man's wage. Da won't eat if I don't earn.'

Jayne gave another of her patient smiles. 'Ah, yes. Of course.'

'See you on the morrow, then.'

'Aye, tomorrow,' Jayne murmured, watching her go, arms swinging and her bare feet already dirty with the dust of their new home.

Chapter Sixteen

The men were just ahead of her. She could see their dark heads bobbing as they walked along the road in a straggled line. Apart but together. It hadn't occurred to Norman Ferguson to knock for her as he passed on his way by, and she was both furious and relieved about it.

She walked briskly over the moor – not for her the road – resenting the boots that were already rubbing her heels. It had been a morning of false starts, following a night of broken sleep and restless dreams. The floor beneath her bedstead was uneven, the bed listing with her every move, and just when her exhausted body had accepted and succumbed to the intermittent rocking, the early-rising sun had poked at her with bright fingers, a perfect beam of light falling across her cheeks through the same small window which had offered no such hospitality on their arrival yesterday. Breakfast had been the last of the oatcakes and weak tea brewed with spring water from the burn.

Her father had got a fire going with the wood, though he kept muttering it was a travesty to be burning the stuff; timber's scarcity on Hirta – only washing ashore as driftwood or shipwrecks – meant it had a rarity value that back home would have seen it put to far better use, such as a new table leg or a window lintel.

The day wasn't cold, nor set to be – the hen harriers soaring on the thermals told her there would be another day of warm winds – but the flames dispatched the brackish damp from the rooms and when she had left, her father was sitting in his chair by the door and whittling a stick with his pocket knife. The loom, no longer needed and with no yarn to weave, sat idle in the front corner beside the spinning wheel, taking up space needlessly. What would he do with himself today, while she worked?

From the map Mr Croucher had given them and her recollection of the road they had taken when being driven from the village, she had been able to work out her route to work this morning. It wasn't a foolproof plan. It hadn't been able to forewarn her of the bog just past the bridge and she'd had to sink a leg almost to her knee to find it out herself. It also hadn't forewarned her there was a colony of ground-nesting bonxies until they dive-bombed her out of their territory; one had managed to get a claw to her hair and no matter how much she pressed it smooth, it still stuck up.

Still, she was but a quarter mile behind the men. The land rolled in heathered waves all around and had any of them looked back, they would have caught sight of her solitary figure; but they had disappeared from view now and she hastened to a jog, the distant purple hills inching closer. She summited a small hillock and looked down into the shallow dip where the forestry yard was sited. It was just a courtyard with several large storage buildings in it – larger than she'd ever seen – and huge stacked piles of logs that had once been trees. Shorn of their bushy heads and enquiring arms, they lay denuded and inert and she couldn't help but think of the life that had once flourished within and on them, and had been cast out to find other homes. There were several trucks parked at one end and a sequence of long, low huts with tin roofs. She could see some of the men she had grown up with standing in the doorway of the middle one, their attention on something within.

She broke into a sprint for the final few hundred yards, not wanting to miss anything.

'Hey,' she panted, drawing up beside Finlay and Angus McKinnon standing at the back. 'Did I miss anything?'

Angus looked down at her, an open look of scorn crossing his face as he took in the sight of her. She was taken aback to see it. She knew their rivalry back home had sometimes crossed lines but she had hoped that here, where they were all among strangers, a familiar face would be accepted as a friendly one. 'What are you doing here?' he sneered.

'Same as you. Reporting for work,' she tossed back, standing on tiptoe and looking forward as she tried to see who was in charge.

A laugh of disbelief escaped him.

'This isn't the parliament now, Effie,' his brother Fin hissed as she put a hand to his shoulder for balance. 'Get, now. Things are different here. You can't stay. The women are in the town.'

'That's no good for me,' she whispered back.

Fin shrugged his shoulder, trying to dislodge her. 'Effie, stop with your games. This is serious now. We've all to adapt and that includes you.'

The voice that had been speaking stopped.

'. . . You. At the back. Is something wrong?' a man enquired from the other side of the room. Effie wasn't tall enough to see to whom it belonged.

'Actually, yes, sir,' Angus replied, lifting his chin so that everyone could see he was the one talking. 'There's someone here who says she's come to report for work.'

'Sssht, get,' Finlay hissed at her again as everyone turned. He was younger than his eldest brother by three years and two years older than her. '. . . We've all to make a good fist of it. Don't cause a nuisance, Effie, just for once in your life.'

'I've every right to be here,' she hissed back, resisting as he tried to push her out into the courtyard with his elbow. They had scrapped plenty of times as children and she'd won her fair share until he was double her weight. She jammed her foot against the door frame, hooking and locking her leg against it; she was determined not to be jostled back out but Finlay simply stepped in front of her, blocking her from sight instead.

There was a ripple of murmured voices at the commotion.

'What's happening back here? You, man, what's your name?'

'. . . McKinnon, sir. Finlay McKinnon.'

'And what's all the bother?'

'It's not Fin making the fuss sir,' Angus said, elbowing his brother aside. Effie stared back at the room of men, all of whom she knew. Except one.

The foreman looked taken aback by the sight of her, although whether it was because she was a girl dressed in a man's suit, or on account of her muddied leg and clawed hair, she wasn't sure.

There was a silence as they regarded one another. He had a moustache and pale, doughy skin that was pocked on the cheeks. He was wearing a shirt with the sleeves rolled up and she could see a vivid scar, almost like a crocodile bite, down the length of his right forearm.

'And you are?'

'Euphemia Gillies. Effie Gillies. I've come to work.'

A flicker of amusement danced through his eyes. 'Well, Miss Gillies, I'm sorry to have to inform you we only employ men at the forestry commission.'

She tipped her head to the side but didn't blink. 'Why?'

He seemed surprised by the question. 'Because the labour is manual and requires a man's strength.'

'That's what they said back home about fowling on the cliffs, but I showed them there and I can show you too. I'm as able as any man here,' she said staunchly, refusing to look away, even though she could hear Angus sniggering beside her.

The foreman's eyes slid between the two old neighbours for a moment. 'Miss Gillies, I don't doubt your . . . fitness, but the women have been found work in the village, helping Mrs—'

'It's not women's work I'm after, sir. I need a man's wage. It's just me and my father, you see. He's not good on his feet now so it's up to me to put the meal on the table. I can't do that on the wages I'll get for women's work. You'll see I'm as hard-working and strong as any of these men. More so! I was the fastest climber on Hirta—'

A snort of disbelief escaped Angus.

'And because of my size, I could get into crevices they couldn't. I'll be helpful to you, I promise. You'll vouch for me, won't you, friends?' She looked at the faces she had known all her days: Archie MacQueen, Flora's father; Callum McKinnon, the middle of Mhairi's brothers and always the most reasonable; even Norman Ferguson. They had prayed beside her in kirk or sat beside her in the schoolroom, they had cragged and hunted and wrung necks together; but the weather-worn, sunburnt faces she had known all her life were

233

turned now to the ground. They were honourable men, brave and stoic, but to her amazement, what she saw on them now was fear – and shame of their fear. They could not defend her when they had no power here. They were no longer the masters of their fate, as they had been back home. A cash wage, and the easy survival it bought, came at a cost to dignity.

A silence grew as no one stepped forward, no one spoke out and she felt her stomach lurch as their silence – betrayal – solidified into something firm. Denial.

'Things are different here, lass,' the foreman said as her cheeks grew red. 'What may have been acceptable – necessary even – over on the islands, can't be done here.'

'Why not?' Was she to be the only one even to question it?

'Let's just say there's an etiquette to how things are done.'

Effie stared at him blankly. She'd never heard this word 'etiquette' before. It meant nothing. 'If you could just give me a chance to prove myself—'

'But even if you did, it wouldn't make a difference. I can't have a slip of a thing like you working here. We'd be a laughing stock. This is men's work.'

Effie felt her breathing become shallow as the full hopelessness of what he was saying dawned. She was wholly condemned by virtue of her sex?

'How about we settle it over an arm-wrestle?' Angus McKinnon suggested, cruel mockery in his voice.

'That won't be necessary,' the foreman said coolly. 'Miss Gillies understands the situation, don't you, lass?'

For a moment she said nothing. She cast her gaze around the room and the men – most of them – had the decency to look away, ashamed of having denied her the chance to prove herself, when they knew full well that whatever they could do . . .

'Aye, sir,' she said bitterly.

'Mrs Buchanan will be waiting on you. You'd best hurry along now, she'll be thinking you're late and she's a stickler for good timekeeping.' He looked at her clothes again. At her wet foot and the mud tideline up to her knee. 'I expect she'll have a change of clothes you can wear too.'

'That won't be necessary.'

'On the contrary, I think you'll find she'll insist upon it.'

'I'm not wearing someone else's clothes.'

'Uh . . . you already are,' Angus stage-whispered.

'Look,' the foreman said. 'You said yourself you need to earn a wage to put food on the table. And how else can you do that if you won't meet Mrs Buchanan's standards?'

'Well, not the *other* way, that's for sure. No one'd pay for her,' Angus drawled, emboldened by the men's enduring silence.

If he thought he was quick-witted, Effie proved her fists were faster and she connected a strong sucker-punch to his kidneys – just the way John had taught her – before he'd finished laughing at his own joke. He staggered sideways for a few steps before he could recover himself.

'Beaten up by a girl?' she crowed through the red mist as he advanced towards her with an open hand.

The foreman positioned himself between the two warring St Kildans.

'That will do,' he said firmly, standing eyeball to eyeball with the younger man and making his intention plain. Angus's hand dropped.

Effie breathed heavily as she stared at Angus over the foreman's shoulder. She felt wild. She wanted to continue the fight, to show him – all of them – that she wasn't what they said she was: weak, frail, feeble. She would defend herself no matter what. He had no idea what she was capable of, the things she had done . . . Her bloodlust was still up. It had been since the night before evacuation, outside the kirk, and nothing since could make it settle. Her heart was jumpy, her nerves scattered.

But the argument was already lost. No matter how strong or brave or hard-working she might be, whatever merits she might offer, this was simply a question of how things looked, and she couldn't fight that. Her presence there would be an embarrassment. This was how things were over here. These were the things that mattered.

Without another word, she turned and left the hut.

'You're crazy, you know that? You're out of control!' Angus shouted after her. 'You think you're something special but you're not. You're nothing, Effie Gillies! You hear me? Nothing!'

She could hear the low whirr of the spinning wheels, the clack of the looms, before she'd even stepped through the door, a buzz of chatter bouncing over the machines the way a woodpecker flew, in a rising and falling rhythm.

Effie watched the scene with angry eyes. Women's work. Women working. Heads bent, hands moving in synchronicity. Light fell in from high windows, shining on their hair, which had been smoothly tied back into buns. The building was a large, converted barn and Effie could see the pale tide of the mud splatter still at the bottom of the walls from when the animals had called this their home. Bolts of tweed were carefully stacked on trestle tables, a soft, feminine version of the giant logs piled high at the forestry yard.

At the far end of the space, a group of women were standing in a cluster around a desk; they were distinctive from the women already at the looms by the red shawls on their shoulders. Effie's eyes narrowed to points. Only yesterday those same shawls had been on the women's heads, but now they had slipped to their shoulders? Of course, there weren't the same ferocious winds here to harry their hair, but that they had spent less than twelve hours on these shores and the old ways were already, quite literally, slipping . . . It made her heart tremble to see how quickly her tribe was disappearing into the mainland mass, disbanded and anonymous. Even *Flora*? Her head was bowed, her distinctive black hair tied back. For once, she blended with the crowd.

Effie watched the women standing so obediently as they took their orders. Was she the only one who felt torn from her own life? Who felt a need to retain her sense of self? Why was no one else . . . fighting?

'You.'

The voice startled her from her thoughts and she focused her gaze to find a small woman staring at her. The top of her head would come no higher than Effie's shoulder but she commanded the room. 'You're late.'

'Aye,' Effie replied flatly. 'I went to the wrong place.'

There was a pause. A sense of expectancy hung in it, like a cradled baby in a hammock.

'. . . Then perhaps you might think to apologize for the inconvenience you've caused,' the short woman said finally, looking displeased that she had had to spell it out.

'Do I not look inconvenienced to you?' Effie asked back, indicating her muddied leg and clawed hair. She was tired and irate. Last night's fractured sleep was already digging its sharp fingers into her. The room felt airless.

Another silence followed her words, their impudence causing the women at the looms to fall still as the short woman walked slowly towards her, hands fastened in front of her crisp white apron like she was in a funeral procession. She stopped in front of Effie and stared up at her. The height difference between them was almost comical, but it was clear with whom the power lay.

There were deep fold lines around the older woman's mouth and between her brow. The corners of her mouth dipped downwards; her eyes were a dark blue but the whites around them were faintly yellow. Effie could see she had never been a beautiful woman, but her plainness had ripened with age to a bright sourness. She enjoyed her bitterness. It imbued her with a character her face had not.

'You are Euphemia Gillies.'

'Yes.'

'I've just been hearing about you.'

Effie didn't reply but her gaze flickered towards her old neighbours, now standing in a gaggle, watching them. Like the men, there was pity in their eyes, but none would step forward to defend her. They were gathered meekly in a huddle like the very sheep they had once chased, herded, plucked, and she realized why they weren't fighting. They were terrified that this new life – miserable and meagre though it may be – might be ripped from their arms at any moment and they would be left with nothing at all.

'No. It wasn't them as said anything,' the woman said, watching her eyes track her old neighbours. 'Mr Lennox rang ahead, saying you'd caused trouble at the forestry.'

'I didn't cause anything! I went seeking employ—'

The sudden slap stung her cheek. For a moment she thought she'd been hit with a paddle.

'You've a tongue on you, I can see that. And there's fire in your eyes.' The woman was scrutinizing her through narrowed slits of her own. 'You're trouble, Effie Gillies. I know your sort. Don't flatter yourself that you're an original.' Her voice lowered threateningly. 'You'd do well to understand folks have put themselves out for you. Homes have been found. Jobs too.' A quick toss of her head indicated the weaving machinery set up behind her. 'But there'll be no favours either. No talking back, no shirking, no arriving late. You'll work hard, and to my rules, or there'll be no work at all. Am I clear?'

Effie's eyes watered. Her blood was boiling. Every part of her wanted to scream. She owed nothing to this woman. She was free to work where she chose; this job may have been allocated to her by some bowler-hatted bureaucrat in London, but why should she accept it? She would turn it down and work where she pleased. Her life was her own.

At least, it would be . . . but not yet. She couldn't just leave. She was hamstrung by the economic reality over here of earning a wage. There had been more freedom, more equality, back home, where she could catch their own meals and live in their ancestors' house. But their new home had been given to them, and these jobs too. Until she could arrange something else, she must submit, like all the rest.

'Am – I – clear?' The words were enunciated slowly, threat lurking like shadows in the backs of them.

Effie knew she had to nod. If there was going to be a meal for her father's table tonight, she had to nod. But she could see in this woman's eyes that she wanted more than a 'yes'. She wanted wholesale submission. Humiliation. A line had been drawn in the sand and – contempt established – Effie knew she would get no peace from this woman now.

Another expectant silence quivered even though there could only be one outcome.

Finally, she nodded.

'Good.' The woman gave a small, victorious sniff as though a trifle had been settled. 'My name is Mrs Buchanan, I am the manageress. Your neighbours already have been trained to use the looms, you'll have to catch up.' Slowly, she looked Effie up and down in her men's garb. 'And I don't know what passes for civility where you're from, but over here, men and women don't share each other's clothes.'

A titter of amusement escaped from behind one of the looms. Effie's head whipped round but all eyes were downcast.

'It's lucky for you we've no visitors today as Mr McCaughrean, our buyer in Glasgow, has just cancelled. I'll not lose any more time to accommodating your antics. You'll stay as you are for today and turn up properly dressed tomorrow – if you want to be paid.' She went to turn away but looked back with a glimmer of amusement in her rheumy eyes. 'They tell me that on the isle, only the men wove. The women only carded and spun the yarns?'

Effie blinked a vague assent.

'So then it's men's work you'll be doing here after all. That should please you.' Sarcasm sparkled off her words. 'Everyone, back to work!'

Effie watched her go as the clatter of the looms started up again.

Flora came over – she appeared to be limping – and clutched Effie's hand in her own whilst smoothing her reddened cheek with her palm. 'Eff, are you well?' she whispered. Her long black hair that had blown free in the wind like a pirate's flag on the ship yesterday was pulled back in a braid and pinned up. Effie read it as a sign of submission from her fiery, beautiful friend. A ready – and bewildering – surrender.

'No!' Effie hissed below her breath, her gaze skirting sideways

240

and taking in the curious stares of the women on the looms. She was a wildling to them, no more than a savage. She could still feel the heat in her cheek at her public striking. Where Angus McKinnon had failed, little Mrs Buchanan had succeeded, and Effie didn't doubt he'd hear about it soon enough. 'I hate it here, Flora! I can't stand it!'

'Sssh, you need to keep control of yourself,' her friend said, steering her away towards a corner. 'It doesn't have to be forever. Just let things be for a wee while, let the waters settle. I know it's hard.'

'*Hard?* I've left my home and seen my dog killed, all so that I could live in a house worse than the one we left? Up a track with only Norman Ferguson for help? Doing a job that'll kill me within the month?'

'Why should it kill you?' Flora frowned. 'There was nothing ever so dangerous as climbing the cliffs.'

'The boredom, Flora! I'll die of being inside! Of wearing these damned boots all day!'

A couple of heads turned at her cuss, watching as she kicked at the ground.

'Sheesht!' Flora whispered, eyes glittering with concern that Mrs Buchanan should be called over again. 'This is no time for starting a revolution.'

Effie glowered at her friend. 'Since when did you become so *docile*?'

'You know I'm not that.'

But her friend's voice was flat and toneless and she was still pale from the journey. She was struggling too. They were all of them like landed fish, gasping against the shock of air. 'Flora, why are you still here? I thought you were going straight to the city?'

Flora nodded. 'And so I will. But I can't just leave my

family behind without a backward glance. I'll get them settled first before I go.'

Effie watched the shuttles pass across the looms, biting back furious tears. 'It's all right for you. You can swallow this when you know James has something better waiting for you. But . . .' She met her friend's gaze. 'I can't stay here. I have to leave. I have to find somewhere else—'

'Gillies.' The bark was a command.

She turned to find Mrs Buchanan standing by the door, her dwarfed figure in silhouette as the sunshine glowed in the courtyard behind her.

'Sssht. Keep quiet. Don't make things worse,' Flora murmured, before bringing a light to her own eyes and smiling brightly. 'I was just explaining to her about the looms, Mrs Buchanan, as you asked.'

But Mrs Buchanan was in no mood to be appeased by the charm of a beautiful girl. 'The privy's blocked,' the older woman called, raising her voice so that everyone could hear. 'Deal with it, Gillies, seeing as you've already played in the muck today anyway.'

Effie's body tensed as Flora's hand on her arm tightened in warning. If there was a time to fight, there was also a time *not* to. She must pick her battles. They could do nothing on an empty stomach and she needed to put a meal on the table tonight. Everything else – including her pride – would have to wait.

Chapter Seventeen

'You're back,' her father said as she opened the gate. He was sitting by the door in his chair, smoking his pipe. A figure, crudely carved, was beginning to emerge from the stick resting on his lap. She wondered how long he'd been working on it today.

She forced a wan smile. 'Aye. And I have dinner.' She held up the bag of mutton chops the butcher had given her 'on account' till her first wages were paid. After work, she had stood and queued in a room lined with white shiny walls with Flora, Jayne, Lorna and Mhairi's mother, Rachel. There'd been no sign of Mhairi still. 'Her nerves,' Rachel had tutted, as they stood meekly awaiting the butcher's beneficence. 'The journey did for her.' One of the men had come through from the back at that moment and she'd glimpsed great carcasses hanging from hooks, blood running like a river into the drain. It had seemed a grotesque emblem for this land of plenty where food, and therefore survival, could be assumed.

'It's a treat and no mistake,' she said, walking through to the kitchen and dropping the brown paper parcel on the table. It rocked slightly, the four legs – like her bed – not quite touching at once on the uneven floor. 'We got mutton chops but there's a butcher in the village with a choice like you've never seen. We could have had kidneys, or hogget . . .' The butcher had laughed as the St Kildan women had looked on at the trays of assorted cuts with astonished expressions – so much choice; so much *just there*. 'Well, not today. He was doling it out, like it or not today, but once my wages are in hand, we can choose what we get.' She pulled out the potatoes and leeks and set them on the table. 'Can you imagine that? What will you want when we can choose?'

Her father shuffled in, the pipe still dangling from his lips as he bore his weight down on his stick. 'Whatever'll survive your boiling it to leather.'

'Ha!' she said flatly. 'Rachel McKinnon got given a shoulder and Jayne's got kidneys. They were so shiny! Like . . . lips!' She pulled a face. 'I'm not sure about those. She's going to tell me how they taste.'

She bent down to undo her laces, pulling off her boots and socks and spreading her feet on the bare stone. She felt the day's tension lift off her shoulders, returning something of her to herself.

'You smell bad,' her father muttered, sniffing the air.

Effie didn't respond immediately. It had been the excuse the local women had given to steer clear of her all day, their noses in the air as they passed by as though she was somehow lesser than them. 'Aye. It's dirty work pushing a loom all day, let me tell you.' She'd spent two hours clearing and then cleaning the privy.

'Loom? I thought you were working at the forestry?'

'So did I.'

There was a pause as their eyes met briefly but she looked away again, not wanting to see his disappointment. They both knew her factory job with the women meant less money.

'You'd best clean yourself before dinner. I canna eat with that stench. Scat. I'll bring out the hot pan once it's boiled.'

With an impatient huff, he turned away. She slipped out through the back door and pressed on the well lever, watching as water rushed into the tub, running rust-coloured for the first minute before it began to come clear. The copper was streaked green, with some upside-down beetles, a long-legged spider in the bottom, and a couple of fossilized fern leaves stuck to the sides. A large rhododendron served as a privacy screen of sorts, not that there was anyone around to see – or want to see – her naked.

She watched the tub fill slowly, remembering the baths that had punctuated her brief time with Sholto back home – the day she'd leapt for the boat off the cliff and half landed in the water, the next day when they'd had a water fight in the bay, two days after that when he'd given her another swimming lesson as an excuse to put his hands on her, to be with her. Every time she'd come back shivering. Wanting more.

'Coming through,' her father said, rounding the rhoddie and unceremoniously dumping the hot water into the tub. The steam instantly dissipated. 'Towel for you,' he said, draping the ragged cloth over the bush. He limped away again and she quickly stripped off her clothes and climbed in. The water was still breathtakingly cold, the hot pan only just enough to nudge the temperature off turgid. The depth barely came to her hip bones as she sat down but she wasn't one to linger and she began splashing the water over her arms and face, her teeth gritted. There was an old milk pail on the grass and she reached for it, scooping the water over her head, spluttering and gasping as the biting cold plunged over her shoulders and down her back. She gasped with every splash, her skin rippled with goosebumps as she moved quickly to remove the stench of the day. The mud from the bog had seeped through her trousers, painting her leg brown up to the knee like a woollen sock, and she scrubbed as best she could. Mrs Buchanan had made it clear she was to arrive for work in the morning dressed in women's clothes, her hair brushed and neatly tied back.

Effie took a deep breath and leant back, bending her knees and sliding down the tub until she could get her back flat and her head and ears under the water. It was as cold as swimming in the sea but she forced herself to remain under as she scrubbed her scalp with her fingertips, her long hair floating around her face like seaweed.

A minute later she emerged with another gasp. Frozen, but clean at least. She stepped out of the bath and clutched the thin towel around her, shivering as the water dripped, not wanting to release the towel from her shoulders and brush herself dry.

Something came to her ear as she stood there, rigid with cold. Voices? There was no window to see through at the back, and the words were indistinct through the thick stone walls, but she could hear it was a man. She could guess who, too – Norman Ferguson, come to rat on her and enlighten her father as to this morning's latest shame as she came to blows with Angus McKinnon. If he was to hear about Mrs Buchanan as well . . .

She dried herself quickly, determined to give her account and not let his stand as the official record of events. She let herself into the bedroom through the back door and pulled some clean clothes from the trunk. She could hear the voices in the other room, though they were still indistinct through the closed door. She pulled on a patched shirt and John's soft moss-green trousers that were slightly too short for her now.

She opened the bedroom door and headed for the kitchen, but as she stepped through the lobby, her gaze caught something vast and shiny, something burgundy-coloured, in her peripheral vision. It was just a cursory glance and she was in the other room before her brain had processed that it was a car – and that the man talking to her father was not Norman Ferguson.

He greeted her with a look of relief, and she remembered he spoke not a word of Gaelic.

'Your Lordship!' she exclaimed.

'Miss Gillies, there you are. I was just asking after you.' The Earl of Dumfries was wearing an expensive suit and a homburg hat. 'What a pleasure it is to see you again.'

'And you, sir,' she said hesitantly, unable even to swivel her eyes and look openly around the room. Was his son here? Outside? It had been 106 days since the sloop's three-lighted masts had disappeared around Dun – catching a tide, racing a storm – and Sholto Crichton-Stuart had disappeared into the blackness. She'd heard nothing from him since. Lorna had grown used to her loitering by the postal hut whenever a ship came by and the mail was delivered, hoping there might be something for her . . . but a louder silence had never whistled through the Minch. The facts were plain – he had returned to his world and left her alone in her own.

'As I was just telling your father . . .' he began, and Effie could only imagine the torment for both men as they waited for her, unable to understand one another. Little wonder the earl seemed pleased to see her. 'I'm on my way back from a few days' shooting at MacLeod's estate, and I thought I would look in and see how you're finding things.'

I, singular. He wasn't here, then. The adrenaline that had shot through her body like a bullet slowed to a stop. She felt her body sag with dismay. '. . . You thought of us, sir?'

'Of course. Sir John can talk of nothing else at the moment, naturally. He and I have been discussing . . . certain matters pertaining to the archipelago.' He smiled obliquely. 'But it put you in my mind again and I thought, seeing as I was passing, I would look in. I hope you don't mind the intrusion. I know I ought really to have called ahead.'

'Not at all sir. You're always welcome here.' She tried to gather her wits, to remember the manners her mother had always insisted upon. 'Would you like to join us for dinner, sir? We've plenty.' Her stomach grumbled, as if in protest at the lie.

'You're too kind, but I'm afraid I must leave forthwith for an arrangement in Glasgow that has been long-standing. It is most tedious but nothing can be done.'

'Of course, sir.' She couldn't help but be relieved that she wouldn't have to forfeit her chop after all – her first 'easy' meal in the land of plenty, a dinner she hadn't had to hunt, catch, kill and pluck first, although given what she'd had to endure to get it, she wasn't sure anything about it was easy.

Lord Dumfries allowed his gaze to skirt the tiny room. 'Well, I must say, all things considered, they've done a . . . fine job, finding homes for everyone.'

Effie bit her lip. Her views on that matter were firmly opposite. 'Aye, sir.'

'It's a dashed tricky logistical exercise, moving man and beast across the water like that, providing homes and jobs. It's no mean feat. No mean feat at all.' He looked back at her, a convivial light in his eyes that reminded her of his son. 'Although I'll be honest . . . I think perhaps I could offer you better. The light is somewhat . . . poor, here.'

A silence opened up as she – and her father, who was understanding not a word – looked back at him in bafflement.

'You see, I have a proposal for you, Miss Gillies—'

Her heart lurched at his words.

'—I want you to come and work for me. Come to my estate in Dumfries and do what you do best.'

'Fowling?'

He gave an amused laugh. 'Ha, no, sadly not! We've nothing like the numbers of birds you're used to, for one thing.'

'Oh. So you mean cragging, then?'

He hesitated. 'No, not that either. I'm afraid you'll be very disappointed with our hills. They're pale imitations of what you're used to.'

She waited for him to tell her what he wanted her to do, then. Feed his animals? Weave his tweeds?

'Miss Gillies, I want you to come to Dumfries House and curate my ornithological collection.'

'What?'

Lord Dumfries smiled. 'You know my passion for bird life was what brought us to your shores originally this summer. I thought I was something of an expert, but I don't mind admitting that in the space of under a week I – or rather, *we –*' he said, referencing his absent son, 'learnt more from you than we ever did from a book, professor or birder.'

Effie blinked.

'The truth is, I'm being courted by a museum in London. They believe my personal collection of eggs, feathers and whatnots merits an exhibition and, whilst I am still undecided, it has concentrated my mind on organizing the collection with the care it deserves. I have a great many specimens but I'm not too proud to admit my interest lies in the chase and procurement; cataloguing is rather too time-consuming for my diary and things have become somewhat muddled.' He looked at her carefully. 'What do you think?'

She had a feeling of her world shifting, its walls vibrating, though whether they should fall in or outwards, she wasn't sure.

'You would be given lodgings on the estate in Ayrshire, several hours south from here. And a decent wage, of course.' He named a sum that made Effie's mouth fall open. It was more than the men were receiving at the forestry; Jayne had told her what Norman was earning as they were standing in line at the butcher's earlier.

She felt her blood rush. This proposal was more than she could have dreamt – not just that she would be given a man's wage for doing what she loved, but being in the earl's employ was the very escape she sought. She might not be out of sight there – word would get around – but it would put her out of reach. The earl would be untouchable. She would be safe there.

She glanced at her father. He was standing by, mute and inert, and she knew he felt humiliated that it was she who was conducting the conversation with the earl and not him. It had been bad enough back home that he could not earn, but now here, not even to communicate . . . His voice had been the only remaining strength he had.

She saw the pain in his eyes that he could not contribute in any single way. Strained though their relationship might be, there was no question of leaving him.

'You are so generous, sir, and kind too, to think of me when there are so many others better qualified.'

'Nonsense. You have real-world knowledge. An instinct for the subject.' He regarded her, seeing her downcast eyes. 'Miss Gillies, I hope this isn't leading to a "but".'

She shook her head slowly. 'I'm sorry, sir, but I can't leave my father.'

'Of course you cannot! And you must not! It was never my intention to separate you from your father. Where you go, he goes. There would be room for you both, naturally. We will most surely have a cottage on the estate that could be made ready for you both.'

She blinked, marvelling at how easy everything was in his world. 'Really?' She hardly dared to hope it could be true. They could leave this dank, dreary house – just like that? She would never have to see – or work for – that harridan Mrs Buchanan again? They could turn their backs on this new life that had been foisted upon them and choose one of their own making?

But . . . 'Does Lord Sholto know you're asking this?'

'Sholto?' He seemed surprised by the question. 'No, not yet. He's been in France for the summer. He's back now, living it up in London, though we've yet to see him. The countess keeps trying to get him over the border; he must have worn himself out with all those silly parties. Still, her birthday's coming up, so he'll have to be back for that, and I'll tell him then. But I know he'll be delighted. He's very fond of you, told me on the journey home you'd become great chums.'

Chums? She'd never heard the word before, but it didn't *sound* like what he'd been to her. She remembered how it had felt to rise on those mornings in that week in May, knowing he was down the street, that she would spend the day with him. The days had felt golden and for the only time in her life, she had understood what it meant to be rich, to have more than anyone else. But then he had gone – to France, and now London. While she'd cried and malingered for him on Hirta, he had been at parties, laughing and dancing . . . ?

The earl replaced his hat and looked at her. 'So that's a yes, then – yes?'

Her mouth parted. She felt rushed. It was so much to take in – she suddenly had a solution to her one overwhelming problem, but it also created a problem with what had been a solution. Sholto's enduring silence may have told her what she hadn't wanted to hear, but at least it had been absolute. To come and live on his estate, when he had no knowledge of it; no say . . . She would be as welcome as the boiled fulmar on his plate. But what other choice did she have? They couldn't stay in this place, and she couldn't earn enough for the two of them on her woman's wage here.

'. . . So long as my father agrees, sir. I'll need to discuss it with him first. It's only right.'

'Of course, of course, though I'm sure he'll see the sense in it.' His eyes flitted lightly around the damp room again. 'I'll wait for your answer, but please don't delay. Preparations will need to get underway before you arrive and it's probably best to give notice to your new employer sooner rather than later. Although they've only had you for a day, so they can't be too disgruntled with me for stealing you away.'

'They're already sick of the sight of me,' she said.

He laughed as though she'd told a joke. 'I'm afraid I must dash, but I'm pleased to have taken the trouble in finding you here. Someone will be in touch in the next few days for your answer.' He tipped his hat. 'Mr Gillies. Miss Gillies.'

'Sir,' Effie nodded, her father dumbly doing the same.

The two of them walked to the doorway and watched as the earl passed through the garden gate and stepped into his gleaming car, the door held open for him by a man in uniform with silver buttons. Effie was rapt – the car and the driver were her first glimpses into his real life, the one that had been hidden from her on St Kilda. What else would be different, she wondered, when they got there? Fewer seabirds, disappointing hills; that was all she knew.

The car pulled away with a purr and Effie waved haltingly.

'So? Are you going to t' tell me what that was all about?' her father demanded, pulling his pipe from his jacket pocket and dangling it from his lower lip.

'He offered me a job,' she said quietly. 'Organizing his bird egg collection.'

Her father looked unimpressed and she knew the foibles of the rich must seem ridiculous to him. 'What nonsense,' he muttered.

'A museum in London wants to put on an exhibition of them. It sounds important. He's prepared to pay me a man's wage but we'd have to move to a cottage on his estate in Dumfries; it would mean leaving here. I said I'd have to ask you first. It's your decision, Father.' Her heart thudded as she gave away control of the situation and she didn't know what frightened her most – if he'd say yes, or if he'd say no.

He was quiet for several moments as he lit his pipe. 'A man's wage, you say?'

'Aye.'

'And we'd have our own cottage?'

'That's what he said. But in Ayrshire, a hundred miles from here.'

Her father's eyes rolled over the damp stone walls, the rough floor, the barren landscape outside the window. '. . . Tell him yes, then.'

She felt her heart – which must have been holding its beats – gather into a gallop. 'You're sure?'

'If it comes down to being hungry here or well-fed there, then I'm sure. We need the money now.'

253

She swallowed. 'But what about Old Fin and the others?'

His lips turned down. 'What about them? If they're two hundred yards away and I can only walk twenty, then they may as well be two hundred miles away.' His voice was flat, his eyes hooded with despair. 'The old days are gone, lass, and there's no point in wishing otherwise. We asked for this and now we must live w' it. Lochaline or Dumfries, if it's no' Hirta, then it makes no difference t' me.'

Chapter Eighteen

The door opened with a creak, revealing a long but narrow room that tapered at the far end. A double-sash window that filled the end wall allowed in the soft afternoon light. It was grey outside and fast growing dark, but there was no gloom here as the housekeeper flicked a toggle on the wall and lamps were instantly, magically lit.

The walls were a pale green and there was a brightly coloured rug on the flagged floor beside the single wooden bedstead. Effie had never seen so many colours woven together in such an intricate pattern before – so unlike the muted vegetable-dyed tweeds she knew – and she walked over to it with a look of wonder. It was decorous and pretty and utterly curious; in her world, things had only ever been functional.

The bed, alongside the left wall, was made with white linens and covered with a cream blanket that had 'DH' woven in brick-red bold type across the middle. Opposite were a table and chair. A slim sheaf of paper was piled neatly on top, with a curious turned pole on the corner edge.

Effie reached an enquiring hand to it, before looking back at the housekeeper with a quizzical expression.

'A hatstand,' Mrs McKenzie replied after a moment, as she understood that Effie was at a loss. Her gaze pointedly moved to Effie's bare head, her long pale hair loosely held back with a broken piece of bootstring.

Effie turned away, still absorbing the pretty room. She had never had a room of her own before, not a proper one – only ever the byre, then the closet with no windows, then for one week, the shared one with her father with the sheet hanging down the middle. She saw, in the embrace of the window nook, a wash-stand with a blue and yellow floral painted jug, some rails with towels draped on them. And something else . . . She squinted quizzically, before walking over. The thing was oval and set upon the wall; it had a small shelf below, but above it—

Oh!

She stepped back in surprise as a face suddenly appeared on the other side. The other girl looked surprised and stepped back too. There was a moment's silence as they stared at one another and it occurred to Effie that this was a peculiar place to set a window.

A couple of moments passed before she realized the girl appeared to be copying her—

'It's a mirror, Miss Gillies,' Mrs McKenzie said into the silence as Effie moved her head, first one way and then the other. 'You've surely . . . seen yourself before?'

A mirror? She had read about them in books, naturally, but there had been no need for people to look at themselves back home. Vanity was a sin, the minister always told them at Sunday service.

Effie peered more closely, raising a hand and tentatively touching the mirrored glass. She tapped a nail against it. Back home, she could sometimes see an essence of herself in the summer waters in the bay, when the wind dropped in the late afternoon, but this time, the impression didn't scatter at her touch. The girl just blinked back at her. She had big round eyes that were the blue of March, hair the colour of barley. She pressed her fingers to the skin of her cheeks, but the freckles didn't disappear and she saw – compared to the housekeeper, the strangers on her journey, and the villagers of Lochaline – how very much more brown her skin was than theirs. It was because of the way the wind carried heat, as well as salt, to their island. All her neighbours had the same brazened look too. She bared her teeth – they were pearly bright; the whites of her eyes too – and finished with her hands on her cheeks as she blinked and pulled fearsome expressions, seeing herself in every attitude for the first time.

The housekeeper cleared her throat. Effie realized she had forgotten all about her, and dropped her hands with a blush.

'Your laundry and linens will be washed once a week, on a Thursday. Make sure they're in the basket by Wednesday night.'

'Oh, I can do my own.' She had never had anyone else wash her clothes before and the idea of it was strange.

'That would be disruptive,' Mrs McKenzie said disapprovingly.

'Oh.' Effie nodded her acquiescence; the housekeeper made 'disruptive' sound very ominous indeed.

'Breakfast is at seven. Dinner at twelve. Tea at six, not a minute later or you'll go without. Mrs McLennan is a stickler for keeping good time, as she might well be. The days are busy enough without being kept waiting for others.'

'Of course.' She turned to face the housekeeper. 'When will our cottage be ready, do you know? I must make arrangements for my father to travel.'

He had remained in Lochaline for the short term in order that the bothy which had been chosen for them, somewhere on the estate, could be restored first. Apparently, upon closer inspection, the roof had partially collapsed, the door was rotted and the chimney needed repointing.

Effie was being put up in one of the rooms in the servant's attic, to begin her new job until the cottage was ready and her father could join her. Jayne had promised to look in and sit with him every day, and to bring him meals in her absence – but still Effie worried. With her meals and board provided here, she would send her wages back to him till he could be put on the train and brought down here; Lord Dumfries had even promised his driver would collect him from Glasgow. It was a luxury she hadn't been afforded – she had walked the hour trek from Auchinleck station herself, the blisters on her heels forcing her to a limp by the time she reached the estate. She had been grateful that her bag was reasonably light in her hands as she followed the unmade road. Her possessions amounted to the clothes on her back, her climbing tweeds, Sunday best, her brushes, paints and books. She had nothing else and she had been glad of it.

'I cannot say, Miss Gillies. That's the domain of Mr McLaren, the estate manager. I concern myself only with the running of the great house.'

The great house. It was certainly that. Effie's bag had dropped clean from her hand as she had caught her first glimpse of it from the bridge – a vast bluff building that chested into the gardens, with bustling chimneys on the roof and windows that stretched from ceiling to floor. The perfect symmetry, heroic ambition and sheer scale of it had astounded her; even in books, she had never seen such a sight. It was a palace, a home for a king! Even the gardens, of a deep and luscious green unknown back home, were clipped and shaped into patterns that swirled from the ground itself, bright-headed flowers nodding in deep beds. For several long, silent moments it had been as though her very eyes had deceived her. She had only ever known nature to be wild and untameable, a punishing force against which they continually battled for survival; but here it was nature that bowed into deep submission to man's whimsy, as though a plaything to be whittled and fashioned.

She had looked on in astonished, aghast wonder, recognizing for the first time the breach between her world and Sholto's and she had wondered what he must have thought when he had stepped into *her* domain. Had he thought it less than this – or more? Wasn't there a majesty to her world? Wasn't its very wildness exhilarating—?

'I'll leave you to settle in, Miss Gillies. My office is downstairs, second on the left.'

Stairs. Even they were a novelty.

The door closed with a precise click and Effie sank onto the bed as if her knees had buckled. How much had her world changed over the course of this past week? She had left not one home but two; she had sat in a car, caught a bus, jumped on a train. She had climbed stairs, looked in a mirror, seen her face fully for the first time in her life. After eighteen years of living to the same rhythm as her neighbours and family, suddenly it felt like life and all its varied experiences were on fast-forward as she tried them for size, one after the other.

She pulled off her wretched boots and examined her latest batch of blisters before nestling her feet in the coloured rug. It would be the last thing she felt as she climbed into bed at night, and the first thing as she got up in the morning. How could she ever have foreseen – this time a little over a week ago, as she had chased after her beautiful dog on a clifftop – that she would come to be sitting here, in a pretty room in a great house? Outside there could be a howling gale, and she would know nothing of it. The roof didn't leak. Lights came on without oil lamps. Heat was funnelled through hot pipes. A basin meant she could wash indoors . . .

Already she could feel her sinews beginning to relax and her body starting to sink into this 'softer' life they had heard of on the mainland, where life wasn't just about survival but beauty and culture, too: music, fashions, art. Things that looked good, felt good . . . A sensuous life, not a hard-bitten one.

She lay back tentatively on the bed. It creaked. A spiderweb clustered in the far corner but there was no sign of its owner and she stared up at the frame that went around the edges of the ceiling. She could hear distant voices and the sound of glass bottles rattling somewhere down the corridor, footsteps crunching over gravel, a household in motion.

His household. *His* home. Could she really be in it? She couldn't sense him here.

Outside, the sky darkened, grey clouds scudding. Was a storm coming? It was harder to read here, without the winds and the birds and the sheep . . .

A vision of the storm cleit flashed through her mind again, the one that woke her almost every night, and she got back up as if jabbed by unseen spikes. She walked to the mirror and regarded her own reflection once more. She couldn't help but feel disappointed by what she saw. She had expected to look somehow fiercer, wilder than this. Had she looked different last week, *before*? She felt the memories of that last night shift and stir like nocturnal creatures rising with the moon – they were always there now, never quite gone, even though she refused to give them space in her mind. It had taken three days for her body to climb down from fight or flight mode – for the shakes to stop, for her breathing to steady, for proper sleep to come. It had been the earl's offer of refuge here that had salved her traumatized mind.

She stared into her own eyes, trying to see into her very soul. All that was behind her now, she told herself. She was free. She had done what she had to do and freed herself. He wouldn't hurt her again. No one would. She remembered how she had taken her leave of Mrs Buchanan five days earlier – she had made a point of walking into the barn late the next morning, dressed defiantly in her brother's climbing tweeds again, no boots. She had let the mealy-mouthed woman fly at her again but this time, when her hand had sliced towards Effie's cheek, she had caught it firmly in her grip – the way she did when she wrung a guillemot's neck – and calmly asked for her single day's wages. Without further explanation, she had then crossed the courtyard, paid the butcher and discharged her meagre debt. She had precious little but she had her honour and she had left as she had arrived, under the weight of curious stares. She *wasn't* like the rest of them, but their mistake had been to assume that she wanted to be.

She went over to the window and pressed her face to the pane instead, rolling from cheek to cheek and trying to cool her skin against the cold glass. Her gaze fell to the gravelled courtyard below. It was well swept and bare save for some barrels lined up against a high brick wall opposite, with an arched gate set in the middle. From where she stood, she couldn't see much of the triumphant gardens beyond it, only scattered treetops with distant birds alighting; but as the gate opened and a gardener walked through, she caught another glimpse – like a fan opening – of hot, riotous colour: orange, red and yellow flowers, some pointing to the sky like wands, others stippling the air like an artist's brushes. It was a garden just like Eden, just like the minister had told them about as he stood at his lectern and warned them against temptation. Against sin.

Too late, she was already a sinner now. There could be nothing in that garden to further her fall. She could walk through it and eat all the apples. It struck her as ironic that it was Sholto who had first given her an apple, first led her into temptation, and now here she was, on the wrong side of his garden. Cast out.

But then she'd always been on the wrong side of life – born a daughter and not a son; a peasant and not an heiress. She stared at her brightening reflection in the glass as the sky dimmed and rain began to tap against her window, droplets wriggling down the pane like silvered worms.

She stood and watched from inside her warm, well lit, pretty room, knowing that on a lonely dark mountain, somewhere in the sea, there would be sheep walking in single file towards the stone-stacked cleits. Like her, that last night, looking for shelter.

Chapter Nineteen

'. . . wants a full polish of the Bowes silver. His lordship's expecting a—'

Everyone was already seated at a large table when she walked into the servants' hall; twelve faces turned as one, as though pushed by the wind, eyes grazing up and down the length of her as they took in their newest recruit.

'Who's this?' someone asked, a young boy with an impish look.

The men were dressed in dark-tailed suits and vests with crisp white shirts; the women wore black dresses with white aprons. Everyone was pale, significantly paler than Effie, and her brown cloth trousers seemed rough and lumpy in comparison to their starched uniforms.

'This is Miss Gillies,' the housekeeper said through a puckered mouth. 'You're just in time, Miss Gillies – you can sit at the end there between Mr Graves and William.'

Effie saw an empty chair beside a sandy-haired footman who was looking at her with ill-concealed dismay, and a man at the head of the table with grey hair, a long face, a beaked nose and spectacles. There was something of the eagle about him.

'Everyone, this is Miss Euphemia Gillies, lately of the isle of St Kilda. She will be residing with us whilst the bothy is refurbished for her and her father. Miss Gillies is to work with his lordship on his ornithology collection.'

A quizzical silence enveloped her as she took the seat with an apprehensive smile. Was she really so fearsome?

'Hello,' she said to the room, her gaze alighting upon that of a housemaid opposite, around her age. She was deeply freckled with light brown hair pulled back in looped braids. She had an open, round face and enquiring hazel eyes; Effie could imagine how she looked when she laughed – but the girl looked away immediately as if for fear of being read. Effie wondered what it was about her specifically that prompted such strong reactions. Was she too coarse, too brown, too rough, too unfeminine? Too wild? Could they sense the danger in her?

A plate of food was set down before her by a kitchen maid as Mr Graves bowed his head and said grace. Everyone followed his lead and began to eat and for several moments, the only sound in the room was the tinkle of steel upon china. Effie stared down at her plate, not sure what it was she was going to be eating. It was some sort of meat pie, she could glean that, but there were small bits in bright colours she'd never seen before – green, orange. She separated them from the meat and pushed at them quizzically with her fork.

'Do the carrots and asparagus meet with your approval, Miss Gillies?' Mr Graves enquired with a disapproving tone.

Carrots? Asparagus? That's what they were! She looked back at him with a smile and nodded. The only vegetables she'd ever had were potatoes or turnips; and the only green thing she'd eaten was kelp from the sea. Tentatively, she cut a morsel and took a tiny bite. Flavours exploded on her tongue and she pressed a hand to her mouth as if trying to keep them in. She had never known food could taste like that.

'. . . As I was saying,' Mr Graves faltered, after a moment, looking back from her to the housekeeper. 'Her ladyship wants to use the Bowes silver tomorrow, with the Coronation service.'

'Well, make sure you include the fish knives. They're having salmon. Mr Dalwhinnie's outdone himself. Landed as big a fish as I've ever seen. We scarce had enough ice in the ice house,' said a very round woman in a grey dress, full apron and sleeves rolled up to her elbows. It was clear she was the cook Mrs McKenzie had warned Effie about – Mrs McLennan. Her face was slightly floured, her cheeks ruddy from working in a steamy kitchen. 'Are they still at nine heads?'

'At present, but account for one more in case. You know how *flexible* dinner arrangements are becoming,' Mr Graves murmured.

'The modern way,' Mrs McKenzie sighed.

Effie kept her eyes on the plate, too distracted by her meal to tune in to the conversation. Her body was almost tingling to the rich, creamy tastes. It had always been a treat to have roast puffin when they flew over to nest in spring but this meal was more than just fuel; she felt something in her body wake up, as though a part of herself was blooming into colour.

'Will her royal brightness be in attendance?' someone asked from further down the table. Effie couldn't see who, but she immediately picked up on the note of sarcasm in the question.

Someone else tittered.

'Thank you, Billy,' Mrs McKenzie said sharply. 'That's quite enough.'

'I'm only asking because last time her cat shredded the silk chaise in the Yellow Room and I had my wages docked for not declawing it first. But have you seen the teeth on that thing? How was I supposed to get near its *feet*?'

'Billy, I said enough,' the housekeeper snapped as there were more titters.

Effie allowed herself a grin; the stuffy politeness of the room was beginning to break up as people became more concerned with filling their stomachs than scrutinizing her.

She looked down the table and tried to catch sight of this rogue Billy, briefly making eye contact with the bright eyes in the impish face she'd seen earlier. He looked a year or two younger than her, she thought. He looked like trouble always found him, too.

'So, Miss Gillies, you are a St Kildan,' Mr Graves said, as though this explained some things.

'Yes.'

'That makes you almost a celebrity,' said a housemaid opposite. 'You've all been in the papers for weeks.' She gave a sudden smile. 'I'm Jenny.'

'Hallo, Jenny. I'm Effie.'

'Are you finding things . . . different, here in civilization?' Mr Graves asked. Effie watched as he cut a slice of his pie and placed it carefully in his mouth.

'No,' she replied quickly, feeling an instant heat in her blood. 'Because we were perfectly civilized on the isle too. We attended school and kirk, like you. We just had to work in a different way to feed ourselves.'

There was a small silence as the indignation in her words was received, and sidelong smirks were passed around the table.

'Indeed. Although I understand you had never seen your own reflection before this afternoon?' Mr Graves replied.

Effie shot a look back at the housekeeper, who at least had the decency to avert her eyes. Another titter rippled around the room, but this time no one was told to keep quiet.

'The mirror was a novelty, I admit,' Effie said quietly, with as much dignity as she could muster. 'As were the stairs. And electricity. I am coming across things I previously only read about in books.'

'You can read?' Jenny asked, sounding genuinely surprised.

'Is it true there are no trees over there?' asked William to her right.

'Quite true.'

'So you've never eaten an apple or pear?'

'An apple, yes; but not a pear . . . Not yet.'

The timid maid looked on with a look of curiosity and pity. 'What did you do for shade?'

'Shade?'

'On a hot day. Here, we sit under a tree if it's too warm outside.'

Effie thought for a moment. She'd never considered the lack of shade before. 'We have the stone walls that throw down shadows, or we'd sit in the cleits. If it was really too much to bear, we'd go down to the water.'

'I heard a funny thing,' another man said, everyone growing bolder now as her novelty value cast off inhibitions. 'That you're an island community, yet none can swim.'

'Aye, that was largely true,' she nodded, seeing the ridicule in his eyes. 'Often the water's too heavy for fishing or swimming. Although I can swim now and I'd started to teach the bairns before the evacuation. If we'd stayed, we would all have learnt. I'd have seen to it myself.'

'How did you *suddenly* learn to swim?' Mr Graves asked, with what she could see was his customary scepticism.

'Sholto taught me,' she shrugged.

Every set of eyes around the table widened.

'. . . What?' she asked, seeing their incredulousness.

No one replied, but she caught the looks that sped like pond-skaters between the staff, and she understood that somehow she had confounded them all.

'His lordship taught you to swim?' Mr Graves clarified.

Hadn't she just said that? 'Yes. In return for showing him and his father how to climb and set snares.'

'So you are an . . . expert on those things?' Mr Graves couldn't have looked more disbelieving if she had said she was the prime minister.

'I wouldn't have said so, particularly, but the earl seemed to value my opinion on them.'

'Would that explain, then . . . the clothes?'

Mr Graves was looking at her with an expression that seemed intended to convey another message: one of disapproval. She pulled at the coarse wool cloth that had once been her beloved brother's. 'Of course. You can't climb in a skirt. It wouldn't be very seemly.' She sensed that word carried weight here.

There was another silence, eyes back on the plates again.

'It was my understanding that on your isle only the men climbed.'

'Usually. But an exception was made, in my case.'

A pregnant silence bloomed but she left her full explanation hanging; she felt no need to give her family history to this room full of strangers.

'So are we to understand, given your attire, that you'll be doing much climbing here then?'

'I'm not sure yet . . .'

'Well, I would be intrigued to hear of where, exactly. Last time I looked, the land here was quite flat.' More titters rippled the air as Mr Graves allowed himself a satisfied smile. It was his snide way of telling her to dress differently.

268

'If his lordship doesn't object to my way of dressing, then I don't see why it should concern you,' she said bluntly.

She knew from the silence that followed that she had affronted the butler, the most senior man in the room – but she refused to recognize his rank as superior to her, when she wasn't a servant. The earl was employing her, yes, but in a capacity quite different to theirs. She wondered what they would say if they were to learn that the earl's son had kissed her, pursued her, yearned for her . . . even if only for a little while.

'When will Sholto be back from London?' she asked, unable to delay asking any longer. She didn't care what they thought of her. Let them think she was wild, primitive, savage, odd . . . It was the only thing she wanted to know. She was here. How long must she wait?

'*Lord* Sholto is expected back tomorrow, Miss Gillies,' the butler said with particular stress. 'Though he may be delayed – partly on your account, I should add.'

'Mine?'

'Yes.' The butler sighed wearily. 'Apparently your old landlord's factor has gone missing. No one's seen him since before the evacuation and Lord MacLeod is working up a lather wanting to know what's happened to his man. It's quite the brouhaha.'

Effie felt the blood drain from her face, a twist in her guts.

'There's a press man on the case now, I believe,' Mr Graves continued. 'A Mr Bonner. Do you know him . . . Miss Gillies? Apparently he was covering the evacuation for *The Times* of London and stayed on the isle for the last week.'

And now he was investigating Frank Mathieson's disappearance? Mathieson was still missing? Effie's mind was racing, her pulse too fast. '. . . But why should that be anything to do with m-me?'

Mr Graves gave a quizzical smile that didn't reach his eyes. 'I was speaking figuratively – about you St Kildans as a whole. I didn't mean you personally, Miss Gillies.'

'Oh.' She stared at her plate. The pie was only half touched but she suddenly felt sickened by the rich palate. Overwhelmed. The room felt airless, friendless. She pulled at her collar and stretched her neck. It was so hot in here. Wasn't it hot in here? She pressed her feet to the floor, wanting to feel the ground, to root herself as images began flashing through her head again, but the leather soles of her boots were too thick to allow anything but a dull resistance. The walls of the room seemed to be pressing inwards, the floor beginning to spin. She closed her eyes, but that only made the visions more vivid. She felt so hot. So— She retched suddenly and the company around her flinched as one, like a shoal of fish.

'Miss Gillies!' Mrs McKenzie cried as though this was some sort of game.

Effie couldn't reply. With her hand pressed to her mouth, she roughly pushed back her chair and ran through to the large kitchen, disgorging the contents of her stomach into the copper sink as Mrs McKenzie and Mrs McLennan followed, furiously scolding behind her. But her body was in revolt. She retched and heaved till only bile came up, her hand reaching blindly for the tap as horror washed through her.

'Miss Gillies, what on earth has come over you?' Mrs McKenzie demanded. 'You must compose yourself!'

Effie, her head hanging down, watched as the bright morsels of carrots and beans began to swirl before her watering eyes, circling the drain, her breath coming fast and shallow. Frank Mathieson was still missing? It couldn't be.

'For heaven's sake, child!' The cook suddenly placed her firm hands on Effie's skinny arms and roughly moved her two paces to the side. 'You'll block the pipes and then we'll have no end of bother.'

The tap was turned off amid a flurry of tuts and *God's truths*. Effie was trembling, her body enslaved to the whip-cracks of her mind. It couldn't be true . . .

'Well? What have you got to say for yourself?' Mrs McKenzie demanded, folding her arms across a pillowy bosom. 'Making a scene like that.'

Effie desperately tried to gather her thoughts, scattered though they were like broken glass. 'The food was too rich for me,' she whispered, scarcely able to get the words out. 'Please excuse me.' And she stumbled from the room, leaving the servants gawping in her wake.

She burst outside. It was raining hard and she was glad for it. She ran through the courtyard below her own window and opened the arched gate into the garden. The bright, fiery colours seemed even more vivid in the wet as she ran on gravel paths past planted beds and high brick walls. Tears were streaming down her cheeks. If she could have caught her breath, she would have screamed, but her body could only fill with a silent, gaping horror.

She ran the width of the back of the great house, tall empty windows staring down on her with ghostly censure, the lawns rolling to a stop at a deep ha-ha, with sheep grazing beyond and the landscape rolling out to a distant haze. A voice in her head told her to keep running into it, to just keep going forward into obscurity and lose herself in an unknown land. She could still escape. There was still a chance to become someone new. Leave the past and the horrors it contained behind her.

Her legs couldn't stop wheeling, carrying her past the formal gardens towards a wood densely planted with ancient mossed trees. It looked like somewhere to disappear into and she ran headlong into the shadows, never stopping. Her hands reached out to brush the trunks as she passed, an instinctive reflex she didn't even notice at first, her heavy-booted feet continually catching on protruding roots and making her stumble. She could feel that something was chasing her, something at her back like a shadow she couldn't unstitch. Because even as the ship had hauled anchor and the islanders had waved their handkerchiefs at a home they were deserting, she had known it wasn't deserted.

Not then and still not now.

She stopped running at last, her legs giving out with the realization of what this meant, her hands falling into the mud as she tried to catch her breath. She sat back on her haunches and tipped her face to the sky, feeling the raindrops on her face as they fell in a chicane through the leafy canopies.

The tourist ship SS *Dunara* had been scheduled to make a planned crossing – the last of the season – three days after the islanders had left. She knew that high winds over the open sea could, and very often did, scupper the timetables, but the skipper would always be looking for any break in the weather so that the tourists could have their fill of what was now the ghost isle; the delay was usually only a day or two. But if the weather break *hadn't* come . . . Autumn could be rolling in across the Atlantic this very moment. The seasonal switch was usually abrupt and when it came – if it was already here – there was every chance the seas would be too high now till next spring. And then what?

She knew what.

She knew it very well. With the livestock shipped out and the paltry harvest already lifted from the ground, natural resources on the island were even more scarce. The battle for survival, always hard-fought there anyway, was tipped in the wrong direction.

It had now been eight days since the evacuation – but she had calculated on a rescue within four.

She pressed her forehead to the wet ground and sobbed. Oh God. What had she done?

Chapter Twenty

'You're too late,' Mrs McLennan said over her shoulder, already carrying the breakfast plates back through to the kitchen, as Effie appeared at the doorway to the servants' hall.

'Oh . . . no, I . . .' Effie demurred, her voice croaky. She had skipped breakfast quite deliberately, standing with her ear to the door as she heard the footsteps of the rest of the maids passing down the corridor, beginning their days. The last thing she had wanted was to share another meal with these strangers after last night's humiliation. 'I wasn't hungry.'

The cook stopped walking as if she'd cursed and stared at her suspiciously. 'You can't not eat.'

'I'm not hungry. Really.'

The cook's eyes narrowed. 'This is because of last night. It was too rich and now you've got the fear.'

'No, it's not that—'

'Sit down,' said the cook firmly, walking off with a tut. 'I thought this might happen.'

'Excuse me,' a maid said impatiently, trying to get past her with a large vase full of drooping flowers.

Effie jumped out of her way, almost colliding with a valet coming in the opposite direction with an overcoat. 'Sorry. Sorry,' she muttered, hurrying over to sit alone at the long table, out of the way.

The servants moved past her with cold looks. The hall was a hive of activity, with footsteps echoing and voices carrying, the staff already engaged in their duties – footmen carrying in logs and polishing leather boots; maids arranging flowers on worktables, folding piles of laundry, the cooks chopping and stirring, the scullery maid drying copper pans that hung on hooks.

It amazed her that they were doing all this for *Sholto*. Well, his family, but to think that it required this many people to look after him – them – when over the course of that short week in May, he and his father had survived perfectly well in the factor's house. They had had no staff, no cooks beyond the minister's wife's cooking. They had eaten boiled fulmar along with the rest of the village, bathed in the stream . . .

'Here.'

She looked up to find the cook holding out a small plate with the brick-red border and 'DH' stamped in the middle. On it were two small oatcakes. In her other hand was a glass of milk.

'Plain enough for you?'

Effie took it listlessly. Her stomach was completely empty. 'Thank you.'

'Hmph,' Mrs McLennan retorted as she bustled off again. 'There's not enough of you as it is.'

Effie ate with rare timidity, feeling small. She wanted to fold herself down into tiny parts, to hide away from the world and what she'd done. She had spent most of the night – before exhaustion had won out – praying for the winds to drop, for the ship to sail, for a man to be rescued – but why should her prayers be answered now when they never had been before? She had lost her mother and brother, her beloved pet, and she had *loved* them.

When she had finished, she walked through to the kitchen and one of the scullery maids took the plate and glass from her hands before she could even open her mouth. Everyone was so hurried and busy, their mouths set in lines of grim determination.

Effie remembered what Mr Graves had said last night about Sholto and his father returning today.

'What time will Sholto be back?' she asked the maid.

The girl frowned deeply. 'What business is it of yours?' she snapped, turning her back and moving off.

Effie recoiled. She felt made of glass and like she might break into a thousand pieces with just one knock.

'Well, well, I almost didn't recognize you there, dressed as a girl.' She turned to find the dancing brown eyes of Billy, the hallboy, twinkling back at her. His gaze fell to her feet. 'Well, nearly. Part girl. Part . . . miner.'

She was wearing her Sunday best even though she wasn't going to kirk; it felt . . . prudent that she shouldn't stick out or make trouble. He gave an easy laugh, but she was in no mood for jokes, and his smile faded. 'Mrs McKenzie's ordered me to give you the tour and show you where you'll be working.'

'Oh. Yes.' She exhaled, her body relaxing a little. It would be good to have something to do. She wasn't used to standing idle and being in the way. She needed to be useful if she was to justify her place here. 'Fine. Lead on.'

Billy laughed again and gave a whistle as she walked up to him. '*Lead on*? Tell me something, what exactly are you to his lordship – servant or guest?'

'Neither. I'm their friend.'

At that Billy threw his head back and laughed. 'Oh boy.'

'Why is that funny?' she asked as he led the way out of the servants' hall.

He stopped in the small passage at the foot of a staircase and dropped his voice. 'Listen, a word of advice. You're sleeping and eating in the servants' quarters, but you keep calling his lordship by his given name. Calling him your friend. It gets people's backs up. You have to be one or the other, see? People don't like not knowing where the boundaries are. If you're down here with us, then use his title.'

She blinked, her cheeks hot. It hurt her to be reduced to just another member of staff when she and Sholto had met – if not quite as equals on Hirta – certainly as two free people instinctively drawn to one another. To be reduced to a servant, them and us . . . But staring back at Billy, she simply nodded. It was not Sholto who had brought her here but his father. She would only know 'what' she was when she saw his son again.

'Good. Things will be easier for you that way.' Billy stepped out into a long hallway. 'So this is the servants' passage. It runs the full width of the house and links the east and west wings, or pavilions, as the family say. They don't ever come down here and it allows us to get about quickly without being seen.'

He turned right and began walking. 'That's the butler's pantry, which leads into the silver room,' he said, motioning to a door on his left. 'Next to it there is the lamp room, with access to the beer cellar. On this side . . .' He turned slightly towards another narrow hallway leading off on the right. 'Over here's the decanting cellar, the wine cellar, and that room at the back there is the big boss, the steward's room – his name's Mr Weir. Weir by name, weird by nature, we like to say.' His eyes twinkled again. 'Don't worry, he's not here at the moment. He's gone to London to meet with Lord Sholto. That's the still room,' he added, vaguely motioning a hand to his left, but she had no interest in this myriad of rooms that she would surely never need to go into.

'Billy,' she said, following as he turned out of the passage into a curved lobby that marked the entrance to the west pavilion and led to another series of bisecting narrow passages. 'Is Mr Weir in London with Sh—' She stopped herself just in time. 'Lord Sholto, because of Mr Mathieson's disappearance?'

'Aye, so I understand.' He gestured towards a closed door. 'Brushing room.'

'Why are they in London, though, if Mr Mathieson disappeared in Scotland?'

'Lord MacLeod's down there at Scotland Yard, trying to get the best detectives on the case.'

Best detectives? The words were like iced water over her head. 'But why's Mr Weir involved? Mathieson was Lord MacLeod's factor, not the earl's.'

'Aye, but he and Mr Weir are friends.'

'They are?'

'Of course. The lairds are friends and their roles overlap. They both think they're the Big I Ams, don't they? Anyway, apparently Mr Weir thinks he knows something he should share with the fuzz—'

The fuzz?

'So he's gone to give a report. There's the coal cellar, gun room down that passage there, strong room—'

'Billy!' she said sharply. 'Please! I don't care about all these rooms!'

The hallboy looked offended.

'I'm sorry, but I've not been brought here as a servant. I don't need to know where the coal's kept. But surely you can understand that as a St Kildan, I want to know what is happening with Mr Mathieson? He was . . .' She thought the word might choke her. 'He *is* our friend.'

He didn't reply but his mouth was pursed. 'What is it you want to know?' he asked finally.

She balled up her courage, willing herself to speak, to make things right. 'If the factor was last seen on Hirta and no one's seen him on any of the boats coming back, surely the obvious place to look for him is on Hirta? He might have been left behind, somehow . . .'

'How could anyone have been left behind? People in Tasmania knew when the boat was leaving!'

She swallowed. 'Well, he could have had an accident and no one realized. Can't they send a boat back?'

He sighed. 'They're trying, but the winds up there have been too fierce.'

'Oh.' As she'd feared.

'But the forecast's better in the next few days.'

'It is? When?'

He shrugged. 'I'm just a hallboy. What do I know?'

She flinched, her heart pounding. Someone had to know, surely?

He began walking again and she followed him up a staircase, emerging onto a corridor on the first floor. Immediately the grand proportions of the family's part of the house presented themselves. Daylight fell in celestial sunbeams through domed roof windows, puddling in bright spots upon the floor. Giant portraits of the family hung from chains on the walls – the earl she recognized; the countess she guessed by her blue eyes, inherited by her son. Effie fell still as she stared at Sholto's portrait, feeling her stomach roll over. It was a good likeness and clearly recently done; it was the first sighting she had had of him since her father had walked her away on the Street that May afternoon. If she had known then it would be the last time she would see him, the last moment of happiness she would know before her entire life crumbled . . .

'He's a fine-looking fellow,' Billy said and Effie turned to find him watching her with a grin. 'Don't be getting any ideas, though.'

He gave a laugh as her eyes flashed. She followed him down a long corridor hung with more, older gilt-framed portraits and she felt herself shrink beneath the severe gazes of the long-dead people bearing down from the walls; they seemed to watch her with otherworldly omniscience, as though they knew her secret. They passed by giant colourful pots filled with flowers, wooden cabinets polished to a shine. Even the walls themselves were decorous with froths of plasterwork trailing floral tendrils. It was like walking through a king's dream, she thought.

This was where Sholto lived? Where he belonged? If she had seen the scale of the house last night, only now was she gauging its grandeur. He was wholly lost to her, she instinctively knew that. She understood finally – at last – why he could never have been hers, nor she his. Never ever. But she had been the only one who'd not known it and she felt a shot of anger that he could have allowed her to believe, even for a few moments, that their stolen kisses might have meant something.

Billy stopped outside a pair of double doors. He knocked twice and waited several moments before opening it, but the confidence with which he moved suggested he already knew the room was vacant. 'Your kingdom, Miss Gillies.'

It might have been ironic were it not true. She stepped into a room larger than all of the cottages on Hirta put together. The ceiling soared higher than a kirk spire, wooden cabinets fitted floor to ceiling along every wall, some with drawers and others half-glazed, a ladder required to reach the uppermost ones. Behind the glass were stuffed animals in frozen poses. Effie stared at them in alarm for several moments; she'd never seen the like and it was a difficult thing to comprehend.

'What is this place?' she murmured, her heavy boots echoing on the floor as she slowly walked in.

'This is the collection room; his lordship's had it fitted out to accommodate his . . . collection,' Billy said with a shrug.

In the middle of the room was a five-man-long polished table with a shelf beneath; it was laden with books and a tower of boxes piled high seemingly indiscriminately. She went over and pulled off the lid of the topmost carton. Inside, nestled in tufts of hay, lay three very small eggs, a pinky-cream colour, covered with tiny dark freckles. 'Grasshopper warbler,' she murmured, feeling the corners of her mouth lift in a small smile that she could identify it so easily, though she had never seen the bird herself.

She replaced the lid and wandered over to the cabinets. Idly, she pulled open the nearest drawer and was jolted out of her gentle, wondrous reverie by the sight of dozens upon dozens more eggs boxed in groups. She pulled open another drawer. The same. She looked quickly around the room at the sheer number of drawers – there had to be six drawers per cabinet. She counted quickly – twenty-two cabinets.

'How many eggs does he have?' she asked, her eyes wide.

'I guess you'll be the one telling us,' Billy shrugged, tipping his head as he took his leave of her. 'Have fun.'

'Fun,' she murmured. What was that?

The door closed behind him, leaving her alone. She stood there for several moments with no idea where to start. What exactly was it that the earl wanted her to do?

She ambled to another drawer and pulled it open, picking up an open box with two small eggs inside – they were pale grey and covered with dark brown trails, like a spider that had walked through ink. They were labelled 'Reed Bunting', but she frowned, picking one up and examining it more closely – those would be smaller than these eggs; these were Yellow Bunting, she was sure.

She put the egg back, then scrutinized the ones in the next box. It was the same thing – Linnet eggs confused for Bullfinch.

She checked every box in the drawer, and the next. There were widespread cataloguing errors, not in every box but largely across the board.

'Oh,' she sighed, looking around the room and knowing she had found her start.

She was sitting cross-legged on the floor, her socks and boots pulled off and left under the table, when the door suddenly opened. She had been cross-referencing the first lot of drawers for a couple of hours and was feeling stiff from the lack of movement. She'd never been so still for so long before.

The pale eyes of the maid she had sat opposite last night widened at the sight of her as Effie looked up from examining a sparrowhawk egg. It had been inexpertly blown and there was a faint crack to the bottom. It sat cradled in her palm like a bubble.

'I didn't know anyone was in here!' the girl exclaimed.

Effie's mouth parted but it was a moment before she spoke. '. . . I am.'

'Yes. I can see.' There was a short silence. 'I came in to dust.'

'Well, you still can. I won't stop you,' Effie said cautiously. She remembered all too well how the girl had turned away from her last night when she had been looking for a friendly face.

The maid hesitated, then stepped in with a decisive nod, as if she'd resolved something in her mind. She shut the door behind her and began tickling the surfaces with her feathered duster.

'Why have you taken your boots off?' she enquired after a few moments, reaching to catch a cobweb in an upper corner.

'. . . I don't like wearing them,' Effie muttered.

For several long minutes, they co-existed in silence. Effie bent her head to continue examining the egg but she was aware of the girl's stilted movements and she could almost feel the stirring of air as she kept looking over, intrigued by Effie's quiet industry.

'How can you tell them apart?' the maid asked finally, her curiosity getting the better of her.

Effie kept her head down. 'Practice,' she murmured.

'But how do you know them all?' the maid persisted. 'You couldn't have had all these birds on your island, surely?'

'No, but I read a lot of books too.'

'You had bookshops over there?'

'. . . No.' She gave an involuntary shudder at the memories now attached to the books; it caught the maid's attention. 'Chilly,' she murmured, looking away again.

The maid stopped pretending she was dusting and came over to inspect the egg now in Effie's hand. 'So what's that one, then?'

Effie looked up at her impatiently. 'It's a sparrowhawk egg.'

'And that one?' She crouched down close, hugging her knees, and pointed to its neighbour in the next box.

'That's a common tern.'

'That one too?' Her finger pushed lightly at the one beside it.

'No, that's a moorhen.'

The maid frowned. 'But it looks just the same.'

'Superficially, perhaps. But the moorhen has speckles that are finer and more evenly spread around the whole egg. The common tern has a plainer base with markings that are bolder and more like brushstroke tips. See?' She pointed out the differences.

'You need a good eye for detail doing this.'

'I suppose so,' Effie murmured.

The girl was staring at her openly now, last night's timidity seemingly gone. She smiled brightly, quite suddenly. '. . . My name's Fanny, by the way.'

Effie was surprised by the rapprochement. 'Effie.'

'I know. I remember. You made quite an impression, one way an' another.'

Effie looked quickly away again. She should have known this wasn't friendliness but plain curiosity.

'Hey, it's all right, you know. There's always a drama going on down there.'

'Is that why you were so quiet, then?' Effie asked bullishly.

'Yes! I stay out of it! Last night the excitement was all about you but it'll be someone else tonight . . . Probably Billy. Or one of them upstairs, seeing as they're all due back.'

Effie didn't reply but she felt the quickening of her heartrate. Was Sholto travelling back here, even now? She replaced the sparrowhawk egg in the box and put the lid back on.

'So are you really friends with Lord Sholto, then?' Fanny asked, as if reading her mind.

'I wouldn't have said it if it wasn't true.'

'It's just that . . . people like them aren't usually friends with people like us.'

'Us?'

'Aye, commoners. I know his lordship's a modern man, but even he has limits.'

'I wouldn't know about any of that,' Effie said after a pause. 'Where I'm from, you take people as you find them. Everyone's equal, more or less, though there's some as have more sheep.' She shrugged.

Fanny, who had been watching her closely, laughed suddenly. 'That's probably exactly what he likes about you, then. If you don't fuss over him, there's a novelty for him. He can't move for tripping over servants here.'

'Aye, I'd noticed.'

Fanny cupped her chin in her hand, watching her interestedly. 'Do you mean you *really* had no idea that he and his family were so important?'

'Aye. All I knew was they were friends of the laird, our landlord. But they didn't act . . . uppity or anything like that.'

Fanny's thin eyebrows shot almost up over the top of her head. 'So this place must have come as a shock.'

'You could say that.' There had certainly been a lot to absorb in the past twenty-four hours. '. . . How long have you worked here for?'

'Me? Four years,' the maid said proudly. 'I went into service when I was fifteen. My family lives in the next village. I've worked my way up from scullery maid already and if I keep my head down, I'll make lady's maid twenty years from now.'

'Twenty years,' Effie echoed. It sounded like a prison sentence.

'We're lucky, getting to work here. Their lordships are good people, they treat their staff well. It's not always the case, y'know.'

'I'm sure.' But she didn't want to engage again as a servant, and Effie picked up the next box and opened it to find a chiff-chaff egg. It was the first one she'd ever seen in real life and at least a fifth of the size of the sparrowhawk egg. The scale and delicacy of it surprised her. She supposed books could only show so much.

There was another pause and Effie could sense weight in Fanny's stare. She glanced up. '. . . What?'

'Have you found the banshee yet?' There was a look of mischief in Fanny's eyes.

'The banshee?'

'Aye.' Fanny rose and walked over to a cabinet along the far wall which had drawers all the way to the ceiling. 'Look here.' She pulled on a knob but instead of a drawer opening, an entire panel swung forward. 'They call it a jib door.'

Fanny looked supremely pleased with herself as Effie gasped with outright surprise.

'What's . . . what's in there?' she whispered, hardly daring to stand.

'Come and have a look for yourself,' Fanny said, walking through.

Effie drew her feet in and peered through. The room was half the size of the other one but in here, all the cabinets were fully glazed. Birds of every type and size were arranged on mounts, magnificent in death: a white-tailed eagle, goldfinch, blue-headed wagtail, nightjar, snowy owl, kingfisher, bittern, red-footed falcon . . . But there was one that was no pretty songbird, no apex predator – standing three foot tall, at first glance it looked like a giant penguin with angulated flippers and a macaw-like beak.

She frowned. It couldn't be, surely . . . ? 'A great auk?'

'Is that what it is?' Fanny shrugged, nonplussed. 'Well, if you say so. It gives everyone here the creeps. Mrs McLennan calls it the banshee.'

'But they've been extinct for . . . almost a hundred years!'

'Is that so?' Fanny seemed impressed by that revelation. 'So it must be valuable then.'

'I think there's only several dozen specimens left in the world, and they're all in museums.'

'Aye, well, his lordship does have a long reach.'

Effie didn't reply. She couldn't take her eyes off the bird. She had sunk to her haunches and was gazing at it through the glass, assessing the plumage, the markings on the beak, that distinctive shaping of the flightless wings. Was nothing impossible here, in this great house of beauty and grandeur, where a man could live like a king, where Mother Nature bent the knee and the dead lived on?

'*What* is going on in here?'

The suddenness, as well as the sharpness, of the voice startled them both. Fanny jumped and Effie lost her balance and fell backwards as they both turned to find the housekeeper darkening the doorway.

'M-Mrs McKenzie,' Fanny stuttered, bringing her duster upright like a soldier to attention. 'I was just dusting.'

But the housekeeper was no fool. She knew exactly what had been going on. 'If his lordship wanted that . . . *that* . . . on display, it would be on display, would it not?'

'Yes, Mrs McKenzie,' Fanny murmured. She began tickling the cabinets again, but it was to Effie that the housekeeper was directing her look of acute disappointment.

'The show's over. Out of here now and get back to work, both of you. Fanny, you're needed in the white drawing room.'

'Yes, Mrs McKenzie.'

Fanny followed after the housekeeper's brisk footsteps, but as she glanced back, her cheeks were pink and her eyes bright with a sense of adventure. Effie wouldn't have called that an adventure; she'd just have called it getting caught not working. They might be similar ages, but she was beyond girlish games. Life had already shown her what could happen when things went wrong.

She watched as the door closed behind the two women with a loud click, leaving her alone again with the collections of stuffed animals and blown eggs, memories of the last summer playing in her head.

Chapter Twenty-One

She was lost. Navigating a mountain was one thing, a house like this quite another. Everything was so geometric and repetitive – one corridor looked much like another to her eye and she had no idea where to go next. She'd been distracted by Billy's talk of Mr Weir and Mr Mathieson on the way over, that was the problem. Her brain had stopped paying attention to her feet.

A door to her left was ajar. If she could look in and see what it was, she might get her bearings . . . She peered into the large room, her eyes moving up, down and around, but it took only the merest glance to discern what it was and know that she'd never been here. She wandered in, wide-eyed, automatically setting her socks and boots down by the door as she absorbed the sight of the walls lined with books from ceiling to floor.

The room was dimly lit, the evening already drawing in, and the tall windows gave onto the shaded garden. A threadbare carpet lay underfoot and there were assorted groupings of high-backed leather chairs scattered about, as though someone had been playing a game of hide and seek with them. A tooled leather-topped reading desk was set in the middle of the room with an atlas opened onto . . .

She checked . . .

Onto the Outer Hebrides. A coincidence? Who had been looking at her home, she wondered. Father or son? Her finger automatically pressed on the tiny green dot amid the blue that had been her life. How small it looked from here. How insignificant. Why should the wider world ever have cared about their woes? It was a wonder to her that anyone had ever heard of her archipelago at all.

She looked around again at the shelves. There were more volumes than one person could ever read in a lifetime, all leather-bound and gilt-leaved. She walked over to the nearest stack and let her finger trip over the spines, feeling the indentations of the hand-stamped titles. She reached for one – Baudelaire's *L'Albatros* – and opened it. She couldn't understand a word but the mottled pages released a distinct and yet intangible scent. Instinctively, she raised it to her face and inhaled, savouring the smell. Several others she tried all yielded the same musty scent too. She walked further around, her hand trailing over the spines and her head tipped to the side as she read the titles, looking for words of interest.

Her attention fell upon a large book further along, set into a niche and placed on display on a wooden reading stand much like the minister had used in the kirk for his sermons. The book was opened onto an illustration that showed a large bird standing with its immense wings outstretched, like a phoenix. The image had been finely drawn and vividly coloured, the calligraphic text unintelligible at this distance. But she knew its contents; in fact, she knew them by heart, for she had the very same book, the very same edition. Right this moment it was carefully stowed in her bag beneath her bed and wrapped in an old woollen shawl that had belonged to her mother.

She felt an uneasiness turn over in the pit of the stomach.

She had instinctively known Mathieson's last gift was too good for someone like her, though she'd kept it anyway. She hadn't been able to hand it back, no matter how much her pride had advised otherwise. And she had paid the price. She had never asked him from where he bought her books, partly because it would have made no difference to her back then; she wouldn't have known one bookshop from any other, she'd had no perspective. But being here now and knowing she owned something that belonged in a house like this one . . . She knew he couldn't have afforded it, so how had he come by it? Had it been a gift to him first?

Carefully, she lifted it from the stand, feeling the same weight in her hands. It was too big to hold unsupported but she wanted to see more, to be sure the books were exact copies. She walked over to the nearest of the armchairs so that she might rest it in her lap—

The scream escaped her, the book a moment later as it fell to the ground, landing heavily face down, the cover splayed.

'What . . . wha . . . ?' she gasped, stumbling backwards into the side of another chair as the cheetah stared back at her. It had risen from its prone position at her approach and was now sitting upright, lower jaw hanging down and panting. Around its neck was a bejewelled sapphire-blue leather collar and the attached lead hung slack in a young, sleeping woman's hand.

'Hmmm?' she murmured, inhaling deeply and blinking slowly several times, gazing back at Effie through dreamy brown doe eyes. 'Oh heavens, don't say I fell into another nap?'

Effie gawped back. She couldn't take her eyes off the big cat. It was sitting less than six feet away from her, easily within pouncing distance. 'That's a cheetah,' she whispered, her voice faint with fear.

The woman seemed to come to. '. . . Why, yes,' she smiled languidly. 'I suppose she is. Her name's Margaux. Isn't she darling?'

When Effie didn't reply, the woman looked back at her.

'Heavens, you're awfully white. Oughtn't you to sit down? You look like you may faint, dear. Would you like some tea? Or something stronger? I find a G&T at this time terribly reviving.'

'I . . . I . . .' Effie's hands reached behind her, grasping for the route around the chair, but she wouldn't take her eyes off the cheetah for a single moment. Her bare feet poked at the ground for obstacles as she slowly navigated her way backwards until the library chair sat between them.

Feeling safer, knowing that if nothing else, she could at least duck, she slid her eyes towards the woman. She was sitting up now, quite awake, perched on the front of the chair with her knees pressed together and watching Effie with an expression of bafflement; she seemed completely unperturbed by the big cat sitting, panting, beside her. Her dark hair was styled in primped waves that scalloped around her doll-like face and she was wearing a mustard knitted jacket and skirt, with a knitted striped camisole and strings of luminous white beads around her neck. Effie had never seen anyone who looked quite like her before. She had an air of careless elegance about her.

'My name's Sibyl, Sibyl Wainwright, but all my friends call me Sid.'

'Sid?'

'It's cuckoo, I know, but my father did so want a son. It was no secret, poor Papa; at least this way one could oblige.'

'Oh.' Effie could relate to that.

The woman was smiling expectantly and Effie realized an

introduction was expected from her too. 'I'm Euphemia Gillies, but everyone calls me Effie.'

'How do you do. I say, are you just back from France?'

'France?' Effie was struggling to keep up with this woman's conversation, the threads picking up and being left off at odd tangents.

'I'm just back from there myself. We went for a quick blast on Dickie Grainger's new yacht. He's devilishly pleased with it, though I can't say I blame him. It is rather sweet and I find I colour so much more easily on the water . . .'

Effie was almost able to forget there was a cheetah sitting next to this woman as she chattered aimlessly.

'You've got such a wicked tan. It's all well and good getting out of our corsets and buying Madame Chanel's clothes,' she said, pinching lightly at her skirt, 'but I think it's the suntan that's really pip. So where do you go?'

'Go?'

'In France? I'm not really given to the Atlantic coast personally. Deauville's just a little too breezy for me and Île de Ré's wretched to get to without your own ketch. Parts of Provence are rather sweet though. Don't you think the smell of lavender in the air is just divine?'

'Divine?' A voice from the other side of the door echoed and in the next moment it was opened. 'Good Lord, Sid, what on earth are you doing in h—?'

Sholto walked in, the words dropping from him like birds shot from the sky as he saw Effie standing there, half hidden by a chair.

Effie couldn't blink. Nor breathe. Nor move. She certainly couldn't speak. She had thought the portrait of him vivid enough but she realized it had poorly served him after all, dishing up only a faint outline of the man standing before her now. His skin was a glowing golden brown, quite unlike her reddish, wind-burnt hue, and his blonde hair shone like spun gold; he looked lit from the inside.

'Effie.' The word was a croak.

'Hello, sir,' she faltered.

'Sir?' Sibyl – Sid? – looked surprised by the deference. Her eyes narrowed, as if she'd been duped. 'Why, the way you drifted through here, I thought you were a friend!'

It was an opportunity for Sholto to claim she was, but the moment came and went before he even stirred. 'I . . . I wasn't . . . expecting you.' Just like that, his tan had paled.

'Your father didn't tell you I was coming?'

'. . . I haven't seen him . . . yet . . . What are you . . . ?'

Neither one of them looked away. The thick, ancient walls seemed to have dissipated, the exotic cat no longer sitting on a Persian rug in a Scottish country house, the chattering woman sinking into silence . . . It was just the two of them again, as it had been in their last moments together on the island. *If we could talk . . . make a plan . . .*

'Are you quite all right, Sholto?' Sibyl asked, sitting back in her chair and crossing one leg over the other, swinging her foot. 'You look like you've seen a ghost.'

The woman's words seemed to jolt him from the trance of shock. He cleared his throat, glancing across at her and running a hand through his hair. Effie didn't dare move. She couldn't tell if he was happy to see her or not. He was clearly stunned, but . . .

'Not a ghost, no,' he murmured. 'I'm just a little surprised, that's all. I didn't expect to find *you* in here, much less . . .' His voice trailed off again and he stared at the floor for a moment.

He inhaled sharply, as if catching himself from falling

asleep. 'Anyway, it's good to see you again, Miss Gillies. Find us easily enough?' he asked with the same briskness she'd heard him use with Mathieson once or twice. He stopped before her with a brief nod of his head, seeming taller somehow. He was wearing a black suit with a white shirt and a curious necktie fashioned like a bow. Why was he dressed like that?

She nodded back, looking up into those blue eyes she had thought she would never see again. Her voice seemed to have almost completely deserted her. She had a sense he was playing a role and that she was supposed to say certain things back, but she had no script for this. She didn't know what she was supposed to do or who she was supposed to be in this grand room in this great house. Did the girl he'd known even exist anymore, when she could no longer do the things he'd once admired her for?

Behind him, Sibyl reached into her bag and pulled out some cigarettes. Effie recognized them because Flora's fiancé smoked them and had told her all the Hollywood stars smoked. 'Darling, would you?'

Sholto blinked, breaking the seal between them. Turning away abruptly, he went to walk over, startling at the sight of Margaux, now lying down on the rug. 'Oh for heaven's sake, Sid, you promised you'd keep her in the stables.'

'The groom wasn't keen.'

'Well, nor will Mama be when she sees her in here. You know what a bother we had last time.'

'But I've had her declawed, I told you. Check for yourself if you don't believe me.'

'No thanks.' Circumventing the cat, Sholto walked over to her and pulled a box from his jacket pocket, struck a match and held it towards her. Sibyl leant in, catching his gaze as he put the flame to her cigarette. Effie saw her wink at him. Small intimacies; their ease with one another. Was she . . . ?

Sholto straightened. 'Why aren't you dressed yet, anyway? You know dinner's at eight.'

'I do, but I thought I'd pinch a little book to read in bed tonight. I glanced through a few pages and next thing I knew, I was woken to the sound of screaming.'

He looked concerned. 'Your own?'

'No, silly bean. Miss Gillies's.'

'Effie?' He turned now to look at her again. 'What was wrong?'

Effie frowned. Wasn't it perfectly obvious? '. . . The cheetah gave me a fright.'

'Oh yes. Of course. Well, don't worry about her. She's usually fine.'

Usually?

He plunged a hand into his trouser pocket and set off towards the drinks table. 'Would you care for a drink? I need a stiff—' He stopped abruptly again. He was standing right in front of the niche cabinet and the empty book display. 'Sid?' he asked questioningly, but there was an edge to his tone that made even Sibyl sharpen up.

The woman followed his eyeline, then suddenly gasped as she looked down at the forgotten-about, upended book splayed on the floor. It had fallen to a spot half hidden under one of the chairs.

'Oh calamity!' she cried, looking back at Effie with a look of horror and pity. Sholto followed suit. 'Miss Gillies, what have you done?'

'. . . I was just looking at the pictures,' Effie faltered, not quite sure why the dropped book should elicit more fear than the carnivore sitting six feet away.

There was an appalled silence, then Sholto dropped to his knees and began gathering what she could see now were loose leaves. Several had been creased in the fall and now had perfect fold lines across them. Effie rushed over, taking care to remain out of lunging reach of the cat, and tried helping.

'I'm so sorry. What have I . . . what have I done wrong?' she asked, feeling desperate.

Sholto looked back at her with an angry expression. His eyes were blazing and his jaw clenched, but he shook his head, replying with studied neutrality. 'Nothing. You couldn't have known.'

'Known what?'

Sholto looked down and away and she felt a keen sense of her ignorance, knowing she was missing something – again! – but was too dumb to know better.

'One doesn't tend to read *that* book,' Sibyl offered mercifully into the silence.

Effie looked back at Sholto again, as though this dotty woman was making even less sense. 'But aren't books for reading?'

'Apparently,' Sibyl shrugged. 'Only that's rather a valuable one. More "look, don't touch". It's one of only eight copies, made for the clan heads. One sold last year at auction for a record sum. Everyone was fantastically excited about it. As I recall, it was published in the 1760s and took ten years to complete, all hand-drawn. Something like that anyway.' Sibyl dragged on her cigarette for several seconds, before exhaling a ribbon of smoke through her rouged lips.

Effie looked at Sholto, aghast. And she had one? And she'd damaged another? Her heart was beating fast. She knew it was terribly wrong that one of these books should be in her possession. Sholto saw her upset and relented. 'Effie, it's fine. Don't worry, I'll deal with it.'

'But your father—'

'It's only a book. I'll tell him I dropped it.'

'You can't do that.'

'Why not?'

'Because it's a lie. *I* dropped it.'

'I don't think I'll go to hell for fibbing about who dropped it.'

'Dock it from my wages then,' she said urgently as he rose to standing again and she jumped up too.

His mouth parted as though he was about to say something, but it was Sibyl's sudden laughter that rang through the room. Sholto's expression hardened as he shot her a silencing look. Had she said something funny?

He looked back at Effie. 'Miss Gillies, it's fine,' he said stiffly. 'Accidents happen. My father won't care a jot.'

Effie could do nothing more but nod, but as she looked into his eyes, she saw his anger was still there, that beneath his manners lay a darker mood and she knew he wasn't just angry about the book; he was angry that she was here.

The sound of a small gasp rescued her.

'My dear, where are your *shoes*?' Sibyl asked, staring down at Effie's bare legs and feet. The scandalized tone of her words made Effie feel as if she was standing there completely nude.

'. . . I . . . have blisters,' Effie faltered, feeling her cheeks flame as her next transgression was revealed. Why hadn't she put them back on before leaving the collection room? Why had she thought she could get back to her room without incident? Skirting Margaux again, she ran lightly back to the door and picked up her boots, clutching them to her chest. 'I should go.'

She wanted him to implore her to stay but Sholto didn't stir, his expression tight and closed. Without another word he turned away and began arranging the book as best he could on the display stand. Effie watched him for a moment. It was clear the prize book was a prize no longer, but what could she do?

Meeting Sibyl's thoroughly entertained gaze, she gave a polite nod and slipped from the room. But even with the door closed behind her, she could hear the woman's words at her back. 'Sholto, darling, where did you *find* her? She's a riot!'

Effie walked into the servants' hall, ashen-faced. She had stopped on a servant's stairway on her way down to put on her boots before disgracing herself any further. Most of the servants were already gathered at their places around the table as the meal was brought through by the kitchen maids, everyone talking animatedly to their neighbours. Billy's bright eyes followed her as she made her way to the empty chair beside William again.

'Enjoy yourself today, Miss Gillies?' he asked, as she pulled her chair in. 'I expect you heard his lordship is back?'

'Not just him, sadly,' someone else muttered before she could reply.

Not that she was up to talking. The reunion with Sholto just now had left her shaken and upset. He hadn't once smiled at her; in fact, he'd looked ambushed, he'd been angry and embarrassed. She was no better than the factor, trying to curry his favour.

Mr Graves strode in, disrupting her thoughts as everyone rose, and the general murmur of conversation quietened to a hush. Heads bent as he said grace.

'You missed dinner, Miss Gillies,' he said afterwards as

everyone sat and picked up their cutlery, the first few mouth-fuls savoured in silence.

'Dinner?' Her voice was distracted and flat.

'At noon. Our main meal of the day.'

'Oh.' It would take a while to adapt to the idea that food was readily available at any moment, that sitting down for dinner didn't first involve a hike and a hunt. 'I'm sorry. I worked through, without realizing.'

'Three meals a day, Miss Gillies. Ours is strenuous work. We all must keep our strength up.'

Effie simply nodded, not rising to the chastisement. She ate in tiny bites, determined not to disgrace herself tonight. Her ambitions were modest – to eat and escape back to her room, with as little interaction as possible. To cry into a pillow where no one could hear.

'So the cat's back, then,' Henry, the footman, said to no one in particular.

'I thought she was giving it to the Regent's Park Zoo?' asked Jenny.

'Something about she didn't like the view from the enclo-sure.'

'Ah.'

'Declawed though, now. Apparently.'

'There's still the teeth,' Billy muttered.

There was another silence as everyone ate. Effie caught several of the staff watching Mr Graves, as though his speed of eating dictated theirs.

'Fanny, did you place the flowers in Lord Sholto's room as I asked?'

'Yes, Mrs McKenzie. On the table by the window.'

'Good.' She went to take another bite. 'But you removed the lilies? He's allergic to lilies.'

'Yes, Mrs McKenzie. They were added to her ladyship's arrangement.'

'Very good.' The housekeeper's head snapped up suddenly. '. . . Wait, you do mean her ladyship, the countess?'

'No, ma'am. Lady Sibyl's room.'

Mrs McKenzie looked momentarily stricken as all eyes swivelled towards her. Her head inclined at a small angle as she sat very still.

'Did I do something wrong, ma'am?' Fanny asked trepidatiously. 'Should I remove them?' She made to get up, but Mrs McKenzie had gathered herself.

'. . . Not at all. Eat your supper, Fanny. Her ladyship will be resting before dinner and we don't wish to disturb her.'

Effie frowned as she saw Fanny hesitate, then sit back down and resume eating – but she looked unhappy about it, as though she knew she'd done wrong. Confused, Effie looked up the table to see if anyone else could make sense of what had just happened. She had a sense of an underwater explosion – noise and chaos in the deep but only a few bubbles rising to the surface. She caught Billy's eyes, which were silently dancing as he wolfed down his supper. He seemed to know exactly what was going on, but would he tell her if she asked?

'Talking of . . . did anyone read about the BYPs' latest scandal?' Jenny asked.

'At Number Ten the other night? How could we miss it?' Henry replied.

'It's a disgrace,' Mrs McKenzie muttered, sipping from her glass. 'Stealing the prime minister's spectacles.'

'I don't think they saw it as stealing, Mrs McKenzie – it was a treasure hunt,' Jenny said with bright eyes. 'Besides, I'm sure the PM has another pair.'

'That's beside the point. Not everything can be justified in the pursuit of *fun*.' Mrs McKenzie's mouth was puckered to a seal. 'It's undignified to have carrying-ons like that at the very seat of the country's political power.'

No one spoke for several moments, but amused glances were swapped.

'I suppose there's a good chance the spectacles might now be here,' Henry murmured.

'There is *no* suggestion that Lady Sybil was even involved,' the housekeeper snapped, defending Sibyl even though she hadn't been explicitly named.

'But there's been plenty of photographs of her in the press with the PM's daughter. Everyone knows they're friends,' the footman shrugged. 'I don't suppose you saw anything when you were unpacking her case, Barra?'

'Do you think I would tell it to you if I did?' the lady's maid replied coolly as Effie watched her from below lowered lashes. Dark-haired with a wiry physique, she was nonetheless composed and deliberate in her actions. Clearly no pushover. 'It would be all over Knockroon before you could say—'

'Bogus!' The word burst forth in the round as half the servants fell into laughter. Effie gleaned it was at Lady Sybil Wainwright's expense; certainly she had a . . . flamboyant way of speaking that had made it hard to keep up.

'If I hear that word one more time,' Barra muttered, sharing a half-smile.

'That's quite enough impertinence, all of you,' Mrs McKenzie said firmly. 'Lady Sybil is at leisure to speak how she wishes. Furthermore, nothing else is to be said on the matter of stolen spectacles. You will not ascribe any further illegal or inappropriate behaviour to this household's guests.'

'I concur. It's in very poor taste,' a man said standing at

the far end of the table. 'His lordship would be appalled to hear his friends being talked about in such a tasteless manner. To defame them is to insult him.'

There was a scraping back of chairs as everyone stood, Effie a full beat behind as she saw the man who had spoken was not dining with them, but standing in the doorway, holding an overcoat and hat.

From the silence that fell upon the staff at the stiff rebuke – even Mr Graves's head was bowed – Effie understood exactly who he was. And seemingly he knew her too, because their eyes met in silent recognition. For a moment, nothing was said, as they appraised one another; she saw a man whose face was fleshy with deep lines around the mouth, round spectacles that magnified pale grey eyes and blonde lashes, strawberry-blonde hair clipped short. She saw a man who was calm and unhurried, logical, unemotional.

She wondered what he saw as he regarded her. None of those things, certainly.

'Miss Gillies, welcome to Dumfries House,' he said in the same tone as he'd delivered his scolding. 'His lordship told me you would be arriving. Perhaps you would be so kind as to step into my room when you have finished dining? There are some issues we should discuss.'

'Aye, Mr Weir, I'd be happy to,' she mumbled.

He turned and walked away, the sound of his shoes fading as he turned into the passage and past the wine cellar, the rest of the meal passing in silence.

He was writing at his desk when she knocked.

'Come in,' he said, not looking up. 'And close the door behind you.'

Effie did as she was told – and waited.

303

'Sit down,' he murmured, as he finished making his records in a log book, before finally looking up. 'Miss Gillies. Miss Gillies,' he repeated slowly as he met her eyes. 'Finally we meet.'

Finally? He made it sound like he'd been waiting to meet her, but she'd never heard of the man before this morning. His eyes narrowed to slits as he regarded her and she had a sense he was trying to marry up the sight of her with something else. An idea of her? '. . . How have your first few days been here?'

'I only arrived yesterday, but it's been fine, sir. Nae bother.'

He sneered slightly at her vernacular. 'Nae bother,' he echoed. 'Indeed.' He sighed, looking away and back again, his fingers clasped together in front of him. 'I'm tired from the journey so you'll forgive me if I get straight to the point. I assume you've heard the news about Frank Mathieson?'

'That he's missing? Aye, sir.' She held herself very still; she was practised at it – years of fowling, of not startling the quarry, were good for something.

'Do you know anything about his disappearance?'

She hesitated. '. . . No. Why would I?'

'I thought you were . . . close. Good friends.'

She felt her body grow cold. 'Mr Mathieson was our factor and I respected him, sir, but I wouldn't say we were friends.'

'No?'

'No.' She pressed one hand on top of the other, to keep from fidgeting. She felt an urge to wriggle, keep moving.

'Hmm. That's curious. He implied otherwise.'

She shook her head.

'I thought I heard him say that on occasion he liked to *indulge* you with special gifts.'

Effie stared at him. The urge to move had become an urge to run. Her heart was beginning to pound. 'No, sir.'

'So he never brought you anything?'

Just from the way he asked it, she knew he knew. '. . . Well, once in a while he would bring books over – for our education. Our resources were so limited, you see. He was a kind man like that. But they weren't just for me; they were for all the children on the isle. Maybe that's what he was referring to?'

'Books.'

'Aye.'

'Nothing more?'

What did he know, exactly? Enough to suspect her involvement somehow. She sensed she had to keep as close to the truth as possible. '. . . Um, well, one time he brought some paint and brushes for us too. That was a wee while ago. But that was it. We were dependent upon the kindness of friends, to better ourselves.' She sensed the last bit would satisfy him.

'He told me once he was courting someone special on St Kilda.'

The blood in her veins slowed to a crawl. *Courting?* 'Not me, sir. It must have been someone else. I was only a child all those years and that would have been wrong, wouldn't it? It would be wrong even to suggest it.'

His eyes narrowed at the insinuation. 'Quite. Mr Mathieson may be a hard businessman but he's an honourable man with an upstanding reputation.'

'Aye, sir. That's what I thought.'

She felt Mr Weir regard her more keenly. 'Nonetheless, there is something about you, Miss Gillies.'

'No, sir, I'm not special,' she said quickly.

'No? I'll be honest, I don't see it myself, but you do seem to . . . cast a curious spell, Miss Gillies. Their lordships were very taken with you on their return from St Kilda too. And the earl himself went out of his way to offer you a post here. That is not usual behaviour.'

'He thinks I can help him with a special project.'

'And can you?'

'I'll do my best for him.'

'Of course, of course you will.' He tapped his index fingers together thoughtfully. 'Tell me, Miss Gillies, when was the last time *you* recall seeing Mr Mathieson?'

'It was around the time of the evacuation,' she shrugged. 'He was helping us pack up and leave. We were all busy, as you can imagine.'

'But specifically, Miss Gillies, just think back for me – when was the last time you actually remember seeing him. Which day? Where exactly?'

She could feel herself beginning to tremble. She didn't want to remember it. Any of it. '. . . Am I in trouble, sir?'

'*Should* you be?'

'No, sir. I've done nothing wrong.'

'Then it's a simple question.'

She stared at him. It had been nine days since she'd left but there was a chance he could still be clinging on. He was strong enough, young enough to put up a fight. If she admitted what she'd done right now, a boat could be sent over. The tourist ships weren't sailing but that wasn't to say the trawlers weren't. Or the navy. If word could be passed to them to divert, to drop anchor and shout for him, she could show them exactly where to look. He would be saved.

But in so doing, she would implicate herself. She would have to confess how she knew he was still there, she would have to reveal not just what she'd done, but why.

And what if he was already dead? She would sacrifice herself for nothing. She would be arrested, she might even swing – and who would look after her father then?

'I can't . . . I can't remember exactly when was the last time, I'm sorry. I'd need to think. There was a lot going on.'

'Well, shall I tell you what *I've* heard?' He paused, watching her intently as she hung on his every word.

Slowly, she nodded.

'I heard you caused a distraction in the final minutes before everyone left.'

'A distraction?'

'You gave everyone the runaround, set about wailing and causing a fuss. Tell me, why should you do such a thing? You don't strike me as a hysterical girl.'

'It was no distraction, sir.' Her voice had a tremor to it. 'I was trying to save my dog.'

'Which was killed anyway, I understand? Along with all the others.'

She swallowed, then nodded.

'So you engaged in a wholly futile charade—'

'It wasn't futile to me, sir.' Her voice cracked.

'And yet you want me to believe it's merely a coincidence that no one, not a single person asked so far, can remember seeing the factor getting on the boat – or not – because they were so taken up with *your* escapade, which could have no possible alternative outcome?'

He stared at her for several long moments but she couldn't speak. Words fell like lead weights through her. 'You have nothing more to say?'

She shook her head. She had nothing more to say to *him*.

He sighed, looking resigned to her denials. 'Very well, but you should know Scotland Yard are now involved and

Frank Mathieson is officially registered as a missing person. The police will be coming to interview you about what you know.'

'*Me*, sir?'

'Yes, Miss Gillies. I gave them your name as a person of interest.'

A person of . . . ? 'But why? I don't know anything!' she cried.

'Then you have nothing to hide.'

'But why would you give them *my* name when you'd never met me before now?'

'It's nothing personal, Miss Gillies, but as I said, Mr Mathieson is a colleague and purely out of professional respect, I must do what I can to help him. He and I had conversations over the years – in this very room, in fact – and he made some confidences to me which I felt were pertinent to an investigation. I've told the police what *I* know, and now you must do the same. When a man is missing and very possibly in grave danger, we must all pull together to help him; I'm sure you agree?'

She didn't reply, but she was already standing, her feet walking her backwards towards the door. She was breathing quickly and beginning to feel light-headed. She needed some air. She needed to get away from here.

'I'll let you know when the detective wants to interview you, Miss Gillies,' Mr Weir said, watching her depart through narrowed eyes.

She closed the door behind her and ran down the passage, missing – in her panic – the staircase up to her room. She ran down the corridors until there was nowhere else to go and she found herself in the game larder, surrounded by hanging pheasants, ducks, partridges and quails, but she saw nothing.

She could only hear his words echoing in her head – *I've told them what I know.*

What did he know? How much had Mathieson told him?

Because if he knew what she'd suffered at his hands, then he'd know women had killed for a lot less.

Chapter Twenty-Two

Effie stood at the window, as motionless as the marble statue just behind her. She was standing in the hall, the plainest thing in it – at her back were dainty chairs, those brooding life-size portraits, polished tables, a tumbled stone floor; ornate plaster panels were set high up in a frieze and rich gold tracery spun out in the corners of the vaulted ceiling. It was an imposing entrance to an already intimidating house, but for the girl who had until two days ago never known such grandeur existed, it was irrelevant. She couldn't tear her gaze from the gardens, where Sholto and Sibyl were walking arm in arm. Sibyl had a flower in her hand and was talking animatedly, gesticulating as she spoke. Sholto, by comparison, had his free hand in his jacket pocket and his gaze turned to the ground. He was walking at half his usual speed, his shoes scuffing the gravel. Effie's heart ached at the mere sight of him. Even at a distance, he shone. Even distracted, he was arresting.

'Right then, are you ready?'

She turned to find Billy waiting for her.

'Oh no, you're not back to that, are you?'

'What?' But she knew he was referring to her clothes: brown trousers and an ivory shirt. Clean. Pressed. They fit. Keeping a low-profile in her Sunday best yesterday hadn't exactly worked out well for her.

Billy himself was looking smart in his shirt and mole-coloured waistcoat, a long clean apron falling to his shins and shoes polished to a high shine. 'It's like you want to cause trouble for yourself.'

'I told you, I'm not a servant, Billy,' she said tiredly. 'I don't have to wear a uniform.'

'Women's clothes is all they're asking for! Weir will have a fit if he sees you in that.'

'Then he can take it up with the earl, who has never seen me in anything else,' she said stubbornly. It wasn't her clothes the steward was concerned with.

'It's your funeral,' he sighed, his gaze falling to her sturdy boots. 'At least those are suitable. The track can get muddy. C'mon then, this way.'

Reluctantly, allowing herself a last glance out the window, she moved away from the vast door, following him back to the staircase that led down to the servants' passage on the ground floor. It would be far quicker to step through the door and go straight down the sweeping staircase that led to the gardens, but they would pass Lord Sholto and Lady Sibyl that way and already she was beginning to absorb the assumption that she must be hidden from view.

'It's good of you to take me,' she said, as Billy stepped out into the garden, holding the door open for her.

'Nae bother. It gets me out of filling the coal buckets just yet and I get to be outside for a wee while.'

'Have you worked here long?' she asked distractedly as they walked, Effie glancing around for sight of Sholto and Sibyl, but there was no sign of them now.

'Seven months. My longest stay yet. I'm usually out on m' ear after five.'

'Why?'

He shrugged. 'Trouble has a way of finding me.' He arched an eyebrow. 'Bit like you, I reckon.'

She had thought exactly the same about him but she had no intention of letting him know that. 'Excuse me?'

He shot her a crafty, sidelong glance. 'This morning I over-heard Lord Sholto bribing Mrs McKenzie into locking the library doors for the day to keep his father out. Minutes later, Mr Weir left in a great hurry with a parcel under his arm addressed to an antiquarian bookseller in Glasgow.' He glanced at her. 'I don't suppose you'd know anything about that?'

She swallowed. 'Why would you suppose I do?'

'Because his lordship was adamant Mrs McKenzie wasn't to let *you* know about it.'

She looked at him. 'But it's fine for you to tell me?'

He shrugged, smiling. 'You're avoiding the question. Why aren't you to know?'

'Do you always spy in the corridors, Billy?'

'You're still avoiding the question.'

She gave a careless shrug but she knew exactly what Sholto was doing – cleaning up after her mess. Making things right again.

Was the book repairable, she wondered? And even if the pages could be sewed back in, would it still retain its value? Or was it now damaged, and therefore worthless? As she had lain in bed last night, she had mulled over the notion of offering Sholto her copy – a straight swap; that way his father need never know. But there was no way she could see to do that without explaining how she had come to be in possession of such a rare gift herself, and she couldn't bear to even mention Frank Mathieson's name. Shame had her in a strangle-hold from which she couldn't escape.

She realized she was lost in her thoughts. '. . . So tell me, Billy – have you worked here long?'

He gave a surprised laugh. 'You already asked me that!'

She blushed. 'I'm sorry. What I meant was—' She tried to rally her mind. 'Are you from here?'

'So you want me to answer your questions but you won't answer mine?' He gave her a bemused look as he sighed. 'Very well. I'm from Tarbet, Lomondside. Not so far. Not so far as you.'

'I'm not sure anyone's as far from home as me.'

'Are you missing it?'

'Aye.'

'How long's it been now since you left?'

'Ten days and three hours. But who's counting, right?'

He grinned as they walked and she knew she was already forgiven for her slippery behaviour. She had a feeling of familiarity with him, like he was a little brother. 'Would you go back if you could?'

She didn't hesitate. 'Aye.'

'But why? Everything's so much harder there! You can't even wrap your head around the idea of eating three times a day.'

'Oh don't worry, Mrs McLennan's not letting me get away with skipping any meals.' Just that morning, as Effie had tried to scuttle past the kitchen again without being seen, the wily cook – as if waiting for her – had marched her over to the table where she was told to take some porridge oats and a glass of milk before she went anywhere. It didn't matter that she had no appetite, that even Mrs McLennan's delicious food tasted like ashes in her mouth: she'd been forced to eat. The woman seemed determined to care for her.

'So then why would you go back to a life of hardship and want and struggle?'

'Because I don't belong here.' She raised her hands up, motioning vaguely to the extravagant estate. 'I don't. My brain can't process all this.'

Billy grinned. 'Oh trust me, you'll get used to it. I thought the same when I first went into service. I started out with the Duke of Argyll and half thought I must be working for the king.'

'Exactly!'

'But it becomes normal, fast.'

'Billy, I come from a place where iron nails were a luxury! Where we celebrated if a piece of driftwood washed up on the beach! I will never adapt to gold ceilings and . . . cheetahs sitting on a leash!'

He threw his head back and laughed. 'It's gonna take you longer to adapt, I grant you that, but it's not always so dramatic. Only when *she's* around; Lady Sibyl Wainwright is not your run-of-the-mill socialite.'

'Socia-what?'

'Socialite. A rich, eligible young woman, doing the season,' he chuckled. 'She's one of the BYPs.'

'I have no idea what you're talking about,' she sighed, shaking her head.

'Bright young people! They're the young rich set who like to live fast – and, it would seem, die young. One lady died falling from a chandelier not long ago. The newspapers are obsessed with the lot of them.'

'And she's one of them?' Effie felt a primal stirring against the beautiful woman with the big cat, who stole spectacles from the prime minister and laughed about it.

'Much to her ladyship's horror. The countess thinks it's all *frightful*' – he made a funny voice – 'but she's friends with Lady Sibyl's mother and doesn't like to make a fuss. Nothing's worse than that! I think she's hoping she'll settle down once they're married.'

Effie stopped walking, pale-faced. 'You mean . . . she and Sholto are engaged?'

'*Lord* Sholto! Effie, what did I tell you about that?' He rolled his eyes. 'And no, not yet. But it's only a matter of time.'

She felt suddenly as though there was a weight on her chest. 'Have they . . . been together long?'

'Depends what you mean by "been together". They've known each other since they were children, by all accounts. You know how it is with the rich – they keep a tight circle of friends. From what I heard, they were on and off for a few years, flitting about, flirting with anything with a pulse. But his lordship's twenty-three now; he knows what's ahead of him when the earl goes.'

'Goes? . . . Oh.'

'C'mon, we'll need to hurry. I've got Graves's boots to polish before he goes into the village.' He began walking more quickly and she hurried after, blind to the wildflowers growing in bushy banks along the path, a red squirrel scampering up a tree, blackbirds singing melodies in higher branches. Her brain – her heart – had snagged on the topic of Sholto's imminent engagement to Lady Sibyl Wainwright and wouldn't let go. '. . . It's just up here.'

'Billy,' she ventured, as he came to a stop outside a stone cottage. She blankly registered it had an upstairs and four windows. A brick-red front door.

'Aye?'

'Last night, at supper . . . when Fanny took the lilies and put them in Lady Sibyl's room . . . what was so wrong with that?'

Billy looked across at her, an incredulous grin on his lips. 'Are you really such an innocent that you can't guess?'

She blinked. She must be.

'Corridor creeping.' His eyes were dancing with scandalized delight. 'When he pays her a visit after midnight . . . ?'

'But . . .' Her voice was choked. 'They're not married.' The minister's words still rang in her ears, a lifetime of warnings against sin not so easy to drown out.

'But they're going to be, I just told you. And besides, this is 1930. The world is changing—'

The world is changing. They were the same words Sholto had said to her.

'Look at the papers – men dress as women; seemingly women dress as men!' He indicated to her own clothes. 'As long as they're discreet, what happens behind closed doors, stays behind closed doors.' He pressed a finger to his lips and winked at her.

It was a moment before Effie realized a man had come to the door of the cottage and was standing there, watching them.

'Oh hallo there, Mr Felton,' Billy said, straightening up as he noticed him too. 'I thought we might find you here. This is Miss Gillies. She's going to be the new tenant of the cottage.'

'Along with my father,' she said, recovering herself. 'Hello, Mr Felton.'

The man nodded in reply. He looked to have ten years or so on her. He had thick almost-black hair, bright hard eyes, calloused hands and his skin was so like hers – tanned a nut-brown from working outside – that he could have been a St Kildan himself. She half expected to see him barefoot with a few dead fulmars hanging from his shoulders.

'Miss Gillies is organizing his lordship's egg collection. Apparently she's an expert birder and fowler.'

'Oh, aye?' The man raised an eyebrow.

'Mr Felton is the gamekeeper,' Billy explained. 'The pheasantry is through the trees back there, a hundred yards or so away. He agreed to take on the restoration of the bothy for his lordship.'

'I had a little time, seeing as the birds have been placed in the release pens now,' Mr Felton explained.

'Oh. I can't imagine *releasing* birds,' she said. 'My life used to depend upon trapping and catching them.'

'It's the thrill of the chase here for his lordship. He likes the sport of the shoot as much as the reward.'

She remembered standing in the game larder the evening before, surrounded by the spoils, Mr Weir's threats still ringing in her ears.

'Well, I wasn't expecting to see you or I'd have tidied the chippings,' Mr Felton said, glancing behind him. 'You must be wanting to see in?'

'If it's not too much bother.'

'No. Go in.'

He stepped aside and she passed by. There was a small entrance vestibule on the front of the building, like a nose – somewhere to hang a coat, hat and their ropes (not that they would be needed here, but she couldn't imagine *not* having them). It led onto a narrow corridor that ran straight through to the back of the building. Through a stable door, she could see into a garden behind, some fruit trees in the corners. In the house itself, the kitchen followed the same plan as the Lochaline bothy by sitting to the right, but instead of a bedroom opposite, there was a parlour. Each room had a fireplace but the floors were wooden, not stone, and the windows were significantly larger, swallowing the light in great gulps. She stood at the bottom of the staircase and looked up.

A staircase. It was a hitherto unimaginable luxury, but . . .

'That will be too narrow and steep for my father,' she said regretfully. 'He won't manage it.'

'I can help you with moving the furniture when it comes,' Mr Felton said, standing by the bottom of the stairs with her. 'Would he be happy making this his bedroom, perhaps?'

She looked back at the large and bright parlour. 'Delighted. He's done it all his life. Why change now?'

'Change is overrated, if you ask me.'

'No one did,' Billy called through with his impertinent smile. 'Right, I must head back. I've been dawdling too long and Mr Graves will bawl me out if I don't get his boots done. Can you make your own way back, Miss Gillies?' he asked her.

'Of course. I'll just follow the path.' The track bordered the vast grazing pastures beyond the ha-ha, the old wood sitting behind them here. It would be actively difficult to become lost.

'Or I can walk you,' Mr Felton said. 'I've to collect some things from the house anyway.'

'. . . As you wish,' she shrugged.

Billy took off. Effie led the way upstairs, amazed to see that the cottage boasted the same creature comforts as her room in the great house – a plumbed sink, radiators, an indoor bathroom. The rooms were so much bigger than she was used to. She walked to a window and opened it, taking in a view across the fields towards a distant wood, sheep grazing in quiet contentment.

Mr Felton went and stood by the other window, both of them quiet for a moment. It wasn't a landscape she was used to; it lacked the drama and majesty of home, but there was something reassuring in its benign, gentle curves. If she looked left, she could see the east pavilion and two-thirds of the body of the great house. Even from here, almost a half-mile distant, it was a colossus.

'So . . . you know a thing or two about birds?' he asked, leaning forward so that they were talking outside of the glass.

She peered round the window frame as well and perched on the sill. 'A thing or two.'

He was quiet for a second. 'Well, then I've something you'd perhaps like to see sometime.'

'Where is it?'

'In the woods.' He caught her wary look and laughed. 'Nothing untoward, Miss Gillies. Strictly to do with birds.'

'What is it?'

He shook his head. 'I can't tell you that. It's a secret.'

She looked away. 'I'm afraid I don't like secrets, Mr Felton.'

'Shall we call it a surprise, then?'

'Surprises can be nasty,' she said quickly, not meeting his eyes. She knew her replies were ungracious, that he was only being friendly.

He watched her for a few moments before turning back into the room. '. . . Well, this is almost ready for you and your father. The chimney work's finished and a new door hung. There's just some slates left to fix on the roof and she'll be all set for whatever the winter wants to throw at her.'

Effie looked back out of the window, wondering what winter looked like here – was it all sedate blankets of snow and crackling fires? Or the fearsome monster she knew of howling gales, wind-whipped waves and ice on the beach?

'When will you move in?'

She shrugged. 'My father stayed behind in Lochaline to

319

await the sale of our livestock at Oban, but that's done now. If this is almost ready, then sometime in the next week.'

'It was a big thing, all of you moving over, as you did.'

So he knew she was a St Kildan? Word travelled, it seemed. 'Aye, it was. But for the best,' she said quickly, knowing he would only ask otherwise. There was no doubt living here, in this sturdy, pretty cottage, was a distinct step up from what they'd had before. The earl had been true to his word; he had been able to offer her better.

A sound came to her ear, a rhythmic drubbing that she couldn't place. 'What's that?' she asked, twisting back to see a dark, gathered mass rocketing along the field.

Mr Felton didn't answer immediately. 'Someone out for a ride,' he said, straightening up.

It was too late for him to get downstairs, however. In the space of a few seconds, the rider had pulled the horse to a dramatic stop and it was now trotting in excited circles on the grass below. Its coat was a gleaming blackish brown, with chestnut nostrils and socks. It was also huge; Effie wasn't sure she'd be able to see over its back, much less get up on it. She had never seen a horse close up before, nor in full gallop; there had been none on the isle during her lifetime, although Ma Peg had told her there'd been a shire when she was girl, to help with the ploughing.

Sholto stared up at them, breathing hard and flushed. He was wearing a tweed hacking jacket and a pair of brown riding trousers with long black boots that came up to his knees; he seemed to have no awareness of the imposing figure he cut as he frowned at the sight of them both upstairs talking out of the bedroom windows.

'Miss Gillies. Felton,' he said briskly. 'Mrs McKenzie said I would find you here.'

'You want to see me, sir?' the gamekeeper asked.

'What? . . . No, no,' Sholto said, shaking his head irritably. 'Miss Gillies.' He scowled at the two of them. 'What are you doing up there?'

'I wanted to see the cottage before we move in,' she said quickly. 'My father will be down in the next week or so and I wanted to check it would be ready.'

The horse picked up its hooves and took two paces back. 'And does it pass muster?' he asked, the reins slack in his hands.

'It's wonderf—'

'Felton, how much remains to do on it?'

'Another day of work, sir, that's all.'

'Right. Good. Well, that's something.' Sholto's manner was abrupt and decidedly distant; if she had thought their reunion in the library cold, this felt distinctly arctic. For the first time, Effie saw him as a lord, a landlord, an employer, her superior. He felt not just far away from the bright-eyed, easy-smiling visitor of May, but an entirely different man altogether. Why was he being so stony towards her? It felt almost ludicrous that what had happened between them, could have happened. Had she dreamt it? Kissing on a rope, holding each other in the sea, hungry eyes and pink lips . . . ?

She realized she was staring at him. 'Did you need to see me . . . sir?' she asked, composing her voice. There was no sign of Sibyl that she could see. Had he wanted to see her alone? Did he want to talk without Lady Sibyl listening in?

'Yes.' The horse was still frisky from the gallop and he walked it around, away from her. He pulled on the reins, leading it round in another circle to face front again. 'I'm afraid my mother would like you to join us for dinner tonight.'

Effie was horrified. 'Me?'

'Yes, I'm sorry. I know it will be dull for you but she wants to hear all about St Kilda. My father's bored her rigid with it for the past few months and she'd like to hear about it from a native's perspective—'

Native? There was a short silence and she wondered if he realized how polarizing the word was, how 'different' it made her feel.

He patted the horse on its neck. '—He's thinking of buying the archipelago from Sir John, you see.'

'What?' The word escaped her as a bark, startling the game-keeper. She was vaguely aware of a lack of deference on her part, but to hear St Kilda might be sold . . . ?

'Well, it's not much use to Sir John now, with no rent coming in, and Father's rather keen on the idea of turning it into some sort of protected bird sanctuary. I don't quite know all the ins and outs but I expect he'll spare no detail telling us over dinner.' His horse took itself for another small circular walk. He looked back at her over his other shoulder. 'So can I tell her you'll come?'

Effie stared at him. Did she even have a choice? She nodded wanly.

'Good. Good,' he muttered, but he was looking at her with an expression that could only be regarded as hostile. 'Mother will be most pleased.' But not him. That was the clear intimation.

He nodded, as if making to go, when he pulled back again.

'Uh . . . I should add – she can be of quite a nervous dispos-ition, the countess.' He hesitated. 'It might be best not to mention anything about her only son and heir dangling from a rope above the Atlantic . . .'

'Of course.'

'In fact, just don't mention the ropes, at all. It's irrelevant now anyway.'

She stared at him, knowing what he was really telling her. He was telling her that what had happened between them was irrelevant. Regretted.

'Of course,' she said again, her voice choked. 'I won't mention the ropes.'

His eyes narrowed, as though he was debating whether she could be trusted. 'Good. Eight o'clock, then. In the parlour.' He glanced back at the gamekeeper. 'Felton. Miss Gillies.' And with a jab of his heels, the horse took off again, galloping back down the straight the way he'd come, scattering the sheep and obscuring him from sight in a cloud of dust.

Chapter Twenty-Three

Every head turned as she walked into the servants' hall, stopping Effie in her tracks. Was she late? Mr Graves had said noon for dinner hadn't he? It was three minutes before now.

'Miss Gillies.' Mrs McKenzie drew her shoulders back as she spoke. 'You're joining us.'

She hesitated. 'Shouldn't I?'

'. . . Not at all, you are most welcome.'

Effie hesitated again; it seemed a strange thing for the housekeeper to say. She looked at the staff already assembled and was grateful to see Mr Weir wasn't present. Under the scrutiny of twelve pairs of eyes, she took her usual place at the table beside William. He was looking at her again with the same look from her first evening. Was it the trousers, she wondered? They did seem to elicit such strong feeling.

'Mutton,' she was told curtly as the plate was set down by the same kitchen maid who had snapped at her the previous morning. May, was it?

'Thank you.'

Grace was said and everyone began to eat, but there was a distinct atmosphere. She felt the weight of suspense linger in the air, like gunsmoke after the bang – only it appeared she'd missed the bang. Billy was eating and catching her eye with his customary half-smile. Henry threw constant furtive looks her way; Jenny just looked bewildered by her. Fanny kept looking across at her like she'd been caught dancing with the great auk.

'And have you had a pleasant morning, Miss Gillies?' Mr Graves asked into the silence.

'Thank you, yes. I went out to see the cottage where my father and I will live. Then I resumed cataloguing his lordship's collection.'

'Indeed. Were you able to find the cottage?'

'Billy showed me.'

'And all is progressing well?'

'Very well. My father and I shall be able to move in after tomorrow. Mr Felton is just finishing up.'

'Ah yes, Mr Felton. A hard worker and out in all weathers. He's an example to us all. Some of our footmen don't even like to get their hair wet.'

The comment appeared to be pointed and Effie was aware of William shifting in his seat beside her.

'Mrs McKenzie,' Jenny piped up. 'I went to do the fire in the library just now, but the door was locked.'

The housekeeper straightened up. 'Yes, that's correct. A bird came down the chimney earlier. We tried to get it out but it is being very aggressive. We're letting it settle before we go in again and try to capture it.'

'That'll make a fine mess,' Barra tutted.

'Felton's the man to get it out,' Mr Graves said. 'I'll speak to h—'

'No, not to worry, Mr Graves,' Mrs McKenzie said quickly. 'I've already spoken with him. It's all in hand.'

The butler nodded, but he wore a light frown. 'As you wish.'

The housekeeper's gaze flitted quickly in Effie's direction

and immediately away again. Billy looked up the table and grinned at her. He could hardly have been more indiscreet, that smile implicating her without words.

'And I've been given to understand, Miss Gillies, that you have an invitation for dinner tonight?' Mrs McKenzie's face was stretched just beyond a benign expression so that it looked like her skin and the muscles around her mouth were being pulled back. 'Upstairs.'

So that was it. Every set of eyes was upon her. She swallowed nervously. '. . . Yes. Lord Sholto says the countess wishes to hear more about my home.'

'Does she now?' Mr Graves enquired.

'Her ladyship has already informed me,' the housekeeper said. 'Though I must say, I would have appreciated hearing it from you first.'

'I didn't know myself until . . .' Her voice trailed off as she remembered Sholto's peremptory manner outside the cottage. He had resented having to ask her. She knew he didn't want her to be there – but why? Did he hate himself for kissing her? Did he hate her for kissing him back? Or was it simply that her presence here, in the same house as Lady Sibyl, was a constant reminder of his infidelity? 'I've not met her ladyship yet.'

'Well, now you will.'

'Yes.' Effie stared down at her plate, forgetting to eat. She was going to meet Sholto's mother. It didn't matter that she already knew his father and he was kind to her – she had met him when she hadn't understood the gravitas of this family. But sitting here, with their small army of servants . . . there was no escaping their importance now.

No one spoke for several moments. There seemed to be a general air of disbelief – if not anger – that someone who was sitting at this table, downstairs, would tonight be sitting at the table upstairs.

'I know you know your own mind, Miss Gillies, but if I may give a friendly word of advice – I wouldn't wear trousers,' Mrs McKenzie said lightly. 'The countess is more . . . traditional.'

'Of course,' Effie murmured. Even she could see that her clothes wouldn't do, but . . . she remembered Sholto's strange suit last night. 'What *should* I wear?'

'Your best dress will suffice.'

'I don't have any dresses.'

'What? At all?' Jenny asked.

Effie shook her head.

'But what about Sunday best?' Fanny asked.

'Yes, I wore that yesterday,' Effie said, reassured. 'I'll wear that.'

Fanny's expression changed. 'Wait – you mean the wool skirt you had on that was so big on the waist, it needed a bent nail to keep it up?'

'A *nail*?' The housekeeper looked horrified. She looked straight over to Barra, who was sitting erect, just one eyebrow hitched up. The women shared looks again in silent dismay. 'You can't wear that! Suppose it was to catch on the chaise?'

'A nail?' William echoed, aghast.

A silence stretched out.

'. . . I may have something that would fit,' Barra said finally, with a roll of her eyes. 'My previous mistress gave it to me when I was leaving her service; she knew I had always admired it. I haven't yet had an opportunity to wear it myself, but seeing as this is an emergency . . .'

'I don't want to impose,' Effie said quickly.

'Not at all. That's very kind of you, Barra,' Mrs McKenzie said.

'Yes, that would be so kind,' Effie echoed gratefully.

'So then, shoes.' There was another pause.

'I have only my boots,' she said hesitantly. Beside her, William leant back to take in the sight of her feet. He sat up again with a look of alarm.

'What is your size?' Mrs McKenzie asked.

'Size?' Effie looked back at them blankly.

More looks were exchanged.

'We're similar heights,' Barra said. 'I should have something that will fit.'

'If not, we can always pool what options we have this evening, when Miss Gillies is dressed?' the housekeeper added.

Everyone nodded. It was an imperfect solution but none-theless – it was a solution.

'Talking of getting dressed, you will also need some help with your toilette,' Mrs McKenzie said.

Effie instinctively sensed she shouldn't query what her 'toilette' was.

'Barra will of course be assisting her ladyship and Jenny is helping Lady Sybil while she is with us – but Fanny, perhaps you could help Miss Gillies this evening?'

'Of course, Mrs McKenzie.' Fanny looked back at her with that excited look of adventure again; but this still wasn't what Effie would call an adventure. 'Your hair's long, so we should be able to style it into something pretty.'

Effie nodded, struck mute. No one had ever styled her hair in her life. Brushing it was an achievement.

'Do you have any jewellery, at least?' Fanny asked hopefully.

'No.' The married women on St Kilda had had brooches for their shawls but that was it.

Fanny's gaze slid again towards the housekeeper, who sighed. 'I have a necklace you may borrow.'

'Thank you, Mrs McKenzie.'

'Yes, thank you,' Effie said, looking at them all in turn. 'You're all so kind. I wouldn't have known the first thing . . .'

'Eat up now,' Mrs McKenzie simply said, not wanting a fuss, the other women already concentrating on their meals again.

Mrs McLennan came in with another jug of gravy; she eyed Effie's half-eaten meal. 'Eat!' she said sternly.

'Knock, knock.' Fanny peered around the door before Effie had even lifted her head off the pillow. She had been staring at the ceiling for a good hour now and still had no answers to the pressing question of what she would say to these people tonight. The men she could deal with, but if Sholto's mother was anything like Lady Sibyl . . . 'Did you bathe already?'

'Aye.' Effie pushed herself up to sitting as Fanny came into the room carrying a dress in her arms. It was covered with tissue, but a peep of a fluttery hem caught her eye.

'What *is* that?' Effie asked, her hands reaching for the pale primrose fabric. She had never seen anything so light; it was like butterfly wings.

'Silk chiffon. Barra used to work for Miss Mitford. Nancy.'

Who? Effie had never heard of the woman but it was simple enough to infer that Ms Mitford was rich. And thin. 'I won't fit into that!' she cried as Fanny removed the cover to reveal a long, narrow dress with frills criss-crossing below the bust and over the hips.

'Well, if you won't, then no one will,' the maid replied calmly. 'I've seen sparrows with more meat on them than you.'

'But—'

'Relax. I know it looks skimpy here but Barra said it stretches when it's on, don't ask me how. Something about how they cut it. She says it's from Paris.'

'Oh.' They both stared at the gown. It looked too delicate to actually wear.

'Go on, then. Put it on,' Fanny said as she began arranging some brushes and pins on the dressing table. 'Barra says you just pull it on over your head.'

Effie was dubious as she shrugged off her robe. On the hanger, the dress hung like a sock, limp and skinny. She couldn't imagine getting it past her shoulders, and yet . . . she pulled it down, feeling the silky fabric skim her skin, falling easily, framing her perfectly.

'Oh!' Fanny exclaimed as she turned back to find Effie standing before her, the dress settling around her ankles. 'Well, haven't you got just the figure.'

'What?'

'And the colour suits your tan. Turn around, give a twirl,' Fanny said bossily, pushing her around on the spot.

Effie *twirled*.

Fanny said nothing, but the look in her eyes suggested she was somehow impressed. Effie's fingers skimmed the fabric in amazement. The gown was a feat of dressmaking brilliance, somehow going in and out exactly where she did. She had never worn clothes that fit before; they were always either too big or too short, patched or itchy . . . How could she wear something like this? It was far too fine for her. It belonged to a girl with a house full of music and beautiful books, not—

A memory stirred, reminding her of the night she had stolen down to the featherstore – Sholto swimming in the moonlight, the precious book on her lap. She could almost see her own pale face at the window, wholly unaware she was already in the slipstream of two conflicting futures that would collide just a few nights later . . . How much had changed since then? How much had happened?

Another image presented itself – frenzied, desperate – and she gave a shudder that made Fanny startle.

'It suits you. Don't look so worried.' Fanny walked her over to the writing table, sitting her down in the chair.

Effie tried to meet the eyes of the young woman staring back at her in the mirror, a young woman dressed in a Paris-made gown who had left a man to die. It had been forty-eight hours since she'd heard he was still missing – and she had done nothing. He'd been alone there now for ten days and in spite of her anguish upon learning the boats hadn't sailed, she had nonetheless made a choice and remained silent: she'd chosen her life over his. And yet the reflection in the glass showed a lady, not a monster. Could there really be no visible trace of the darkness of her soul?

'We need to decide what to do with your hair. The style is for finger waves, but your hair is so long, we'd be here all night,' Fanny murmured, putting her hands through Effie's hair and feeling the weight and texture. 'I can't do all the fancy things Miss Barra does, but I'll be damned if I'm going to let her Royal Brightness steal your thunder in that dress.'

Effie couldn't imagine stealing anything from Sibyl Wainwright – her thunder, her lover . . . 'Do you call her that because she's part of that group?' she asked.

'Of course. They're notorious.' Fanny pulled her hair back. 'Even you must have heard of them?'

'Not before this morning.'

Fanny pulled a face. 'Were you living on a rock – or under it?' she grinned. 'How did you hear?'

'Billy enlightened me.'

'Och, don't ever look to Billy for enlightenment! It's quite frightening to think where that could lead!' Fanny picked up the hairbrush and began brushing her hair, carefully pulling out the tangles – of which there were many. 'Don't look so nervous. You're white as a sheet.'

Effie stared at her own reflection again, caught between worlds. 'I don't know what to say to them.'

'It's for them to lead the conversation, all you'll have to do is answer. Trust me, they're good at chit-chat. It's what they do.'

'But what if I do something wrong?'

'Like what?'

'I don't know – sit when I should stand, stand when I should sit?'

'Just follow their cues. Drink when they do, sit when they do, laugh at their jokes. It's pretty simple.' Fanny's hands stopped moving suddenly. 'Did anyone talk you through the dinner table?'

'What about it?'

Fanny's eyes narrowed. 'Salad forks, fish knives . . . ?'

Effie looked back at her blankly.

'Och . . .' Fanny sighed, brushing again. 'Well, just work from the outside in. That'll get you through.'

'The outside in,' Effie repeated, but she didn't really understand what she needed to bring inside. The factor lurked in the shadows of her mind, contaminating everything.

'Will she like me?'

'Who? Brightness?'

'The countess.'

'I should imagine she likes anyone who isn't like Lady Sibyl.'

'She doesn't approve of her?'

'Well, she's the right *sort*, just not made of the right *stuff*. Her ladyship disapproves of all those treasure hunts and fancy dress parties. There's always so much scandal that accompanies that set and if there's one thing her ladyship does not like, it's a scandal.'

Effie swallowed. Would Sholto's mother recognize her as a scandal averted, then? 'And Sholto's a part of all that?'

'He's not really. She's right at the heart of it, but his lordship's less bothered. You see him in the papers sometimes but he finds it all a bit tiresome. That's what Henry says anyway. He's Lord Sholto's valet too.'

Effie swallowed, staring down at her lap. 'Perhaps she'll settle down when they get married.'

'Who says they will?' Fanny put down the brush and picked up the hair framing either side of Effie's face. She pulled it back, positioning it high, low . . . experimenting with different ways of pinning it.

'Billy. He said everyone's waiting for it.'

'Knowing Billy, he's got a wager on it,' Fanny muttered.

'So you don't think they will?'

Fanny shrugged. 'No, they probably will. There's enough about it that works.'

'I saw them walking in the garden this morning,' Effie murmured. 'They look right together.'

'Looking right together. Aye, that's what matters for people like them.' Fanny began twisting her hair into small sections. 'A good marriage doesn't need to have much to do with love. It's all about securing fortunes, consolidating estates, good names, doing their duty for the generations to follow.'

Effie frowned. 'But . . . you do think he loves her?'

'I think he loves her enough,' she shrugged. 'I'm just not sure he knows what *real* love is. Rudolph Valentino love.'

'Who?' Effie looked at her blankly.

'You've a lot to learn,' Fanny sighed.

After that, Effie sat patiently as she was gradually transformed.

Eventually Fanny positioned a last pin in her hair and stood back. She gave a nod, looking pleased. 'Right, the last part. I'm guessing you've never worn make-up before either? Turn and face me.'

Fanny applied powders to her skin, stain on her lips. It felt dusty and the very opposite of how she felt washing in the burn, but when the maid turned her back to the mirror, she was astonished by the difference. She was still herself, but somehow fine-tuned into sharper relief. For a moment, she was able to admire what she saw – a delicate bone structure, thick lashes, a long neck emphasized by the way Fanny had loosely pinned her hair up, pulling a few wavy tendrils free at the front.

'Fanny, what have you done?'

'You don't like it?'

'I don't . . . I don't recognize myself.'

'Well, that's nothing new,' Fanny laughed, reminding her of her display at the mirror in front of Mrs McKenzie a few short days ago.

Effie felt small bubbles form in her stomach, an effervescence coming from inside. 'You must be a magician. You've transformed me!' Was it really her? She couldn't believe it.

'Nonsense, it was easy. You're beautiful, Effie. Just . . . wild.'

Effie gave a sudden smile. She couldn't deny that. 'So what now?'

Fanny put her hands on her hips, looking pleased with herself. 'Simple. You put on the shoes and you go up there.'

'Up there,' she echoed, seeing how Fanny's eyes were bright, her cheeks pink, and knowing hers were the same. The two women looked at one another.

This was an adventure.

Chapter Twenty-Four

Her heels clicked on the floor as she went back downstairs. There was no through access from the maids' bedrooms to the principal rooms on the same floor, so she had no choice but to go past the scullery and kitchen dressed to the nines. She felt conspicuous and out of place. Even just moving, dressed like this, was different – for someone who'd spent the first eighteen years of her life only wearing shoes every seventh day, it was hard enough wearing them daily. But heels . . . She felt like she was balancing on pins.

Fanny was walking ahead of her, as if clearing the path, as Effie pinched her skirt to see her feet on the stairs. Even before they got to the bottom step, they could hear the usual commotion in the kitchen, dinner preparations well underway.

Mrs McKenzie was coming out of the servants' hall when she saw them round the corner.

'Well, well,' she said, stopping and looking on in amazement. 'That's quite a transformation, Fanny.'

'Thank you, Mrs McKenzie.'

The housekeeper walked slowly around Effie, taking in the flawless skim of the dress, the careful pinning of her hair. She seemed especially pleased that the necklace she had loaned Effie added some sparkle to the outfit.

'We'll make a lady's maid of you yet.'

Fanny beamed.

The sound of whistling alerted them to Billy coming down the passage carrying some silver salvers. He stopped dead too, just as the housekeeper had. Apparently Paris-made dresses hadn't been seen downstairs before.

'Crikey. You should wear girl clothes more often.'

'Don't be so impertinent, Billy,' Mrs McKenzie scolded him. 'Take those to Mr Graves and then you can escort Miss Gillies upstairs and hold the door for her. Climbing stairs in long dresses is a particular skill.'

Billy hurried past, winking as he caught Effie's eye.

Barra appeared down the spiral stairs, stopping as she caught sight of the crowd. 'What's going on—?' She saw Effie dressed in her own gown and nodded approvingly. 'It suits you very well.'

'Thank you.'

'Her ladyship's just gone through.'

'You should get up there, then,' Fanny said with wide eyes.

Billy returned, with Mrs McLennan and the kitchen and scullery maids in tow too. The young girls cooed at the delicate dress but Mrs McLennan frowned. 'You need more hot dinners, lass! Make sure you get down what'll be put before you tonight – and no drama!'

'Oh for heaven's sake, this isn't a cabaret show,' the housekeeper said, just as Jenny appeared on the stairs too, carrying a blouse for mending. Effie knew that meant Sibyl was dressed as well. They would all be up there, in the parlour, talking, waiting . . . She mustn't be late and yet, she didn't want to move her feet. If everyone down here was looking at her like she was a curiosity, she could only imagine the disbelief upstairs. They'd laugh. She was a caricature of a dinner guest. 'Hurry along now. Don't keep them waiting.'

'This way then,' Billy said. 'We'll use the wooden stairs so you come out in the hall. Seems more proper this evening. Can't have you emerging from dark corners dressed like that.'

Effie nodded, aware of a murmur of muffled conversation at her back as Billy led her round to the wooden staircase off the main passage. He turned to go up and as she went to follow after, she heard the sound of boots on the floor and saw the gamekeeper come round the corner at the far end. He had a cocked shotgun in one hand and a bag over his shoulder. Like everyone else, he stopped dead, as though he'd found the countess herself down here.

Effie could only raise her hand in silent, distant greeting before she disappeared from sight, trailing after Billy.

'Well, I guess now I've got my answer,' he said, several paces ahead of her and opening the door at the top that led onto the great hall.

'Answer to what?'

'Whether you're servant or guest. Us or them.'

'I told you, I'm neither.'

'Doesn't look like that from where I'm standing,' he shrugged as she passed by. 'You even smell like them.'

It was true. Effie had smelt it too as she pulled on the gown; there was still a trace of scent lingering from the previous owner. She smelt rich.

The door to the adjoining room, the dining room, opened and Henry walked out. He looked at them suspiciously, his eyes narrowing at the sight of Effie.

'Would you take Miss Gillies to the parlour, Henry?' Billy asked, knowing he could go no further at this time of the evening. The hallboys were very much to be not seen and not heard.

There was a pause. 'Certainly.'

Effie swallowed, feeling ever more nervous. Did Sholto understand what his simple dinner invitation entailed for her? Not just a full-scale mobilization of the ladies' maids to get her appropriately attired, but then having to endure a parade before the servants that underlined her dislocation here in the most blatant terms.

Henry led her the short distance across the hall to the parlour. 'Good luck,' he murmured, one eyebrow arched and suggesting she would need it, as he put a hand on the brass knob and turned it.

'Miss Euphemia Gillies,' he announced in a formal voice, stepping back so that she might pass.

'Ah good, good!' She could hear Lord Dumfries's voice before she could see the man. 'Miss Gillies, I was just telling—'

His words fell like stones as she rounded the door and stepped into the room. The walls were the same thick, rich white as in the great hall, but every chair and gathered drape was stitched from a bold canary-yellow silk so that the room appeared to glow from the inside out.

Candles threw an amber light that flattered the incumbents as they sat grouped around an unlit fire, drinks in their hands. Sholto, who was lounging against the mantelpiece in the same suit – black tie, Fanny had told her – as last night, straightened fixedly as she walked over. Small steps, Fanny had warned as they practised walking Effie up and down the short length of her bedroom in heels – part of her brief induction into the rudiments of behaving like a lady, which had also covered cutlery, how to hold a glass and words not to say.

She reached the group in silence, wondering if she had done something wrong already. 'Good evening,' she said in a quiet voice, her eyes invariably travelling towards Sholto. He was staring as if he'd never seen her before.

'Good heavens, young lady, I never would have recognized you! I had to take a moment to check my dashed eyes weren't playing tricks,' Lord Dumfries said, recovering first and greeting her with a gallant head bow. As if she were a lady. 'Last time I saw you, you'd run through a hedge or . . . been for a swim, I think.'

'Your Lordship. My lady,' she said, turning towards the older woman sitting at the far end of the chaise. Fanny had instructed her to greet Sholto's parents first. His mother was wearing a burgundy silk dress with silver threads, her fair hair worn upswept in the older style. 'Lady Sibyl.'

Effie smiled at Sibyl, hoping for some sign of alliance at least, after their introduction yesterday in the library. The young woman looked dazzling, both sophisticated and fashionable. Her glossy dark hair was styled in tight, precisely-set finger waves that must have made Jenny's arms ache, and she was wearing a sapphire satin gown with a cut like Effie's. At her neck were ropes of pearls, all worn at different lengths, and her lips were a vivid scarlet. Effie could see a ghostly impression of them on the rim of her glass.

'Miss Gillies,' the countess said with a distinct note of surprise. 'When my husband and son spoke of you from their sojourn earlier this summer, I'm afraid they wholly failed to mention you are a lady.'

Effie felt her cheeks sting pink at the compliment. 'Oh, no, I'm no lady. I'm from St Kilda. We're all equal there.'

There was an astonished silence and Effie could see Sholto hide a smile behind his drink.

'Well, I think that rather remains to be seen. You have a natural grace, my dear,' the matriarch replied, also with a bemused smile. 'Come and sit beside me. I should like to get to know you better.'

Effie made her way carefully to the other end of the chaise. Now that she'd had a moment to get her bearings and adjust to the grand surroundings, she was beginning to absorb the finer details – William was standing in a corner holding Margaux on a lead. The big cat was sitting up and panting, perfectly docile, but the footman's eyes kept glancing towards his charge every few moments, as though he was taking nothing for granted. If she hadn't been so terrified, Effie might have laughed at the sight.

Mr Graves, too, was there. He had been standing by a drinks table and now approached with a tray and a bubbling glass upon it. 'Would you care for some champagne, Miss Gillies?' he asked, his eyes meeting hers briefly. Only a few hours earlier she had been sitting beside him, eating mutton.

'Thank you,' she smiled, taking the champagne even though she had no intention of drinking it. Fanny had fiercely warned her about this too. 'It'll make your head fuzzy and the room swimmy. You've not got the stomach for it, not if you can't keep down a steak and kidney pie. Just pretend to sip it.'

Sibyl, on the other hand, drained her glass, tipping her head right back before holding out a straightened arm for a refill and sending the butler back to the drinks table again.

'Miss Gillies, I must confess I would not have recognized you from our meeting yesterday. You're an entirely different creature. You look simply divine,' Sibyl said. 'Who's your couturier?'

Effie stared at her blankly.

'Only I swear I've seen that gown before. A dear friend of mine had one awfully similar. Nancy? Nancy Mitford?'

Effie felt the shame bloom in her cheeks. She had been in the room all of a minute. She hesitated, wondering what to say. Fanny hadn't coached her for this eventuality. 'Yes,' she said finally. 'I believe this was hers.'

There followed a silence that seemed to be one part appalled, two parts delighted. 'You mean . . . the very *same* dress? The actual one? But how could that possibly be?'

She swallowed. There was nothing for it but to come clean, lest Sibyl should run away with the even worse assumption that the dress had been stolen. 'I've borrowed it for the evening, from Barra. Miss Mitford gave it to her when she left her service.'

Sibyl's mouth opened wide. 'Oh! Oh that is too fabulous. Just wait until I tell her I'm having dinner with her dress! She'll scream! She'll die!'

Effie was alarmed. She sincerely hoped not.

'I wouldn't,' Sholto said, motionless at the fireplace. 'It would only upset her to hear that Miss Gillies looks supremely better in it than she ever did.'

Sibyl's mouth snapped shut, her little joke abruptly falling flat. Effie shot him a grateful look but he had already looked away.

'Now tell me, Miss Gillies, how have you found it since leaving your home?' the countess asked her interestedly.

Images raced through her mind: Poppit flying through the air; Mhairi collapsing on deck; a sheet hanging across a dank bedroom; Mrs Buchanan's open hand; the butcher's swinging carcasses; shiny cars, mirrors, stairs, a pretty rug . . .

'There's been a lot to learn,' she replied. 'And the more I'm seeing, the more I'm realizing how much more there is to learn. I'm only just beginning to understand now how very small our world was.' Her eyes skated over to Sholto again but he was still staring at the ground.

'It didn't feel like that at the time?'

She shook her head. 'No. It felt like we *were* the whole world. We didn't know what we were missing, because we'd never had it.'

'Quite so. I've always said it – travel is so important for broadening horizons. The earl and I try to travel for at least three months of the year.'

'Sholto and I had the most wonderful few weeks in Provence with Dickie Grainger,' Sibyl said. 'We all stayed in this sweet *guingette* that's just reopened under a new name – the Colombe d'Or. They're terribly keen on painters so we thought we might masquerade as some ourselves just for the larks, but Mr Picasso was there, which rather ruined the fun.'

The countess had a frozen smile on her face.

'Then we went to Vence, just next door, naturally, to pay our respects to darling Lorenzo. So terribly sad.'

'Who is Lorenzo?' the earl asked, looking confused.

'Why, David. David Lawrence.'

'The writer, Father,' Sholto murmured. 'D. H. Lawrence.'

'Oh—'

'He died just a few months ago in Vence. The TB caught up with him in the end. His wife managed to get him out of the san the day before, but there were only ten people at the funeral. Ten! Isn't it pitiful?' Sibyl twirled a hand in supposed sympathy. 'Anyway, it felt right we should pay our respects, didn't it, darling?'

Effie's eyes slid over to Sholto at the casual way Sibyl called him 'darling'. He looked a little startled, but nothing more. This casual intimacy before his parents was apparently normal.

'Yes.' It was more a drawl than an enunciated word, as though the very effort was too much for him.

There was a pause. Effie was vaguely aware that Sibyl had hijacked the conversation away from her.

Seemingly, so was the countess. 'And what do you like most about the mainland?' she asked, as though the diversion through France hadn't happened.

'Umm.' Effie thought for a moment. 'Well, I do really like trees. And hot running water.'

Everyone laughed, as if she'd told a joke.

'You surely don't miss having to descend a rope to catch your dinner?' the earl chuckled. 'Graves makes things so much easier, don't you, Graves?'

'I do my best, sir,' Graves intoned.

'Heavens! Is that what you used to have to do? Go out on ropes and catch dinner?' his wife gasped. 'But you simply don't look capable.'

Effie bridled, though she was sure the countess hadn't meant it as an insult. She glanced at Sholto to find him watching her now. He looked nervous. Could he tell she'd been offended by his mother's words? Did he remember how important it was to her to be capable? Or was it the mention of ropes that had him scared?

'Being light worked to my advantage on the rope, my lady.' She looked back at the earl. 'And actually, sir, I do miss it, the climbing and the hunting . . . It's nice not to be hungry or scared about going hungry; but I miss the physicality of my old life – feeling the ground beneath my feet and being out in the elements.' Since arriving here and starting work in the collection room, she had spent more hours inside than she ever had in her life. 'Everything here is much more . . .' She looked down at the delicate fabric of her dress, her feet encased in high-heeled satin shoes. 'Removed from the natural world.'

'Clarice, it's a continuing sadness to me that you couldn't have seen this young lady in action on the sea cliffs,' Lord

Dumfries said to his wife. 'What a spectacle it was! When we first turned up, the islanders put on a climbing "exhibition" for us—'

Effie let her eyes drift again towards the fireplace. Sholto's gaze was cast down towards the floor again, his jaw balled. He looked stiff with tension. Resentful at being made to remember the moment they had first met, supposedly the moment he had 'fallen' for her.

'—sea cliffs that would make your stomach drop just to look at, and believe me when I tell you, no one held a candle to her. Miss Gillies could shimmy up and down those ropes like a monkey in a tree. We'd never seen anything like it, had we?'

Sholto automatically shook his head, but his gaze remained down.

'There was, I think, some consternation among the men when we said we wanted her as our guide, but I was resolute. And I was right. What a week it was.'

'Not quite a week, sir, sadly. The storm chased you off a few days early. We were very sorry to see you go.' This time she didn't take her eyes off the earl but Sholto had to know she was addressing him, surely? It was as bold as she dared to be. An olive branch extended, something to bridge the divide between them.

'Thanks to you, I was able to add the much-prized sooty tern egg to my collection.'

'Were you, sir?' She was surprised. She didn't remember that.

'Ah yes. It was when there was the emergency on Boreray and you two had run down the mountain to raise the alarm.'

'Heavens, how dramatic! *Running* down a mountain? The only way I can get down them is by skiing,' Sibyl drawled.

'I was making my way down when I saw it circling about,' the earl continued, seemingly oblivious to his house guest's remark. 'You'd mentioned you'd seen them but you thought they were migrating.'

'Aye, they don't usually land in the Hebrides. There must have been a storm that blew them off course.'

'Well, lucky for me they had nested there after all and I nabbed the egg! I got a nasty twisted ankle for my trouble and it took me nigh on eight hours to get down again.'

'Honestly,' the countess tutted. 'Risking life and limb for an *egg*.'

The earl just grinned at Effie, as though she understood his obsession. 'It was a small price to pay, my dear, given I had thought I might have to sail up to the Faroes to get one. I've not got the stomach for that kind of swell anymore.'

'Nor me, sir. I've only crossed open water one time, during the evacuation, but I don't think I should like to make a habit of it.'

'You shan't be going back, then?'

She thought of what would await her there if she should, and shook her head quickly. 'Sadly not.'

'Well, then it's just as well we've got plenty here to keep you distracted. I understand you've made a start on cataloguing already?'

'I hope that's all right, sir? It seemed like a good way to become acquainted with the collection.'

'An excellent idea. It's a daunting proposition, I know. The collection's second only to Charles Rothschild's library, but once we've got it in proper order, I daresay it could be of interest to the public.'

'It's very exciting, sir.'

The earl frowned. 'Talking of libraries . . .' He twisted slightly, looking for the butler. 'Have they managed to get that jackdaw out of there yet, Graves?'

Mr Graves stepped forward from the shadows. 'I believe there was some difficulty, sir. The bird was rather aggressive.'

'But I've left my reading spectacles in there and I'm as blind as a mole without them.'

'I'd be happy to retrieve them for you, sir,' Effie said quickly, catching Sholto's gaze, though he didn't know she knew what he'd asked the housekeeper to do.

'My dear girl, you can't possibly approach an aggressive bird,' the countess protested.

'But I'm very used to dealing with aggressive birds, m' lady.' She remembered Sholto being attacked by the fulmar; it spitting oil and what that had led to . . . She glanced over to him and this time, he was already looking at her. Was he remembering too?

'Not looking like that,' his mother replied, and Effie realized these exquisite clothes made her . . . useless. Merely decorative. If she'd been sitting in here in her tweed breeches, barefoot and with a rope looped around her torso, the conversation would be very different.

'It's quite all right, Mama. It should have exhausted itself by now. I'm sure that between us, Graves and I will manage to get it out,' Sholto said.

Graves inclined his head, but he looked less than pleased by the idea.

'I've got some specs you could use,' Sibyl offered.

'I didn't know you wore spectacles?' Lady Dumfries said.

'Oh, no, they're not mine,' Sibyl replied breezily.

The door opened and Effie felt herself freeze as Mr Weir came in. His eyes found her immediately, dressed above her station and sitting beside the countess, but he walked straight over to the earl.

'I apologize for the intrusion but there's a telegram for you, sir,' he said in lowered tones. 'It's urgent, I'm afraid.'

The earl took it from the silver salver with a tut. 'Thank you, Weir.' He opened it distractedly, shook the paper open, then held it away. And further away again. 'Do you see? This is what I mean about my spectacles.'

'I'll get them for you,' Sholto offered, putting down his glass and looking ready to bolt from the room.

'No, no, just read it for me, would you?'

He handed the sheet of paper over and there was a momentary hush as Sholto cast an eye over it. '. . . Oh.'

'What is it?' the countess asked, sitting more upright at his tone.

Sholto looked up with a frown. 'It's from Sir John. His factor's been found.'

'Oh, at last!' his mother said with relief. 'Thank heavens for that! It was beginning to be quite worrisome. Well, where was he all this time?'

'He's dead.'

'What?' The earl looked at his son in disbelief.

'Oh, how beastly!' Sibyl cried, fanning herself with her hand.

'It says his body was found today on St Kilda. A tourist boat landed this morning and he was found on the beach on the far side a few hours later.'

As if as one, every head in the room turned in Effie's direction, the butler and footmen and Margaux included. Mr Weir had been watching her throughout, as if waiting to witness her reaction. Had she given him a good show?

She felt strangely untethered from them all, like a bubble rising into the sky. Her head felt fuzzy and the room was swimming, though the champagne glass was still full in her hand. Their voices sounded underwater, distant and shapeless.

Someone was in front of her now, a pale face with red lips peering at her, but the detail was blurring and within a few seconds, the white parlour had turned black.

'In here.' The voice was male but unfamiliar to her. She had a sensation of moving – or rather, of being moved – but the effort to open her eyes seemed too great. She was set down on something soft and felt someone pull off her shoes. She gave a groan, as she always did when her feet were free again.

'I think she's coming round.'

Her eyelids flickered a few times, then the dying light of day announced itself. A pale face, no red lips. Sholto?

She blinked again.

'Back in the land of the living, then?'

Effie felt the room snap into focus as Henry pulled back. He was standing there with Mr Weir and Mr Graves. She looked around for Sholto but saw only salmon-pink walls, a large wardrobe; the bed had a roof on it . . . This wasn't her bedroom.

'How are you feeling, Miss Gillies?' the butler asked her.

'Where am I?'

'You fainted. His lordship told us to bring you to the nearest available bedroom.'

She stared back at him. She supposed they could hardly carry her up and down two flights of stairs and halfway across the length of the house back to her own, but . . .

She remembered why it had happened, the confirmation she had been dreading since she'd arrived here hitting her like a brick again. The full awfulness of it rained down upon her head and another moan escaped her. She went to get off the bed, almost whimpering with fear. No, it couldn't be true—

'No,' Mr Graves said firmly, stepping forward. 'The countess has said you are to rest. You will stay here for tonight.'

Effie's gaze slid to Mr Weir, who was looking on with open disdain. It was bad enough that she was not only dining upstairs, but now sleeping there too. But that wasn't why he was regarding her with such contempt. She knew he suspected her for certain now. Why had she fainted? It was like putting a 'guilty' sign on her head. Mathieson had to have told him something, just enough, to put her in the frame as a suspect in his own murder. But what?

There was a knock at the door and Sholto strode in, like a sunbeam in the dark. 'How is she?'

'Recovered, sir,' Graves replied. 'She's awake again.'

'There's no need for me to stay up here,' she said quickly to Sholto, throwing back the cover again. 'I'm fine.'

'I've tried telling her, my lord.'

'If she wants to go back to her quarters,' Mr Weir said, stepping in, 'she's clearly well enough.'

'No.' Sholto shook his head firmly, looking directly at her for one of the only times that evening. 'You've had a nasty shock, Miss Gillies. You should stay up here and rest, in case.'

In case of what?

'Graves, if you could ask Mrs McKenzie to arrange for Miss Gillies's night things to be brought up.'

'Are you sure this is strictly necessary, my lord?' Weir asked, stepping in again. 'Miss Gillies is fully revived, her colour has returned—'

Sholto frowned as he turned to stare at the steward. A silence like a thunderclap boomed between them. '. . . Where is your humanity, man? Miss Gillies has just learnt of the tragic death of a man who was a friend to all St Kildans. She knew him far better than you or I. Every year, for six years, he was their direct and constant link to the mainland. Why should you presume she is not suffering? Clearly she is in shock.'

Weir backtracked. 'Of course, sir. Forgive me.'

'I'll speak to Mrs McKenzie now. Henry, with me, please,' Graves said, leaving the room.

Weir and Sholto both hovered, watching her in the bed. Effie sensed they both wanted to say something, though it wasn't appropriate for either one of them to remain.

'. . . Well, we shall leave you to rest, Miss Gillies. Ring the bell if there's anything you need. I assure you someone will attend to you directly.' Sholto turned his gaze straight back towards the steward in a clear warning.

'I'll draw the curtains first, shall I, sir?' the steward asked, walking towards the window. She couldn't very well sleep there with them left open.

'Yes. Very good, Weir,' Sholto muttered, standing by the door for a moment before reluctantly walking out.

Effie watched him go, her voice stoppered in her throat. She desperately didn't want to be left alone with the steward, but what could she say?

She swallowed and looked back at Weir. He was pulling the curtain cords with exquisite slowness.

'This is a troubling development indeed,' he said quietly, pulling at a pleat and shaking it out so that it fell in a way more pleasing to him. 'A missing persons case has now become a suspicious death inquiry.'

She swallowed. '*Is* it suspicious?' she asked quietly. 'It's awful, of course, that Mr Mathieson was somehow left behind, but it's a tragic accident surely? Nothing more. No one's to blame.'

Weir turned to face her. The evening light shone behind

the curtains, silhouetting him. 'That's the question though, isn't it, Miss Gillies? How *did* he get left behind?'

She knew now was the moment she had to convince him of her innocence. If she didn't do it now, he would keep coming after her. 'I don't know. But it was so busy; there was so much going on that none of us slept much the last week. We were all exhausted, doing what had to be done for our own families; we weren't keeping tabs on the factor.'

He walked slowly across the floor, staring at the shine on his shoes. 'I'm afraid I just don't believe that. Frank would never have been 'left behind'. He wouldn't have got the timings wrong.' He sneered, the motion crumpling his face. 'He was a professional manager: organized, efficient – and at times, ruthless. I'm quite aware he was a man with enemies.' He stopped at the end of the bed and stared at her. 'But he had been masterminding the logistics of the move for weeks. Months. He didn't get left on the wrong side of the island *by mistake*. There was no one who knew the drill better than him.'

'I don't know what you want me to say,' she said quietly. 'I'm very sorry about all of it.'

'Oh, I know you are. From where I'm standing, you look very sorry indeed. You look like the kid who kicked the cat; you know you've done something wrong and now you're just waiting to be found out . . .'

She shook her head. 'It's not true.' It was the truth.

He walked up the side of the bed now and for the first time she saw he had something in his hand. He stared down at her for several moments and she pulled the blankets tighter around her neck. She hated that she had been put in the bed and she could see him reading her fear. '. . . This came for you this morning,' he said finally.

He held out the object she had glimpsed. A letter.

She took it without thanks. Had he read it? She wouldn't put anything past him.

He stared down at her forbiddingly for a few moments more, and she realized he made her feel exactly as the factor always had: threatened and off balance. A determined and contrived abuse of power.

'. . . Sleep well, Miss Gillies,' he said, leaving the room. 'While you still can.'

The door closed behind him and Effie sank back into the pillows. For several seconds she lay motionless, going over everything he'd said to her, the questions he had asked, the innuendo in his voice. What had Frank told him? Everything? Some of it? Or was this all a bluff?

She remembered the letter, twisted in her hands, and felt a stab of longing for some loving words from an old friend: Flora. Mhairi . . . Slowly she opened it.

Dear Effie,

We hope this letter finds you well. We miss you here, things are quiet without you.

The auction went well and everything is arranged. Your possessions have been sent on, to arrive in the morning, and your father will be on the four o'clock train tomorrow. Please meet him at the station.

Write with your news when you can. We'd be glad of some adventure.

Your loving friend,
Jayne

Tomorrow? It was several days sooner than expected. She'd need to get down to the cottage in the morning to give it a good clean before their possessions were delivered.

She went to refold the slip of paper, her gaze falling to something written in the bottom corner that had been obscured by her thumb.

I dreamt of the factor again.

Again? Effie dropped her head at the confirmation, come too late. When had the first dream come? If Effie had still been in Lochaline, living beside her, Jayne might have told her and a couple of days could have been saved; Effie might then have balled up her courage and done the right thing, told people what she'd done and insisted on a trawler going out. Or the navy. Anyone who could get over there to save him.

But the truth was that even with foresight and hindsight combined, Frank Mathieson was never going to be saved, for one simple reason: Effie had wanted him dead. She was glad he was dead. She had just never known she had it in her to be the one to kill him.

The moon was full, bathing the room in a silvered light as Effie slept in a soft bed that might well have been feathered by St Kildan fulmars. Feathers she herself might have plucked, from birds she herself might have caught. Feathers that had lain in sacks and kept secret gifts she never should have been given. Nor accepted.

Everything seemed to connect somehow, drawing her back to her past and home, yet also leading her here, away from it. She didn't know if she was lost or found. Could she hide here? Or should she run? She was not a servant, but still staff. She was a friend, but still staff. She lived in the margins, as she always had. Indefinable. Unpredictable. Impossible to catch. Wild.

She lay in a sea of silky cotton, spreading herself over more space than her sleeping body had ever known. Embroidered silk drapes fell in waterfalls beside the pillows and a bouquet of pink and yellow roses scented the night air. This was luxury unimaginable only two weeks ago, but she couldn't find rest in the comfort. Her dreams were vivid and she was fitful, tossing and moaning as images tore through her fevered mind like racing demons: Frank Mathieson lying on the ground. Poppit pawing the air. Carcasses swinging on hooks. A cheetah on a lead. A gilded book on the floor. A pale face and red lips. A man in her room.

A man in her room.

Her breathing came hurriedly as sounds began to imprint themselves over pictures in fractured segments: the pad of a bare foot.

The creak of a floorboard.

The rustle of a sheet.

A breath in the dark.

Her eyes flew open as she gasped. Silvered light. A pleated ceiling. Curtained walls. Where was she? Her heart was like a caged nightingale, its wings beating frantically, urgently, as she tried to make sense of her surroundings. This was no byre, no closet, that she knew.

The fireplace. The oil paintings.

Her body softened as it all came back. She was safe. It was just a bad dream. She closed her eyes again, allowing her head to sink deeper into the pillow once more.

Just a bad dream—

A door clicked shut.

Not any door. The door. Her door.

She sat up with another gasp, fully awake now, the night-ingale frantic again as her eyes strained in the gloom looking for a shadow, as her ears strained for another breath in the dark.

Nothing stirred, the night holding itself in perfect contraction. For several moments she was held too, her body rigid and tight – but then she threw back the covers and ran across the carpet. She flung open the door and looked out.

The long jade-green corridor didn't even blink back: ancestors on the wall, ancient chairs, polished tables. No signs of life. No fleeing figure on either the stone staircase or its wooden counterpart at the opposite end. Everyone was sleeping, all doors closed. She had no idea who was in which rooms – was it Sholto beside her, right there? Or was it Lady Sibyl? How many bedrooms were there in this vast house? She stared at the door opposite, then beside her, but there was not so much as a creak to suggest anyone else was up.

Heart thudding, she stepped back into the room and shut the door, turning the key in the lock behind her. She crept back into the soft feathered bed and pulled the silky sheets around her neck. Was she imagining things? Going mad? Had the steward got into her head, as she knew he wanted. Or was this the revenge of the dead, the torment of sleepless nights? She'd not rested well in weeks now, her spirit heavy with malaise.

She closed her eyes but saw only the scene she had left the last time she had seen the factor – his body on the ground, blood on the rocks. Her eyes opened again, her gaze falling dully on the far wall. No, there would be no rest in sleep. She could do nothing but wait for the sun to come up.

Chapter Twenty-Five

'What did I say about no drama?' the cook asked as Effie tried to steal her way past the kitchen. She had hoped to be first up and back to her room before anyone could see her. She had had the unenviable choice of flying through the house in either the yellow chiffon gown or her nightshirt. She'd chosen the latter. The gown wasn't for wearing bare-footed and bare-faced. It wasn't a dress for her to just slip on any time she liked. It demanded an occasion.

'I'm sorry, Miss McLennan. I tried my best.'

'You're no end of trouble, lass,' Mrs McLennan tutted, sighing. A gleam came into her eyes and she winked. 'But you've a way about you. Henry said you were doing well till the bad news came.'

'He did?'

'Aye. He also said he's lifted heavier coal buckets, so you'd best eat the oatcakes I've left for you in your room. Then I want you down here for breakfast in the half hour or I'll come and find ye myself.'

Effie nodded. 'Yes, Mrs McLennan.'

'Now scat, before anyone else sees ye. Fancy running about the place in just that nightshirt, I don't know.'

The cook had a point. If Billy was to catch sight of her, she'd never hear the end of it. And William would probably die on the spot. She took the stairs two at a time, hurrying down the corridor past the maids' bedrooms and just clicking shut her door as Fanny's opened and then closed a moment later. Footsteps trod down the hall. Effie leant against the door and closed her eyes. At least she could get dressed without causing a scandal.

She opened her eyes, grateful to be back in her narrow room. It was meagre compared to the opulence of the family's bedrooms but it was comforting to her. She liked its simplicity and cosiness.

She frowned. She sensed there was something . . . different about it. There was nothing visibly wrong or broken, no new odour she could detect but like a stare had weight, so she somehow had a feeling of the air having been disturbed. A silent turbulence in her absence.

Her gaze grazed the room – the bed was made, her coat hanging on the hook, her towel folded on the rail by the window. The pretty rug was . . . it was slightly askew, with a slight ruck, as though someone had been standing there and caught it with their foot. Her, most likely. Caught in a hurry. Rushing out.

But her instincts told her not.

She walked slowly to the bed. Her heart was already pounding. She dropped to her knees and lifted out the suitcase, but she already knew what she would find.

The pad of a bare foot.

The creak of a floorboard.

The rustle of a sheet.

A breath in the dark.

She had been right last night. It hadn't been a bad dream. There had been a man, looking for something in her room. But not just that one—

She opened the case and looked inside. Her heart dropped like a dead bird.

He'd come to this one too.

Twenty minutes later, she was bathed, dressed and back in the servants' hall. A quiet broke out as she walked slowly through, dressed in her Sunday best navy wool skirt and blouse.

'Well, it's not quite on last night's level,' Mrs McKenzie said. 'But to what great occasion do we owe thanks for putting you in a skirt? Even if it is the skirt that's being held up by a . . . *bent nail*?' She tutted at the sight. 'For heaven's sake.'

Billy spluttered with laughter. Jenny and Fanny giggled. Even Barra was smiling.

'We had nothing else back home, Mrs McKenzie,' Effie said simply, walking over to her chair. She felt spectral. Completely empty.

'I'm sure not, but you're not at home anymore, Miss Gillies. Bring it to me later and I'll sew another button on for you. That thing is a liability. You could be injured by it. What if you were to get tetanus?'

'Death by skirt,' Billy grinned. 'There's a new one.'

She didn't have it in her to smile at his quip and she took her seat in silence as a plate of steaming porridge was set before her by one of the kitchen maids. She stared at it, knowing there was no way she could eat.

'So, Miss Gillies?' Mr Graves prompted, reminding her of Mrs McKenzie's original question. 'The great occasion?'

She looked at him dully. It was hard to think straight. Could he see her hands were shaking? '. . . Oh. My father's arriving today, from Lochaline. I'm to collect him from the station.'

'Ah. Well, that will be nice for you, to be reunited with him and have some family near.'

But for how long? How could they stay now? What she had just discovered had shaken her to her core. She felt paranoid, and defeated.

She forced herself to respond, to somehow move through the motions. 'Aye. I'm going to go down to the cottage after this, to clean it before our furniture arrives.' Her voice was as colourless as her cheeks. Where was he, her intruder? Would he confront her in here? Shame her before everyone? He had all the proof he needed.

'Does that mean you'll be moving out of your room upstairs?' Mrs McKenzie asked.

Effie nodded. It would take all of three minutes for her to pack her possessions. What remained of them.

'Shame,' Fanny murmured, looking sad. Effie couldn't meet her eyes.

'Well, that's very well timed,' Mr Graves said. 'Mr Felton came up last night to say the cottage was ready.'

There was a pause and Effie realized she was staring at him. Staring but not seeing. She couldn't seem to rein in her mind; it wandered like an aimless child.

'Are you quite all right, Miss Gillies?' the butler asked her. 'You're very pale. Are you still troubled by last night's news?'

She looked away quickly, terrified she could be read like an open book. 'I'm fine, thank you. Just . . . shocked.' Effie raised the spoon to her mouth and willed herself to take a bite. She had to be as normal as she could, until she worked out her next move. '. . . Mr Graves, when his lordship first approached me about coming to work here, he said he would arrange for his driver to collect my father from the station. His bones are bad and he can't walk far. Do you think—?'

'Of course. I'll see to it that Fraser is notified. On which train is your father arriving?'

'The four o'clock.'

'Very well. Be at the garage half an hour before and he'll take you to collect him. I know his lordship's not got any plans to leave the estate today.'

'Thank you.' She took another bite of her breakfast. The sweet honey flooded her tastebuds and she closed her eyes reflexively, grateful that this at least broke past the dullness that had settled upon her in the bedroom, a scattered mind in a stunned body.

'So,' Billy said with a leading tone. 'Last night.'

'I can't believe you ended up sleeping in one of the bedrooms!' Jenny said, looking delighted they had finally got round to the topic of interest. 'What was it like? The beds are so soft, it must be like sleeping in a cloud.'

'It was . . . nice,' Effie stammered. Every word was an effort. 'And so kind, but I'd have been better in m' own room.' She *should* have been in her own room. If she had, then—

'You were very pale,' Mr Graves murmured, still watching her closely. 'The countess wanted to call the doctor. It was Lord Sholto who convinced her you'd just had a shock but I must say you still don't look quite right.'

'I'm fine.'

He sighed, not pushing it. 'Such a shame. You acquitted yourself well, all things considered,' the butler said. 'You were doing a fine job of engaging her ladyship. I thought she was rather taken with you.'

'You did?' Her voice was flat and toneless.

'*Un*like Her Royal Brightness,' Henry put in with a dark smile. 'She looked like she might throttle you.'

'Henry!' Mrs McKenzie scolded.

'It's true, Mrs McKenzie,' he shrugged. 'She was in a frenzy of jealousy because Lord Sholto couldn't take his eyes off her.'

Fanny gave a gasp, her cheeks pinking with delight on Effie's behalf.

'Only because he'd never seen me like that before,' Effie said quickly. Every time she'd looked over, he'd been staring at the floor.

'Or because he'd never seen you *in that way* before – as a woman,' Henry countered. 'I was there. I saw it all. So did Mr Graves, didn't you?'

'I saw no such thing,' the butler contradicted. 'Everyone was quite appropriate in their behaviour. His lordship would never dream of . . . crossing the line.'

Effie said nothing. Gossip, tittle-tattle, innuendo . . . If they only knew the story she was sitting on.

'Stop teasing, Henry,' the housekeeper said. 'It was a shame for the evening to end the way it did, on such tragic news. Did you know the man well, Miss Gillies?'

Effie didn't reply immediately. He had been monstrous in life. Was she to speak well of him in death? 'Well, I didn't know him that well,' she said edgily. 'I was only wee when he became factor and first started coming over.'

'Oh? How . . . wee?'

'Eleven? Twelve? He spent most of his time with my Uncle Hamish and Ian McKinnon, the postmaster. And the minister too of course, although I don't think he was a religious man.' Her words seemed tied together, quiet and indistinct, running into one another.

'Still, you must have been happy to see him on his visits over. His lordship said the factor was your principal contact with the wider world?'

Happy to see him? He'd been the very last person she wanted

to see. 'He only came over twice a year, so like I said, I really didn't know him that well. But he'd arrive in the late spring, just as soon as the water calmed, and he'd bring us provisions, so we were pleased for that. Then he'd come again for a week at the end of August to collect our rents before we were cut off again.'

'So you had no contact at all through the winter months?' Barra asked, looking pitying.

'Occasionally we'd get whaling ships or trawlers stopping in the bay if there was a storm, but for anything smaller, from September to May, the sea was too rough.'

'How did you pay rents?' William asked. 'With what?'

'Feathers, fulmar oil, tweed, knitted socks and sheep's wool.'

'It all sounds so primitive,' Billy muttered.

'I think it sounds romantic,' Fanny sighed.

'Romantic?' Billy laughed. 'Where's the romance in poverty? I'd like to see how long you'd feel romantic with an empty stomach and skirts held up with bent nails.'

Fanny gasped, shocked by his rudeness, but Effie was beyond affrontery. 'I never felt poor till I came here,' she said simply. 'You can't long for what you don't know. Sometimes I think it might be better to live in ignorance and just be happy with your lot.'

'So you think ignorance is bliss?' Henry asked.

'Aye, maybe.'

He shook his head firmly. 'No. We're not made that way. I think it's human nature to want more than we've got.'

'You certainly do,' Barra groaned, rolling her eyes.

'Not just me! Even if a man's got every single thing he could possibly desire, he always wants more – he'll always take a bite of the forbidden apple.' He met Effie's eyes with a secretive, knowing look. 'I'd put money on it.'

* * *

She was heading for the garage later that afternoon when she saw the gamekeeper emerging from the woods, a pack of dogs bustling and running around his legs.

'Miss Gillies!' he called, raising his arm in the air to catch her attention.

She stopped where she was and waited as he altered course to come over. Only as he drew nearer did she see that the dogs were in fact juveniles, barely out of puppyhood.

'Oh my goodness,' she whispered, immediately crouching and holding her arms out as they swarmed, almost knocking her over. They had long silken black coats, with chestnut brown socks, chests and facial markings. She smiled – and it felt like cracking a nut. One dog in particular nuzzled into the crook of her elbow, its muzzle down and head pressed to her arm affectionately. 'And what's your name?' she wondered as she stroked its velvety head.

'That one's Slipper,' Mr Felton said, coming to stand near.

She looked up at him. 'Slipper?'

'Aye. Because she's always under m' feet.'

Effie smiled again. This time it didn't feel quite so alien. 'I like it. It suits her. How old are they?'

'Seven months now. They're getting leggy . . . and very boisterous.'

'Ah but they're beautiful. How many have you got?'

'Nine. This one here's the mother, Storm.' He pointed to the dog with the greying muzzle. 'I've had her since she was born. And her mother before her. They're from good stock.'

'What breed are they? I've never seen the like before.'

'Gordon setters. Intelligent, biddable, soft mouths. Excellent gundogs. They've an instinct for the birds. His lordship wouldn't have any other kind.'

He'd have had Poppit, she thought, if he'd known how clever she was, how attuned to the wildlife and birdlife around them, how loving and responsive and kind and brave . . . The sadness surged in her again. How much had she lost? And for what exactly? She had gained nothing by being here. . .

Slipper was still nuzzling her, the other dogs losing interest as they picked up on other smells. 'Can I pick her up?'

'If you wish.'

She lifted the dog, feeling something inside her ease as she felt the soft warm weight of the animal in her arms. The last time she had felt it, everything had been falling apart. Her world disintegrating around her . . . It was still disintegrating even now. She closed her eyes, holding the puppy closer to her cheek.

'Y' like dogs then.'

'We always had them back home,' she said quietly, angling her head as Slipper burrowed into the crook of her neck, tickling her with a cold, wet nose. 'They weren't pets, working dogs only, but ours I had to rear by hand after her mother rejected her so we had a special bond.'

'Aye, that can happen.' He watched her as she cuddled the animal.

'Where are you taking them?'

'On a walk. They need to stretch their legs and I've some pen mending to do so they can keep me company. You can too if you wish.'

'Thank you, but I'm just on my way to the station to collect my father,' she demurred. 'He's travelling down from Lochaline today and I can't be late. He's no English.'

'It sounds like I finished the bothy just in time then—' She saw the gamekeeper's eyes lift off her and onto something behind. 'Good day, sir.'

'Felton.'

She turned to see Sholto approaching. He was wearing a suit and looking grim-faced. 'Miss Gillies.'

She swallowed at his coldness. Last night in the parlour there had been glimmers of his old kindness, but it seemed that with the rising of the sun . . .

'They're coming along well,' Sholto said as the dogs clamoured around his ankles now, seeing how she was holding onto Slipper.

'Aye, sir. They're growing fast now,' Felton replied. 'They're a good pack. Clever animals. I'm pleased with them.'

Slipper wriggled in her arms, beginning to sniff her hair and Effie gave a low, unexpected giggle as she was tickled. 'You monkey,' she whispered, planting a kiss on the dog's head.

Both men watched as though she'd done something unusual.

'Well,' Sholto's smile was tight, tension around the edges of his eyes. It was clear he didn't see dogs as pets. 'I won't keep you.'

He walked off, Felton giving a single short whistle that brought the dogs immediately to his side.

The two of them watched him go for a moment.

'I understand you dined with the family last night,' Mr Felton said, looking back at her.

Effie kept her gaze on Sholto's back. So upright. So correct. So determined to avoid any one-on-one interaction with her. 'Aye. The countess wanted to hear about my home,' she said quietly. 'Apparently they're thinking about . . . buying the isles.'

His face was impassive but she knew his inward reaction probably mirrored hers. Who *bought* islands?

'I saw you on your way up last night. I didn't recognize you at first,' he said.

'I didn't recognize myself either.'

366

'You certainly looked the part.'

'Well, maybe for a moment, but that was all,' she said quietly. 'I'm nothing like them.'

'Not many of us are, Miss Gillies.' He was watching her closely.

She sighed, giving Slipper another kiss on her head and reluctantly setting her down. 'I should get on, I mustn't keep the driver waiting. But thank you for everything you did on the cottage. I've been down there all morning as they delivered our furniture and it looks wonderful.'

'Then I'm pleased you're pleased, Miss Gillies.' He nodded his head. 'Good day to you.'

Effie headed towards the garage, as instructed by Billy earlier, but she turned back several times to watch the dogs running ahead of Felton, noticing his easy lope through the grounds as he went about his day. His world seemed simple. Safe.

The doors to the garage were arched and double-height, painted in the same brick-red as was found on the kitchen plates and servants' blankets and her new cottage door. The estate colours. She stepped through.

'Hello?' She turned – to find Sholto in conversation with the chauffeur. They were standing beside a glossy back car that had no roof. 'Oh, I'm sorry, I didn't mean to intrude.'

Sholto looked back at her as though she was deliberately testing him. 'Fraser tells me he's scheduled to take you to the station to collect your father,' he said irritably.

'Aye, sir. He's on the four o clock train.' She looked across at the driver, who was looking distinctly uncomfortable. 'Is there . . . a problem?'

'I need to go to the station too, to collect a parcel. On the four o'clock.'

'Well, can we collect it for you?'

'No. No, I ought to take personal possession of it,' he said quickly.

Was it the book, she wondered? Had it been repaired? Did he not trust her to take good care of it?

'There's room for three of us, although it'll be a squeeze, but if we're taking your father back too, there won't be room for four.'

'Oh . . .' She felt she ought to bow out, that that was what he was asking from her – but how could she let her father arrive in a foreign place, where he spoke none of the language, and she not be there? Sholto didn't speak Gaelic either, so there was no consolation there.

She stayed quiet.

'I'm afraid there's only one thing for it, then. *I'll* have to drive.' Sholto looked back at the driver. 'I'm sorry, Fraser. I don't mean to deprive you of your duties.'

'Can't be helped, sir,' the chauffeur said. 'She's all ready for you.' He handed over the keys.

Sholto took them and looked back at Effie coldly. It made her stomach pitch and swoop, her blood still in her veins. '. . . Shall we, then?'

The driver opened the door for her and she climbed in. The car was unlike the one she had travelled in at Lochaline in that there was only one bench seat, not a front and a back. She sat down as Sholto climbed in on the driver's side. He started up the engine, the sound of it amplified in the garage like a thunderclap in a bottle, and they pulled away, leaving the chauffeur staring after them.

She was silent as he turned out of the garage and started along the estate road, his hands gripping the wheel, eyes dead ahead. They picked up speed quickly, the house already receding behind them, trees whizzing past, her hair lifting off her neck and beginning to fly. She saw him glance at her as she tried to catch it.

They drove over the sweeping Robert Adam bridge and she saw a swan gliding on the deep, black waters below them, moorhens in the reeds. For a moment, as the road curved, she could see the house between the trees – all its vastness, all its glory – before they swept out of sight, through the woods.

She stared at the road, watching the huge estate gates loom ever larger, squat lodges flanking either side. She knew he must concentrate, that driving a car would be complicated and difficult – though he made it look easy – but could he not talk at all? Was he going to drive the whole way in silence?

She glanced across, her mouth already parted to say something, but there was something about the set of his jaw that stopped her. She fell back into silence too, her gaze dropping to her hands, idle in her lap, his thigh just a handspan away from hers.

They were on the public road now and she tried to focus on the landscape she had been living in and yet still not explored. There were distant hills to the west, more stone cottages like hers with brick-red front doors, some people standing talking on a green, other cars less shiny and sporty than this one . . .

She could stand it no longer. 'Thank you, for helping me last night.'

He glanced across, but his eyes were hard. 'It was nothing. You'd had a shock. You needed to rest.'

'No, I didn't mean that. I was referring to your kindness when Lady Sibyl was laughing about my dress.' She put her hands to her head, trying to trap down her hair as she looked at him.

'Oh. That.' He tapped a finger on the wheel. 'Yes, well, she was being unkind. It wasn't fair. She can be a . . . bully, sometimes.'

'Well, I was grateful to you.'

'I don't want your gratitude, Miss Gillies.'

She stared at him, stung by his sharp words. Calling her *Miss Gillies* even when they were alone? 'Miss Gillies?' she echoed. '. . . Are we not even to be friends, then?'

His grip tightened on the wheel as he glanced over with another icy look. 'I hardly think we need worry that you'll be short of friends.'

She frowned. 'I don't under—'

'You're very tight with Felton.'

What? An astonished gasp escaped her. 'But. . . I've only spoken to him a few times!'

'So?' A few times could be all it took. Hadn't it been exactly that for them? One look, in fact. One smile.

He shot her a look, and this time there was more to see in his eyes. He wasn't cold at all, she realized. He was boiling hot, burning up. But with what? Rage?

The Auchinleck village sign flashed past the window. Already? The car moved so fast. She looked at him again. 'Sholto—'

'Don't get me wrong, it's good news. Very good. I can see it between you. He's certainly keen and you'd be a good match together.' He nodded as if agreeing with himself. 'Shared interests, similar backgrounds.'

She couldn't believe what she was hearing. 'You sound like my father – marrying me off.'

His fingers tapped on the wheel, rigid and rhythmic. 'Well, there's no point fighting the inevitable.'

Fighting the inevitable. Was that to be her destiny, then? Married? Or married to a man of her own kind? She stared at him. 'And what if I don't want to get married?'

He shook his head as though she was a tiresome child. 'Don't be ridiculous. You need to secure your future.'

She turned away from him, feeling a rush of emotion she wasn't sure she could hold back. Her very life was teetering on a precipice but she had thought she might endure it if she had him as a friend. Someone she could trust. But for him to say those things, to push her towards someone else and not make a single mention of what had happened between *them* . . . Had he really forgotten the last thing he'd said to her on the island? He had wanted to make a plan, to find a way forward with her. And now he was palming her off to his own gamekeeper? Who was this version of the man she had thought she knew?

She could see the signs for the station up ahead now and she let her hands drop, allowing her hair to fly around her head, grateful for the protection it gave her from his enquiring glances. She would not cry in front of him. She would not. She clasped her hands together till the knuckles were white.

He glanced over, seeing her rigid form. 'Oh for God's sake, Effie, what do you want me to say?' he snapped. 'I never asked you to come here!' He indicated right and pulled up alongside the station front.

'No, your father did.'

'But he wouldn't have done. Not if he knew.' He cut the engine and the car shuddered to a halt as he faced her at last, his eyes burning with an honesty that hadn't been allowed since she'd arrived.

'Knew what?' She stared at him, her eyes growing wide as she understood his meaning. 'You mean if he knew that you kissed me?' Was it really so terrible? Was she that shameful?

'He wouldn't have you here if he knew what it risked,' he said in a low voice.

'What is it risking?' she asked, incredulous and baffled.

He looked away. The train was pulling into the station, people walking through to the platforms. There was a loud hiss of steam as the brakes were applied.

'What is being risked?' she demanded, louder now. Her emotions were threatening to overflow, uncontainable. Messy. 'You won't talk to me. You won't even look at me!'

As if dared, he turned back again, meeting her eyes and holding them with his own. And for a second, she thought she could catch it again, the spark that had leapt between them on Hirta. But it was a leprechaun of a feeling, darting and mischievous, impossible to catch.

'What have I done to make you hate me?' she whispered.

'I don't hate you.'

'But you don't like me anymore.' It was a simple enough statement. A quiet truth. 'Not even as a friend.'

His head inclined away slightly and she saw him swallow, but for several moments he said nothing at all. 'I just don't think it's a good idea you being here, not for either one of us,' he said finally. '*You* need a completely fresh start. You need to build a new life, away from . . . here.' He swallowed again. 'My father should never have asked you to come.'

Her mouth fell open, a first twinge of apprehension beginning to rush through her blood at his words, the recurrence of this thought: you shouldn't have come. 'So what are you saying? That we should go?'

He looked directly at her. 'I think it would be for the best, yes.'

She stared at him, feeling the walls of her life begin to shake. He couldn't mean it. 'But my father's going to be coming through those doors any moment. He's just left our new home, sold all our animals . . . We've given up everything to come down here. You can't honestly be saying . . .' She couldn't believe her ears. 'Sholto? You're not going to throw us out? We've nowhere to go.' It was true. All day she had racked her brain trying to think where they could go to next, to hide away from here. But there was no outrunning the trail of evidence that the steward had found to connect her and Frank Mathieson, and when the police came for her – and they surely would – what would happen to her father then? Her only hope was that the Earl would show mercy to an old man, left abandoned and destitute through no fault of his own. They had to stay here and she had to wait for her fate to catch up with her. 'Please. For my father's sake. He'll end up in the poor house.'

Sholto wouldn't look at her but the ball of his jaw was pulsing. He looked pinched with strain, unspoken thoughts racing through his mind. 'I didn't mean . . . Of course I'm not . . . throwing you out.' He shook his head and sighed. 'Of course not. It's fine. Stay.'

'Really?' The word was a sob of relief as she clutched his arm. '. . . You promise?' Why wouldn't he look at her?

He turned away, out of her reach and opened his car door. 'Forgive me. I shouldn't have said anything. It was selfish of me. You'll be in the cottage now anyway. It'll be fine.' He got out and shot her the briefest of glances. 'I'll meet you back here when you're ready.'

And before she could say another word, he turned and walked into the station, spine erect, shoulders back.

Effie watched him go, trying to absorb what had just happened. Leave. Stay. Stay out of my way . . . For several seconds, she sat where she was, heart clattering at the near miss. How could he have said those things to her? Who was this version of the man she had thought she loved – running cold where once he'd been hot? Distant where once he'd been intimate? Rigid, no longer languid. Humourless, no longer laughing.

People were beginning to come through from the platform, porters carrying trunks and bags.

'—Father!' With a start, remembering why she was even here, she jumped out of the car and ran through, her skirt hanging low on her hips, the bent nail not quite bent enough. Steam billowed like a drunken sea mist as she looked up and then down the platform. She could see no sign of Sholto but it cleared just enough for her to catch sight of a silhouetted man making his way unsteadily, leaning heavily on his stick. Her father was stooped and seemed smaller than she remembered, even his cloth cap seeming too big for his head.

She ran towards the frail figure with a gasp. Until that moment, she hadn't realized how much she'd missed him. How much more she had left to lose. What would he do without her when justice came?

'Father!' she cried.

'Effie,' he breathed, looking relieved to see her. She threw her arms around his neck and inhaled the smell of him – black twist tobacco and peat smoke; the smell of home . . . It was all too much. She began to sob for what she'd lost, for what she'd got back, for what she could never have.

Her father patted her back as he'd always done when she was little. 'There, there,' he said kindly. He hadn't hugged her in four years, not since John had died, but his large, rough hands felt familiar and comforting, reminding her of happier times before their family had been cleaved by death. It only made her cry harder. 'We're together again lass. Things will be better now.'

They'd never been parted in eighteen years and if he only

knew how much had happened in the past eleven days. 'I missed you, Father,' she said, pulling back eventually and wiping the tears from her eyes.

'And I you,' he said softly. 'It's not been the same wi'out you about the place. Too quiet. Too clean.'

She laughed, but the sound was still a half-sob. She noticed something around his neck. It was a placard hung on string.

'Bearer speaks no English. See through to Auchinleck.'

'Jayne's idea,' he said as Effie pulled it over his head.

'Well, you won't be needing that now,' she said protectively, throwing it into a bin. She was all he had and he was all she had.

She took his bag in one hand and linked her other arm through his. 'Have we far t' go?' he asked. 'It looks awful flat.'

'Not far. His lordship's going to drive us home,' she said, trying to keep her tone neutral. But she was angry now, and growing angrier at how close they'd just come to having nowhere to go, their livelihood utterly dependent upon the whims of a capricious man.

How could he have said those things? She had thought she could trust him. She had thought they could be friends at least, but the truth was that from the moment she'd arrived, he'd been a stranger, distant and cold. And now he'd been cruel; he'd retracted it in the face of her alarm, but for how long? He was with Lady Sibyl now and he didn't want her, a wildling, here, reminding him of his indiscretion on St Kilda.

They walked through the station doors and out onto the street, where Sholto was placing a brown paper parcel into the trunk.

'Welcome to Dumfries, Mr Gillies,' he said, hurrying over and taking the bag from her, not meeting her eye. Not that she was looking either. They moved around each other like marble statues.

She helped her father into the car but he hadn't the flexibility to shuffle sideways along the bench and she shut the door beside him.

'You'd better come in through my side, Miss Gillies,' Sholto said, holding open the driver's door.

Effie slipped past him wordlessly and slid along the seat beside her father. He was already looking around with bafflement. 'Shouldn't it have a roof?' he asked her.

'I don't think this one does,' she replied. 'It's the style. Hold onto your cap.'

'What's your father saying?' Sholto enquired as he switched on the engine again.

'He's admiring the car,' she muttered.

He glanced at her, as if something of her new feeling sounded in her tone and she saw him squint as he took in the reddened eyes and wet lashes that she couldn't hide. She didn't need to. It no longer mattered what he thought. She stared ahead, aware that their legs were pressed side by side; she could even feel his thigh muscles flex as his feet pressed on the pedals. She moved her leg away as much as possible, not caring if he noticed.

For all the fresh air around them in the open-top car, a heavy atmosphere descended.

'. . . Right, well, Mr Gillies,' Sholto said with studied politeness. 'Let's get you home.'

Chapter Twenty-Six

The old proverb turned out to be true. Absence really had made their hearts grow fonder and over the following couple of weeks, Effie and her father settled in well to their new home. As the shock of their abrupt move began to abate and the news of Frank Mathieson's death became muttered fact, she and her father settled into a new rhythm that passed off as remarkably normal. The cottage was bigger than anything her father had ever known before; Felton had done a fine job of the repairs, keeping the warmth in and the cold and rain out. It had no damp, which stopped her father's bones from aching so much, and sunlight seemed to squirrel its way into the furthest corners. His mood was higher than it had been in years, even motivating him into digging some lazybeds in their garden while Effie worked up at the house. She had arranged the furniture into a homely setting, and every few days she would pick wildflowers – cow parsley, heather, violets – growing at the edges of the wood behind them and place them in an old milk bottle. It had seemed strange to her at first. Much like birds' eggs, she felt flowers were intrinsically best left untouched and most beautiful when left where they grew, but she couldn't deny they brought a certain cheer into the little home. Jayne's quiet, unwitting influence upon her, she supposed.

Jayne, Flora, Mhairi . . . She missed her old friends desperately. Effie had written to Flora and Mhairi, sending them her address and asking for their news by return. Flora had yet to reply – which was no surprise at all – but Mhairi had come back, talking flatly about their new house and the jobs at the factory: Mrs Buchanan was a 'harridan'; Norman Ferguson had been promoted to deputy foreman at the forestry; Mad Annie now had a bike; her siblings were enjoying the village school playground . . . but like Effie, she made no mention of the things that really mattered between them – secrets that couldn't be put to paper – and Effie had finished the letter feeling more isolated from her friend than before.

It was impossible to write with full honesty, Effie knew that. She could imagine how her own reply would read when she put pen to paper, for on the surface of things, life appeared to be on the up. Mr Felton had taken to dropping in most days as he passed and often she would find him sitting with her father, talking in Gaelic together, as she came back in the evenings. She sensed that it would be the gamekeeper who would be the most comfort to her father when the time came for her to leave and she felt a growing affection for this man who made him smile. But not only him. The gamekeeper would bring the dogs with him and every time Effie would scoop Slipper into her arms and cover her head with kisses, loving the warmth and weight of her. It was blatant favouritism, but she missed Poppit so much, it made her stomach ache. Some days the gamekeeper dropped around a fresh pheasant for them to hang by the door; on others, Mrs McLennan would send Billy over to the cottage when he was passing on his bike to run errands in the village, putting a small pie of leftovers for them in the basket. Such were the green shoots of new friendships and they were a solace to her that she had been right to stay here after all, to defy Sholto's wishes and lay the foundations for a new life for her father at the very least.

Everything was for him now. She had stopped eating in the servants' hall and even at dinner – in the middle of the day and when she was working in the big house – she would walk back to the cottage and dine with her father; unable to converse in English, there would be no companionship for him around that long, bustling table and she didn't like to think of him spending his entire days alone.

She missed her meals with the servants – though they had not passed without incident in the time she had stayed in the house, the gossip and chatter of a body of people who dined together three times a day had given her a fleeting sense of community that she had lost upon leaving St Kilda. But a perpetual sense of dread hung over her as she awaited her fate and she would not willingly put herself in Mr Weir's path.

It was lonely working in that room all day, every day, cataloguing eggs in silence. The hours dragged. The house was so big, she was often the only person in the whole of the west pavilion. She had seen and spoken to Billy only twice since moving out; Jenny had waved once from the other end of a hall. She had seen nothing at all of Barra, Mrs McKenzie or Mr Graves; they kept below stairs whenever possible but Fanny would try to dart in whenever she was passing with her duster or a vase of flowers, and share with her the latest news – the earl and countess were shortly leaving for Skye to visit Sir John MacLeod; Sibyl and Sholto were throwing a party but couldn't decide on a theme . . .

Effie saw some things for herself from the window where she worked and she watched the household's lives continuing on the other side of the glass – Henry 'walking' Margaux on her lead across the lawns each morning, the cheetah straining and panting happily at the sight of the plump sheep grazing. Sholto and Sibyl walking around the flower beds after lunch or playing croquet in the late afternoon. It was always the same between them – Sibyl lively and full of the joys, her laughter carrying like a bird's song across the terraces, Sholto quietly smiling with infinite patience, moving sedately through the days. Once he had glanced up at the window, as if sensing Effie's stare, but she had quickly ducked down out of sight. Another time she had almost run into him as she was taking the stairs two at a time and he passed by in the corridor above. He hadn't seen her but she had waited in the stairwell, heart thumping, until she could no longer hear his footsteps. They hadn't seen nor spoken a word to one another since their confrontation at the station. She wouldn't forgive what he'd said. Everything that had once been alive between them was now dead and he had been right that it was better not to see one another at all.

She put her boots back on and closed the collection room door behind her, making her way outside. Another day was done and summer was being squeezed out by autumn, the long days growing shorter, the sun dropping behind the hills on Bute before seven now. They would be eating pheasant stew tonight; she had put it on at dinnertime and left it simmering all afternoon.

'Oh! Hello, Fanny,' she said, surprised to find the maid standing out on the terrace at the top of the steps. She was staring up at the roof, her arms reaching towards the sky. 'Is everything all right?'

'Oh Effie,' Fanny groaned. 'I've been out here almost an hour trying to get Miss Petunia down. But she's stuck!'

'Miss P—?' Effie looked skywards in alarm, to find a fluffy white cat huddled on the roof; specifically, she was tucked into the corner of the intricately carved stone pediment that protruded at a perpendicular angle to the slate roof. '. . . Oh.'

She was an entirely different beast to the cats back home. On St Kilda they were sleek creatures, tiger-striped and mottled tabbies with bright yellow eyes, excellent at catching the mice. Miss . . . *Petunia* didn't look capable of catching anything but a cold.

'She can't stay up there all night. She's an indoor cat. I don't even know how she got up there. She must have climbed through one of the windows in the bedrooms when I was airing earlier and onto the drainpipe.' The maid's voice wavered. 'Oh, what will I do? I can't tell her ladyship Miss Petunia is stuck on the roof. She's her pride and joy. If she was to fall . . .'

'Cats are pretty good at landing the right way up,' Effie said, seeing how the cat curled herself into a tighter ball as they talked. She was mewing and clearly in distress. 'But I agree, that is a long way down.'

She stepped back and took a closer look at the roof. The slate tiles were too smooth and steeply pitched to climb down from above, but the chimneys up top were set upon a flat area in the centre and looked solid and secure. 'Mmm . . . I reckon I can get her for you.'

Fanny gasped. 'You do? How?'

'I'll climb up there and get her.'

'Effie, no! You could be killed!'

Effie grinned at her dramatics. 'Fanny, believe me, I've climbed much higher and harder than this wee wall.' She tipped her head to the side. 'But I will need a rope.'

'A *rope*?' Fanny was looking at her like she'd asked for a gun.

'Mm-hmm.'

'. . . All right,' Fanny breathed, looking scared.

'The longest you can find, please. And Billy. Get me him too. There must be an access to the roof from the top floor?'

'Yes. Through the attic.'

'Then give him the rope and ask him to get onto the roof with it. But he must stay on the flat. No heroics, y' hear me?'

Fanny nodded. 'Rope. Stay on the flat.'

'Get him to shout down when he's up there.'

Fanny ran back into the house, leaving Effie standing by the top of the steps.

'Well, you're causing an awful fuss and no mistake,' Effie called up softly to the cat as she crouched down to unlace her boots and remove her socks. Miss Petunia meowed in reply. She seemed distinctly out of place, cowering on the Palladian roof. She looked like she ought to be napping on a silk chaise before a log fire.

Fanny must have flown around the building because within a few minutes, Billy's cheeky face appeared at the parapet. 'Miss Gillies!' he cried down. 'You called?'

She chuckled, looking back up at him with her hands on her hips. 'Thanks, Billy. Have you the rope?'

'Aye!'

'Then if you could loop it round the nearest chimney and throw both ends down to me.'

There was a brief pause. 'Is that all? You don't want me to shin down? I reckon I could!'

'Just throw it, thanks, Billy! I don't want to have to rescue you too!'

She heard his scoffing laughter but a few moments later, the rope ends came dangling down like snakes.

'Effie, are you entirely sure about this?' Fanny asked her

worriedly as she tied the ropes into the slide and grip knots favoured back home. She felt a rush of thrill to be doing again the thing she loved – and had missed so much.

Effie just winked at her. '*This* is an adventure, Fanny.' Pulling sharply on the rope a few times, she got a foot up to the windowsill on the window beside the door and, without a moment's hesitation, began to calmly 'walk' barefoot up the wall.

Fanny gasped again, her hands pressed to her mouth as Effie moved seemingly effortlessly up the vertical stone face of the house. She passed the jambs of the front door, then began scaling to the bedroom windows on the second floor. A movement inside one of them briefly caught her eye but she didn't look in, needing all her concentration on her destination, even if it was an easy climb.

The windows were trimmed with stone frames that gave her enough of a foothold to support herself as she drew level with the bottom of the pediment and placed her forearm along the ledge. It wasn't an ideal position; the rope still lay somewhat to the right of where the cat was huddled.

'Now you're quite sure you don't need my help there, Miss Gillies?'

She looked up to find Billy grinning at her from his position on the roof, but she could see a flicker of concern in his eyes. 'I might if this was a sheep and not a cat, but I think I'll be fine thanks, Billy.'

'That's a shame then, but we've definitely not had any sheep stranded up here, as far as I'm aware.'

She grinned. '. . . Here, puss-puss,' she coaxed, reaching towards it with her free arm. It meant she wasn't holding onto the rope with both hands and she heard Fanny's latest audible gasp as in the next instant, Effie gave a single balletic lunge, hopping sideways on the rope and grabbing the cat in a fluid movement. She scooped her into her body before the cat could even panic and tucked her into the front of her woollen vest. 'There,' she said soothingly as the cat's claws sharpened against her shirt, looking for purchase.

She looked back at the hallboy and winked at him. 'Wait for my call. I'll give two sharp tugs when I'm free and you can pull the rope back up.'

'Aye aye, cap'n,' he said, saluting her.

Effie got both hands back to the rope again and with a simple push off the window frame, began to descend. The figure she had glimpsed inside the bedroom had opened the window while she'd been retrieving the cat and there was a moment of surprise for both parties as Effie suddenly, fleetingly, found herself face to face with Sibyl.

'Oh, hallo, my lady,' she smiled as she casually passed on her way down, the other woman open-mouthed and mute, for once, with shock.

As Effie's feet touched the pediment of the front door, she glanced down to gauge the remaining distance – only to find a small crowd had gathered. The rescue had taken less than five minutes, but in that time Fanny appeared to have been joined on the terrace by half the servants – Jenny, Mrs McKenzie, Mrs McLennan, William and Henry were all there, but it wasn't their scrutiny that suddenly put the nervous fizz in her stomach that hadn't been there at the top of the rope. She was being watched by the countess and her son, who were walking in the rose garden.

Moments later, Effie's bare feet made contact with the terrace again and she untied herself from the rope, thinking fast. Would Fanny be in trouble for letting her do this? It had been Effie's idea after all but she knew her ladyship could hardly be pleased to find ropes dangling down her house and a feral girl playing upon them. There was scarcely a moment to think however; the countess and Sholto were already climbing the steps up to the terrace as Effie reached into her vest and brought out the cat. 'Miss Petunia was stuck, Your Ladyship,' she said quickly.

But she hadn't finished speaking before people began clapping. Jenny and Fanny were jumping with excitement, the footmen looking bemused yet impressed. A yell came from up top, too – Billy, out of sight but not out of earshot as he heard their celebrations and realized she was safely down.

'Dear girl,' the countess exclaimed, regarding her with a look of open astonishment. 'Now I understand what my husband has been trying to tell me. That was extraordinary. *You're* extraordinary.'

'Oh, no,' Effie demurred, but her eyes were bright from the adventure. 'It was nothing, really. We just wanted to get her down quickly before the light went. It seemed the easiest solution.'

She kept her gaze upon the countess but she was keenly aware of Sholto's attention.

'Easy?' the countess laughed. 'I don't know how to thank you.'

'There's no need, my lady. It was my pleasure.' It was no word of a lie; it really had been. For the first time in weeks, she felt herself again. The Effie of old. Effie Gillies of St Kilda.

The countess took her hand and gripped it for a moment, looking at her intently. 'You are a remarkable young woman,' she reiterated. 'Quite unlike anyone I've met. Don't let life over here dim your light, will you?'

Effie swallowed. 'I'll try my best.'

'Good. And thank heavens you were wearing trousers!' the

countess smiled. She dropped Effie's hand and brought the cat up to her face, enjoying the feel of her luxuriant fur. 'Now Miss Petunia, we must get you warm,' she said, drifting back towards the house and sending the footmen scrabbling to open the door.

'Just what is it with you and drama, lass?' Mrs McLennan muttered, smiling, as she and the housekeeper turned to go back in too.

'That was amazing!' Fanny hissed, her eyes bright as she and Jenny followed the senior servants until only Sholto was left.

Effie turned away from him, giving the ropes the two sharp tugs she had promised. 'You can pull the ropes up now, Billy,' she called for good measure, hoping Sholto would take her distraction with the ropes as the cue to leave. She watched the ropes being hoisted back up the building's facade, but when she turned back again, he was still standing there.

He'd said not a word throughout, but his eyes burned with something that looked like pride. 'Well, you'll have a friend for life in my mother now,' he said eventually, leaning into the silence.

'Oh?' she asked coolly.

'Yes. Sometimes I think she loves that cat more than she loves me.'

Effie didn't reply and she let another silence swell, seeing the uncertainty grow in his eyes as he took in her new distance. She wouldn't forgive him for how lightly he had toyed with her job here, her home. She wouldn't beg for his friendship again. She didn't want his kindness or company. She was here by his father's authority, not his. Her future was uncertain enough without his caprices.

He shifted his weight. 'At least now she will understand

what my father's talking about when he regales their friends about your climbing exhibition.'

'I doubt it merits any such glory. It was really nothing special to any of us.' Her eyes flashed defiantly. 'Just an easy way to make money off the tourists. They were always easily impressed.'

She saw his eyes narrow at her insult.

'—Miss Gillies!'

She looked down to see Felton crossing the gardens. He was walking with purpose towards them but for once the dogs weren't with him. 'Was that really you up there?' he asked, slightly out of breath and his eyes shining. He sounded uncharacteristically . . . jovial. He wasn't a man given to ready smiles and easy compliments. 'I couldn't believe my eyes!' he enthused as he got to the bottom of the steps. '—Oh, Your Lordship. I apologize,' he said, stiffening. 'I didn't see you there.'

Effie realized that Sholto had been obscured from his sight-line by a rosebush in an urn.

'Good evening, Felton,' Sholto nodded, stepping forward slightly from the shadows.

There followed an awkward moment. No one seemed to know who should speak first.

'Am I intruding, sir? Shall I come back later?' the game-keeper asked more formally.

'Was it me you wished to see?'

'Uh . . . Miss Gillies, actually. But I can wait.'

Effie saw Sholto's jaw ball with irritation, a movement that would be invisible at distance. He glanced at her again and she felt the same swipe at her knees that she always felt when their eyes met. Even when he was angry. Even when she was. For a moment, he looked like he wanted to speak, but then something – an instinct – made him look up.

Effie looked too.

Sibyl was leaning out of the window and watching their conversation with a scowl.

Sholto looked back at the gamekeeper again. 'Not at all, Felton,' he said peremptorily. 'She's all yours.'

The words felt like a slap as he moved past her, back into the house. Effie felt her eyes sting but she didn't stir until she heard the door close behind him and the window above slid shut a moment later.

'I couldn't believe my eyes when I saw you coming down the front of the house like that,' Felton said, picking up where they had left off, wholly unaware of how her entire world had just changed with those three words: *She's all yours*. 'My heart was in my mouth.'

'It wasn't a hard climb,' she said flatly, picking up her boots and joining him on the grass. 'Are you heading home? I was just on my way back.'

'Ah, but before you go.' He put a hand on her arm, stopping her from walking by. It was the first time he had ever touched her. 'Do you remember when we first met, I mentioned I had a surprise I'd like to show you?'

'Aye.' Her eyes narrowed. 'And I remember telling you I don't like surprises.'

'Well, I hope you feel, as I do, that we've become friends since then.'

She shrugged. 'Aye.'

'Please, then. Won't you indulge me with this? I have no wish to alarm you, but I know it will delight you and there's really no more time. It's now or never.'

'Delight me? Those are strong words, Mr Felton.'

'I'm confident I can deliver on them.' He smiled and it enlivened his eyes, softening his face from the gentle frown it settled into at rest. 'It's just through here,' he said, pointing towards the woods. 'Will you follow me?'

Effie felt herself tense. The last time she had found herself alone with a man she thought she could trust . . . 'It will be dark soon.'

'Which is why we mustn't delay.' He smiled and she saw the man who sat and talked with her father, who helped chop their logs.

'Fine,' she nodded.

A relieved smile enlivened his face. 'Good. Follow me.'

Effie looked back towards the house as they began walking through the gardens, but amber lights in the long vaulted corridors glowed through the windows in silent reply. They were observed by unseeing eyes only.

They walked into the woods. It grew dark quickly, in the trees. Shadows ceased to have edges, the first fallen leaves rustled beneath their feet. He walked briskly with his eyes down, making no attempt at conversation. The birds were singing wildly at the tops of their voices in a final symphonic blast before night fell, and Effie noticed how cloistered their songs were, trapped by the tree canopies.

She saw a nuthatch and a green woodpecker but most of the birds were hidden in the leaves. She had grown up under open skies, where gannets, shags, cormorants, fulmars, guillemots and puffins soared, dove and danced in the blue; aerial mating displays, dogfights and bullying all took place in plain sight, the experience more visual than aural. But here, largely out of view, melodies soared, skittered, chattered and tripped in an invisible choir and she realized that while her books had educated her in plumage, migration patterns, egg identifiers and so on, the birds' songs were an intangible beauty that couldn't be described. She could no sooner pinpoint the song of the blackbird than pocket a sunbeam and bring it home.

They didn't stop walking till they arrived at a clearing. The wood ended in a clean slice, the ground before them dropping away in a narrow gorge to a river a hundred feet below. She had had no sense of climbing but as Felton crouched low before some boulders, she looked around and saw the horizon had indeed dropped. She knelt down beside him. 'What are we looking at?' she asked in a low voice.

'There,' he said, pointing, his eyes trained on the rough cliffs opposite. A pine tree was growing out from the rocks at an extraordinary angle and it was several moments before she noticed the large, twiggy nest balanced in the crutch of the trunk and several large branches.

She squinted, peering closer. Her breath held . . . It couldn't be.

The hairs on her arms stood up as she got lower, lying on the ground on her stomach, staring with an intensity that even the birds seemed to detect. She watched as the adult moved its head in their direction, twitching its wings. Its legs were long, the beak deeply hooked, dark brown wings flanking a white breast. A stripe at the eye made it look masked, and she was surprised by the size of it, almost as big as a goose.

For several seconds, neither she nor Felton stirred. Only when the parent bird began to fuss at the nest again did she dare to breathe.

'Osprey?' she whispered.

Felton just nodded.

'But they went extinct here in '16,' she whispered.

He nodded again. 'Until this summer.'

She watched as the juvenile sat on a branch, looking out

to the distant sea. She could see the white spots on its back that distinguished it from the parent.

'The mother left a few weeks ago. They're getting ready to migrate. Any day now.' He glanced at her. 'It was why I had to bring you here, do you see?'

She nodded. 'Thank you. I'm so grateful. I never thought I'd get to see one. How many eggs were there?'

'Two. One failed,' he murmured. She could feel the timbre of his voice vibrate through the ground to her.

'Have you shown the earl?' she asked quickly.

He shook his head.

'But he loves—'

'No. I don't approve of what he does,' he said quickly.

'You mean, collecting eggs?'

'Taking them just for display . . .'

She nodded. It chimed with the reticence she had felt back home, an instinct she couldn't quite suppress as the earl had gathered egg after egg. Avaricious and covetous.

'It's one thing to capture and kill for survival; even for sport and profit if it provides jobs as well as a meal. But just to put it in a box to be able to say you have it . . .' He looked at her. 'Because that's what they do, you know, that family; they have to own everything, possess anything that's beautiful and wild and rare – they have to make it theirs, along with everything else.'

He stared at her intently and she had a feeling he wasn't talking about birds anymore. Had he heard Henry's gossip?

She looked back at the nest. 'So no one else knows?' she asked quietly. 'Just us?'

'Well . . .' He hesitated. 'Only Lord Sholto.'

Her head whipped round again.

He cleared his throat. 'Actually it was *he* who showed them to me. He brought me out here and asked me to keep an eye on them, to make sure they were protected from poachers. You can imagine the racket we'd have if word got out. The eggs would go for a king's ransom.'

'But he hasn't told his father? Even though they're on their own estate?'

The gamekeeper shrugged. 'He asked me to keep it between just the two of us. That was what he said.'

She looked back at him. So it wasn't quite true, then, what he had said about Sholto's family – having to possess for mere display? The son did not necessarily share the sins of the father. Sholto understood the birds' rarity meant they needed protection, not possession.

'I shouldn't have broken my word to him by taking you here but I knew you'd understand how special they are.'

'I do. I really do.' She looked back at the birds that told her so much about the nature of the man – men – protecting them.

He placed a hand upon her own and she almost jumped at his touch. 'I'm trusting you to keep the secret, Effie.'

Effie? It was the first time he'd called her by her given name, another step towards an intimacy she had known was coming. Nothing had been explicitly said, but she saw it in his and her father's eyes when she came home to them in the evenings; an expectation was growing.

'We're alike, you and me. Birds of a feather, if you will. We understand one another.'

It was true, she couldn't deny it. She'd known him before he'd ever said a word. He was her stock, the kind of man she'd been bred to marry: no airs, no graces, just plain-speaking and inured to the prospect of a life of toil. A future with him stretched out long and clear with no bends in the road. She already knew, just from the way he greeted him, that her father approved the match. Sholto had seen it too, the seemingly inevitable divergence of their two paths. He was destined for a socialite, she a gamekeeper. Or at least, she would have been, were it not for Frank Mathieson.

But it was too late for her now, and as he gripped her hand, it didn't matter that her heart fluttered against her ribs like a caged bird. Felton was a good man, he deserved better.

She looked back to the ospreys, seeing how they were getting ready to fly, preparing to escape here for somewhere safer, far, far away. If she had wings and no ties too, she knew she'd be doing exactly the same.

It was dark by the time they walked back. Felton had a couple of small travelling lanterns in his bag and he lit them, a small pool of light illuminating each single step along the path back to the cottage. They didn't say much. They both knew he had set down his cards and said what he wanted to say. They also both knew that at some point, she must reply. But not tonight. If their destiny was so inevitable, why rush? Her true fate would be revealed soon enough.

They walked in the easy silence that had been paved by their forebears as the great house glowed at their backs. Its golden eyes still gazed onto the grounds as before, but one now blinked as a figure watched in stillness at the two lights bouncing along the path, as though they were fireflies dancing in the night.

Chapter Twenty-Seven

'There you are.'

She turned to find Billy standing in the doorway, grinning at her.

'Billy,' she smiled, pleased to see him. The drudge of long days, spent largely alone, was beginning to wear on her. 'What brings you this far west?'

'You're wanted in the stables.'

'Me?' she frowned. 'Why am *I* wanted in the stables?'

He shrugged.

'Well, who wants me?'

He shrugged again. 'Mr Weir just told me to find you and tell you that you were wanted in the stables.'

Weir. Her blood ran cold at the mention of his name. She replaced the egg she was holding – a pine finch – in its box with a trembling hand. She knew it was the moment she'd been waiting for, the one she had known for weeks was coming, heading for her like a bullet – once fired, unstoppable. The stables would be private and discreet, well away from the main house.

'He said to be quick about it,' Billy added as she stared at him in horror.

She felt a cold chill ripple down her arms as she walked from the room and followed him down the stairs while he

394

recounted the gossip in the servants hall following her 'daring' rescue of Miss Petunia last night. She didn't hear a word of it.

'You know where to go?' he asked, standing in the passage, ready to head back to the kitchens.

She nodded sombrely, pushing on the door and walking outside. The first tendrils of autumn were reaching through the air now, stray russet leaves scratching along the ground, the breeze tickling with cool fingers. Somewhere in the back of her mind, she was pleased to have pulled on a woollen vest over her shirt this morning; she had knitted it for John long ago (without any of Jayne's proficiency, dropping stitches and falling into purl when she lost focus) but it was particularly soft and he hadn't minded that the armholes were different sizes.

The stables were a short walk, several minutes downhill from the house, but she was still mildly breathless when she arrived, her heart hammering, her adrenaline levels up. She peered around the brick-red doors to find eight long faces nodding over stable doors. But no steward.

'There you are,' a voice said from on high.

She looked up to see Sholto standing on a rough-hewn stone mounting block at the far end, beside the enormous horse she had seen him riding the other week. 'I was beginning to wonder if I was going to be stood up for a basket of eggs.'

What? She blinked, then blinked again.

'Weir got hold of you, did he? I thought we'd go for a ride.' He said it casually, as though it was something they'd discussed over breakfast. Not like someone who, during their last proper conversation two weeks earlier, had almost thrown her out on her ear and left her destitute.

She stared at him, mouth agape. He was wearing the riding jacket and tobacco jodhpurs he'd worn a few weeks earlier. If she hadn't recognized him as a peer of the realm when he'd landed in St Kilda, she saw it now – absolutely everything about him was superior and commanding – but was that because he had changed? Or because she had?

She was too shocked, too confused, to reply. The relief alone that it wasn't Weir waiting here almost felled her.

He looked her up and down. She was in her usual brown trousers; they were soft and, being baggy, perfectly comfortable for hours spent sitting cross-legged on the floor, sorting through almost-identical eggs. 'Yes, those should do fine,' he said, slipping a foot into the stirrup and throwing a leg over the horse's back. 'You've ridden before, haven't you?'

Effie looked at him as if he was completely mad, beginning to gather her wits again. 'Where? Where would I have ridden a horse? You know we had none on the island.'

The groom made a sudden move, as if startled by her impertinent tone. Sholto threw a glance down at him, then back at her, and she saw that this was all an act for the servant: his casually offhand manner, resumptive friendliness . . . He didn't want the groom to detect any of the tension that belied their every look, their every word.

'Well, if you can tend a bull, you can certainly ride a horse. There's nothing to it.' He clicked his heels and his horse obediently moved forward several paces, allowing another groom, who was holding a saddled-up grey, to come alongside the stone block instead. 'Gannon will help you up. I assume you're happy to ride astride? All the ladies do now, really.'

She stared at him, knowing his dignity rested upon her playing along; her job probably did too, but she felt caught between the desire not to humiliate him by walking out and the desire to humiliate him by walking out. *She's all yours.* The words still rang in her ears. His casual cruelty.

For several moments, she hovered indecisively. Her pride told her to turn away, to leave him sitting there, but her body seemingly had a will of its own and she climbed the steps, putting her feet and hands where the groom instructed. She allowed him to thread the reins through her fingers, listening as he explained the basic manoeuvres of stop, go and turn, but she saw the relief on Sholto's face that she was playing along. She wanted to ask him what this was all about – she was busy and she had work to do – but with the groom in their orbit, she stayed quiet.

'Don't worry, she's bomb-proof,' Sholto said, clicking his heels again and indicating for her to do the same. 'But I'll keep an eye on her. If she wants to take off, she'll have to take me with her.'

'You make that sound like it's supposed to be reassuring,' she muttered, drawing from him another glance. Did he see, now, that they weren't friends anymore? That this was where he had put them?

Her horse, Norma, stepped carefully over the cobbles, passing below an arch and out into the grounds. Effie had never been this far off the ground without a rope, but she instinctively sensed the animal was placid and quite happy to have her on its back.

'I doubt she can even feel you up there,' Sholto said, seeing her hesitancy.

'Where are we going?' she asked, daring to look up.

'Nowhere really.'

She glanced at him. Only he could make riding out over one of the finest estates in Scotland sound inconsequential.

They walked on, Effie's gaze focused entirely on the narrow

gap between Norma's ears. She realized she enjoyed the sound of the hooves upon the drive, the rolling rhythm as the horse trod, head nodding and giving occasional whickers. She felt Sholto's glances across to her, watching her form and checking her confidence, but he didn't speak, allowing her to settle in the saddle.

Once they were passing by the back of the great house, she sneaked a look at him, so handsome in profile and absolutely at home in this landscape. His face was relaxed, his eyes on the horizon, hands resting on the pommel of the saddle. She supposed he had been riding since birth.

Not climbing, though. She had that on him, at least.

She waited for him to offer up some sort of explanation as to why he was giving her a riding lesson she'd never asked for, but it didn't seem to be on his mind or his lips.

'What are we doing?'

He glanced at her. 'We're riding.'

'I mean – why?'

'I thought you might enjoy it. And I fancied some company.'

He *fancied some company*? She couldn't quite believe she was hearing this. 'You said we weren't to see one another.'

'I know.'

'So then . . . ?' Her tone was confrontational.

There was a pause and he sighed. 'It just seems a little extreme, don't you think? Rather dramatic that we should have to go around avoiding one another.'

'That was your decision. Not mine.'

'I know. And I was wrong. I was just a little . . . thrown, that's all. But I've got my head around it now. We can be friends, of course we can! We *should*.' He sounded like he was trying to convince someone.

They walked on in awkward silence. It wasn't exactly the

rapprochement she'd yearned for. She couldn't keep up with him and the way he blew hot and cold. He was more changeable than the wind. How could she trust him, after everything she'd been through? Was still going through? He had no idea what his presence in St Kilda had meant for her last May.

'Do you like it here?' he asked.

It seemed an odd question but she just shrugged. 'There's a distinct lack of mountains.'

'Yes. Sadly no mountains. My ancestors couldn't quite manage that.'

Moving mountains was seemingly the only thing beyond their reach, Effie thought as they hacked past groundsmen who all tipped their caps. The determination to subdue nature was an ongoing commitment. Billy had told her there was a maze somewhere, too; apparently that was the most impressive feat.

They could both see Henry on the other side of the terrace, walking the cheetah.

'Does Lady Sibyl always travel with her?' she asked, more from curiosity than any sophisticated desire to make conversation.

'Margaux?' he sighed. 'Yes. It's such a bore. She's been barred from Claridge's, you know.'

She didn't know. 'Who's Claridge?'

He laughed as though she'd said something funny. 'You are a breath of fresh air, Effie Gillies.'

She still didn't know what was so amusing, but there was something in his sudden laughter that pulled at her, an echo from another time that cracked the glaze of her new shell. She didn't want them not to be friends. When they weren't trying to fight, everything was so easy and natural between them.

Sholto began pointing out landmarks, telling her about the works and plans executed by his ancestors: the fifth Earl of Dumfries did this, the fourth Marquess of Bute did that. She was amazed to learn they had more than one title, more than one name – Crichton-Dalrymple – as well as another seat, Mount Stuart, the home of the Stuarts on the Isle of Bute thanks to an ancestor's favourable marriage: the Crichtons had honour but the Stuarts had money. His father was primarily known as the Marquess of Bute, the Dumfries earldom being a courtesy title only invoked when he stayed here, though he told her his parents preferred Dumfries House because it was more 'homely' and easier for the cities. They passed through what he called Cow Park, which was being grazed by several hundred of the glossy brown beasts, all nose down and shuffling slowly through the grass. She remembered her cheek pressed to Iona's belly that May morning when the sloop had first nosed around the headland. How long ago that seemed now. How very far from here.

And yet, here they were, riding out together.

She looked across at him again, wishing he wasn't quite so handsome. Just a little less golden.

'And that's Broad Wood over there,' he said, pointing to a thicket. 'Very good for badgers. I've lost one or two terriers down those setts over the years.'

In a flash, another memory was in Effie's mind – Poppit nuzzling her hand with her muzzle, her ears hiked up in excitement when she found a puffin's nest . . .

'You know every last inch of this estate,' she said, forcing her mind away from the past, even though the shadows slunk over her at every turn.

'Of course. Didn't you know every last inch of your home? And that was an entire isle!'

'I suppose that's true enough.'

'I can't imagine ever leaving here,' he murmured, looking out into the distance at the faint smudge of distant hills, the rolling pastures, Dumfries House now but a bright spot behind them. He looked over at her. 'It makes me realize what a brave thing you've done.'

'I wasn't brave. I just didn't have any choice. I'd have stayed if I could.'

'Really?'

'Really,' she said firmly. 'I always said I had nothing to come to here – and I was right.'

She deliberately invoked the spectre of Sibyl. Between her and this place, they had never stood a chance. There could never have been *a plan*.

There was another pause. 'Well, for what it's worth,' he said stiffly. 'I'm glad you didn't stay. Even if you felt there was nothing here for you when you left, I hope you feel you have a home now. Friends.'

'Friends?'

'Yes.'

'You mean like Mr Felton?'

He met her gaze, flashing her a brief rictus smile. 'Quite.'

'You're right. I do.'

They walked in silence for a few yards before he pulled sharply on his reins, veering away from the wood. 'Come on. We're heading this way.'

She thought she could already tell their destination, for ahead in the middle distance lay a copse so perfectly round and so artfully contrived, it could never have come from Nature herself. They were drawn to it as though magnetized.

'It's called Stairs Mount,' he said, seeing how she scrutinized it as they drew nearer.

'It's very round.'

'Yes. Perfectly, mathematically so.'

'Why?'

'The landscape aesthetics and visual artistry of a talented man called Capability Brown. When we get closer you'll see there are avenues within it that bisect the plantings. They create sight lines back to the house in one direction, and over to Cumnock on the other.'

'Oh.' Was the landscape not already beautiful enough to just enjoy, without having to be directed and shaped? But she didn't voice the thought. What did she know about beauty? About anything, really, other than how to climb a rope, catch a bird, tend a bull?

The ground, though gently undulating, was largely level over the expanse, but as they neared the Mount it rose like a pimple, with steep banks. She could see now the avenues he had described, how the eye travelled through the tunnelled tree stems to the light beyond. It had the effect of focusing the eye, creating a diorama.

The horses broke into a slow canter as they travelled up the slope but Effie forgot to be concerned, having almost forgotten her feet were not on the ground. The vast views, Sholto's languid conversation and Norma's nodding walk had contrived to lull her into relaxation.

'You're a natural. I knew you would be,' Sholto said admiringly as they walked down one of the paths. 'We can dismount here,' he added as they neared the halfway point and she saw how the trees peeled back from the very centre, creating another perfectly round space within, a majestic oak in the centre.

She felt flattered by the compliment but said nothing. She was too distracted by the sight of a straw basket – a picnic basket – left on a rug, below the oak.

She watched as he slid a foot from the stirrup and leant his body forward as he simultaneously threw a leg back, swinging it over the horse's rump, and slid himself to the ground. Did she have to do that?

He tied the horse's reins around one of the smaller tree trunks before coming over and helping her down too, reaching his arms up and holding her by the waist as she came down. She hesitated, but there was no other alternative and, a second later, she landed softly, like a cat.

'Is that for us?' she asked quickly, eyes averted and stepping out of his embrace.

He watched her walk over to it. 'Yes. I asked for it to be dropped off. Wasn't sure whether I'd need my hands free to stop you from bolting all over the place.'

'You just said you knew I'd be a natural.'

'Yes.' A wry grin escaped him as he tied up her horse too. 'But you can never be wholly certain.'

She turned on the spot, looking out at the trees that fanned around them in perfect, sculpted symmetry, playing peek-a-boo with the world.

'Are you hungry?'

She nodded, sitting opposite him on the rug and watching as he opened the basket and pulled out a pastry-topped pie, some chicken drumsticks and cold vegetables, some of which she recognized – tomatoes, cucumbers, pickles, carrots, beetroot . . . The assortment alone was dizzying. She hadn't known food could come in so many colours, textures . . . 'What's that?' she asked as he set down a small round dish.

'Pâté.'

'Oh.'

'Had it before?'

'Nup.'

'Heard of it before?'

'Nup.' She looked at it doubtfully.

'It's delicious.' He looked back at it too, his face slowly pulling into a grimace. 'But I admit, it does look . . . rather unsavoury.'

Effie watched as he sliced the pie, serving onto china plates. 'Mrs McLennan's provided us with some elderflower cordial and trifle and lemon cake too, so we shan't starve.'

Starve? This was more food than she'd ever seen in one place in her entire life. She picked up something small and red. It was round and hard, with a skinny tail.

'Radish?' she asked.

He nodded.

She took a bite, surprised by its crunchiness. But it tasted . . . clean. Of the earth. She smiled, liking it.

They began to eat, Sholto shrugging off his jacket and lying outstretched on his side as he picked up some asparagus. Effie sat cross-legged, trying everything at least once. She started out picking warily, but it was all delicious and she was hungrier than she had realized. She took another of the baby beets. They were so soft and sweet.

'By the way, I managed to get the book repaired,' he said, watching her as she saw, too late, the stains upon her fingers. She saw his gaze fall to her mouth and she wondered if it was on her lips too. Did she look ridiculous? 'Oh . . . Good.' Just the mention of the book made her tense.

'Yes, they've done a splendid job, sewed everything back in again. Apart from one or two slightly creased pages, it's as it was.'

She stared at the ground. 'I'm still awful sorry about it.'

'Don't be, it was an accident.' His eyes fluttered up to her and off again. 'Besides, it was hardly the most shocking thing to happen that day.'

'Wasn't it? What was more shocking than that?' She had felt sick about it for days.

'Why, you!' He laughed. 'I almost dropped dead of shock when I walked in and saw you standing there.'

'Oh.'

'You did look pretty shocked yourself,' he added, seeming to want corroboration from her that it had been shocking. Awful.

'I was pretty concerned to find m'self six feet from a cheetah, if that's what you mean.'

He grinned as he reached for another asparagus stem but she sensed the conversation was hovering above something else – close to, but not quite touching it.

'Did you manage to keep your father away from the library?'

'Yes, actually, although it took some doing. He was quite insistent about getting in there. I started out telling him a bird had come down the chimney but in the end, I had to say an entire jackdaw's nest had come down too. Whole thing. Fledglings. The lot. Hence the aggressive parents.'

Effie stared at him, her next radish poised in mid-air. 'And he believed that?'

He shrugged. 'Seemed to.' He saw how she was staring at him. 'What?'

'Jackdaws fledge in June . . . July at the latest.'

Sholto stared back at her, his eyes beginning to dance with amusement. '. . . They do?'

'How can you not know that?' she cried.

'Ah.'

'You are useless! You have a hundred thousand eggs in that

house and you don't even know when jackdaws fledge?' An exasperated laugh escaped her and without thinking what she was doing, she flung the radish at him. It was done before she even knew it.

He dodged it with a laugh. 'What can I say? We're just humble collectors. You're the expert!' He reached forward and threw a cranberry back at her. It whistled past her ear.

She gasped. He looked shocked too, and for several moments they sat poised on a precipice, eyes locked. Had he gone too far? Had she? The formality and distance that had existed between them since her arrival, throughout this ride, was suddenly gone. Here was the Sholto she knew again, the one from St Kilda who swam in the moonlight and rowed the sea, who climbed ropes and chased her up hillsides.

She saw him see the gleam light up in her eyes and he grinned devilishly. He lobbed another cranberry that whistled past her hair, making her scream. She threw back another radish as she got to her feet, laughing now. It hit him on the temple and he yelled, catching her on the shoulder with a baby beet. He threw with impressive accuracy as she began dodging around the trees for protection but she realized too late that she should never have left the rug – for now he alone had the ammunition with which to pelt her.

For several long moments, he launched a sustained attack of gooseberry fire, but she drew him out, running back into the trees and forcing him to chase after her, allowing her to nimbly double back to the basket and pick up more supplies.

'Hey!' he laughed as she grabbed a bunch of grapes with the same nimble ease as a great skua on a fly-by. Sholto caught her square on several times with more cranberries, which burst like little blood blisters on her vest. She scored some direct hits with the grapes but everything changed when he suddenly stopped by the basket on a 'loading-up' run and then straightened slowly, something hidden behind his back.

She could tell from the look on his face that it was far more than a bunch of berries.

'No . . . !' she laughed warningly, hiding behind a tree and hearing his footsteps approach. 'What have you got there? Show me!' She peered around to find him tiptoeing over and he froze as their eyes met. There was a cream cake in his hands and the look on his face made plain he had no intention of eating it.

She squealed, running away to the central oak and hearing him laugh behind her as he gave chase. Should she peer left or right? She knew that with every tree she hid behind, she had a fifty–fifty chance of peering around the wrong side.

She looked up instead. A vast, shimmering green canopy of interlocking branches spread above her head. If she could just get up to them . . . The height was nothing to her but the trunk was vast, far wider than she could get her arms around, and with her feet encased in leather boots, she wouldn't have her usual dexterity. Still, she could hear his low laugh as he approached; she knew he thought she was just standing there. She'd show him she was a St Kildan yet!

She dug a toe into the rough, pleated bark. She had to angle her knee awkwardly but there was a low, stray branch just above her head. It wasn't strong enough to support her alone, but the two combined would allow her to get off the ground and find another toehold, another branch or knot . . .

She had made three moves when he rounded the trunk.

'Oh no you don't!' he cried as he saw her scaling the tree, within an arm's length of reaching the safety of the branches. He reached an arm out, grabbing her leg and making her scream in fright and delight. Gripping the tree tightly, she turned to find him with one hand upon her ankle. He wouldn't pull her down, she knew that, but she couldn't escape him now either. She was stuck fast, pinned to the tree.

'I should have known you'd start climbing!' he laughed, still holding the cake in his other hand. It was raised up by his head, ready to throw.

Effie's grin widened. Without hesitation, she twisted and leapt down towards him, her arms outstretched – just as she had done off the cliffs towards the boat that first day – and pushing the cake into his own face.

He stumbled backwards, falling over, as she landed heavily on all fours by his feet. There was a moment of pause, Sholto blinking in disbelief through a mask of cream and jam.

Effie looked up at him and immediately creased at the sight. 'Got you!' she cried, doubled over with laughter, but as she went to get up to sprint back to the picnic rug, he caught her again – a hand on her leg, pulling her back along the grass on her stomach.

'Not so fast!' he panted, gasping with laughter too as she tried to wriggle free. 'You really must try some cake!' And his hand reached around her head, smearing cream all over her face.

She shrieked and twisted around onto her back, trying to avoid the dairy onslaught by thrashing her head from side to side. He changed tactics, falling still instead, and she opened her eyes to see what was coming next.

He was half crouched, half lying above her, one hand in the air ready to resume smearing her. He had cake all over his face, but as his eyes fixed upon hers, she felt the laughter die in her throat. In a flash, they were back there, spinning on the rope, covered in oil. Everything had changed, but nothing had changed. She saw the realization flood his eyes too, dismay and desire in equal measure . . .

'I say! What fun!'

The voice made them both stop in their tracks.

'Is this a private bunfight or can anyone join in?'

Sibyl was sitting astride a dun horse in the avenue which had a direct line of sight back to the house.

'Sid!' Sholto's arm dropped down. He rose as if he'd been lying on a chaise, smoothing the cream off his face and hands with casual flicks. 'You're here!'

Sibyl cocked her head to the side questioningly. Wasn't that self-evident? She was looking elegant in a long navy fitted jacket, cream jodhpurs and silk stock with a cloche hat. Effie immediately jumped to her feet. She looked down and saw her clothes were stained with moss and grass and exploded cranberries. 'That's all right isn't it?'

'Perfectly. It's . . . wonderful. Although I'm afraid—' He walked back to the rug and peered down into the wicker basket. 'You've missed lunch. Unless . . . trifle?'

Sibyl shrugged. 'Oh, I'm sure cook can rustle something together for me.'

Effie blinked. Both Sholto and Sibyl seemed to have moved into a mirrored gear of languor, as though it was being too late for lunch that was the calamity here. Was she the only one whose heart felt like it might explode? She was trembling, but she wasn't sure if it was because Sibyl had disturbed them or because of what might have happened if she hadn't.

The dun horse took a few steps back, but Sibyl was unperturbed. Effie could see she sat well in the saddle and, from her sanguine demeanour, that she was an accomplished horsewoman. She could feel the other woman's nimble scrutiny and Effie knew she must look . . . wild by comparison. 'Well, I do wish you'd said you were planning a food fight,' Sibyl pouted. 'I'd have joined you like a shot. You know how I hate missing out on the fun.'

'This . . . wasn't planned,' Effie said, becoming aware of a cranberry in her hair and reaching up to remove it. 'It was my fault. I started it.'

'Did you indeed?'

'Barra told me you were sleeping, Sid, and I didn't like to disturb.'

'You know I don't mind being disturbed by you,' Sibyl said in a lower voice as though her words were only for him. But Effie didn't think that was true.

'I thought you'd want to rest as best you could before the party.' Sholto was wiping the cream off his face; only a tiny amount remained on his neck, like shaving cream. He ran his hands through his hair and it stayed slicked back, sticky but sleek.

'That's just it! I had a darling idea for what to wear tonight! It came to me in my dreams and that was it, I was awake.'

'That's what got you up?' Sholto sighed, reaching down for his jacket and shrugging it back on. He looked like a different man – an old man – to the one who had just laughed and chased Effie through the trees. 'What is it, then?'

'It's a surprise. You'll see!' she teased coquettishly.

He didn't look terribly excited. He glanced towards Effie but his eyes didn't quite meet hers. 'Well, I expect we ought to be getting back.'

He walked over to where he had tied the horses.

'What about all this?' Effie asked, indicating the basket and rug, the plates still loaded with food.

He looked back, the sight of it seemingly almost painful to him now. 'Oh . . . just leave it. One of the grooms will be up later to fetch it.'

It seemed wrong, to Effie, to leave it there, but she knew she couldn't very well carry all that back and ride at the same time. She needed both hands, both legs and her brain very much engaged if she was going to sit on a horse's back again. She repacked the basket again as best she could. It seemed the least she could do.

'Here.' She turned to find Sholto standing beside her mare, his hands clasped together, creating a small step of sorts. 'I'll give you a leg-up.'

It worked, allowing her to throw her other leg over and settle in the saddle with an element of grace, for climbing had made her limber as well as strong. She watched, impressed, as he jumped on his own horse without any assistance and took the reins expertly, thoughtlessly, in his hands. Back in his jacket, his hair slicked back, no trace of the food fight remained upon him. He looked as dignified as ever. She, on the other hand, looked like she'd gone to war with a hedge.

'Shall we, then?' Sibyl asked, clicking her heels and walking her horse on.

They moved in single file through the avenue, the horses treading carefully down the steep banks. Instinctively Effie angled her weight back but by the time she got to the flat, Sibyl was already circling them.

'What do you say? Shall we stretch their legs?'

'No, this is Effie's first time riding,' Sholto said quickly.

'Is it?' Sibyl looked surprised. 'I never could have guessed. You've a wonderful seat, my dear.'

'She's a natural,' Sholto said.

'Well, of course she is. She's brilliant at everything. Look what she managed last night, rescuing Miss Petunia like that,' Sibyl said, smiling. 'Let's just step into a pretty canter then.

It'll take an age to walk back and I do so hate trotting. It makes my brain rattle.'

Sholto looked at Effie.

'Fine,' she replied before he could demur on her behalf again.

'Good girl, that's the spirit,' Sibyl said, tugging on her reins and heading a straight line back to the house; it was but a bright speck in the distance from here. With a hard kick of her heels and a single flick of the crop, her horse broke into a canter.

Effie did the same, not allowing herself a moment to falter; indecision led to paralysis, she knew that from the ropes. Keep moving, it was nature's way. The mare obligingly broke into an easy, flowing rhythm and from pure instinct, Effie felt her body tense, her arms and legs becoming rigid against the momentum.

'Stay relaxed,' Sholto said, cantering beside her.

Breathing out through her mouth, she forced herself to release her thigh and arm muscles, to let the horse's stride ripple through her, rather than trying to resist it.

'That's it,' he nodded. 'That's all it is.'

Sibyl was leading the charge, cheering up front and looking over her shoulder to check on them every now and then. The great house began to grow greater as they passed through Cow Park and towards the ha-ha, the building's sense of heft and noble intention beginning to impress itself once more. She could make out the southerly sweeping staircase, the east and west pavilions . . .

Suddenly there was a step-change. Effie felt it immediately as Sibyl's horse pulled away – but only for a few seconds. Moments later, the gap was narrowing again as Norma too switched up to a gallop. Effie gasped as her eyes began to stream. The estate blurred in her peripheral vision and she felt the wind buffeting against her ears as her hair streamed behind her.

'Sid, slow down!' she heard Sholto yell, but Sibyl couldn't hear over the thunder of hooves. Beside her, she saw Sholto hit the horse several times with his crop, his body becoming hunched as he urged his horse on faster.

Steadily, he moved ahead of her, leaving her behind as he tried to draw level with Sibyl. Effie knew what he was doing but she felt the fear begin to set in as she was left alone now. She could do nothing but hold on. She couldn't look down, the rushing ground was too dizzying. She tried pulling on the reins but Norma's chase instinct was up; she would run for as long as the others ran.

Just hold on, she told herself. Just hold on.

She could see Sholto drawing closer, his horse's head dipping with the exertion but his presence on Sibyl's mare's shoulder only encouraged her to go faster again.

'Sid! Slow down! Slow down!'

He was pulling level but Sibyl didn't even look at him. She was up in the stirrups, hips high and her head down low, her gaze cast squarely on Dumfries House.

Effie's body felt cast from stone. She was rigid and unpliable. If she should fall, she was certain she would smash into a thousand pieces. She could see Sholto beginning to draw level, but he was so focused upon drawing up to Sibyl, he didn't seem to have noticed the ha-ha looming ahead of them.

'Sholto! Look out!' she screamed, pulling desperately on the reins and drawing back as much as she could, trying to slow the horse.

She saw Sholto look up and see the looming ditch. His body tensed and gathered, but she didn't see what happened next. Her own horse, spooked by the ha-ha, veered suddenly to the left and began running alongside it.

'No!' Effie cried, but her voice was strangled as she saw she was wholly alone now.

Still her little grey kept galloping, panicked, her spirits and nerves frayed by exhaustion and fright. The formal gardens and all their sense of order were just a few feet away above them, but Effie couldn't get to them and she was aware of groundsmen beginning to stand up and wave their arms, of distant shouts.

But nothing could soothe or stop the horse. There was the path ahead by which she and Sholto had travelled on the way out. Was her horse heading home? Or towards the woods beyond? Effie knew there was no way she could stay on in the trees.

The horse's hooves drummed on the road as they left the grass and . . .

The wind dropped. As suddenly as it had come, it stopped streaming her hair and she felt a forward momentum that seemed certain to propel her over the reins.

'Whoa!'

The word wasn't coming from her, a man was standing right in front of their path, his arms wide and waving in huge arcs so that he appeared to fill the track. 'Whoa!' Felton said again, his voice big but also low. There was comfort, not panic, in the timbre and as Norma went to pass by, he lunged for the rein. 'Steady, girl, steady,' he said, his arms strong but voice soft, immediately patting her flank and reassuring her that she could rest here.

The sudden stillness felt like a slap. Effie was dizzy, almost faint. She had been breathing in terrified shallow sips and the lack of oxygen, combined with adrenaline, was overwhelming her. She slumped, completely drained, barely registering the clatter of hooves behind them, of her own feet being removed from the stirrups.

'Jump down, Effie.'

Felton had his arms raised up to catch her. She half-slid, half-fell off Norma's back but as she landed, her knees wouldn't lock and she almost dropped to the ground. His arms closed around her in time, holding her up. 'Don't worry, you're safe now,' he said into her hair, his cheek against her head.

'Effie! My God! My God!' Sholto jumped down from his horse, as flushed as she was pale.

'What were you thinking?' Felton burst out angrily. Effie could feel his arms shaking with rage around her. His body felt as taut as a drum. She tried to push herself free but he didn't even notice her. 'Letting her on a horse like that? She could'a been killed! You had no right putting her in that position!'

Sholto stopped in his tracks, stunned by the outburst. For several moments no one could speak, all of them breathless and their bodies taut as drums.

'It wasn't his fau—' she said, feebly trying to release herself from his grip.

'He had no right!' Felton looked back at his employer. 'You had no right and you know it!'

Effie pushed herself out of Felton's embrace; she wasn't sure he even remembered he was holding her. All his attention was upon Sholto as he squared up to his employer. 'Huw, I'm fine,' she protested.

She saw both men react to her calling him Huw, before they heard the sound of approaching horse's hooves, almost dancing on the gravel.

'I say, brava!' Sibyl's shrill voice pierced the air.

There was a moment of pure silence.

'. . . Brava?' Disbelief inflected the sound as Sholto turned around to face her. 'What the blazes were you thinking?' His voice was low but harsh, he as angry with her as Felton had been with him.

'What? We agreed to have a run back.'

'Not at full gallop! She could have been killed!' he cried. 'You knew perfectly well it was her first time. What were you thinking?'

'I thought she'd enjoy it!' Sibyl protested, looking taken aback that he was dressing her down in front of staff. 'She was doing so well with the canter and we all saw what a daredevil she is. What's having a little trot to climbing on ropes?'

'That was not a little trot, as you know perfectly well! Look at her, she's as white as a sheet.'

'No harm was meant. I don't know why you're making such a fuss.'

'A *fuss*?' he echoed, under his breath.

No one spoke. Even in her dazed state, Effie sensed they made an unhappy four, caught in a push–pull tension where the movement of one affected the three others. She watched Sibyl's horse's hooves pick and tread on the gravel, a step forward, two steps back. Then they went forward, out of sight. 'I'm going in,' Sibyl said with a sigh. 'I'm hungry.'

Effie felt Felton staring at her.

'Felton,' Sholto said roughly, demanding his attention. He waited for the gamekeeper's hard, blue-eyed stare to alight from her and land on him. '. . . Thank you for your assistance in helping Miss Gillies just now. I'll see you receive extra in your wages this week—'

Felton bristled as Sholto redrew the lines between lord and servant. They both knew he hadn't acted out of financial interest just now, but they were no longer speaking man to man. Not anymore. The immediate crisis had passed and they must all revert to their roles.

'Now take the horses back to the stables.'

The gamekeeper stirred angrily. It wasn't in his remit to deal with the horses but Effie sensed his job and home, his entire livelihood, depended upon his next move. She caught his eye. 'Please,' she whispered. He could not lose everything on her account.

'. . . Aye, sir.' He took the reins of his master's horse too and resentfully headed back towards the stables.

They were alone again. Sholto stared at her, looking as shaken as she felt. She couldn't comprehend what had just happened – the moment that had passed between them on the mount, Sibyl's dangerous cruelty, Felton's reckless protection . . .

Sholto gave a small, sudden laugh, like he'd been hit on the back, forcing it from him. 'Well, it really can't be done, can it?' he asked. There was something off in his voice, a brightness in his eyes that unnerved her.

'What can't?'

'I was a fool to think . . .' He stopped himself short.

'Think what?'

He shook his head.

Did he blame himself for taking her riding? 'Sholto, it wasn't your fault the horse took off—'

'I'm not talking about the horse,' he said abruptly. She had never heard him sound like this before. His voice was hollow. He blinked, staring back at her like she was something unfathomable. 'Every time I think there's a chance, a way for us to somehow be in each other's lives . . . something happens to show me it's madness. That it can never be. I can't stand it, Effie. Other people can't stand it.'

She frowned, frightened by the look in his eyes. 'Sholto—'

He gave another forced laugh, but it held no joy. 'I mean, you do see it, don't you?' He ran a hand through his hair, looking stricken. 'You understand what I'm saying . . . Everything's against us.' He bit his lip. 'Everyone.'

Who was everyone? His parents? Her father? Felton? Sibyl? Because when it had been the two of them on the mount, it had felt like there was nothing in their way at all. It had felt like all the power in the universe was pushing them towards one another. If Sibyl hadn't come along when she did . . . She took a step towards him but he took several back, increasing the distance between them. 'No.' He shook his head. 'No.'

He was looking at her now like *she* was the danger. She watched the distance between them increase.

'I'll get . . . I'll get Mrs Mac to run a bath for you. And a stiff drink. You'll need that,' he muttered. 'The shock lingers in the body for a while.'

'But—' she said as he turned away and began walking back to the house. 'Sholto!' she called, but he didn't turn back; just carried on walking, leaving her alone on the path. The shock lingering.

Chapter Twenty-Eight

'Mrs McKenzie, this really isn't necessary,' Effie said, holding the liqueur glass.

'His lordship's orders,' the housekeeper said from the dressing room, swirling the bath water so that the bubbles foamed. 'You've had a shock.'

If she heard that one more time . . . Did they think she was made of glass? 'It was just a fright. I didn't even come off. I'm fine.'

'All the same. And these are for you.' Mrs McKenzie handed her a soft tower of plumped-up towels. 'Now, do as you're told and rest in there a while. If nothing else, I can tell his lordship I've done as he asked and get on. It's not like we're not busy enough with two hundred people descending here in a few hours.'

Effie couldn't imagine that number of people; she came from a world of thirty-six. 'Thank you.'

'Don't thank me, I'm just doing my job. Let me know when you're finished so I can send Fanny in here after.' The housekeeper glided out. She had an ability to move in silence, as if on castors.

Effie looked around the salmon-pink bedroom again, at the half poster bed with monogrammed cotton sheets tucked tightly and the satin eiderdown gently puffed. The flowers had been changed from when she'd spent the night here, a new arrangement of snapdragons and foxgloves in the vase. The room looked softer in the daylight, the colours less moody, but for all its beauty, it still gave her the shivers – confirmation of Frank Mathieson's death, nightmares that had forced her from her bed . . . And now, recovering from a near escape on a spooked horse? She would have far preferred escaping back to her old bedroom at the very least, but Mrs McKenzie had said the new scullery maid had already moved in.

She walked through to the water closet, putting the towels on a small flowery armchair beside the pink-enamelled bath, and undressed. She climbed in and automatically hugged her knees to her chest, braced for the shivers. For her, baths had always been cold (at best, tepid) and shallow, and she had to share her bathwater with dead spiders and fossilized leaves; but this one was warm and deep, the bubbles scented and frothy on her skin, smelling of roses. A small sigh escaped her. It was yet another small luxury she had never known she was doing without, another distinction between her life and theirs.

Her muscles softened like slowly melting butter and she began to realize how tightly she'd been holding herself. For all her protestations of being fine, when the horse had been in full gallop she had compressed her body as tightly as a coil and she would feel it tomorrow, she knew.

She stretched out her neck, dropping her ear to her shoulder on each side, before sinking back into the tub with a sigh. It really did feel so good . . .

'Knock, knock.'

A voice called through from the bedroom. A woman's voice.

Effie jolted in the water, twisting back to see Lady Sibyl walking across the carpet. She stopped at the door and looked in without a hint of embarrassment, still wearing her riding clothes.

'Mrs McKenzie said she had put you in here,' she said briskly. 'I am glad.'

Effie didn't reply. She was completely covered by the rosy bubbles but she felt distinctly disadvantaged to be lying naked in the bath. What was that woman doing here?

'How are you feeling?'

'I'm fine. None of this is necessary.' Effie's reply was clipped with embarrassment – but anger too.

'Nonsense, you had a horrid fright and it's all my fault. I feel wretched about it. I get so carried away on horseback. It's my great passion, you see. I just assume everyone loves it as much as I do.' She placed a hand above her heart. 'But it must have been so fear-making for you and I feel terrible, truly I do. It was thoughtless of me and I've come to beg your forgiveness.'

Beg? Effie blinked. '. . . That's not necessary either, m'lady—'

'You simply must call me Sid,' she said, coming into the room and moving the towels onto the floor, settling herself in the small armchair beside the tub. Effie eyed the towels, now further away than before; there was no chance of her getting out now. 'I insist.'

'Sid?'

'Of course. All my friends do, and I want us to be friends, Effie, really I do. I know we got off to an awkward start, what with Margaux giving you a fright like that.' She smiled and Effie thought how perfectly symmetrical her face was; she was like a doll really, pretty and neat, not a hair out of place.

She leant in closer. 'Can I tell you a secret?'

Effie blinked again. 'What?' she asked quietly.

'When we first met, I was fiendishly jealous of you.'

421

'Of me?'

'Of course! The earl was forever telling me about this extraordinary young woman who'd guided them on their trip. Then you turned up with that fantastic tan and a figure like a mannequin. Sholto was quite right, you know, when he said Nancy never looked half so good in that dress as you.'

Effie could hardly believe what she was hearing.

'I know he admires you terribly too, just like his father, and he wants us to be friends. Can we? Can you forgive me for being so beastly? I was a silly girl for being so petty.'

Us. Being Friends. I was a fool to think . . . Everything's against us. Everyone.

If she and Sibyl could be friends . . . 'There's nothing to forgive, m'lady.'

'Uh-uh. Sid.'

'. . . Sid.'

'Oh good!' Sibyl beamed suddenly, clapping her hands together, and her brown eyes shone. 'I'm so pleased! And now to celebrate our new friendship, you must come to the party tonight.'

'What? No!'

'Yes. You must. You absolutely must. Everyone's going to be there and I want to introduce you to them all. You'll love them! They're such a riot!'

'But I can't. I can't talk to those people.'

Sibyl reached forward, placing her hands atop Effie's lying on the sides of the bath. 'I won't leave you alone for a single second. I'll be by your side all night. Everyone's going to love you.' Her eyes were shining. 'We'll tell them about your climbing! I nearly died when you scooted past the window last night and all our friends love a skill, you know! They so wish they could have some of their own. They'll be enthralled by you!'

Effie felt a surge of panic. 'But I have nothing to wear,' she said desperately. There had to be a way to get out of it.

'Of course you do! You must borrow something of mine. Whatever you like. What is mine is yours. Go and choose. The jewellery too.' Her eyes brightened further. 'And we'll get Jenny to do your hair and maquillage too; she can do it just the same as she does mine and we can be like sisters.'

'It really isn't necessary—'

'Of course it is! You simply have to let me make things up to you. I don't know how I can forgive myself if you don't.'

Effie felt steam-rollered. She had seen the young woman's excitement from afar but to be in the full glare of it . . . It was like sitting in a hurricane and letting the winds blow. But if this was what it was to be friends with her. If this meant she and Sholto could be allowed to be friends too . . . She knew he meant to avoid her again. Weeks might go by before she could even set sights upon him. 'All right.'

'Marvellous!' Sibyl beamed, playfully flicking a small spray of bubbles towards her. 'Take your time in here. I need to refresh and change my clothes too but come to my room when you're ready. Oh this will be such fun!' She jumped from the chair, noticing Effie's clothes lying in a heap on the floor. 'And I'll give these to Jenny too, while I'm at it.' Her nose wrinkled slightly at the sticky stains. 'Then she can have them laundered for you, all clean for tomorrow.'

'That's really not necessary. I can do it.'

'Don't be silly. There's some stains here that will need some work if we're to get them out.' She inspected the beetroot bleed on Effie's hand-knitted woollen vest before looking back at her with kind eyes. 'It's the very least I can do. Let me spoil you. I'm trying to show you I'm sorry, remember?'

Effie gave a wry smile. 'It's not that. I'm grateful for all your kindness, but if you take those clothes – I've nothing to wear when I come out of here.'

Sibyl gave a laugh of realization. 'Oh!' She looked around the room quickly. 'Look, over there – there's a robe on the door you can put on. Come over to my room and we'll find you some day clothes too, although it may have to be a dress, I'm afraid?' She pulled a face. 'I know you're not awfully keen.'

It was Effie's turn to smile. 'A dress is fine.'

'Super!'

Effie watched her go, a whirlwind of energy and good intentions. Suddenly she understood why Sholto always looked so tired in her company. It was exhausting. She lay slowly back in the bath, listening to the bubbles pop and wondering what on earth she had just agreed to.

The music drifted up the stairs, all the way to the top of the house. Effie was still cloistered in the salmon-pink room, at Lady Sibyl's insistence. 'You can't possibly walk all that way from your cottage in those shoes,' she had said as she had handed over a pair of her silver satin Mary Janes. The heel was several inches high and she was right – Effie would be doing well to cross a room in them, much less a country estate.

The dress she had loaned, to go with them, was hanging on the wardrobe door. Effie couldn't keep her gaze from returning to it. The colour of June skies, it was cut in a liquid satin that seemed to drip as much as to drape and finished in a gently flared long skirt. The bold blue hue had drawn her at once as she had stared into Sibyl's wardrobe and she had only realized after she'd picked it that a demure front belied a risqué cutaway back with just a single ribbon of fabric running down the spine. Sibyl had laughed off her protestations, telling her it was the fashion, but Effie had already determined to spend her time with her back to the wall. She sat very still as Jenny tonged her new short dark hairstyle into the same tight, sleek finger waves that Sibyl favoured. It was a shock every time she caught a glimpse of herself but Sibyl had been adamant she could carry it off. Her make-up was already done: brows drawn, cheeks rouged and her lips painted a bold red. She could see the overall effect worked; it was just so odd, being *painted*. She had never worn make-up in eighteen years, and now she had worn it twice in a few weeks.

Effie could tell the maid was unhappy about having to tend to her; she'd said barely a word and wouldn't meet her eyes. But was it Effie's fault that Sibyl had said she would see to herself for tonight? That she was prostrating herself for forgiveness after this afternoon's disaster?

'How many people are down there?' she asked, as they heard the sound of yet more cars drawing up outside on the gravel. It was a constant stream, it seemed.

'It was supposed to be two hundred, but I think Lady Sibyl added a few more at the last minute. Apparently there are even news reporters at the gates.'

Effie flinched. 'But why?'

'For the society pages. People like reading about them.'

'Oh . . . yes. Of course.' The mere mention of reporters made her nervous.

'There.' Jenny stepped back, admiring her own work. 'You could be Lady Sibyl's twin.'

Effie stared at her unfamiliar reflection too. They would be sisters indeed tonight. 'Well, that can only be a good thing,' she murmured. 'The less like me I am, the better.'

'Shall I help you with the dress?' Jenny asked.

Effie nodded. 'I hardly know where to start with it.'

She slipped off the robe and stood still as Jenny carefully lowered it over her head, taking care not to ruin her hair; it gleamed like moonlight, as silken as a cat. Effie watched the fabric settle around her, the colour bringing out her own blue eyes as Jenny placed the finishing touch Sibyl had left for her – a paste sapphire necklace – around her neck.

The frantic tooting of a car horn outside made them both jump. Jenny ran to the window and looked down. She sighed. 'There's so many people. You had better go down. I'm needed to help the footmen tonight.'

Effie gave a nod, wishing she could hide below stairs too. But she knew she had to be brave, for Sholto's sake. The hardest part would be walking in alone, but Sibyl had said she would be waiting for her by the fireplace in the tapestry room. For as long as she was in Sibyl's company, she could stand quietly beside her and simply let the hostess shine. She probably wouldn't even have to say a single word. No one could compete with Lady Sibyl Wainwright for sheer social dynamism and who would want to? Effie would only be there to show Sholto they were friends, she and Sibyl; and that it meant they could be too, that something was surely better than nothing . . . ?

Effie pushed her feet into the shoes, adding another few inches to her already lofty height. 'Wish me luck, then.'

The maid gave her an odd look. 'Good luck.'

They walked out of the room and along the jade green corridor, past the grand portraits of long-dead Crichton-Dalrymples and down the wooden staircase to the first floor. The volume increased like it was being turned on a dial. A woman in an ivory satin dress skittered past; she was wearing a white-blonde wig and had plucked every single last hair from her brows; her mouth was shaped into a tiny pucker.

There was something . . . extreme about her look. Effie realized a moment later that the woman was being chased by a man with a moustache and a cane and hat, and a funny wobbling walk.

Effie stared as the pair laughed hysterically and made their way down the corridor, past the stone stairs at the other end. They disappeared momentarily from view but Effie knew they would have to come back this way in a moment, for the corridor on this floor only led to the chapel – and they didn't look like they wanted to pray. Effie wished she could ask Jenny what it was about them that had been so strange but she had already gone too, slipping down the servants' stairs to the corridors on the ground floor.

Steeling herself, Effie turned into the pewter corridor – it was her favourite part of the house; a run of vaulted ceilings adorned with delicate stencils in celery green, duck-egg blue and shell pink, highlighted with dots of gold – and she made her way across to the tapestry room. She walked to the sound of her satin shoes click-clacking on the floors, catching sight of her reflection in one of the round windows as she passed. She stopped, stunned by the sight of herself in motion. It was one thing to sit before a mirror and be presented with a static image, like a painting, but to see herself moving, in these clothes, through this house . . . She had never had any aware-ness of how she looked before these past few weeks, but she could scarcely believe she was *her*. No matter that her heart was clattering beneath her ribs; that wasn't what the reflection showed. The young dark-haired woman staring back was beautiful and poised and Effie suddenly realized who it was she had become – even if it was only for tonight, she was the girl with the hand-drawn book, who wore silk dresses and lived in the house of music. There was no indication of her former self, dressed in patched clothes and huddled in the dark in the featherstore. She put a hand to her hair, to her lips, and slowly smiled. Perhaps she really could walk in there and belong . . . ?

Ahead, she saw Henry emerge through the doorway with a tray, looking more flustered than she had seen before, even when dealing with Margaux. He did a double take as he saw her and looked distinctly shocked – the new dark hair, no doubt – but his feet didn't stop and he disappeared in the next moment, down the spiral staircase that would take him to the servants' passage.

Effie took a deep breath and moved forward into the fray. She stepped through the doorway, to be greeted by a scene that took her breath away. She had never seen so many people in one space before. Bodies were pressed together, mouths wide and eyes bright as everyone talked and laughed, all at once. Life seemed concentrated into its most dazzling form in this one room – colours were brighter, sounds louder.

She stood there for several moments, taking it all in, until the woman in the creamy dress dashed past her again, knocking against her, still screaming with laughter. The man with the funny walk wasn't far behind.

Effie jumped out of his way before he ran into her too, only to jump another foot to the right as something cold wriggled down her bare spine. She whirled around to find a man, sucking on an ice cube as he held his drink. Had he . . . ? He was staring straight at her and there was a look in his eyes she didn't like. And why was he dressed as Winston Churchill? He wasn't Winston Churchill, she knew that, but . . . It was creepy.

She moved into the crowd to escape him, to escape his stare. She hid herself among the people revelling, the swarming mass of strangers. She needed to find Sibyl and her friends. She moved towards the centre of the room, heading for the fireplace at the far end. Sibyl had said she would be there, waiting for her.

It was so hot, the noise disorienting. She felt hands on her bare arms and shoulders as she passed, as though these people knew her, or were claiming her. There was a man in front of her. He was wearing a red ceremonial costume, with a blue sash.

'Excuse me,' she said, trying to get past.

The man turned and she found herself face to face with the king.

'Your Royal Highness,' she breathed.

The king stared back at her sternly for several moments. Had she said the wrong thing? Should she do something?

But then he laughed. He threw his head back and laughed and she saw the elastic holding on his beard around his ears. She saw his eyes were brown, not blue.

'And who have you come as, my dear?' he asked, clutching a hand onto her elbow and stepping back to fully appraise her. 'Wait. Let me guess.'

Who had she . . . ? She looked around the room, seeing suddenly not clothes but costumes.

'Oh my goodness, I've got it!' he cried, eyes bright. '—'

'Miss Gillies!' She turned at the sudden mention of her name to find a familiar-looking man coming towards her through the crowd, one arm raised up as if to catch her attention. 'It is Miss Gillies, isn't it? They said you were here.' He squinted. 'Only . . . your hair is different, I think?'

The party dropped away as her past caught up with her at last.

'*You?*' she asked, her voice barely more than a breath.

'So you remember me, then?'

The ice cube on her back was nothing to the freeze, now, in her veins.

'I wanted to talk to you about the factor. Ask some questions—'

'Ah, I've got it!' the man dressed as the king exclaimed, butting in. 'You're Mr Thompson, of Thomson and Thompson. The double act. Thick moustache, bowler hat. Confused expression . . .'

Effie watched the man frown back at him distractedly. 'What?'

'You know – Thompson, from *Tintin*.'

There was a pause. 'Actually, Your Majesty, it's Mr Bonner. From *The Times*,' the reporter said in a sardonic tone.

The king frowned, peering at him through narrowed eyes, before a slow smile began to open up his face once more. 'Oh, very good! I like it. Yes. Mr Bonner from *The Times*. How novel!'

'*Effie?*'

She felt another hand on her arm and turned again, this time to see Sholto staring at her with a look of disbelief. And something else, too . . . concern?

'What are you doing here?'

She no longer had any idea what she was doing here. She had never imagined a party might be like this. She wanted to tell him she'd come to show him she and Sibyl were friends. That she'd come for him, but—

'My God, your hair . . .' he said quietly, a hand automatically lifting to touch it. 'What did you do?'

A part of her brain wanted to ask if he liked it; the dress too? She wanted to tell him Sibyl had done it all for her so that they could be friends at last. But she couldn't find her words. Mr Bonner from *The Times* was *here*, and he'd been looking for her.

'Did Sibyl do this?'

She managed to nod. Why wasn't he pleased?

'Effie . . .' His eyes lifted off her, looking around the room for someone. Who?

'I say, Sholly old chap, who are you supposed to be?' the king asked him now. 'Isn't that rather your usual get-up?' He gestured at Sholto's outfit of a black tailcoat and white tie.

'Lord Chatterley,' Sholto muttered. '*Before* the accident.'

The king laughed. 'Ha, splendid, old boy. Good call, yes, before the accident. Makes all the difference tonight; you wouldn't catch me at knee-height to this crowd, I can tell you. I know you don't like these themes.'

'No, Ernest, I don't,' Sholto said tersely, his eyes already back on Effie. He looked desperate.

'Lord Chatterley before the accident. I shall remember that one.' The king tapped his head, getting the hint at long last and wandering off into the crowd.

'Effie, you shouldn't be here,' Sholto said with urgency.

She felt her heart plummet. 'But why not? Sibyl specifically asked—'

'She shouldn't have,' he said firmly. 'It wasn't . . . it wasn't kind.'

'I don't understand. She's been nothing *but* kind – ever since the riding thing earlier, she's looked after me. These are her shoes, her dress, her jewels . . .'

He was staring at her with a look she couldn't read.

'What is it?'

Sholto noticed the man still standing beside them, openly listening in on their conversation. 'I say, have we met?' he asked curtly.

'Not properly, sir, no. Miss Gillies and I were just talking.'

'Do you know this man?' Sholto asked her.

'Miss Gillies and I met on St Kilda, Lord Sholto. I was there for the final week before evacuation.'

'Oh. I see.' He looked irritated.

'Yes. It was a busy time, of course, and stressful. There was a lot of high emotion, which was to be expected. Then, of course, the landlord's factor was found dead.'

'Mmm, yes. Bad business,' Sholto muttered distractedly, his jaw pulsing, his patience – and manners – hanging by a thread. 'Well, would you excu—?'

'Actually, Miss Gillies and I were just talking about him.' The reporter looked from Sholto back to Effie again. 'Because I did remember noticing an . . . *altercation* between you and Mr Mathieson—'

She stood, frozen. This couldn't be happening. Not here. Not in front of all these people. In front of Sholto.

'—outside the church, the night before the evacuation. You were walking back to the village and he caught up with you. It looked like he wanted to talk with you.'

'. . . He probably did.' Her voice was small. 'He was forever on at us about something.' She looked past him, looking for the police. Were they here too?

'But then he took you by the hand. Or rather, he tried to, and you jumped like you'd been burnt.'

She swallowed. 'I expect he must have surprised me.'

'It seemed an extreme response to a harmless gesture.'

'What makes you think Mr Mathieson was harmless?'

The comment was out before she could stop it. His eyes narrowed. 'You looked like you hated him.'

She didn't doubt she probably still did. She couldn't hide what she felt about that man any longer, not after the things he'd done. 'Most of us did. He wasn't popular.'

432

Sholto looked between them. 'Now see here – I met the man myself, and there was no love lost between us either. I shan't speak ill of the dead, but don't ask for a eulogy for him. Besides, what's the meaning of all these . . . *morbid* questions? It's a party. Go and find a drink, man.' Sholto went to shoo him off, but Mr Bonner made no move to go.

Effie felt the tension ratchet up a notch. Her stomach tightened to a knot.

'I thought Miss Gillies might want to give me her account of what happened to Mr Mathieson?'

'Why would sh—?' Sholto's expression changed as he caught on that this was no social conversation. 'You're a bloody *reporter*!' He looked around the room, almost immediately catching Henry's eye. With a sharp nod of his head, he brought the footman rushing over, as fast as was possible through the crowd. 'I specifically forbade any of your lot coming past the gates. This is private land and a private party. How dare you! Get out!'

'I'm not here to report on your party, sir,' Mr Bonner said hurriedly. 'But it can't have escaped your attention that there was a lot of interest in the evacuation. The St Kildans occupy a unique place in the national consciousness. It was felt something significant was being lost by their departure. We had a strong response to the coverage and now that there's a police investigation we must—'

Henry was upon them.

'Get him out of here,' Sholto said furiously. 'He's a bloody reporter! And make sure no one else is getting past the gates either.'

'Of course, sir,' Henry said, raising himself to his full impressive height and grabbing the man by the arm. 'You. Come with me. Now.'

'All right, all right. I'm going.' Mr Bonner offered up no physical protest, but he shot Effie an angry look that left her in no doubt he'd be back. 'Another time, then, Miss Gillies.'

'The damned nerve . . .' Sholto muttered, watching them go.

The crowd pushed them together suddenly and his hands automatically gripped her bare arms as people jostled to get past. Effie looked up at him, shaken and overwhelmed by what had just happened – and was still happening. She felt like she'd been thrown into a writhing pit. Was this so very different to the minister's descriptions of hell? The crowd had a manic edge, as if everyone was teetering on the brink of hysteria, and she was aware of a growing ruckus, a steadily increasing din.

Sibyl's laugh carried over to them, but to Effie's surprise it wasn't coming from the direction of the fireplace. She wasn't already holding court with her two hundred closest friends . . . she was only just coming in. Effie turned to see what was going on but she couldn't see past the wired, flowing scarf of Amelia Earhart. Instead, she saw a ripple in the crowd, like a snake swimming in a river, making its way through, coming closer . . .

Laughs and shouts accompanied her progress. 'But who *are* you?' someone called, as the sense of scandal deepened.

Suddenly, the snake was upon them. Effie gasped as Sibyl blinked back at her, almost unrecognizable. Her face was smeared with mud, her hair was a wild tangle and her clothes – a boy's shirt, vest and trousers – were covered with food stains. Her feet were bare and a rope was looped around her torso, a dead pheasant dangling from it at her shoulders.

'What do you think?' she asked, flicking at the dead bird.

434

'I know it's supposed to be a seagull or whatnot, but I couldn't get one at such short notice. The gamekeeper was most obliging, though.'

'You're in my clothes,' Effie whispered in disbelief, looking her up and down.

'And you're in mine! Isn't it just too fabulous?'

Effie felt her eyes sting with tears as she realized what Sholto had been trying to tell her. She felt her humiliation bloom as people looked between the two of them, slowly beginning to understand the ruse. She felt suddenly not beautiful but ridiculous to be made up as that woman, humiliated that Sibyl had depicted her as some sort of primitive savage. 'Why would you do this?'

'Darling, it's an impersonation party! I'm you and you're me.'

'But you never told me that!' The words escaped her as a cry, betraying her hurt so that Sholto looked over at her with a pained expression.

'Why, I thought it would be a surprise. Don't you love it?' For the first time Effie noticed a flatness to Sibyl's voice, a deadness behind her eyes. There had never been kindness or friendship in her actions. She was cruel. Malicious.

'Sibyl, what the hell are you doing?' Sholto's voice was a growl, white spots of rage in his cheeks. 'You know this is completely unacceptable.'

Sibyl's smile disappeared like the sun behind a cloud, throwing a shadow onto her face as she saw his anger. 'Why? Why is it? She's dressed as me. Why can't I be her?' Her eyes flashed. 'Isn't that what you really want, Sholto? Her, but me? Or is it me, but her?'

He swallowed at her bold words, the party pulsating around them like it was a heart and they were a blockage. Something stuck. Something dangerous.

'Stop it,' he snapped. 'Not here, Sid. Not now.'

He went to turn away, but Sibyl lunged for him. 'No? Not the right time?' She had her hand on Sholto's arm. 'Tell me, then. Seeing as timing is *such* an issue for you, darling, when exactly would be a good time to tell all our friends here that we're engaged to be married – and have been for six months? Why exactly are we keeping it a secret? What is it that we're waiting for?'

Her voice had risen to a shriek, and several people around them gasped. One man – his moustache twirled to point upwards, a monocle at one eye – pressed his hand to his mouth in exaggerated shock.

Effie recoiled. He was grotesque. They all were. Even Sholto. Even in all his refinement and decorum . . .

Tears sat gathered in her throat and pooled at her eyes as she looked across at him. It wasn't hearing he was engaged now that devastated her; it was that he had been even when he'd come to St Kilda, when he'd kissed her and asked her to make a plan . . . Even by the time he'd found her on her rock in the sea, he was already lost to her.

And what had she suffered because of him? Aside from her own heartbreak, the jealousy he had spurred in Frank Mathieson had sparked a ripple effect with devastating consequences, far beyond anything he could ever imagine: Mathieson himself was dead, Poppit was dead, and she was left broken by what she had had to do to survive. Her entire life was in tatters for someone wholly unworthy; she had invested in a lie.

She tore the wig from her head and threw it at him. His mouth parted as she stood before him, herself again, wild and defiant.

'You disgust me!' she cried. 'You're not better than me! You're worse!'

'Effie—'

'Where is your honour?' she demanded.

Sholto blanched at the question but she wasn't interested in hearing his answer. She looked around desperately for a way through the bodies, an escape route to the door. She couldn't breathe in here. She couldn't think.

'Effie, just wait—' Sholto reached for her, holding her back.

'Get your hands off me!'

'Don't go,' he implored her.

'Better a good retreat than a bad stand,' she spat.

'Please! Just listen to me—'

'Sholto!' Sibyl's voice was fractured with shock at his actions. 'What are you *doing*?'

Effie jerked her chin towards Sibyl. 'She's right. What are you *doing*?' she scoffed, her eyes blazing. 'People are *looking*!'

He looked back at her desperately. 'Effie – I can explain—'

'You and she deserve each other.'

'No—'

'Yes!' she cried suddenly. 'Yes! Stop pretending there's a different ending! It was always going to be this way. You belong with her. And I belong to another anyway.'

His mouth flattened. 'Felton isn't—'

'Not him,' she spat, cutting him off. 'You're engaged . . . and I'm already wed!'

His hand dropped from her arm like he'd been burnt, the wig falling to his feet. '*What?*'

The pain flared in his eyes and she was pleased to see it. He had treated her like a fool but she was nobody's victim; she felt her own tears threaten, but they would not fall, not for as long as she stood here. Let him suffer for once! Let him know how it felt to lose!

She glanced at Sibyl and without a word turned imperiously

upon her heel, driving the satin stiletto into the cruel woman's bare foot. A scream pitched through the cedar-panelled room but Effie walked on – the only true wildling in a room full of pretenders.

Chapter Twenty-Nine

The skies were clear, stars already peeping as Effie tore through the night, the very edges of her jagged and sharp. She felt contaminated by the louche debauchery of those people for whom nothing and no one mattered. It was almost more than she could bear that Sibyl was still back there, in her brother's clothes, holding court while everyone laughed at Effie and at John, and all they were proud to be – but nothing would make her return. The scales had fallen away. She had always known that she didn't belong here but only now did she realize that she didn't want to—

'Effie!' Sholto's voice carried over the gardens.

She whipped round in surprise. He couldn't have followed her out here? It was an impossible thing. She had cut him down before all those people.

His blonde hair was shining in the lights as he stood at the top of the steps, scanning the grounds for sight of her – but there were so many people, lovers everywhere carousing, high on life, good fortune and even better champagne. A couple was sitting on the wall by the fountain, the tips of long lighted cigarettes dancing in the dark, their laughter tinkling like the water.

Every instinct told her to run home, to race across the grass in the shortest possible distance. He would see her in the lights, but she was fast, fast enough to outrun him, she was sure of it. Almost sure. Besides, he wouldn't make a scene and chase her . . . Would he?

His eyes found her. 'Effie!'

With a gasp she took off, but not in the direction of the cottage. He would expect her to run home so she knew she must confound him and lose him in the shadows. She ran a few metres but the ridiculous shoes hobbled her and she had to kick them off after a few metres, losing valuable time. Still, she was fast and she sprinted barefoot over the grass, her arms pumping and her blonde hair streaming behind her. She ran down the slope, the house at her back, heading for the gracious hump of the Adam bridge. Beyond it lay the ponds and the walled garden. She could lose him there, surely . . . ?

She headed for it, passing under ancient beeches and oaks, but lanterns flickered, lighting the path, whereas to her right a dense tall hedge curved around and away, back towards the house but slipping into darkness.

She glanced back but there was no sign of him. Not yet.

She ran to the hedge and felt the shadows claim her, the moonlight no longer kissing her dress. She ran around the curve, almost immediately coming to a tall ironwork gate that had a dark avenue leading off behind it.

She peered through – he would never find her in there! – and she pulled at it eagerly. A chain rattled.

'No!' she whispered frantically, looking back to find Sholto rounding a beech tree, heading for the bridge. He stopped at the sound, looking over. She could see him squint, trying to see into the shadows. Even if he couldn't see her yet, he would in another few paces.

She looked up with a gasp. The gate was twelve, fifteen feet high. Nothing to her . . . Without another thought, she hitched up her dress and scaled it quickly. She jumped down on the other side, but the full skirt billowed and caught on a spike as she leapt, tearing a gash through it.

She looked down dispassionately. It no longer held any beauty for her. She would happily throw it into the fire when she got home and watch it burn.

'Effie! Don't!'

The sound of his footsteps drubbing the hard ground came to her ear and she took off again, sprinting silently down a narrow grassy lane. The hedge reared high above her on both sides but with one left turn she was out of sight. It led onto another narrow avenue, less than the span of her open arms, the high bushes lush and thick. She frowned. What was this place?

Bewildered, she ran on, taking a left turn, then a right. A left, a left, then another right – only to come to a towering stone obelisk and a dead end. She stared at it in panic. Where was she? How did she get out of here? Should she turn back or find another way around?

There was another rattling of the gate and she knew he – a skilled climber too – was scaling it. There came the sound of him jumping down, then a moment of silence. She listened to the sound of her own breathing.

'Effie, I know you're in here.' His voice was raised, but also muffled. The green walls loomed around her as she stood in silence, her back against a wall, palms pressed to the leaves as she strained to hear the sound of his footsteps. She consoled herself that if she didn't know where she was, how could he?

'Please. I just want to talk,' he called.

A lonely owl hooted from a distant tree and she turned her face to the sky, staring into a night that had started with such promise. All she had wanted was to show him she could be

441

in his life. She had come to understand – and even accept – the way things were and she would have settled for being just his friend. She needed a friend. Instead she had learnt that not a single moment between them had ever been true . . . that everything had been a lie, that he couldn't be trusted.

'I'm sorry, Effie—'

She heard the emotion in his voice.

'Hurting you was the last thing I ever wanted.'

She shook her head, trying to drown out his words, but a sapphire night wrapped around them like a velvet cloak. They were alone out here.

'You were all I wanted. And everything I couldn't have.'

She pressed her hands to her ears, trying to stop the words from reaching her, but she felt them through the earth, on the wind, and the anger that had propelled her from the party collapsed into something frail and brittle, tears she had been holding back beginning to slide down her cheeks at last. She gave a small sniff, wiping her eyes.

It was only a tiny sound—

'I'm sorry.'

The words were softly spoken, his voice suddenly so close it made her jump. She pivoted and backed away from the wall where she had been standing, but she couldn't see him. She stared into the hedge as if the leaves might wither and wilt, revealing him, but they remained in all their springy verdancy, blocking them from one another.

The silence held. The wall stood. He was close yet still so far, on the other side.

'I'm sorry you had to hear about the engagement like that. I wanted to tell you about my . . . situation before I left St Kilda. It was why I wanted to see you. I wanted to tell you that I was going to call it off with her.'

She said nothing. She didn't move a muscle, she didn't breathe. He was lying.

She heard a sigh, a gentle rustle as though he was sweeping a hand across the branches. 'I left a note at the bull house that night, as I said I would, asking you to meet me.'

She frowned. There *had* been a note from him?

'I waited at An Lag but you didn't come.'

An Lag? *Not* the storm cleit? Mathieson had switched the notes?

'—I assumed your no-show was your answer, that you were facing up to a truth I didn't want to see. I thought you were better able than me to see the reality of our situation and act . . . appropriately.'

There was another silence. 'If I'd known you were . . .' He cleared his throat. 'With someone else . . .'

She pressed her hand harder over her mouth, the tears flowing over her own fingers, shaking her head at his words.

'It was arrogant of me to presume you weren't, of course.' He sighed again. The sound was weary and . . . defeated. 'You're right to hate me. I hate myself. But you have to believe me when I say I'm sorry for all of it, Effie – for kissing you when I had no right, for thinking you might feel for me the way I felt for you. And I'm sorry for the way I behaved when you arrived here, too – my father had brought you in and I had no right making things so difficult for you.'

She couldn't believe what she was hearing.

'But I was angry, you see? I'd spent all those months trying to forget you, the way you'd obviously forgotten me. I'd thought that if I could just give it some time, the memory of you would fade and I'd be able to accept my future with Sid again. We had been happy enough, bumbling along, before St Kilda. But then suddenly there you were, standing in the library, looking at me as though you *hadn't* refused me that night and . . . I knew nothing had changed for me. I still felt the same.'

She squeezed her eyes shut.

'My pride was wounded. Friendship was enough for you but not for me.' He cleared his throat again. 'I went almost out of my mind every time I saw you talking to Felton. I thought you were going to choose him and I . . . I couldn't stand it. I've known him my whole life, we played together as boys, but suddenly I couldn't stand the sight of him. I wanted him gone from here. Out! And for what?' His voice rose suddenly, despair inflected with frustration as she stayed silent. 'When all along, you were married to someone else!'

She splayed her hands over her face. The tears wouldn't – couldn't – stop falling now. Every word he said only made it worse. How could she possibly explain to him . . . ?

'. . . Why didn't you tell me?'

Her head whipped up at the new direction of his voice and she saw him standing a few feet away, at the end of the path. He was no longer in his jacket, no doubt abandoned for scaling the gate, but she saw the scrap of blue silk in his hand.

She blinked in disbelief that he had found her. 'How . . . ?'

'I played in here as a boy,' he murmured. 'I know my way around blindfolded.'

They stared at one another for what seemed like endless minutes. She saw the pain in his eyes, felt the track of her own tears streaming down her cheeks.

He took a step towards her. 'Why didn't you just tell me? It could have saved so much pain—'

'Because it's not what you think,' she said quickly, her voice thick. 'It's not.'

He blinked, looking unconvinced. He was holding his body

444

stiffly, as though he was injured. '. . . Who is he? I have to know. Tell me his name.'

She felt herself begin to tremble. Even just talking about it made her want to fall apart. To disappear. 'It doesn't matter now. He's dead.'

She watched his expression change. '*What?*'

'He died.'

'. . . When? How?'

She looked sharply away. She didn't want to talk about it, to think about it.

'Effie—' He took a few steps closer, looking alarmed, but she stopped him with a step back.

'I'm not sad. I never loved him,' she said quickly. Defiantly. 'I hated him!'

Sholto stared at her, seeing the way her hands were pulled into fists, her eyes shining too brightly. She looked like a cornered fox. 'Effie . . . you have to tell me what happened. You can't leave it like that!'

She shook her head vehemently. 'I can. It's behind me now and I never want to think of him again. I won't say his name . . . He's dead and I'm glad of it and I won't pretend otherwise. I hated him!'

He stared at her with a look that she couldn't bear and she knew her fear was leaking from her, all her terror and revulsion from that night telling him a story she had never wanted him to hear. *You looked like you hated him*, Bonner had said.

A cloud came into his eyes as he paled. '. . . Tell me his name.'

She shook her head as he walked over to her, ignoring her protestations now.

'Effie, tell me his name.' He placed his hands on her arms

but she wouldn't look at him. His voice was hoarse. '. . . Tell me it wasn't . . . *him.*'

She looked up then, her eyes round and shining with tears.

His hand went to his mouth, pinching his cheeks. He rubbed his face, his eyes squeezing shut. 'God no.' He shook his head. 'Not him.'

She felt a clutch of panic at seeing his own despair. 'He took your note from the bull's house and replaced it with his own,' she faltered. 'It sent me to the storm cleit, on the other side of the glen from you.'

Sholto's face crumpled as the factor's deception was revealed. 'No.'

'He was waiting for me there. He made me . . .' She swallowed. 'He made me jump the broom with him—'

'What?'

'He said it made me . . . lawfully his.'

The breath caught in his throat. She could see it snagged there, like her dress on that gate.

'But that's a lie! Broomstick weddings aren't legal!'

'Not here, perhaps. But your ways aren't the old ways. It was different, over there. The law is . . . loose.'

'. . . Did he . . . ?' His breathing was coming heavily, his hands pulled into fists. She could see the agony inside him.

'He tried. But Mhairi and Pop—' A sob burst from her. She couldn't even say the word. '. . . Poppit stopped him. She bit his leg . . . He kicked her, broke her leg and ribs.'

'*That's* why he was limping?' he whispered. 'He said he caught it on a nail.' He looked back at her, horrified, remembering their hospitality on the boat as the factor had hobbled aboard.

'But it's over now. He's gone and I'm glad of it.' She jerked her chin in the air, seeing how his expression changed from sorrow to something closer to fear. The factor was, after all, now dead.

He paled, watching her closely. '. . . Effie? What did you do?'

She stared back at him for several moments. 'What I had to . . . I had to get away from him. He was coming back for me and I . . . I knew I couldn't live a life like that.'

'Yes.' He nodded, placing his hands upon her arms. 'I understand, but you have to tell me what you did. All of it. I have to know so that I can help you. If you keep me in the dark—'

'I can't drag you into this,' she said desperately. 'I won't let you get involved.'

'But I'm already involved! You have to tell me what happened. I can't help you if I don't know.'

She was already far beyond his help. Now that Weir had the book, it was all the evidence he needed to prove the 'unnatural' relationship he suspected between her and Frank Mathieson. It was done, the clock already ticking, but she could see the angst in Sholto's eyes. He was a man in torment. If it would help him, even just for this moment, to believe something could be done . . . She took a breath. 'The night before the evacuation, he caught me outside the kirk – like Bonner said – and told me he was going to tell my father we were wed. He said he'd been "reasonable", giving me that last week on the isle with my father – but that I'd be going to the mainland with him. As his wife.'

Sholto blinked. 'What did you say?'

'I agreed with him. I'd been braced for it for months. Ever since he went away with you that night, I knew he'd be back. So I got myself ready; I dug my bait and planned for it. I tried never to be alone but I knew it was an impossible task; he'd

447

catch up with me eventually, one way or the other. Poppit wouldn't let him anywhere near me during the days but all it took was a few moments alone outside the kirk that last night . . . So I told him I was reconciled to the marriage; that I believed it was a better match than I could have hoped for and that he'd been patient long enough.' She swallowed, trembling as she remembered her bold lies. 'I got him to meet me on the other side at midnight,' she said quietly.

'Glen Bay?' Sholto frowned. 'He didn't query being so far from the village?'

'I told him we should be somewhere private where we could . . . take our time and not be disturbed—'

He blanched, understanding perfectly.

'I got him drunk till he passed out, then tied him up. I put a knife out of reach, but where he could see it. I left him a sheep's bladder full of water – enough for four days if he was careful – and some oatcakes. The SS *Dunara* was due a few days after we left, but . . .' She bit her lip. 'The winds got up and they were late in getting across. Too late for him.'

He frowned. '. . . So you didn't go there to kill him?'

'I just wanted to get away. But it led to the same thing.' She shrugged hopelessly.

'Yes, but motive matters, Effie! At worst, it's manslaughter, not murder. And you were afraid of what he was going to do. We could argue self-defence. That's hugely significant.' He was looking at her intently now. 'Think carefully now – were you seen?'

'I don't think so. It was dark and everyone was so busy.'

'Does anyone know what you did?' He looked back at her, desperation in his eyes.

She bit her lip. 'There's one person who might be able to . . . guess.'

'Who?'

'. . . I asked one of the trawler captains to buy me some whisky from the mainland. There was never any on the isle.'

'Hmm. I see no reason for the captain to link your whisky bottle with the factor's death. What did you tell him you wanted it for?'

'Doping the bull. For the evacuation.'

A hint of a smile came into his eyes, gone again in the next second. He looked away, his gaze distant, lost in his own thoughts. '. . . It's been a couple of weeks now since he was found and no one's come knocking. That must be cause for hope,' he said quietly. 'I'll ask Sir John what the police know anyway. Find out where the investigation's at.'

'Please, you mustn't interfere. The less you're involved—'

'If you think I'm letting anything else happen to you on account of *him*—' His voice was sharp but she knew it wasn't her he was angry with. Immediately, he reached for her hand and pressed it to his cheek. He turned his head and kissed the inside of her wrist. 'I'm sorry. I'm sorry. But I won't let him take you from me again, Effie. He did it in life but I'll be damned if he does it again in death.'

She stared up at him, seeing his desperation to protect her and knowing it was hopeless. Even if the captain hadn't yet any cause to connect her whisky with Mathieson's death, once Weir proved her 'unnatural' relationship with the factor – a compelling reason to kill him – he would make the link soon enough. But there was no benefit to worrying Sholto with something he couldn't control. 'I'll be fine. I'm certain no one saw us. Like you said, they've not come for me yet and every day that passes . . .'

He nodded urgently, kissing her wrist again and holding her like she was something holy, sacred and rare. Something to be protected, but not possessed.

He looked back at her with eyes full of sorrow and regret. How much had they suffered – lost – for these few sweet moments? How many more would they get to have?

Or was this it?

He looked back at her, time suspending. She leant forward and kissed him, feeling the tension in his body as her story settled in him like rocks. She felt his wet cheeks against hers, the sweetness of his lips as he drew her closer and kissed her the way he had on the rope, when they had been hidden from the world and nothing and no one else existed. They were still hiding, but instead of clinging rigidly to rocks, she wasn't afraid now to fall. She let him pull her to the ground, sighing as his hands travelled over her, the lush grass smelling sweet in the night air as the owl in the far-off tree called forlornly for its mate.

Chapter Thirty

'Effie!'

The voice was carried off by the wind, the sheet in her hands flapping and twisting from her like a naughty child as she tried to peg it to the line. Her hair kept striking her cheeks with tiny whip-cracks, but she merely smiled in reply. Nothing would take the happiness from her heart today. She felt reborn, for once her bare feet not spread on the ground but hovering an inch above it as if she'd been kissed by angels.

But she had been kissed by someone altogether more earthly. She could still smell the grass on her skin, the cool damp soil in her hair and as she had lain beneath him, she had felt as if he had pressed her into the very ground, making a new cast for her so that she would belong here now. Let this be her home!

Her eyes closed, her body falling still as she fell into another memory of last night. At last she understood the fevers that had overwhelmed her friend, Flora talking excitedly in a high, fast voice, eyes burning, as Effie had watched on, cross-legged and cross at her exclusive happiness.

'Effie!' Something hard tapped on her shoulder and she whirled round to find her father standing there, regarding her with a quizzical expression. 'Are y' deaf, lass? Or sleeping standing up? Billy's here.'

'Billy?' She left the rest of the laundry in the basket and followed him inside. Her father's lack of English had made him more timid in recent weeks. Felton spoke Gaelic to him, of course, and that was a comfort, but all the new faces, the unspoken pecking order and grandeur of the great estate, left her father overwhelmed.

Sure enough, Billy was standing on the front path, holding a soft bundle wrapped in calico. He had his back to her, his face turned up towards the sun.

'Hallo there, Billy,' she said, coming through the hall, her father falling back at her shoulder now.

Billy whirled around. 'Hallo, Effie. Mrs McKenzie wanted me to bring this over to you.'

He held out the bundle and she took it from him. 'What is it?'

'Your clothes. They've been washed and pressed.'

Effie's eyes met his. Sibyl had been wearing her clothes only last night. To have cleaned and dried them in this time . . . when exactly had the laundry maids started?

'She was adamant that they were to be returned to you as soon as possible,' he said, as if reading her mind.

Effie peeled back the top layer. John's woollen vest, the one she had knitted so poorly for him, lay plump and clean – no more beetroot stains – on top. She immediately understood what was meant by the gesture. It was an act of solidarity, the servants showing a kindness in response to Sibyl's malice last night. It also meant they all knew what had happened, her very public humiliation.

'It's just my washing, Father,' she said in Gaelic, showing him too.

'Ah,' he said, losing all interest and shuffling back inside the cottage to resume sweeping the floor.

Billy watched him go before he spoke again.

'She's gone,' he said firmly, the look in his eyes making it plain who 'she' was.

'Gone?' Sholto had done it, then? He'd said he would – but so soon? She felt her soul pirouette.

'Aye. Fraser drove her to the station this morning.'

'Not Sholto?'

'No. Not him.' For once, he didn't correct her impertinent familiarity.

She stared down at the bundle, trying not to betray how fast her heart was beating, but she knew her cheeks must look flushed, at the very least. Her happiness felt almost uncontainable. Was it contained – or could Billy see it in her? Was her secret in fact nothing of the sort?

'Well . . . then Henry must be pleased,' she said lightly, a hint of a smile hovering over her lips.

His eyes twinkled as he grinned in return. 'Oh, Henry is over the moon.'

Effie chuckled softly at the memories of the footman walking Margaux around the rose gardens every morning. But the big cat was gone now, and her owner with her. Effie brought the clothes in to her chest and clutched them tightly. She had thought she would never get these back again, her only mementoes of her brother.

'I thought you'd want to know,' Billy said, watching her. 'But I should get back. It's frantic up there, tidying up after the party before his lordship and the countess arrive home.'

Effie was surprised. 'They're coming back today?'

'Aye,' he groaned.

'You must be run off your feet! When did the party finish?'

'Oh, not too long after Lord Sholto chased after you in the garden and Lady Sibyl retired to her room,' Billy said boldly, flushing her out with a keen-eyed gaze. He looked at her with the same bemused expression she'd seen that time in the servants' hall, when the matter of where the lilies had been put had thrown the housekeeper into a panic. Effie had been baffled then but she understood it now. She knew Billy knew she had done what she must not, what the minister had inculcated was a grievous sin, what Flora had warned her about, what the factor had paid with his life in trying to stop . . . And she didn't regret a moment of it.

'You know, y' look different these days. You don't look so . . . lost.'

'I thought you were going to say wild!'

He laughed. 'Ha! No! I reckon you'll always be that, no matter what happens.'

No matter what happens. For all her joy this morning, her future still trembled with uncertainty. Total happiness could be hers and yet . . . total despair hovered too. She couldn't pretend she was out of the shadow of her past. It fell upon her even in the sunlight, chilling her bones and stalking her dreams. She was free of Frank Mathieson in one way, perhaps, but that didn't mean she had escaped him entirely. For as long as Weir had that book, the dead could still have their revenge.

'I'll be seeing y', Effie.' He touched his cap and walked back down the path to the estate track. His bicycle was propped against the stone wall and he threw a leg over. 'Oh aye . . . talk of the devil. It looks like you've another visitor,' he said, glancing back at her with his customary impish smile.

'Who is it?' She hastened from the doorway to see a rider cantering towards them.

Billy threw a wink at her. 'Boy, I wish I could stay around for this!'

'Scat!' she chided, laughing.

He rang his bell and pedalled off as Effie clutched the bundle ever more tightly and stood at the gate, waiting for the visitor to arrive. Sholto nodded as Billy cycled past, lifting his cap deferentially.

'Effie,' Sholto said as he approached, pulling on the reins, and at their first look, she could see the joy inside him threatening to escape, just as it did her. It felt irrepressible. It showed her with a single glance that what they had shared last night had been true, not a dream.

She realized she was beaming. That they both were. There was a basket balanced between his legs and he jumped down with it and threw the reins over the gate post as she stepped back to let him pass. His gaze fell to the bundle in her own arms. From his expression, he seemed to know what it contained too.

'How are you this morning?' he asked in a low voice.

'Very well,' she nodded, wishing she could slip into his arms again. 'And you?'

His blue eyes penetrated her like sunbeams. 'Magnificent.'

'Magnificent,' she repeated, liking even just the sound of the word, much less what it implied. No regrets.

'Another picnic?' she enquired, seeing the basket in his arms.

He hesitated. 'Not exactly.'

'What then?'

'Look inside and see.'

With a nervous laugh, she lifted the lid – and a cold wet nose popped out.

'Slipper?' she gasped, instinctively reaching in and pulling her into her arms. The dog wriggled happily. 'But what are you doing with—?'

Another cold, wet nose appeared. She blinked. '. . . You've brought *two*?'

He beamed. It was that same smile she knew from St Kilda. Unsophisticated, heady happiness.

'Sholto, what's going on?' she laughed. 'Does Huw know you've got them?'

'It was Huw who gave them to me. Or rather, I bought one and he gave me the other to give to you. As a gift.'

'But why is he giving me a gift?' she puzzled. 'I don't understand.'

'I went over there this morning. We've known each other since we were boys and I wanted to make things right with him. I had to.'

She swallowed. 'You mean . . . ?'

He nodded. 'I told him. About us.'

'Sholto.' Her voice had dropped to a whisper. 'You can't.'

'But I did,' he said firmly. 'And now I'm going to tell everyone. My parents too.'

She shook her head firmly, feeling a cold clutch of panic. 'No.'

'Effie – yes.' He made her look at him. 'Yes.'

'But what if—'

'If the worst happens, I can protect you better as my wife.'

'*Wife?*'

He blinked. 'I mean it, Effie. I won't lose you again.'

She shook her head. 'You can't. The shame it would bring to your family—'

'Stop. I could never be ashamed of you.'

'Your parents would beg to differ, I can assure you!'

'They're back this afternoon,' he said determinedly. 'We'll tell them then.'

'Sholto—' she protested. She knew she had to tell him about

Weir now, before he went any further. She had to tell him it was hopeless. The police would be coming for her as soon as they had the book. It gave them her motive on a plate – self-defence or not, there was no denying what she'd done.

He pressed a finger to her lips. 'I won't pretend it won't come as a shock to them, but they think you're delightful, and they want me to be happy.'

She shook her head. 'Delightful is not enough,' she hissed, glancing over to check her father was still in the cottage. 'Me marrying you would be shocking enough to people, but your wife being *arrested* . . . ?' Her voice broke. 'No. I did a terrible thing and you have to face it. I'm everything they say I am. I'm too wild.'

He took her hand and kissed it. 'Effie, listen to me. Yes, people will talk, some will even turn their backs – but I don't care. You showed me what freedom is, you make me laugh. I never feel more alive than when I'm with you. It's your very wildness that I love, don't you see?'

She looked back at him. Even now, with no lies left between them, obstacles remained.

'I can't leave my father. He needs me.'

'I know, and I had thought he could live in the house, with us, but Felton said he would hate that.'

She couldn't help but smile. Felton was right. Her father wouldn't manage all the stairs in the big house, far less be comfortable there. He was setting down his roots in this cottage. Every morning he picked an apple from the tree in the back garden for his breakfast, and with the potatoes, broad beans and carrots now planted in the lazybeds, he was digging in flower beds instead. It had taken him a while to accept something could be merely decorative and not purely functional, but a few of the gardeners – also Gaelic speakers, it turned out – had started to come over with some bare root specimens of honeysuckle and roses and gave him some pointers.

'But Felton says he's just through the trees there and he'll still sit with him in the evenings. He's going to train the pup to mind him too, so your father'll not want for company or help. And we'll send one of the maids up to keep house for him, and Mrs McLennan can dispatch Billy with his dinner. And *we'd* only be down there.' His head tipped in the direction of the grand mansion. 'You'd still see him every day.'

Effie blinked. He had thought of everything, but she knew the gamekeeper's company was all the reassurance her father really needed. Day by day, he filled the hole left behind by her brother. Huw Felton was not a sentimental man, but he was a good one. 'What did he say when you told him about us?' she asked quietly.

'He said . . .' Sholto thought for a moment, a small puzzled frown puckering his smooth brow. 'He said "Two never kindled a fire but it lit between them." Does that mean anything to you?'

She just smiled. It was an old Hebridean saying and perhaps another sign of why Felton should have been her match – but her heart would not be told. It had been Sholto from the first moment.

Slipper nuzzled into her neck and Effie dropped her face into her fur again. '. . . Is she really mine?'

'Felton said she was yours from the first moment. She's your wedding present.'

She smiled, hugging the warm, heavy body even closer and feeling something in her heal, a wound closing up. She looked back at him with a sigh. 'So you're really sure, then? I can't talk you out of it?'

His smile grew, eyes sparkling. 'Where's your father?' His eyes alighted from her, fixing upon the house.

Effie turned to see her father standing by the doorway, holding the other puppy – which had run through – with a look of bafflement.

'She's for you, Father,' Effie said in Gaelic, walking over. 'Huw's going to train her up for you.'

'For me?' he asked. 'Why?'

She swallowed. 'For company.'

Her father stared at her, as if he'd heard something more in those two words.

Sholto stepped forward. 'Mr Gillies, I love your daughter,' he said. In Gaelic!

Effie's mouth dropped open. Her father looked stunned, too.

'Would you do me the honour of allowing me to ask for her hand in marriage?'

A stunned silence met the question.

'Where . . . where did you learn to say that?' she whispered.

'Felton,' he murmured, never taking his eyes off her father.

Effie looked at her father too. Well?

He held her gaze for several moments, the silence between them more profound than words could ever be. He had lost so much in his life and had precious few gains.

'Did I not always tell you – go courting afar but marry next door?' he said finally, sweeping his arm from the cottage garden towards the hulk of the great house across the fields.

She laughed. Technically, they *were* next door, albeit with three hundred sheep and eighty hectares between them. 'You're sure, Father?'

'He loves you, and he has sheep,' he shrugged.

'An earldom too. But yes, sheep.' With another laugh, Effie

stepped into his embrace, smelling the peat fires of home still upon him as the two men shook hands solemnly.

'I wonder . . .' Sholto murmured, wandering over to the cottage.

'What's he doing? You're not leaving me already, are you?' her father asked, watching as Sholto disappeared inside.

'No, but . . .' She had no idea what he was doing – until Sholto emerged a moment later with the broomstick in his hand. With a smile, he laid it down upon the ground by her father's feet, looking up questioningly at him.

Her father nodded his approval.

'You know that's not lawful,' she laughed as Sholto took her by the hand and led her around.

'It is if we both want it to be. I'll marry you any and every way I can, Effie Gillies.' His eyes shone and she knew what he was doing. This wasn't just an homage to their island traditions, a nod of respect to the old ways. It was overwriting a terrible wrong.

'Will you jump the broom with me?' he asked.

She beamed. 'As many times as you like.'

Chapter Thirty-One

They walked up the steps to the house. Effie could see the groundsmen glancing over, noticing that they were hand in hand.

'Relax,' Sholto smiled, feeling the tension in her grip.

The door was opened for them by Henry, his chin held high, his gaze dead ahead. He gave not a single indication that he saw their clasped hands or their closeness as they walked, but Effie knew the news would be around the servants' hall within minutes, his every suspicion confirmed. Didn't he have money on it? Or was that Billy?

'Are the earl and countess back?' Sholto asked him.

'They're expected any moment, sir,' Henry replied, still staring at a fixed point on the wall.

'Good. Would you ask them to meet us in the blue drawing room when they arrive?'

'Yes, sir.'

Sholto squeezed her hand as they walked through the hall into the drawing room, Henry's footsteps receding behind them. He went over to the fireplace and pressed the button that would ring the bell downstairs and send Mr Graves up to them.

He turned back to her, so handsome in his suit, his eyes burning as he took in the sight of her standing in the middle of the carpet. 'You look like a stray fawn that's wandered in from the woods,' he laughed softly. 'Come here.'

She walked over, feeling feral in a room of silks.

'Relax. This is your home now.'

'But—'

'No buts. This is your home.' She looked back at him as he put his hands in her hair, cupping her head as he kissed her properly, not the way he had earlier in front of her father when they'd jumped the broom, but like last night in the maze, when there had been no one else around. She felt her body relax. Was he really hers? Was she really his?

They heard the first rattle of the doorknob as it turned and she leapt away, cheeks flaming. If the earl and countess were to find them like this—

'Thank you, Graves,' Sholto laughed, seeing her panic. He shoved a hand into his trouser pocket. 'That was quick, I must say. I've asked Henry to show my parents in here when they arrive. Would you put some champagne on ice?'

Champagne? It was scarcely midday. Effie felt as shocked as the butler looked.

'Actually, my lord, I'm afraid I was already on my way up when the call came.'

Sholto frowned. 'Oh?'

'I'm afraid there's been some . . . commotion, below stairs.'

'Commotion?'

The butler looked pointedly at Effie before looking back at him again, his point clear.

Sholto walked towards her and made a point of clasping her hand again. It felt shocking and bold to her, but Sholto was defiant. 'Anything you have to say, you can say in front of Miss Gillies.'

To his credit, Graves kept his composure and simply

nodded his head. 'Very well, my lord. There's a policeman here. He wishes to speak with you.'

Silence as loud as a thunderclap erupted in the room.

'What?' Sholto's voice was hoarse as he immediately looked across at Effie. She stood rigid and pale. 'Well, what does he want?'

'It's to do with Sir John MacLeod's late factor.'

Sholto's grip tightened. It seemed several moments before he could respond. '. . . Very well.'

The butler nodded and left the room. She sagged immediately, her body deflating as all the hope left her. Sholto put his arms around her, keeping her up. 'Effie, now listen to me – don't say a word, you hear me? I'll deal with him. I'll send him away and we'll get Kerr-Miller onto it. He's our solicitor—'

She tried to keep her focus on him but he sounded so far away, like he was calling from another room. She could feel her breathing was shallow; she felt dizzy, her hands beginning to tingle. So this was it. An hour of happiness was all they would get.

'Effie, look at me – you have nothing to fear! You did not go out that night with the intention of killing him. His death was an accident, brought on by reasons outside your control. Kerr-Miller will show them you acted in self-defence and that it was Mathieson's own depraved actions that led you to it and to his demise—'

The door opened again and she slipped from his embrace as Graves came through with a uniformed police officer. No matter Sholto's great hopes for saving her, she knew what he did not – that Weir had proof of her motive; that she had planned to incapacitate and abandon him; to do him harm.

The policeman took off his hat and nodded at Sholto. 'Lord Sholto? I'm Sergeant Menzies.'

'How may I help you, Sergeant Menzies?' Sholto asked coldly, drawing himself up.

'I've come in connection with the investigation into the death of Frank Mathieson.' He hesitated and looked questioningly at Effie, but neither she nor Sholto stirred. 'It's a . . . sensitive matter. You may wish for some privacy?'

'Not at all.'

Still the policeman hesitated. 'Well, as this is a live investigation, may I ask who this young lady is, sir?'

'Miss Gillies is my f—'

'I'm the earl's ornithology curator,' she said firmly, stopping him from saying more.

Sholto looked at her with consternation but she wouldn't be dissuaded. The moment was upon them and couldn't be denied. She wouldn't heap her shame upon his family.

'Miss *Euphemia* Gillies?' The policeman's eyes narrowed.

'Yes.'

There was a pause. 'Well, how very fortuitous to find you here, Miss Gillies. You are the next person to speak to on my list today—'

Effie sagged again. She felt sure her legs wouldn't support her.

'What is it you want, Sergeant?' Sholto repeated, drawing the officer's attention again.

'Ah yes – well I'd like to ask you some questions, if I may, sir,' he said, pulling a notebook and pencil from his jacket pocket. 'You are friends with Sir John MacLeod, are you not?'

'We are.' The full weight of his distinguished family hung in that small two-letter word.

'And were you aware of the spate of thefts from the Dunvegan estate in recent months?'

464

Sholto frowned. '. . . Of course. Sir John lost several valuable artefacts that were irreplaceable. He was most upset.'

'Do you recall any specific losses?'

Sholto thought for a moment. 'Bonnie Prince Charlie's gold ring was mentioned.'

'Anything about a book?'

Effie felt her pulse skyrocket, though Sholto remained calm in his ignorance.

'Yes, now you mention it. His copy of the Dalwhinnie book was taken. It's rather valuable. There were only ever eight issues printed. We have one of them here.'

'Indeed. And is it still here?'

'Yes.'

'So you've seen it recently?'

Sholto's frown deepened. 'Yes.'

'You're quite sure?'

'I'm absolutely certain. Look, why are you asking me all this?'

'Your steward, Mr Weir, visited an antiquarian bookshop in Glasgow on the ninth of September. Do you know anything about that, sir?'

'Yes.' He cleared his throat, glancing at Effie. 'Um . . . our copy needed some urgent repairs. Some pages had come loose.'

'But it's back here now?'

'Yes. I collected it myself from the station.' Sholto pinned a hard stare on the detective.

'And are you looking to sell it, sir?'

Sholto scowled. 'Of course not! It's been in the family for almost two hundred years. It's one of my family's most treasured possessions. Why?'

'The bookseller reported that the gentleman enquired as to the book's value on the open market.'

Sholto's eyes narrowed. 'What? But why should he do that?'

'I was hoping you could tell me, sir.'

'I have no idea! We have no intention of selling the book. Furthermore, I don't understand what our book being repaired has to do with MacLeod's factor's death?'

The sergeant straightened up and put his notebook and pencil back in his jacket pocket. 'I'm sorry to tell you, sir, that we believe the late Mr Mathieson was stealing valuable, if not priceless, objects from Sir John MacLeod and selling them on to private collectors – and we believe Mr Weir was his accomplice.'

There was an astounded silence. '. . . *What?*'

'The Dunvegan copy of the book which you have just had repaired, was found in a suitcase under Mr Weir's bed following a search of his room just now. He has been arrested for possession and handling of stolen goods and taken into protective custody.'

'I don't believe this!' Sholto looked across at her but Effie couldn't say a word. The blood was rushing through her head, her pulse like a drumbeat. Mathieson and Weir . . . ?

'*Weir?* A thief . . . ?' Sholto looked confounded. 'What's he got to say about it?'

The police sergeant looked straight at her. 'Well, it's a funny thing, but during the course of our interview, Mr Weir repeatedly mentioned you, Miss Gillies.'

'Me?' Her voice was a whisper.

'He said he found the book under *your* bed and had been intending to hand it in as evidence into Mr Mathieson's murder investigation.'

'That's preposterous!' Sholto blustered. 'Evidence of what?'

But the policeman would not be rushed. 'Did you know Mr Mathieson, Miss Gillies?'

'Aye, of course. I'm from St Kilda and he was the landlord's factor.'

'How would you describe your relationship with him?'

' . . . Polite.'

'Polite? Nothing more *intimate* than that?'

Effie managed to gasp. 'Of course not! He's almost twice my age.'

'Sergeant! I object,' Sholto said forcefully.

'I apologize for asking such an indelicate question, but Mr Weir alleges that Mr Mathieson stole the book from Lord MacLeod and gave it to you, Miss Gillies – as a love token.'

Sholto scoffed. 'I think it's perfectly clear that Mr Weir is grasping at straws here. He desperately wants to deflect attention from his criminal activities and is trying to implicate Miss Gillies simply by virtue of the fact that she is from St Kilda, where Frank Mathieson died.'

There was a pause.

The sergeant watched her carefully. 'Do you have anything to say on the matter, Miss Gillies?'

'No, sir. I don't know why Mr Weir would say such a thing.' Her voice tremored under the weight of the lie. She sensed her life was like a spinning coin. On one side was liberty, on the other was loss: loss of freedom, loss of a future, loss of Sholto . . . But which way would she fall?

'How . . . how do you know the book you found belonged to Lord MacLeod?' she asked quietly.

'It is stamped with the MacLeods' bull crest, Miss Gillies. Each family has their own.'

'Ours is the wyvern,' Sholto said distractedly. He looked back at the policeman. 'Do you believe he was intending to steal ours too, then, and offer both to market?'

'Possibly. A pair of such rare books would certainly

command a premium. We think he was sounding out the bookseller for any possible interest.'

Could it be that? Was he as wicked as the factor, his partner in crime? Or had Mathieson worked alone and Weir's chance question, asked in curiosity, had taken his life down a new path in which he was now the villain, not she?

She felt her heart pound as she tried to think through whether he could prove his own innocence, just as he'd tried to prove her guilt. There was nothing in the book to show it had ever come into her possession – no mark, no inscription. It would be her word against his as the very piece of evidence that had linked her to Frank Mathieson now linked him indelibly to his former friend instead. They were two men of similar age and standing, known to be friends, each working in trusted positions for powerful families . . . She could almost taste her freedom; it glided before her like a seabird on the thermals, daring to be caught. She knew she was not innocent but she couldn't say for sure that Weir wasn't either. The story fit and she wouldn't do anything to dismantle it. After all, Weir had come after her. Why should she save him?

She glanced at Sholto, her eyes infused with a pale, flickering hope. She could see the desperation in his, a silent urgency that they be anywhere but here.

'Miss Gillies, while I have you here, I would like to ask you some further questions,' the policeman said, putting out the sputtering flame and delivering another spike to her pulse. 'As I mentioned, I was due to visit you next anyway. I understand you and your father live in a cottage on the estate?'

'Actually—' Sholto began.

'We do, sir,' Effie said, speaking over him again. For as long as the sword swung above her head, he couldn't publicly reveal their relationship. She wouldn't let him.

'Scotland Yard is in the process of interviewing all your former neighbours from the isle. We're trying to identify the owners of the objects in this photograph.' The policeman reached into his jacket and pulled out a small photograph, handing it to her.

She took it with a noticeably trembling hand, her guilt pushing forward like an impudent child. The colours were all shades of grey but the objects within were clearly defined. Just in the top right corner, four fingers of a hand inched into the frame.

Effie's stomach turned as she understood what she was seeing. She didn't want to see it. Him.

But . . .

She frowned, peering closer, a cold sweat prickling her skin as she saw the old rusted knife she had left lying beside a loop of rope – that was now cut. And the heavy whisky bottle – had its base shattered. Splatters of something dark stained the rocks and grass . . . Blood?

She looked up in alarm at the police officer. He was watching her closely. The notepad and pencil were in his hands again.

Sholto, standing beside her, stiffened too. She could tell he could see this didn't correspond to what she'd told him. The bloodied chaos bore no relation to the scene she had left – but how could she tell him that?

'What is this?' Sholto asked in a low voice, the words like ashes in his mouth.

'This is the crime scene – how and where the victim was found, sir. It was a vicious attack.'

'*Attack?*' The word – more of a cry – escaped her like a bullet. 'You mean he was killed?' Her breath came heavily, her body feeling leaden.

'You sound surprised, Miss Gillies.'

'I thought he . . . *died*. That he got left behind and he died of hunger, or thirst. Or exposure. Not . . .' She stared again at the fingertips in the edge of the photograph.

The policeman's eyes narrowed. 'Miss Gillies, Mr Mathieson was murdered. There was nothing accidental about his death.'

Murdered? The word swam in her head.

'Do you feel faint?' Sholto asked her, seeing how she paled. 'This is a terrible shock for her, Sergeant,' he said to the policeman. 'Effie, do you need to sit down?'

'I don't believe it,' she murmured. She began shaking her head, slowly at first. 'No. No. I know every person in that village and none of them – not a single one – is capable of murder. They wouldn't have it in them to do that.'

There was a pause.

'Except one of them clearly did, Miss Gillies. Which is why it's important you tell me whether you recognize anything in the picture.' He stepped forward and tapped a finger on the knife. '. . . How about that?' he asked. 'Have you seen that before?'

'It's just a fishing knife,' she murmured, her mind racing. None of this made sense. She stared at the rope. Had he managed to get himself free? Cut himself loose? But how? He had been unconscious when she left him '. . . There must have been a thousand fishing knives on the isle.'

'What about the bottle?'

She shook her head. It had been empty, not broken, when she'd seen it last. 'We have no alcohol on the island. The minister was always very strict about that.'

'There were a lot of visitors to the isle that last week. Perhaps one of them brought it?'

She swallowed. 'Maybe. I wouldn't know.' The lies came,

470

one after another. Would the captain be interviewed too? He wasn't an islander, merely an occasional visitor. He hadn't been over in the last month before the evacuation. Why should they even think of him? He would be forgotten, surely, his role in bringing over a murder weapon sinking into the obscurity of history?

'Well, what about this, then?'

She looked down, anticipating his finger on the loop of cut rope – but he had tapped on something small, almost indistinct in the picture. The angle was strange, so she hadn't noticed it at first. She brought the photograph closer to her face, feeling herself grow weak as the shape presented itself.

'Do you recognize this?' he asked, watching her closely.

No . . . It made no sense. How could that be there? Her mind was racing, trying to find reasons why it should be there.

'Miss Gillies, have you ever seen this before?' His voice was more insistent again.

'Effie?' Sholto asked, his hand on her arm, desperation in his eyes.

She looked back at them both, her heart a nightingale singing for its life.

The policeman's pen was poised above the paper. 'Miss Gillies? If you know, you must tell me. To whom does this brooch belong?'

Acknowledgements

I feel like I've been waiting a long time to write this series. I had dallied with historical backdrops in a few of my other books – *The Paris Secret*, *The Rome Affair* and *The Spanish Promise* – but I always felt strangely obliged to root the body of the stories in the present day. In *The Spanish Promise* particularly, I felt it was the historic characters that were truly the beating heart of the narrative, and the urge to fully commit to another time and place began to take hold.

But when exactly? And where?

In the end, after a few years of waiting, I chanced upon a tiny comment in the newspaper one Saturday morning. The headline read 'Ninety Years Since St Kilda Gave Up'. I had never heard of St Kilda, but a quick Google search told me it was the outermost of the Outer Hebrides, a tiny archipelago centred upon two-mile-long isle Hirta, one hundred miles off the Scottish mainland. It had been deserted since the islanders requested evacuation in the summer of 1930, but that wasn't what held my interest. It was the use of those two words – *gave up*. Had something broken them? Driven them away?

I was in! I read every book still in print about St Kilda, I watched jerky, silent black-and-white cinefilms taken by early tourists and, of course, I travelled there. Even now, it's an arduous crossing – four hours each way over heavy water, with only a four-hour stay on the island itself, which is nothing.

By the time I got there, I thought I already knew everything there was to know about the place, but even though I had pored over photographs, illustrations and maps, I still wasn't prepared for the scale of it. Though tiny, it is also majestic and the gradients are far, far steeper than I had anticipated. The islands are now owned and protected by National Trust for Scotland, but the Ministry of Defence maintains an observation presence there – sadly – and have built a road to the summit of Mullach Mor. Reputedly it is one of the steepest in the British Isles and I can confirm that, having walked up it in pigeon steps. It really is a remarkable sight to see the cliffs rise above the horizon as you approach, and as you draw closer and the scale becomes apparent, it is just staggering that these towering mountains can be positioned on such a tiny scrap of land in the middle of the North Atlantic.

There are several small boat operators licensed to drop anchor at St Kilda, but we travelled with Go To St Kilda and I'd like to thank our highly experienced skipper, Willie, and his first mate, Gordon, who was hugely knowledgeable about the bird and marine life, as well as the history of the place.

Throughout this book, I have strived to remain faithful to everything I learnt about the islanders' lives, so the locations and details you read here are true – from feeding the cows dock leaves to keep them still when milking, to learning the market cost of puffin feathers for the upholstery trade. However, this is of course a work of fiction, so the characters and what they do within the framework of this series are wholly made up and should not be attributed to anyone real. I have used some commonly found islanders' names – such as Euphemia, Annie, Donald, etc. – and the surnames are also very specific too. A census was taken as the islanders were evacuated and there were found to be just five surnames shared among the last thirty-six islanders: Gillies, Ferguson, MacDonald, McKinnon and McKenzie. It felt right to give each heroine one of those surnames – and her own book – but I have deliberately made a point of not learning about specific villagers themselves so that the pairing of names is entirely spontaneous.

The one name that is historically true is the Earl of Dumfries' title, and his seat is indeed Dumfries House in Ayrshire. It was also the case that MacLeod of MacLeod sold the archipelago to the Earl of Dumfries in 1931, the year after the evacuation. The earl was a very keen ornithologist, and it was he who preserved it as a marine bird sanctuary and later bequeathed the land to National Trust for Scotland. However, in real life the earl was younger than my fictious version, and in 1930 his children were babies. I have used the framework of the earl's interest and later ownership of St Kilda as a foundation for this story, but none of the events or characters you read within these pages are rooted in truth, only imagination.

Interestingly, Dumfries House passed out of the family's ownership years ago, but the estate and buildings were rescued by Prince Charles in 2007 and saved for the nation. Having visited it myself, I would urge you to take the tour if you are ever in the area. It boasts the largest private ownership of Chippendale furniture in the world and we had afternoon tea in the old stable block! Homemade cakes and good tea followed by a wander around the maze.

I studied historic architects' plans to manoeuvre Effie around the house in Part Two, so you really are walking through the corridors with her. However, there is one deviation from the truth here – in real life the ha-ha is situated on the north side of the house, but for logistical dramatic purposes I had to put it on the south side.

This has been a labour of love for me and it has been such a privilege to immerse myself in the history of St Kilda. When I returned from visiting it, I felt as if I'd been to the Galapagos or the Antarctic – it really is that special and rare and remote, so I'd like to thank my publishers, Pan Macmillan, for being so wholeheartedly behind the idea for this series. In spite of my draw to the place, I was nonetheless hesitant about setting the action in a faraway place, a hundred years ago, with no communications, no shops, no nightlife . . . But my editor, Gillian Green, and publisher, Lucy Hale, immediately saw that the lack of external stimulus would mean the story was driven by a cast of strong, vividly drawn characters instead. And on an island with no trees and only thirty-six inhabitants, those characters would have to work very hard and be quite ingenious if they wanted to keep any secrets – because of course they had them!

Everyone on the team has worked so hard to whittle, shape, sell, market, define and refine this book and I sincerely thank you all. I'm so proud of what we've achieved.

Amanda Preston, my incredible agent, who buoys me up when I need it, keeps me calm when I'm stressed and cheers louder than anyone when we get a success – thank you! Teamwork, gal.

And of course, I rely on my family's forbearance when I do one of my deep dives and retreat into my head for a few months at a time. I famously can't finish a sentence, forget to cook and dress in trackies for four months straight, but somehow they still love me. And I love them, all of them, always.

The Hidden Beach

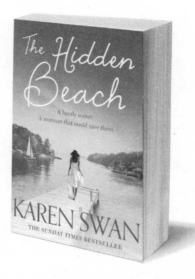

'Novels to sweep you away'
Woman & Home

Secrets, betrayal and shocking revelations await
in Sweden's stunning holiday islands . . .

In Stockholm's oldest quarter, Bell Appleshaw loves her job
working as a nanny for the rich and charming Hanna and
Max Mogert, caring for their three children.

But one morning, everything changes. A doctor from
a clinic Bell has never heard of asks her to pass on
the message that Hanna's husband has woken up.
But the man isn't Max.

As the truth about Hanna's past is revealed, the
consequences are devastating. As the family heads off
to spend their summer on Sweden's idyllic islands, will
Bell be caught in the crossfire?

The Spanish Promise

'The perfect summer read'
Hello!

The Spanish Promise is a sizzling summer novel about family secrets and forbidden love, set in the vibrant streets of Madrid.

One of Spain's richest men is dying – and his family are shocked to discover he plans to give away his wealth to a young woman they've never heard of.

Charlotte Fairfax, an expert in dealing with the world's super rich, is asked to travel to the troubled family home to get to the bottom of the mysterious bequest. She unearths a dark and shocking family past where two people were torn apart by conflict. Now, long-buried secrets are starting to reach into the present. Does love need to forgive and forget to endure? Or does it just need two hearts to keep beating?

The Greek Escape

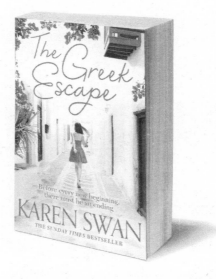

'A beautiful setting and steamy scenes –
what more do you need?'
Fabulous

Set on an idyllic island, *The Greek Escape* is the perfect
getaway, bursting with jaw-dropping twists
and irrepressible romance.

Chloe Marston works at a luxury concierge company, making
other people's lives run perfectly, even if her own has ground to a
halt. She is tasked with finding charismatic Joe Lincoln his dream
holiday house in Greece – and when the man who broke her
heart turns up at home, she jumps on the next flight.

It doesn't take long before she's drawn into the undeniable
chemistry between her and Joe. When another client's wife
mysteriously disappears and serious allegations about him
emerge, will she end up running from more than heartbreak?

The Rome Affair

'Enthralling and magical'
Woman

The cobbled streets and simmering heat of
Italy's capital are brought to life in *The Rome Affair*.

1974 and Viscontessa Elena Damiani lives a gilded life, born to
wealth and a noted beauty. Then she meets the love of her life,
and he is the one man she can never have. 2017 and Francesca
Hackett is living la dolce vita in Rome, forgetting the ghosts
she left behind in London. When a twist of fate brings her into
Elena's orbit, the two women form an unlikely friendship.

As summer unfurls, Elena shares her sensational stories with
Cesca, who agrees to work on Elena's memoir. But when a
priceless diamond ring found in an ancient tunnel below the city
streets is ascribed to Elena, Cesca begins to suspect a shocking
secret lies at the heart of the Viscontessa's life . . .

Summer at TIFFANY'S

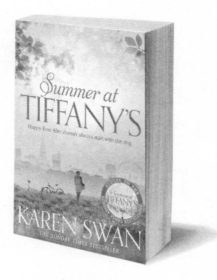

'Glamorous, romantic and totally engrossing'
My Weekly

A wedding to plan. A wedding to stop.
What could go wrong?

With a Tiffany ring on her finger, all Cassie has to do is plan her dream wedding. It should be simple, but when her fiancé Henry pushes for a date, Cassie pulls back. Meanwhile Henry's wild cousin Gem is racing to the aisle for her own wedding at a sprint, determined to marry in the Cornish church where her parents were wed. But the family is set against it, and Cassie resolves to stop the wedding.

When Henry lands an expedition sailing the Pacific for the summer, Cassie decamps to Cornwall, hoping to find the peace of mind she needs to move forwards. But in the dunes and coves of the north Cornish coast, she soon discovers the past isn't finished with her yet . . .

There's a Karen Swan book
for every season . . .

Have you discovered her winter stories yet?